Anne Madden is a M
Somerville College, Oxford
Slavery, Emancipation and
worked as a news journalis *Irish News* and *Belfast Telegraph*, and in communications for a number of charities. She lives with her partner and dog in her home city of Belfast, where she is learning to speak Irish and enjoys cycling. *The Wilderness Way* is her first novel.

 twitter.com/madsteranne

 instagram.com/madsteranne

 facebook.com/AnneMaddenAuthor

THE WILDERNESS WAY

ANNE MADDEN

One More Chapter
a division of HarperCollins*Publishers* Ltd
1 London Bridge Street
London SE1 9GF
www.harpercollins.co.uk
HarperCollins*Publishers*
Macken House, 39/40 Mayor Street Upper,
Dublin 1, D01 C9W8, Ireland

This paperback edition 2023
2
First published in Great Britain in ebook format
by HarperCollins*Publishers* 2023

Anne Madden asserts the moral right to
be identified as the author of this work

A catalogue record of this book is available from the British Library

ISBN: 978-0-00-853531-5

This novel is a work of fiction. Any references to real people, places and events are used fictitiously. All other names, characters and incidents portrayed are a work of the author's imagination and any resemblance to actual persons, living or dead, events or localities is entirely coincidental.

Printed and bound in the UK using 100% Renewable Electricity
by CPI Group (UK) Ltd

To the millions of Irish emigrants of the past and all those around the world today who find themselves homeless through no fault of their own.

Part I

SEPTEMBER 1860

Chapter 1

Huge, angry waves constantly pounded the cliffs of the north-west corner of Ireland, shaping a coastline that on a map appeared to lean backwards in almost terrified awe of the Atlantic Ocean and the New World on the other side. Beyond the shoreline stretched the emerald-green fields of undulating farmland, divided into patches by a labyrinth of drystone walls. Declan Conaghan built and mended these walls, like his father before him and his father before that. He was proud of the walls and maintaining them felt like he was taking care of his da's legacy. At twenty years old, his large rough hands bore the evidence. He loved the landscape he was born into, not just for its wild scenery. He was in awe of its power and ability to make life, or snuff it out.

Sometimes Declan and his brother Michael came down to fish in Portnablagh, off the stone pier their da had helped build. It was like a pilgrimage. They would sit in silence and remember how hard he and the rest of the stone-breaking gang had toiled. They had worked nine-hour days – bashing, belting, battering rocks into bricks. His da had told him it gave the authorities a reason to provide the men with relief rather than just giving them charitable handouts.

"Better than ending up in yon workhouse," he'd said repeatedly and made him promise that if anything should happen to him they wouldn't go into the workhouse. The Great Hunger was behind them but there was always a fear among the tenants that the crops could fail as disastrously again. Beyond the coastal fishing villages, the land swept higher into brown moorland, rich in the dark brown turf that the brothers spent long hours digging. They stacked the turf bricks in pyramids and left them to dry just like their ancestors had done before them. It was a communal effort to cut the turf, with labourers from miles around the area working together at each man's plot in turn to harvest the rich dark fuel.

"One, two, three – no curse on me," Declan muttered to himself as he stepped out of the deep hole. According to legend, St Columba, the great saint who was born in Gartan, had once been trapped in a boghole and so it became traditional to cut three steps into the turf channel "to prevent any other saint or sinner from getting stuck". Declan stretched his back, stiff from the cutting, and looked around. Smoke from burning the turf furled from the chimneys of the white stone cottages that dotted the hillside. Rising above the moorland were some of the tallest peaks in Ireland – he remembered how his da would point out the distinctive peaks of Muckish and Errigal among the Seven Sisters. The stony peak of Mount Errigal commanded the highest view in the Derryveagh range which enjoyed its majestic reflection in the still looking glass of Dunlewey Lough. When they were very young their ma would threaten to send them to the old hag whom she claimed sacrificed bad children on the flat top of Muckish. Even today its table-top shape, often shrouded in mist, gave Declan the shivers. But he and the other tenants were more concerned these days about another character, a real one, who posed a threat to their way of life.

"Have ye heard Adair's back?" said Michael, who was digging in the channel beside him.

"No! That means trouble. Must be back for hunting season."

"Aye, lock up yer livestock!" Michael laughed.

"No laughing matter when he charges ye two shillings to get back a stray sheep or goat," shouted Ruairi Bradley, their neighbour Alex's son, shaking his spade. "Me da's fed up going to that pound."

"Alex must've paid Murray a small fortune by now," agreed Declan and stepped back down to dig.

The new landlord had quickly made a name for himself as a cold character who hired a group of surly shepherds from Scotland to watch over the estate in his absence. It was rare to see Adair in Donegal as he seemed to spend most of his time in Dublin or at his father's home, but he made his presence known when he stayed at Glenveagh. He took a haughty tone with his tenants and was despised by his staff at Glenveagh Lodge who dreaded his return. His new land steward, a Scotsman called Murray, had opened an animal pound on the estate where he held sheep and goats that had strayed, demanding a high fee for their release. But worst of all for Declan's entrepreneurial aspirations, the landlord had declared war on the illegal production of poteen. Ruairi came sliding along the muddy plank to Declan and whispered so the other men couldn't hear.

"Ye should warn the Sweeneys about distillin' on Lough Veagh. I heard from Adair's staff he's planning a raid with the police."

Declan tipped his cap at him and continued to dig but his mind was racing. The Sweeney brothers, Sean and Owen, were small tenant farmers who lived on the neighbouring estate and regarded themselves as the poteen kings of Donegal. Declan had been serving something of an apprenticeship with them. It helped the family get by on the little means they had. The men had been working that day on the Sweeneys' bog patch but he'd seen no sign of them from late afternoon.

When dusk approached, Declan, Michael and Ruairi joined the other labourers from Gartan for a lift home on the rickety cart. It was a clear night and Declan could see there was going to be a full moon. He began to panic that the brilliant light of the harvest moon would shine a spotlight on the illegal still. He remembered Sean Sweeney had vowed he'd have a batch ready in time for Harvest Home, which they planned to celebrate in their barn tomorrow night. The date coincided this year with Declan's da's ten-year anniversary. They must be on Lough Veagh, he thought. He'd have to warn them. The Sweeneys were a fair bit older but since his father had passed they'd often looked out for his family and he'd often depended on them to provide the muscle when he or Michael got into a scrap. As the cart came close to Glenveagh, he mumbled an excuse to his brother.

"Tell Ma I've gone, er … gone to see the priest. I'll be back later."

As he jumped off the cart Michael raised an eyebrow and hollered after him.

"I'm going to see Sinead tonight – think I'll have a better time than ye!"

Declan laughed. Sinead was their sister Cara's childhood friend. Now in her late teens she'd blossomed into quite a beauty and had caught Michael's eye. They had become inseparable. Declan felt some affinity with Sinead – the oldest of the three Dermott children. Their mother had died during the Great Hunger, which had driven their father Francis to drink and he came to rely on her to look after them all as he was drunk most of the time. Declan felt a slight pang of guilt at his part in keeping Donegal awash with booze, but he justified it as it helped keep the roof over their heads.

Heading in the direction of Lough Veagh, Declan smelt the turf before he spied the smoke coming from one of the tiny islands which lay like skimmed stones on the lough's surface.

"Bloody fools!" he muttered.

He found the small boat he'd left hidden in the reeds and scrambled into it, laying low to avoid being seen. He dipped the wooden paddle into the still water, gently easing the boat towards the smoking island while cursing the wind for disappearing. Without the wind the smoke was very visible. The boat glided cleanly through the water with Declan bent practically double, until there was a dull thud against the bottom of the boat as he grounded it. Easing himself into the knee-deep water, he dragged the boat to a dark inlet out of the moon's gaze and tied her tight, his fingers numb from the cold, damp air. He waded to the shore, hunched over, pulling his threadbare jacket tighter around him as he squeezed the water out of his trousers over the stones on the shore. A twig cracked behind him and suddenly a weight landed on his back and sent him face first into the wet grass. Declan tried to holler but only managed to eat soil. The wild beast, whatever it was, had pulled his arms behind his back and was sitting on him.

"Well, well … who do we have here? A tinker looking to raid our still? Yer a brave lad coming on yer own to take on the Sweeney brothers. Or maybe there's more of ye, eh? Got yer jars with ye ready to fill up. What's that?"

Declan let out a long, low groan but his assailant carried on.

"Of course not, sure why bring yer own jars when ye can steal ours!"

He slapped Declan around the back of the head and then hissed, "Owen, take this wee shite and tie him to yon tree. We're nearly done here."

The weight lifted itself off Declan's aching back and as he choked on the smoky air, another hand grabbed at his arms.

"Fock's sake, Owen, it's me Declan!" He wrenched his arms free.

"Christ, Sean, look what the water rats dragged in – if it isn't our very own Mr Conaghan."

"Shhhushh!" both Declan and Sean hissed in unison. Declan looked around and spied the poteen still in the nearby copse of trees. It was a messy kitchen of pots and pipes, with all shapes of jars and barrels strewn on the ground.

"You've gotta dismantle this quickly, now," he said, his hands flapping at the still. His voice dropped to a whisper. "I got a tip-off that Adair knows about it. He's lending the police his boat to search the lough. When I saw the moonlight, I thought they're likely to discover it tonight."

"Shit – bastards – I mean, it's good ye found out, young Declan, but this was going so well," said Sean, who began to look around. "We've made plenty to get us through the winter and out the other side but we'll have to ditch half this if they're on their way."

Declan nodded and poked some of the jars.

"I know, it's a bloody waste of the best liquor in Donegal but ye can't risk getting caught. Adair's on a mission," said Declan. "Look we can load some of it in my boat too. The rest will have to go in the lough."

"Ha! There'll be some happy trout in there tonight," said Owen.

"Shhussh!" the others hissed. They set to work taking apart the still, beginning with quenching the fire with a bucket of water. To Declan's horror the smoke billowed up in an even thicker plume. He carried jars of the poteen to the shore and rolled them into the bottom of his boat. Sean and Owen hid the copper pot in the tall reeds and poured half the poteen away. They were just scratching away their footprints in the soil with a tree branch when they heard a knock and then a splash. The sound grew louder and more consistent. *Knock, splash, knock, splash.* Declan strained his ears and then peered out across the lough. In the shaft of moonlight across the water, a long boat with three or four heads came into view before gliding back into the dark and closer to the island.

"Shit! They're coming," he said. The three men nodded to each other, then crouching low, they headed for their separate boats. Declan was at an advantage as his boat was moored at the far end of the island, furthest from the police, but with two oarsmen in the other boat he expected the Sweeneys would make it. Declan felt the cold water lap up over his knees this time as he waded out to his boat. He imagined being thrown into the police cell in Church Hill and shuddered. His mother's face flashed in front of him. He could hear his excuses and see her shaking her head as she passed her precious rosary beads through the bars of the cell. Suddenly there was a ruffle of feathers as a duck collided with him. In its fright it quacked and shuffled back into the reeds. Declan cursed it and gripped the side of the boat, holding his breath. He thought he heard voices. It couldn't be the Sweeneys, it must be the police. Had they reached the island already? Then out on the water he spied a dark shadow gliding past. There were no oars moving. It must be the Sweeneys; he smiled, pleased, until he realised the other voices must be the police. His heart beat fast as he tried once, twice and then a third time to clamber into the wooden vessel weighed down this time with jars of poteen. His cold fingers fumbled as he untied the rope and pushed off from the island. He crouched low and dipped the oar, which he realised was quivering in his shaking hands. The boat rocked a little, causing the jars to clink together. They hardly made a sound but in the glassy still of the lough it seemed to Declan as loud as bells pealing on a Sunday morning. He jerked his neck around to peer back at the island and squinted at the sight of dark figures moving in the shadows. They had lit a lantern and one of them was holding it above his head. Something caught the light and glinted. Declan swallowed as he spotted a familiar sight. It was the shiny brass head of Murray's crook. The land steward carried it everywhere, pointing it with menace at anyone who passed him. Declan shuddered at how close they were to being caught. It would have meant immediate eviction for his whole family, and that, especially in winter, was like a death sentence.

He grimaced and rowed as quietly as he could towards the bank. Suddenly he thought about the possibility of police waiting on the shore. He cursed to himself, the adrenalin still rushing through his veins. His legs were numb and shivering with the cold but he felt he could still make a run for it if necessary. Then he spied the familiar shapes of the Sweeney brothers rolling jars on to the shore. Sean's smooth bald head bobbed back and forth next to his much hairier brother. Their broad shoulders hulked the cargo to a temporary store created in the yawning roots of a tree. There was no sign of police and Declan sighed with some relief and steered the boat towards them. As it rode up on to the pebbly shore, Sean waded out and hauled the vessel and its precious stash out of the water. He raised his thick hand and clapped Declan on the shoulder.

"Declan, lad," he mumbled. "Good work. We just missed them peelers and no more. Think we owe ye a few drinks."

He winked and nodded to Owen who was panting as he salvaged the jars from the bottom of Declan's boat. Declan looked back again at the island. The lantern was a distant dot of light as clouds had begun to scurry across the moon.

"Sure, I'd say there'll be a few drinks taken tomorrow night, after the Mass and me ma's finished her prayers," said Declan.

"See? Told ye we'd have the poteen ready for his anniversary." Sean grinned as he helped his brother with the last few jars and Declan dragged the boat to conceal it under some overhanging branches.

"How many years is it since Dan passed?" asked Owen.

"Ten – a whole decade," Declan whispered. His eyes blurry from the cold, he blinked a few times.

"A decade? Good Lord. Well there'll be some decades of the rosary said tomorrow and some volume of this stuff drunk too."

"Ye were just a kid," said Sean as he filled two knapsacks with the jars and handed one to his brother. "And look at the man ye are now. Yer da'd be proud. Ye kept the family fed and watered!" He laughed, raising one of the jars into the night air. Then he shook his thick, bulging neck. "Most of all ye kept them out of the workhouse."

Declan smiled and looked back again at the lough. He couldn't see the light on the island anymore.

"Aye, well, if they catch us that might not be the case. Let's go our separate ways, makes it less suspicious."

The three of them grinned and slipped away separately into the dark. Across the water a sonorous echo of metal hitting metal broke the silence, as Murray's brass crook discovered the copper pot amongst the reeds.

Chapter 2

Adair pondered the shiny, green apple. He pulled out his white embroidered handkerchief and gave it a quick wipe. A window of light now reflected off its emerald skin. *Crunch!* He sank his teeth into its flesh and was satisfied with the moist, slightly bitter flavour. Quite delicious. The landlord stared out the window towards Lough Veagh, whose waters glistened in the sunlight. It was a picture of calm. There was certainly no sign of criminal activity. *Infernal peasants coming on to my land and setting up their filthy little business.* He chomped more quickly on his apple. They might have got away with it in the past but they wouldn't while he was landlord.

From the window Adair could survey the scene before him – a panorama of green hills, rocky mountains and the sparkling navy-blue lough. He had first come across Glenveagh on a hunting trip to Donegal and had fallen for its beauty and isolation. It was such a different landscape to his home, further south in Bellegrove, Queen's County. His father had done much to improve the estate but the dreary flatlands of Queen's County could not capture someone's heart like the wild, mountainous scenery of Donegal. Since he'd bought Glenveagh a year ago, he had spent more of his time here than on his other estates and even less time on his business trips to Dublin. He understood why his father would be puzzled. Up until then he had focused on buying parcels of land around Queen's County to enlarge his father's estate. He had started with a small amount of capital, taken out a few loans over the years and bought land going cheap. Through a series of mortgages and exchanges, helped by his Trinity College connections, he was able to turn these into larger estates. He owed some of his success to the advice of his dear Uncle Trench. A notorious land agent, his maternal uncle knew all there was to know about property and had helped him enormously. While they were all struck by the horror of the Great Famine, which had bankrupted many estates, his uncle's words had resonated with him. "Every cloud…" Father, on the other hand, cared too much for his tenants, a concern that could have seen him end up one of those bankrupt landlords. To think the Adairs, gentry who had been settled in the county for two centuries, could have been destroyed by his father's misplaced charity.

"Ah, blessed tenants," he muttered, and flicked his apple core on to the sideboard. He wouldn't have poteen being distilled on *his* lough. The cheek of them! Adair stroked his thick, dark beard and decided to summon his land steward. He pulled the rope at the mantelpiece, which sent a maid scurrying to the lounge.

"Ye rang, sir?"

"Yes, I want to speak to Mr Murray – do you know his whereabouts?"

The maid fidgeted with her apron.

"I believe, sir, he's in the stables, sorting stuff."

"Sorting stuff? You mean cleaning out the stables? Are the stable boys not available? Why is my land steward mucking out the stables?"

She frowned and rolled the apron into a tighter ball.

"He's not cleaning, sir. I-I saw with my own eyes – he's sorting things, bits and pieces ye know."

"No, I don't know." Adair despaired at the poor vocabulary of the locals but at least she spoke some English instead of that peasant tongue, which was still fairly common in Donegal.

"Very well. I shall go see him with my own eyes. And please stop pulling at your apron, I don't wish to look at a crumpled mess. My staff should look tidy and presentable at all times."

"Yes, sir, sorry, sir," she said, attempting to straighten her apron as she backed out of the room. He sighed as he recalled the very attractive housekeeper he'd almost hired only to discover she had no English, at all. *Pleasing to the eye, but not practical.*

Adair picked up his jacket and scarf and headed out to the stables. There he found Murray standing amidst a clutter of pipes and barrels, which he realised was the stash retrieved by police from the island.

"Here you are, sorting things!"

Murray jumped slightly and spun around with a piece of copper piping in his hand.

"Good day sir, I was just checking through the remains of the still to see if I can identify where it might have come from. You know, stamp marks on the pipes … some of it might have been stolen."

He was broader than he was tall and spoke with a strong Scottish accent.

"Turned detective, have you? It all looks like rubbish to me," said Adair, kicking it with the toe of his leather boot.

"Ah, sir, now put all this together and it's quite an operation. See this, they call this the worm … it connects to the barrel, the liquid passes along that pipe and collects through here," he said, pointing at various pieces of piping. Adair listened impatiently. "…and that, Mr Adair, is how the locals make moonshine."

His land steward seemed to speak with undisguised admiration for the equipment.

"Alright, alright. I get the picture – a good little business they've got going on my estate. Shame they didn't work as hard on the land."

"Potent stuff this, Mr Adair – close to ninety per cent alcohol – it'd be hard to do a day's work if you supped on this the night before," said Murray reaching for a jar. "Would you like to try some, sir?"

"Indeed not! I've perfectly decent Scotch whiskey in the house, which I know won't kill or blind me. Shall we take a walk into the hills? I fancy a bit of sport."

"Aye, aye, sir."

Murray went to fetch their rifles and the pair left Glenveagh Lodge, heading past the gushing Astellan waterfall and into the mountainous terrain. They strode with purpose, scanning the horizon for wildfowl. It was a mild autumn morning but the higher they climbed, the blustier it became. Despite the remote landscape, the hillside was speckled with small grey-white cottages – a few abandoned tumbledowns but most with a grey plume of smoke indicating occupancy.

"There'll be a few dry houses down in the valley today, sir." Murray laughed.

"I daresay but I'd be happier without bothersome tenants. How they can even eke out a living in this remote wilderness is beyond me. This is sheep country, pure and simple."

"Well, they have their own livestock, sir, and there's decent farming land down in the valley…"

"Don't you go soft on them. I hope you're still impounding any of their animals that stray onto my land. And what about my missing flock? There must be thieving among the tenants."

"Aye, sir, there always is but the shepherds and I are keeping a close eye and we're clamping down on any sheep-stealing. The word is out that Mr Murray—" He cleared his throat. "I mean, Mr Adair won't stand for it."

"Good!" Adair stopped to breathe in the air. "Look around, this is a splendid estate – no finer hunting ground in all Ireland. But these tenants' cottages, they're … they're spoiling my view."

"Aye, sir, aye."

"What part of Scotland are you from? Remind me?"

"Am from Aberdeenshire, sir."

"So you've seen Balmoral then?"

"Balmoral? The Queen's castle? I haven't seen the castle, sir, but I know the land – a fine estate that is, sir."

"Indeed, I visited it once, not long ago. Don't you think this scenery is as spectacular as the Scottish Highlands?"

Adair looked into the distance, a dreamy look in his eyes.

"Certainly sir, 'tis just as beautiful if not more."

"This could be a very fine hunting estate – a herd of deer, some game birds, leaving the higher ground for sheep. That's my plan, Murray."

"Yes sir, and a fine plan it is, sir."

"But there's one thing missing," Adair cocked his head and stared at his land steward as if testing his ability to know his mind. Murray screwed up his forehead and stared back at his master's gun.

"The gentry to hunt?"

"No!" Adair looked back towards the lough.

"Sorry sir, I don't know, what is missing?"

"A castle, a mansion house like Balmoral."

"You're planning on building a castle? Way out here?"

"Why not? I think it's a fine idea. Why, every splendid estate has a castle and in order to attract hunting parties I would need plenty of rooms for people to stay." Adair made a humming sound, ruminating. "Well, it's just an idea, for now. I'd have to raise the capital first and this place would have to be a lot more profitable than it currently is with the pittance coming in from those tenants."

Murray nodded as the bleat of a distant sheep interrupted them.

"We can bring in more sheep and make a decent profit

on them. I just would need to recruit more shepherds. There's a lot of acres to cover."

"Whatever you need, make it happen," said Adair.

"Certainly, sir! And might I pry and ask if by building a castle you're thinking of settling here? You know, making this your home?"

Adair felt himself blush; he never discussed personal matters. He adjusted his tone to a higher level of haughty to hide his embarrassment.

"Settling? I don't see myself as ever settled, like some soggy autumn leaf! That would involve taking a wife and I'm really not interested in a woman draining my finances."

Murray laughed his wheezy, hoarse heckle.

"Yer right, sir, my missus would spend every penny I have and still not be happy. Women – they bleed ye dry!"

"Quite. A wealthy woman, on the other hand, would be a worthwhile pursuit."

"I daresay you're a very eligible bachelor. The ladies must be tripping over themselves."

As Adair frowned, Murray changed the subject back to hunting.

"There was a great flock arrived just yesterday, sir, when I was surveying the farms. White-fronted geese I believe."

They climbed higher in search of the birds and the landlord squinted into the distance.

"Over yonder, Murray – we should make for those trees," Adair hissed, removing his gun from his shoulder and carrying it low to his waist. Both men changed direction before Adair suddenly stopped. Murray grabbed his rifle, straining to see what his master had spotted. The sun illuminated the land so that from the blades of grass to the granite cliffs everything shimmered. As they watched, new colours of cream and brown began to jar with the shimmering grass. Murray stiffened and pointed at the herd of cattle heading towards them. A dog barked and a man's voice bellowed after the cows.

"Hup, hup, hup!" the farmer swished a cane in the air, just high enough to lift the hairs on the cows' backs.

"Who's that? What's he doing here?" Adair demanded.

"I believe it's that peasant farmer Sean Sweeney, sir. Shall I tell him to beat it?"

Without waiting for him to answer, Murray set off towards the offending herdsman. The cows stumbled into each other as Sweeney shifted his attention towards the figure approaching him.

"Well, well. If t'isn't Mr John Adair Esquire and his humble servant. To what do I owe this honour?" Sweeney forced a smile.

"You're disturbing our hunting."

"I'm disturbing ye? Yer disturbing my cattle. Adair has no hunting rights in these parts. I've always herded my cattle through here." Sweeney's bull neck stiffened as he stood square to Murray, pointing his cane at the surrounding fields. The Scotsman shielded his eyes from the sun with his hand and followed the direction of the farmer's cane.

"What's happening here?" asked Adair, catching up with Murray.

"Good day, Mr Adair sir. I was just telling yer good servant that yer disturbing these animals." Sweeney remained rooted to the spot and lowered his cane to his side.

"But I have sporting rights, you damn fool."

"I may be a fool but least thing I know is yer not meant to be shooting here and I can drive my cattle through here as I please. But I 'preciate yer new to these parts, Mr Adair," said Sweeney.

Adair snorted and slung his shotgun over his shoulder.

"Very well. Murray, we'll not engage with this peasant farmer any longer. We're wasting valuable time," he said and backed away. Murray spat on the grass near Sweeney and obediently followed his master.

For several hours the huntsmen surveyed the landscape of purple and green heather, but the geese were alert to the danger and outwitted them at each attempt. Frustrated, Adair fired his gun in a wild bid at a distant bird.

"Damn! I say that Sweeney peasant has cursed us."

Murray gave a hoarse chortle.

"Aye he'll have cursed you, gone to Mass and then home for some poteen, what little they have now!"

Murray snatched his breath mid-laugh and seemed to hold it. A cloud of dust had risen and through it came several men. Adair followed his gaze.

"Who… What's going on?" He gripped his shotgun.

A mob of men and boys were heading towards them brandishing sticks. Many of them wore old sacks with rough-cut holes for their eyes and mouth. Adair had heard tales of Ribbonmen torturing and even murdering landlords and their agents. He recalled reading about the Molly

Maguires from County Monaghan – men who dressed in women's clothes, their faces blackened and shawled, who snuck up on officials and ducked them into bogholes or beat them to a pulp. He began to tremble. Both men charged their guns and took aim.

"Don't come any closer, you hear!" shouted Murray, raising himself on his toes to his full height. There was a cackle of sound from the advancing crowd but they stopped on seeing the guns pointed towards them.

"Any of you takes another step and I swear I'll shoot," Adair shouted.

The mob stood silently glaring at the hunters. Gradually they fanned out until they had completely encircled the two men. Adair could have been mistaken but the large fellow leading the pack had the same bearing as the farmer, Sweeney. It was difficult to know for certain as his face was hidden under a sack. From it a voice bellowed at them, "G'wan, g'wan!" which the others echoed. The men and the mob glared at each other across fifty yards of heather. Adair whispered to his land steward, "They'll not come any closer. They've no guns."

Pointing his gun ahead, the landlord continued on his path. But the mob encircled them and, keeping their distance, moved as they walked. When Adair and Murray stopped, they stopped too and jeered.

"What sir? What should we do?" the Scotsman hissed.

"We just keep moving. Head back to the lodge," ordered Adair, all the while surveying the mob. Some, especially the smaller ones, went sackless with just thick mud attempting to conceal their faces. He tried to make mental pictures to identify them again. A raggle-taggle bunch with their dirty faces and some without shoes. Next to a grey-haired man wielding a rusty scythe, he spied a young woman whose dark hair was scraped tight under a scarf. He was startled; even the women were uncivilised in this place. At first the hunters advanced cautiously, testing the circle of fierce faces and banging sticks. But they picked up pace like partners learning to dance. The circle expanding and contracting as the hunters moved swiftly in the direction of Glenveagh Lodge. When they finally reached it, Adair found some courage. He waved his shotgun at the now diminished band of pursuers. Some had drifted off back to their cottages as the children had struggled to keep up.

"You will rue the day you menaced me!" he yelled. "I'll have you all prosecuted."

There were jeers and hoots from the mob, drowning out his last words. Adair and Murray at last escaped the threatening circle and when they were safe behind closed doors in the kitchen, Adair punched with the full force of his fist a piece of mutton hanging on a hook from the ceiling. The carcass took the first blow and the second and then sagged as the dead flesh stretched on the hook.

"I will have them!" roared Adair. "Those peasants can't threaten me! I will clear them all, every last one of them. They won't be smirking and jeering then. Oh no, they'll be crying and begging me to let them stay."

"Sir, I would gladly assist you in that pursuit but I'm not sure any of them were even your tenants."

"I don't care who their landlord is. I'll have them locked up," Adair's face was scarlet with rage. "That large fella leading the pack looked to me like Sweeney, if I'm not mistaken."

"Hard to say, sir, what with his face covered, but aye, he had a similar shape to yon peasant."

"To be threatened on one's own estate is a serious enough matter for me to report this to the police."

Murray poured two glasses of whiskey and Adair snatched one and swallowed it neat. His face reddened beneath his beard and he made a rasping sound through his teeth as the whiskey scorched his mouth. He then kicked off his boots and stormed from the kitchen into the lounge where he had a magnificent view of the glen. He slumped into an armchair, muttering to himself with a mixture of rage and relief. Murray left him alone but not before pouring himself another whiskey from Adair's cask.

Chapter 3

Declan woke with a jump the next morning. He had slept uneasily. Tense from their narrow escape from the law, he had dreamed he was back on the tiny island on Lough Veagh. He felt someone pulling his arm in the dark.

"Declan, would ye get up! It's past midday."

A stern face swam in front of his sleepy eyes and as he focused, he leapt up realising it was his ma. She had been shaking him as he lay curled up in the family cot by the cold embers of last night's fire.

"Michael went hours ago. Ye missed the turf cart so ye can help me dig the spuds. Yer sister's disappeared now too. Where were ye 'til so late? Don't lie to me on yer da's anniversary!" Mairead wagged a finger at Declan whose tired brain tried to digest her monologue. He could see the curve of dirt under her fingernail and her arthritic gnarled knuckles. She spent her days bent double over their potato patch checking the drills of soil, tending their meagre land for what it could produce.

"Ah, sorry, Ma, just some business with the Sweeneys," he said, splashing cold water on his face. "Ye know, in preparation for tonight's Harvest Home."

"Those brothers are trouble. The Widow McAward says they're Ribbonmen. Don't ye be getting too mixed up with them."

"No, Ma. I don't court trouble. It's Mickey ye wanna be scoldin'. He's the one courtin' Francis Dermott's daughter." He grinned and picked up the battered loy leaning outside the door.

"Ah now, she's a good girl," Ma said, pointing out the drills to dig. "Nothin' like her drunkard father. Sinead could do worse than our Michael."

She pressed her bony hands around Declan's arm and spoke in a gentler tone.

"Listen, son, I've decided not to go to the harvest tonight. No doubt there'll be drinkin' and dancin' and plenty to eat..." Her voice drifted off. "Well, my heart just isn't in it."

"If yer sure, I can bring ye home some of Briege's biscuits."

He patted her hand and set to digging, plucking up one of the potatoes from the soil when its unusual shape caught his eye. One end of it was bad, its skin damaged and tinged green. He went to toss it away and then stared again. Was that a face in it? Yes, there was the long nose, the haughty chin. He blinked. Adair had clearly got under his skin or maybe he was drinking too much poteen. He couldn't get him out of his head. But no, he swore he could see the landlord's face in the spud. He shuddered. The crop that had nearly finished them was still revered by all the tenants. Was the next threat to their livelihoods drawn in this singular, rotten spud? He felt certain the Widow McAward would believe it was a sign. But he was too sensible to countenance that. He glanced one more time at the strange outline and then flung it towards Lough Gartan. *Too much poteen.* He shook his head.

When dusk fell there was still no sign of the twins so he decided to head on without them. He passed under the sign saying, *Rath Dé ort* above the door, and still shaken by the night on the lough, muttered to himself with relief, "But for the grace of God indeed." On the way to the Sweeneys' barn he called in with the Bradleys, but no one was home. Alex and Briege Bradley were their closest neighbours. Their son Ruairi was the only boy still at home. The rest of them had left Donegal. One died during the Great Hunger, the eldest had emigrated to America and several others were itinerant labourers who rarely returned to Gartan. They were left with a granddaughter, Bridgeen, after her mother disappeared to Derry, while their son, the child's father, sought his fortune in England. Declan wondered what it would be like to just pack up and leave Donegal. Uncle Liam often wrote suggesting he and Michael join him in the States, but Declan had no real desire to leave home. He accepted his role in life was to look after his family.

He dandered up the lane, knowing he'd need to conserve his energy for the night ahead. In a way he was pleased the

Harvest Home celebrations coincided with ten years since his father had passed as it helped him forget the pain of losing him. A whole decade. He missed him, though not as much as his ma of course. She'd never got over losing her beloved husband. Declan used to hear her sob at night when she thought they were all asleep. It was hard not to since the whole family shared the one bed and there wasn't much privacy in a two-room cottage.

The screech of a violin rang out above a growing din of voices and stamping feet, startling some of the ravens roosting nearby. It was pitch dark with dense clouds hiding the moon and the stars. Declan's eye caught the crack of light under the Sweeneys' barn door and he smiled, recognising many of the voices as the cries from the party grew louder. He reached the barn door, which creaked open, and the wall of sound struck him with the same punch to the senses as he felt from a single sip of poteen. It seemed most of the tenants from around Derryveagh were packed into the Sweeneys' slim barn. They were jumping and swinging each other across the sawdust with an energy that was infectious. Immediately his spirits lifted.

"Declan, you made it!"

Sean's large, rough hand came crushing down on his shoulder. In his other fist he held a jar of liquor.

"Where's yer ma? Did ye leave her at home?"

"'Fraid so, she wasn't up to it," Declan mumbled, shrugging his shoulders. "Thought it best to leave her be. When she makes up her mind, that's it. Are Cara and Michael here?"

"They certainly are. Been here since this afternoon. We

had some sport up yon mountain with ol' Adair. We got his blood up, I'll tell ye'."

Declan struggled to hear him over the din but was then distracted by the large feast spread on the table to one side. Candles illuminated thick slices of meat, crusts of fresh-baked breads, oat and honey biscuits and stacks of apples and pears. His stomach overrode his curiosity and he pushed past Sweeney and tucked into the food. For a moment he recalled the ghastly yellow stirabout – his da's last supper – and felt a morsel stick in his throat. He thumped his chest and continued to eat ravenously. It was as good as it looked and smelt, especially the biscuits, which were legendary in Derryveagh thanks to the baking skills of their neighbour Briege. She was the closest thing Gartan had to a baker and Declan thought looked the part with her round, rosy cheeks and stout physique.

"Well Declan, is yer mother not with ye?" asked Briege, offering him the basket of biscuits. She pursed her lips and without waiting for a reply nodded her wise, knowing head. "I didn't think she'd come, y'know. It's a bit lively for an anniversary. Maybe I should head back and keep her company…"

Declan shook his head as he munched on the biscuits.

"That's very thoughtful of ye, Mrs Bradley, but I offered and I think she's happy to be by herself tonight. Sayin' her prayers and just being with him."

"Him? Oh, you mean Him," she said and pointed upwards with solemnity.

Declan frowned, his mouth too stuffed with biscuit to reply. Briege put the basket back on the table and went over to where her husband Alex was playing the fiddle. Declan swallowed.

"No, I meant me da," he muttered to himself and, remembering his promise, stuffed some biscuits into his pockets.

He looked around for his brother and sister. Girls had tied up their long hair with scarves and danced with each other, whooping and yelping to the jig. Little Bridgeen, her hair in pigtails, looked enthralled and was following the older girls' every move. He spotted Michael in the centre of a circle of girls, among them the Widow McAward's granddaughters dancing and laughing. He was clapping and stamping his foot to the music, grinning from ear to ear. His smile melted the ladies, young and old.

"Yer a charmer just like yer da," Mairead would say of Michael. Declan admired his brother's confidence. He noticed how he would smile at a girl, stare for a little while and then saunter over. He complimented even the plainest of dresses and within minutes he was dragging his prey around the floor. Declan, on the other hand, found himself lost for words with women. Of course he could have a conversation with Briege Bradley or the Widow McAward but girls his own age left him flustered. Michael saw him looking and gave him a swift nod before linking arms with Sinead for the next reel. She was the most striking girl in the barn, with her long, shiny black hair and eyes as large as saucers.

Alex played the fiddle, beating time with his foot, while another neighbour – James Gallagher – belted out a ballad.

We were homeward bound one night on the deep,
Swinging in my hammock I fell asleep.
I dreamed a dream and I thought it true,
Concerning Franklin and his gallant crew…

Declan laughed at the antics of the dancers who were jumping to a different beat from Gallagher's throaty lament.

When the dance finished Michael whisked Sinead across the floor and brought her to an abrupt standstill in front of him.

"Ye finally got here," he said, panting. "Thought Ma might've dragged ye to confession."

"Naw, avoided that one. Evening, Sinead!"

She smiled shyly as Michael, all gangly arms and legs, threw himself down on a haystack beside the table. Even close up her skin was flawless. She glanced over his shoulder to Michael but before he could turn around, gave a loud gasp.

"Michael! Watch the flame!"

Declan swung round to see a candle had been knocked on to the haystack where Michael had just leapt from. The dry straw caught fire and began to lick around the table.

"Stand back!" shouted Michael and went to grab Declan's jar of poteen. As Declan let go of it, Sinead pushed between them.

"Don't do that!"

She stopped Michael's arm and doused the contents of a water pitcher from the table over the small fire. Oblivious to the commotion in the corner, Alex continued to play the fiddle, while the dancing and singing grew louder.

A slightly damp Michael stood gaping at Sinead.

"W-what did you do that for? I was putting out the fire," he exclaimed.

"With poteen? Are ye wise? You'd have sent the whole barn up in flames with that stuff."

Sinead stood with her hands on her hips, a scolding look on her face. Declan burst out laughing.

"She's right Mickey, ye bloody eejit! There's not much a Dermott doesn't know about alcohol."

This time she turned her glare on him.

"You men think ye know it all but ye haven't a clue." She then turned on her heel and joined Cara on the dancefloor. Michael shrugged and handed Declan back his jar.

"Beauty and brains, aren't I the lucky fella'?" He smiled sheepishly after her.

The Widow McAward came across to them, tapping her stick.

"A decade since yer da passed. How the years fly by!" she said, peering through her occluded eye. "He was a good man and he left two fine sons. Now when are ye goin' to ask for the hand of one of my girls?"

They both laughed. As the song came to an end, Sean Sweeney lifted his drink and called for the revellers to join him in a toast.

"First to a dear friend who departed ten years ago – Daniel Conaghan!"

The room muttered in unison, "To Dan, to Dan."

Declan raised his jar in appreciation and swigged his poteen.

"Those were desperate years, let us not forget all those

who passed during the Great Hunger and let's celebrate the fine harvest we have this year." Sean bowed his head solemnly.

"Aye, hear, hear!" the barn echoed.

The solemnity quickly passed as Sean raised his jar again.

"One more toast tonight... To Mr Adair's health and happiness!" he slurred with a wide grin.

Sinead's father, Francis, who was leaning against the barn wall, began to splutter on his poteen. "And may the devil hang 'im!" he roared over the cheers. He was a squat man, with large sunken eyes, which were often half closed. Declan remembered when he had a thick head of hair like his daughter, but the resemblance ended there. He wondered how he had sired such a beauty. Owen approached the table beside Declan and poured himself more poteen.

"Glad ye could join us. Did Mickey tell ye about this afternoon?"

Declan shook his head and listened, astonished, as Owen described how Sean, furious at his encounter with Adair and his land steward, had summoned a band of villagers to menace the landlord. Declan set down his jar and stared across at Michael who was back swinging Sinead around on the dancefloor. Beside them Ruairi Bradley had linked arms with Cara who was laughing and clapping in a line of dancers. Owen followed his gaze.

"Yer sister's a great girl. No fear in that lass, she came up the mountain too. T'was fairly beating the ground with her stick at Adair."

Declan spluttered in rage and pushed Owen aside. He rushed over to the dancefloor and grabbed Michael and Cara by the wrists.

"Party's over ye two – we're leaving!"

Michael wriggled his wrist free from his brother's strong grasp and glared hard at him.

"What's the matter with ye? It's Harvest Home, we're celebrating. Get yerself a drink," said Michael, rubbing his arm.

"It's also Da's anniversary – have ye no respect, both of ye?"

Declan, his face flushed, glared at his brother and sister. They stared back open-mouthed and blinking. He could feel his chest tightening and wondered what his father would do in the same situation. Cara pursed her lips and stared at her older brother with that defiant face he had become accustomed to when he scolded her.

"We wasn't doin' nothin' wrong," she began to gush. "I was with Sinead when Michael arrived with scraw for the fire. Then the Sweeneys came by to get Francis and we all followed them up the mountain. It was just a bit of fun. We didn't mean any harm."

"She's right," added Michael, folding his arms and sticking out his chin. "No one was hurt. We just wanted to show 'im he can't treat us like, like dirt."

Declan exploded. "He's the landlord, ye eejits! He can do whatever he likes. He can put up our rent, have ye arrested, evict us and pull down our cabin. All within the law. Did Sinead go too, Cara?"

"No."

"Then ye didn't have to follow them. Seems she's more sense than ye both."

"We were wearing sacks, he couldn't see our faces..." Michael hissed. Declan looked around at the crowd and pulled his sweaty palm through his mop of thick, dark hair. They were all staring at him like a flock of sheep, silent and nosy. Just then his gaze met Sean's. Declan caught Cara's arm and nodded to Michael to follow him. The three of them pushed through the crowd towards Sean whose grin grew broader as they approached.

"Aw Declan, yer not leaving so soon? Ye only just got here."

Declan pushed his nose close to Sean's face and through gritted teeth whispered, "Don't ye be bringing trouble to my family Sean, d'ye hear? It's alright for ye, he's not yer landlord."

Declan clenched his sister's arm tightly and could feel himself shaking. To his surprise Sean stooped his head and appeared apologetic.

"I'm sorry, Declan. I didn't expect—" He stopped mid-sentence and looked around at the musicians.

"Ye gonna start playing something? The party isn't over, ye know." He glared at the watching villagers.

"The party *is* over!" said a stranger with a Scottish accent who had just entered the barn. There was a stomping of feet on the gravel path outside. The revellers looked up as the doors of the barn were flung wide open. A half dozen police burst in, their buttons gleaming in the candlelight. Declan blinked a couple of times, thinking it was the effects of the poteen, then he realised he was looking at a shepherd's crook. It was Murray. The Scotsman swung the crook through his hands and jabbed at Declan's collar with the handle. There was a scar on his forehead, which, up close, gave him a more menacing appearance.

"What's there to celebrate? Upsetting Mr Adair?"

Murray snatched the jar from his hand and gave a dramatic sniff. He handed it to one of the detectives.

"Evidence. Cuff him!"

Murray's fellow shepherd, Dugald Rankin, a tall skinny fellow with a scruffy moustache, appeared behind him. Declan wobbled again as he tried to free himself from the crook but Murray had snared him through a tear in his jacket.

Declan turned to the twins.

"Go home, the pair of ye!" he yelled.

Michael began to protest but was jostled by the crowd of revellers. He grabbed Cara and Sinead, whose faces had turned white. They fled out the door in a stream of shawls and caps.

"Right, party's over! Go home or you'll be arrested," said Rankin, standing legs planted on the table, scattering the food. At Murray's instruction several of the men, including the Sweeneys and Francis, were handcuffed. With Sean's fists safely tied behind his back, Murray squared up to him.

"We were just enjoyin' a nice bit of hunting when you lot showed up!" he snapped. "Ruined my day. Mr Adair is... How would you describe him, Dugald?"

Rankin pursed his lips and slammed his fist into his palm.

"No words, sir. Angry, very angry."

"Innn-candescent!" bellowed Murray into Sean's face, spattering him with hot saliva. "You probably don't know what that means, you ignorant peasant."

Sean struggled against the cuffs but he was tightly chained to the others and led out of the barn. Declan felt the rage rise inside him and he couldn't decide who he was angrier at, the Sweeneys or Murray.

Chapter 4

Declan examined his new metal bracelet with a mixture of horror and disbelief as he trailed behind Francis with the police escort to Church Hill. At the station Sean demanded to know what they were being charged with. Murray seemed to delight in teasing him without fear that the big man in handcuffs could throw a punch.

"Mr Adair is a Justice of the Peace so he can decide whatever charges he likes," said Murray with a smirk. "But let's consider what he could charge you with..." He rubbed his stubbly chin. "Poteen-brewing, harassment... Ah, but sheep-stealing, now that carries a large sentence. Shall we pursue that charge, Dugald, what d'you think?"

Murray and Rankin were clearly enjoying their double act and with one final flourish they slammed shut the heavy iron door. The Sweeney brothers were separated and Declan found himself sharing a cold, stone bench with Owen. Sean Sweeney and Francis Dermott looked across at them through the bars opposite. Declan guessed the police thought one burly Sweeney per cell was enough to deal with. All four sat in the semi-darkness and pondered their fate. Owen kept muttering, "Sheep? I didn't take no sheep, I didn't, they can't put this on me."

"Aye, that's what they all say behind bars – everyone's innocent," growled Sean from out of the gloom.

"We're done for with all that poteen in yer barn," said Declan.

"Relax, young Declan. Our stash is well hidden. The only stuff they'll find in the barn is what's in them jars. We hadn't time to move the barrels from the big tree at Lough Veagh. Most of it's still hidden. So, we were supping on moonshine at Harvest Home." He shrugged his large shoulders. "Every tenant in Donegal is doing the same. Are they going to arrest us all?"

"If you hadn't been harassing Adair none of us would be here," snapped Declan.

Sean began to whistle, which agitated Declan more.

"It was a good Harvest Home until Declan arrived. Right, Owen?"

"Ha! Blame me," said Declan. "Got a lot worse when Murray burst in. It's alright for ye boys but me and Francis are his tenants. He can just evict us, evidence or not."

Sean slammed his fist on the bars.

"Look I know yer mad I led yer brother and sister up the mountain." He raised his voice. "Adair got my blood up. Telling me I was disturbing his shooting. And all this business for months locking up our animals in that pound, accusing us of stealing sheep. Then raiding our poteen still. I just wanted to scare him, that's all."

"Scare him?" Declan was trembling partly from rage and partly from the shock of landing in a police cell. "Ye think ye can scare a wealthy man with guns and staff by gathering a bunch of villagers wearing sacks and beating sticks? He's not like our old landlord Mr Johnston – he was never there half the time, not interested in the estate. Adair has plans, ye can see that about him. Why else would he bring in a land steward and shepherds? He's filling them hills with sheep. He doesn't need or want us. And ye menacin' him on the mountain isn't going to do anything except make him want rid of us more."

They sat in the gloom and listened to the water dripping from the eaves outside. Declan worried about his ma and the twins. What if they did charge him with a crime? He couldn't take care of them from prison. He stared at the four walls of the tiny cell, feeling a tight knot of frustration and anxiety in his stomach. He wouldn't get work if he had a record. He felt in his pocket and found the biscuits he'd saved for his ma. So much for bringing them home to her tonight. He remembered her words about the Sweeneys being trouble and wished he'd never got involved with their poteen racket. He put the biscuits back in his pocket. He'd no appetite. He'd keep them for when he was hungry. *God only knows how long we'll be banged up,* he thought. He rested his head against the wall and prayed for sleep. Perhaps Father O'Flanigan could vouch for his good character. Didn't he go to Mass every Sunday?

"NO! I don't want to owe him any favours," he shouted.

"Great," tutted Owen. "He talks in his sleep."

At some point Declan must have drifted off.

Before dawn had broken, they were marched in chains fifteen miles to the courthouse in Letterkenny, the nearest large town for the arraignment. Declan hung his head in shame as he recognised labourers in the fields they passed. They leaned or sat on the stone walls craning their necks. Women carrying baskets of food to and from village markets stopped to stare as they trudged and clinked past. The four accused had stumbled, one behind the other, across stony rough ground for hours and Declan found himself glaring at the three in front, still angry that they'd dragged him into trouble. At the courthouse they were charged with the illegal brewing of poteen. The magistrate asked how they were pleading.

"Not guilty," whispered Declan, hanging his head.

"Not guilty," said Owen, raising his chin.

"Not sure," said a bewildered Francis. The room erupted, even the sullen-looking defendants waiting for their cases at the back of the courtroom creased themselves laughing.

Then Sean stood up, staring straight at the magistrate, he cleared his throat. "Guilty – of drinking moonshine but not of making it."

There was a rustle of voices around the room. The magistrate conferred with Sergeant McSherry who'd made the arrests. The clerk passed some papers between them before the magistrate called the room to attention.

"Very well. If the Crown can bring the evidence before

this court, we shall begin proceedings in three weeks." He struck his gavel. "Take them back to Church Hill."

They made the long journey back, this time in the rain, where they were thrown into the police station cells, damp and more dejected.

"There's not an ounce of truth in those charges," Francis said. "Did you see the magistrate's face? I never saw eyebrows raised as high. We'll be outta' here in no time."

"Think the raised eyebrows were on account of you, Francis Dermott," Owen mumbled.

The rest of them sat in silence. The gloom of the grey walls had sapped their spirits. Apart from noting the setting of the sun from the light through the air vent, they'd lost track of the hours. They'd been given little to eat except a bowl of thin stirabout. Declan sighed; he couldn't stay mad at his friends and neighbours. They weren't the ones who'd locked him up. He passed around the biscuits, which were met with the sound of grateful munching.

He woke the next day feeling stiff and sore as doors banged above them. There was a sudden clamour of voices. Francis and Sean had raised themselves up on the bars opposite and strained to hear the details.

"Shush, it's Adair," Sean hissed.

The distinctive voice of Adair, with his polished Trinity College accent, rose above the sound of the police inspector, Sergeant McSherry. They were engaged in a heated argument.

"We don't have evidence to prove any of these men were distilling poteen. As I said before we'd need to catch them in the actual act. All we caught them doing was drinking the stuff. The magistrate warned me yesterday not to waste his time on charges of drinking poteen, saying, and I agree with him, he'd have 'every Sean, Mairtin and Paddy up in court for that'."

"Then what about the sheep-stealing. Has there been any progress with that?"

The sergeant cleared his throat.

"Mr Adair, we found sixty-five of your sheep, dead, not two miles from Glenveagh Lodge. Dead, I might add, from exposure, want and neglect on the part of your shepherds. What's more, sir, we searched for the remaining sheep and although we couldn't account for them all, we did discover sixteen sheep hides hanging in your land steward's premises."

"Murray?"

"Yes sir, Mr Murray. He admitted they were your sheep but insisted they died of natural causes and he had slaughtered them for mutton. You should be aware that he had a lot of mutton in his store."

Adair was silenced by the revelation.

"So, so what now?"

"Well, Mr Adair, I shall write a full report on this but I will not be pursuing Mr Murray's malicious injuries claim," said the weary-sounding sergeant. "If anyone should be paying compensation to you, sir, it should be your own land steward."

Adair mumbled, "You're sure none of my tenants have

had a hand in the deaths of my sheep? I mean sixty-five is a lot of…"

"Positive sir. I am sure as a Justice of the Peace for this district that you recognise the importance of evidence and the legal process. Might I add a word of caution, Mr Adair?" The sergeant's voice was now barely audible. "The Derryveagh tenantry are a peaceful folk. We have had very little crime here for many years. Over in Gweedore some years ago at Lord George Hill's estate, the tenants killed hundreds of imported Scots sheep because they feared eviction. Several tenants were convicted of maliciously killing the sheep, one was transported to Australia and several were imprisoned. I know this because I investigated these crimes. I can assure you, you are not dealing with the same sort of tenants."

Adair raised his voice and Declan imagined him spitting the words out at the inspector.

"As a Justice of the Peace, I take crime in the area very seriously. From the brief period I have been landlord I have intercepted several illicit stills, I have been harassed by local people on the mountain and large numbers of my sheep have been stolen. I think, inspector, this does not reflect your claim of a peaceful, law-abiding folk and I will not rest until I get rid of the criminal elements blighting this community."

"We will keep up surveillance of the tenantry, but I hope we can put these claims to rest, sir. Might I add that if you're not happy with any of your tenants there is a much simpler recourse at your disposal – eviction."

There was a pause as Declan and his cellmates strained to hear more but the voices dropped to a mumble and then the door banged as Adair left. The four prisoners stared wide-eyed at each other as they heard footsteps coming closer and the rattle of keys. Sergeant McSherry stood in the doorway grinning from ear to ear.

"Gentlemen." He paused. "You're free to go. I'm sorry it has taken so long but, if you want, you can take it up with the Justice of the Peace."

"Ye jokin'?" cried Sean. "Ye mean with Adair? If I never see that scoundrel again it'd be too soon."

The sergeant frowned. "Take my advice, keep a low profile and stay out of Adair and Murray's way."

All four left the Church Hill police barracks, and emerged blinking into the daylight. Declan took a deep breath of the fresh mountain air and smiled with relief.

"Declan!"

He looked around to see Michael jump from the opposite wall and rush across the lane.

"Thank God!" He slapped him on the back. "I knew they'd release ye."

Declan grinned, finding it hard to stay mad at his brother.

"The constable told us they had no evidence against any of ye. Think Murray just wanted to raid the party, scare us all a bit after, after…"

"Let's not talk about yer adventure up the mountain. Hope ye didn't tell Ma?"

Michael shook his head. He looked like he hadn't slept.

"Everything alright?" asked Declan.

"Just Ma's been worried sick. Cara's been upset, blames

me for being stupid and Sinead, well, she thinks it's all my fault too."

Declan laughed.

"Good! Nothing like the wrath of three women. Let's go home, sounds like you've been punished enough."

Mairead was overcome with joy when he walked up the lane. She threw down the loy she'd been digging with and pressed him close, the earthy smell of her scarf and coat instantly assuring him he was home. That night she made his favourite boxty, baked good and crisp on the griddle. She even sent Cara over to the Bradleys to borrow a box of eggs, which he knew would take her ages to pay back. Still sore from Declan's public scolding, Cara shook her long hair over her eyes and pretended she didn't hear their ma.

"G'wan fetch them eggs, missy!" said Mairead pushing her out the door. "And don't come back without a smile on yer face for yer big brother."

Declan's relief at his release quickly turned to anger at the misery his family had been put through. An anger which seemed to burn in his chest. He worried about the sergeant's suggestion to Adair of eviction. The Conaghans and their neighbours had worked their plots of land for years. It was all they knew. His father's father had broken his back removing the stones and boulders from the earth so they had a patch to cultivate. The Conaghans, not Adair, worked the soil, tended their crops, mended the walls and ditches, he fumed. Did he even know their plot of land? The distinct shape of the fairy mound at the end of the field? Did he know the way the sun set on the land or the birds who fought for the best roosting spot in the trees by their cabin? Adair couldn't know these things so how was the land more his? Just because of some paper deeds in a dusty drawer in faraway Dublin? Who was this landlord that could threaten decades of peace in the area? His thoughts were interrupted by Mairead who had settled in the inglenook by the fire.

"What I want to know is why they arrested ye, Declan? Ye've never been in any bother. Those Sweeneys, on the other hand, are always up to somethin'. I warned ye they were trouble."

Declan shrugged his shoulders, while the twins stared at the floor.

"Ah sorry Ma, I was caught with a jar of poteen so it gave them an excuse to arrest me."

She threw her hands in the air.

"What have I said to ye about suppin' that stuff? The Widow McAward has said it can blind or even kill ye. Well I hope yer sober now!"

Declan sighed and thought of the barrels of poteen still hidden at Glenveagh. When Adair had become their landlord, he'd put up the rent. Little did his ma know poteen was keeping the roof over their heads. She picked up the conversation again.

"Those shepherds are a bad lot too ... no morals, if ye know what I'm saying..."

Cara poked her in the arm.

"Are they thievin' Ma, is that what ye mean?"

"Thievin' aye – stealing Adair's sheep themselves and

keeping the mutton in their own stores. But that's not the worst of it," she said.

"There's worse?" asked Cara, leaning forward, her hair dangling close to the fire.

"Och, yer so innocent," Michael piped up. "I heard rumours about Rankin and Murray's wife being ye know … close?"

Cara gasped.

"Yes, I was leaving butter at the big house when Adair's housekeeper began tellin' me Rankin has been getting cosy with Mrs Murray," said Mairead. "Not that I care for her, God forsaken lot all of them, but what man would carry on with his friend's wife?"

"Maybe they're not friends, he's his master after all. Perhaps he hates him!" said Cara.

"Or just fancies his wife," said Declan, shrugging his shoulders.

"Seem to spend a fair bit of time together, like down the pub, for someone who hates him," Michael said.

"As the Widow McAward would say, 'keep yer enemies close'."

"Think I'd prefer to keep my distance from Adair and all his lot," said Declan. "Find it hard to avoid them shepherds, seems like they're always watching us."

"Be as well for Mr Murray to keep a watch on his own wife and shepherds," said Mairead, having the usual final word on a subject.

As the turf crackled in the grate, Declan began to feel drowsy. He hadn't slept well in the station's cold cell and was just thinking of bed when there was a dull thump on the door.

"What was that?" said Michael, jumping to his feet.

Declan slowly opened the door, nervously looking from side to side into the darkness but there was no one there. Then his eye caught sight of a dark lump that looked like a rock, just feet from the door. He bent down to examine it. To his astonishment it was soft to touch. Turning the woolly ball over, two empty sockets stared up at him. It was a sheep's head, recently slaughtered. He surveyed the quiet lane, still except for the occasional bleat of Alex's goat and the cries of a fox.

"Look at the door, Declan!" cried Michael, holding a candle to it.

Above the splodge of blood where the skull had clearly been thrown, Declan could just make out the initials '*JA*' in the bloody trail.

A shawled figure came out of the darkness. It was Sinead, breathless and looking alarmed.

"They did ye too!" she said, covering her mouth. "I was so relieved when Da got out today but clearly Murray and his men mean trouble. It's a warning, isn't it? Will they evict us? Where will we go?"

Michael went to comfort her but she pushed him away.

"Ye were right Declan, Adair doesn't care about his tenants," she sobbed. "We're done for."

Declan looked at her worried face, which mirrored his own.

"He needs to have a reason to evict us. The police told us just to keep our heads down. Daubing our doors in blood is surely a sign of desperation. Murray just wants to scare us. Don't let him scare ye."

Then he took a run at the skull and kicked it beyond the hedge. There was a rustle, and in the dark they could just make out the red streak of a fox skulk back to its den with the skull in its jaws.

Chapter 5

The morning fog was just rising from the fields as Adair left his appointment with Sergeant McSherry in Church Hill.

"Home, sir?" asked the coachman opening his carriage door.

"Where am I likely to find Murray at this hour?"

The coachman paused and rubbed his bushy eyebrow.

"It's early enough, you could catch him at his cottage, otherwise he'll be at the animal pound – he's rather fond of that place."

"Good, we'll try his cottage first!"

They departed in great haste, as if the coachman sensed Adair's bad mood. His head rushed as he struggled with the revelation that his own land steward had a storeful of mutton. That didn't bother him so much as Murray's inability to find charges to stick against the tenants. How difficult can it be to bring a case against those infernal peasants who threaten me – their landlord, no less? The police were useless but he was starting to question his own staff. He glared out the window at the men, women and children they passed on the laneways carrying baskets of produce or farm implements. As if sensing his gaze, they avoided looking at his carriage except some of the dirty-faced children who waved at the horse or attempted to keep up in short running bursts of energy. They reminded him of the tear-streaked faces of the paupers who clamoured around the gates of his father's estate during the famine. Begging day and night. Each time his father provided some charitable bread, they would return ten-fold, as word got out across Queen's County and beyond. He beseeched his father to desist but to no avail. George was an admired agricultural improver but at the time his son feared his father's generosity would cripple them or attract unsavoury characters.

They arrived at a small group of thatched cabins not far from Glenveagh Lodge where Murray and a number of shepherds lived. There was a thin spiral of smoke coming from Murray's cabin, which was distinctive for the fox's pelt hanging from the door. Adair rarely visited his servants' quarters and was just considering whether he should order the coachman to walk up to the cabin for him when the foxtail swayed and the door slowly opened. A tall figure with hunched shoulders emerged backwards on to the step. Adair squinted through the carriage window. The man had his arms wrapped around a smaller figure and stooped low until their faces met. As he stepped out into the yard Murray's wife became visible, her face flushed and beaming at her suitor. Adair looked away astonished and then back again to confirm that the man leaving the cabin was Dugald Rankin,

Murray's head shepherd. Rankin pulled on his cap, fixed his belt tighter about his waist and trotted down the lane. Mrs Murray quickly closed the door. If they had noticed the carriage, Adair thought, they probably assumed it was empty, as the coachman lived in their quarters. Adair sat for a minute or two and pondered the situation before tapping the roof of the carriage and calling to the coachman.

"Head on to the animal pound! I don't think Murray is home." He exhaled a deep sigh that rustled the silk curtain in the carriage.

"Women – fickle creatures," he muttered.

There were some fine ladies in Dublin society but he'd broken off an engagement with one when his cousin Townsend Trench informed him of her infidelity with one of his business clients. He had avoided affairs of the heart after that. He sat back in the carriage and began to fiddle with his gold pocket watch. The engraving on the back said, "*To George, all my love, Eliza*". His father had given him the watch on his twenty-first birthday; it had been a gift from his mother who died not long after childbirth. 'She would have wanted you to have this,' he always remembered his father saying. His thumb caressed the engraving. He wondered if he could ever love a woman as much as his father had loved his mother.

After a bumpy ride uphill, they approached a barn-like shed amidst a number of stone buildings where the carriage came to a halt. Adair stepped out to hear a medley of animal bleats and grunts. He had never visited the pound before. A police constable who had been leaning against the outer wall straightened.

"Good day, Mr Adair, sir!" He saluted him as he climbed down from the carriage.

"Is it? I'm looking for Murray – is he on the premises?"

"He is indeed, sir." The constable reddened. "I think he went for a pis— Ye know, he'll be back in a minute."

"Very well. I shall just wait inside. Oh, and don't tell him I'm here. I'd like to surprise him."

He motioned to the coachman to bring the carriage around the back and went inside to a small room where the fire was lit. Adair watched from the window as a man, probably one of his tenants, arrived slightly out of breath and leaning on a worn-looking stick.

"Are ye looking for some strays?"

"Am indeed, constable. A couple of my sheep disappeared a week ago. I thought they had just wandered off and would come back. Then I realised they could have been rounded up by Mr Adair's shepherds, again."

"Well, take a look inside and tell me if ye can identify them. I'll have to write a report of this so I'll need some details – oh, and ye know that there is a fine to have them released?"

The man glared at the policeman.

"Aye. Desperate business this, fining farmers for wandering sheep. What does he want us to do – put leads on them like dogs?"

The constable lowered his voice and muttered something that Adair couldn't make out. A door slammed nearby and

Murray appeared, followed by a lively black and white sheepdog yapping at his feet.

"A new customer, constable?"

"It's one of Adair's tenants, Mr Murray – Alex Bradley from Gartan. He thinks his two sheep are here. I was just going to fill out a report. The usual fine then?"

"Aye, 2s.6d." Murray grinned, putting out his rough, blistered hand.

"Two what?!" The tenant looked bewildered and then turned to the policeman. "Constable, the sheep aren't even worth … surely?"

"I'm afraid, sir—"

"Afraid nothin', constable. Yes, it's the law. Mr Adair can't have your bastard animals crawling over his land, so unless you can look after them better, you'd better get used to being fined." Murray tried to raise himself to look taller but his clenched fists and sharp features made him look menacing enough. The dog at his heel started to bark. The man fumbled in his coat pocket. Just as he pulled out a pouch of coins, Murray snatched it.

"Well, what do we have here…?" As quick as lightning Murray spilled the coins into his hand. The man lunged at Murray who neatly ducked away and left him an inch from striking the policeman.

"Right, enough!" The constable jumped backwards and grabbed Murray by the collar. "I will deal with this. Go and release those sheep to Mr Bradley and I will sort out the fine."

Murray winched himself free from the policeman and still leering at the tenant, went into the animal pen. The constable came into the room from where Adair had witnessed the whole scene.

"Sorry, sir, I just have to write up this report for the records ye know. Er, Mr Murray, as ye can see, is back."

"Yes, I saw that. In fact, I saw everything I need to see. I'm glad Mr Murray is running a tight ship up here."

"Who's that you're talking to in there?" Murray entered the room having released the sheep. Adair folded his arms and cleared his throat.

"Constable, can you please leave us? I want to have a word with Mr Murray."

The policeman quickly put the paperwork away in a drawer and left the pair alone.

"Oh and take that yappy hound with you," said Adair, gesturing with his foot at the dog. As the door opened again he caught a fleeting glimpse of the tenant in the distance, sitting on the stone wall with his head in his hands.

"Good day, sir, not like you to call up here." Murray looked puzzled. He rummaged deep into his pockets and pulled out bags of coins.

"There sir, this week's takings from the pound – the tenants haven't learned yet that we mean business."

"And what about the police business I requested?" Adair frowned.

"Aye sir, the charges, well that's proved a lot trickier than I thought … you see, it wasn't that easy to plant the dead sheep on the tenants. The police wouldn't fall for it." He stared at the ground.

"No, but they found sixteen sheep hides in your cottage."

Murray shook his head.

"They were old sheep, dead sheep, sir. None of them were any of the new Scottish ewes."

Adair walked over to where Murray had rested his rifle against the wall. He lifted it, swinging it close to his own face as if giving it an inspection.

"I tried to make a case against some of your most troublesome tenants," Murray began to speak faster. "You said make those tenants go away, better still put them away. You thought the malicious injuries claim was a good idea. I didn't think the police would be coming to *my* door."

"I thought you had strong evidence for a case. I just wanted to make an example of those peasants. Send a message. Now we're a laughing stock. You humiliated me in front of the police. And I am a Justice of the Peace."

"I apologise sir for embarrassing you in any way. I assure you I have not been stealing your sheep. If you are here to … to sack me then so be it but I must warn you, with best intentions, that I am perhaps the only friend you have in these parts. I'm gonna deal with those boys – the Sweeneys, Conaghan and Dermott so they know even if they escaped the court, we haven't finished with them."

Murray stretched out his arms, hands upturned, and stared in earnest at the scowling landlord. Adair studied the scar on his forehead, which he'd once claimed was from a bull that had stampeded him in Scotland. He was full of tales, probably most of them tall, but Adair found him mildly entertaining. He also felt a slight pang of pity for him, knowing that his wife was being unfaithful with one of his staff. He walked to the window and watched as the scrawny-looking tenant dragged his sheep down the lane. Hadn't he just seen Murray in action, enforcing the law with his tenants? He needed a strong hand, someone to whip these tenants into shape. Murray had proved an effective land steward and loyal to boot. He didn't want his friendship; he was his servant after all. Perhaps their hunting trips had allowed Murray to feel he'd crossed the boundary between staff and friendship. He would reassert that, keep his distance a bit. But Adair knew instinctively that he didn't want to lose him.

"Very well." Adair felt the blood cool in his face. "You shall continue your work here. I can see you're doing a good job."

He handed the rifle roughly back to the Scotsman.

"Above all I value your loyalty but don't take mine for granted."

Murray placed the rifle by his side and bowed his head slightly.

"Thank you, sir, I won't disappoint you, sir."

Chapter 6

Declan woke early. The light streaming through the cottage was brighter than usual for November. When he looked out there was a sprinkling of snow across the fields, reflecting the bright rays of the low winter sun. He shuddered, not just at the thought of snow but that it was gale day – the annual day they paid their rent. He didn't like the thought of facing Murray who no doubt would be tasked with collecting their dues. He crossed the lane and met Alex Bradley for the journey to Glenveagh Lodge.

"Mornin'! Have you heard the news? About that bastard Murray?"

Declan looked puzzled.

"Vanished! Disappeared," said Alex who plucked a clump of wool stuck in the hedge and blew it from the palm of his hand. "Poof, just like that!"

"I don't understand, has he gone back to Scotland?"

"Without his wife? She reported him missing."

"Well maybe he's left her, ye know…"

It was Alex's turn to look puzzled; clearly he was one of the few tenants that hadn't heard the gossip, Declan thought.

"Ruairi came back last night and told us the police and shepherds are out looking for him. His dog, ye know the yappy one that's always by his side, well he came back yesterday, they say, with blood on his back. Never cared for him anyway, especially after the way he treated me at thon animal pound."

"He hadn't too many friends but, God, if something's happened to him…" Declan bowed his head as they trudged uphill.

Alex agreed. "There'll be a reckoning from that landlord if he's been done in."

They joined the heads of families from across the Derryveagh district who had hitched rides or dutifully walked across the snowy slopes to Glenveagh Lodge. They hung about the yard in the biting cold until they were summoned one-by-one into a room next to the stables. News came up the line that it was Adair himself who was collecting the rent. No one mentioned Murray. No one dared. Declan looked around the stables and saw one other Scottish shepherd standing near the door. The rest, he figured, were out looking for the land steward. He looked at the queue ahead and studied the pained expressions on the other tenants' faces. They had toiled hard all year to raise money for the rent and provide food for their families. The cold weather seemed apt for the bitterness felt by the tenants after a year's hard slog. Standing in line was ol' man Doherty leaning his bony frame on a stick next to James Gallagher who discussed with him the snow. Doherty lived alone and eked out a living on his tiny plot where he still grew crops despite being at least eighty. The Widow McAward, who was buried deep in a frayed shawl, swayed behind them. Alex Bradley sucked on his pipe and attempted to shield it from the gusts of wind, which threatened to ruin his pleasure. Declan wondered if the Sweeneys knew anything. He clutched his thin coat around him and hopped from one foot to the other in an attempt to keep his blood circulating.

"Ye think this is cold. Our Seamus has it tough in New York. His last letter said they had six feet of snow."

They all winced at the thought of six feet of snow. The Widow McAward cackled. "That would bury me, sure I'm just five foot."

Alex and Declan smiled at her. She might be just five foot, Declan thought, but she was a tough old bird who could withstand any weather.

"So ye heard from him recently?" asked Declan who remembered playing with Alex's eldest son as a boy.

"Aye, sure he sent us some money to help with the rent. What about yer uncle? Have ye heard from him?"

"Aye, he's still in upstate New York. Seems to have a good landlord, Mr Wadsworth, treats 'em well." He frowned, looking towards the stables. "In fact we just received a letter from him. Come over after and we'll read it together. God knows we'll need to warm ourselves by the fire after this."

Letters from America generated a lot of excitement in the village and Declan preferred them to the usual story-tellers that visited the area and got a few shillings for their tales. He liked true stories and seeing the scrawl across the tattered pages, which had come from so far away, seemed to make them more real.

Alex was summoned by a servant at the stable door and a short time later emerged grim-faced from his meeting with Adair. Before Declan could quiz him, he was called in. Seated at a wooden bench inside, the landlord was dressed in a smart suit with silver cufflinks twinkling from his sleeves. Declan had previously only seen him from a distance or the outline of him at the window of his carriage. He was a tall, imposing figure even while seated. He fingered the notes that had been laid carefully in front of him by each shivering tenant. Declan removed his brown cap and stuffed it into his pocket as he approached the table. Adair looked up, his eyes narrowed.

"Good day, sir."

There was silence as Adair, his lips pursed, looked him over.

"Is your mother the Widow Conaghan?"

He looked back down at his list.

"Y-y-yes. My da, y'see, passed some time ago and I'm the head of the house now. My ma would've come only she's not up to it in the cold..."

Adair began tapping his pen on the table.

"B-but it's all here – we have the rent for ye, sir."

Detecting the landlord's impatience, Declan placed the wad of dirty notes in front of him. He thought of his uncle toiling, perhaps in the snow, to send back the money. Adair brushed the messy pile aside with the back of his hand and signalled to a servant to count it. He then sat forward in his chair.

"I had hoped to address your mother but seeing as you're now the 'head of the house'…" he said, clipping each word of the title. "I haven't been landlord here for very long but I must tell you how disappointed I am with the tenancy of this estate. I have uncovered illicit poteen-making on my lough…"

"Illicit?"

"Yes, illegal, unlawful. I shall try to keep this simple for you, Mr Conaghan. Tenants' livestock wander freely everywhere and I've been threatened on the hillside by masked gangs. I wished to meet with each head of household today to demand better behaviour as my tenants or I will be forced to do this…"

Declan stepped backwards and gasped as Adair ripped the page in front of him. The landlord seemed to enjoy his reaction and half-smiled as he held up the blank piece of paper.

"Thankfully for you, Mr Conaghan, this is not your family's tenancy agreement – this time."

Adair cocked his head to one side and seemed to be scrutinising him.

"Conaghan, Conaghan – you were one of the men arrested for sheep-stealing?"

"Yes, sir, but no, sir, we didn't do it, sir."

Declan could feel his armpits fill with sweat.

"Your face is familiar, Mr Conaghan – you didn't happen to stumble upon my land steward and I hunting recently?"

Declan clenched his fists. Adair continued to stare.

"N-no sir. Mr Murray quizzed me about that and as I told him, I wasn't there."

Adair rose to his feet and walked around his desk.

"I'm sure you've heard that Mr Murray is missing. Disappeared on the mountain yesterday. Would you have any knowledge about that?"

"No, sir. Only heard myself today, sir."

Declan looked down at his boots and wished he could disappear.

"And how did you hear?"

"My-my neighbour."

"Your neighbour, I see." Adair walked around the back of Declan. "And how did your neighbour hear the news?"

"I don't know. Everybody knows everything very quickly round here."

Adair stomped his foot, making Declan jump.

"Exactly! Everybody *does* know everything around here," he half-mimicked him. "And it stands to reason then that somebody knows where Mr Murray is or what has happened to him, doesn't it?"

Declan stared at the ground.

"You're friendly with the Sweeneys?"

Declan swallowed hard, he hadn't expected an interrogation.

"Friendly? Y-y-es I know the brothers well. I mean everyone around here does."

"Hmm, yes, everyone knows everyone and everything around here." Adair returned to his seat. "I would hope, Mr Conaghan, that if you have any information about recent events that you would pass it to the relevant authorities."

Declan frowned and reached into his pocket for his crumpled cap.

"The police I mean..." Adair searched his tenant's face and shaking his pen between finger and thumb, dismissed him.

"Yes, sir, certainly, sir. Good day, sir."

He turned and shuffled outside into the chill of the afternoon, hugging his loose coat closer around him.

Alex was waiting for him and they travelled home in concentrated silence, scrambling uphill from Glenveagh to Gartan. Past the lonely waters of Lough Inshagh they could see a line of dark figures combing the mountainside. The search for Murray continued. As they descended into the valley, they hailed a lift on the back of a labourer's cart. The Conaghans' cabin was empty when Declan poked his head around the door.

"There's yer ma with Briege," said Alex, pointing across at his cottage. "C'mon, they'll have some soup for us, I'm sure."

Declan was cold and hungry but he wasn't sure if he could eat anything. He followed Alex across the field and scraped his boots on the stone grate at his door. His appetite returned when his nose picked up the smell from the pot. There was a pleasant wall of heat as they entered the Bradleys' cottage, a result of the roaring fire and the number of people assembled in the room. Ruairi sat hunched beside Michael over the fire. Bridgeen, their granddaughter, sat cross-legged on a rush mat on the floor. Steam rose around

Briege and Ma who were pouring out dishes of soup. Cara came gingerly over to Declan to ask how they were.

"Well," said Declan, pausing and looking at Alex's downcast face. "We've been better."

Briege thrust a bowl of thin soup into his hand.

"Here, take this Declan, son. Ye look like ye could do with it. Let's leave the questions til after, eh?"

Declan thanked her and cradled the bowl in his numb hand. They all stared quietly as Declan and Alex slurped their soup. As Alex finished his last drop, pressing the bowl to his lips, he broke the silence.

"We all got a right roastin' from the landlord – told us if there's any more trouble, we'd be out."

"Yon Black Adair is the devil himself," Ma muttered. "Ruairi told us about Murray disappearing. No more word on him?"

Declan shook his head and described the interrogation he had about Murray from the landlord.

"He'll be arresting ye for that next," said Michael.

Briege had jumped to her feet and took down the St Brigid's cross, which hung over the door.

"This will protect us – all of us – from any harm," she said, clutching the bound reeds to her breast.

A voice piped up from the floor near the fire.

"Is someone going to hurt us, Nana?" It was Bridgeen who looked bewildered at the adults around her. Briege rushed over to where she sat and put her arm around her to reassure her. Declan sighed and pulled out his uncle's letter from his jacket where he'd tucked it away.

"Never mind Adair. This is the latest from Uncle Liam

in the States. Here, Cara, why don't you read it to everyone?"

Declan smiled at his sister who looked delighted to be given the honour. He was proud of the fact that he'd helped her learn to read and write, passing on what he'd learned from the local priest as a child. Michael had been less interested but at least he could sign his own name.

"Yes, Bridgeen don't ye worry. I'm going to read us all a story from my uncle in America." She unfolded the paper gently and cleared her throat.

"*Geneseo, New York State, second day of October 1860,*" she announced.

They all sat around the fire listening as she pored over the words.

"*I find a growing love for this country,*" she read aloud. "*Here you can hold up your head and not take off your hat to any man. There is this idea much touted by our politicians that if you work hard you can prosper. I have worked hard these past thirteen years but I'm still no closer to owning my own land.*"

"Holy Mary, imagine owning yer own land!" interrupted Ma.

"A quare thing that'd be, Mairead," agreed Alex.

Cara returned to the letter. "*Still, I'm grateful, the Wadsworth family remain kind and generous landowners. Mr Wadsworth recently donated a sizeable sum to have a Catholic church built in the town.*"

Briege gasped.

"Imagine Mr Adair building us a church!"

They all laughed and chatted over Cara who continued reading. Only Declan was really listening at this point. He'd already read the letter several times and had used the stash of money sent in the envelope towards paying the rent that morning. He sympathised with his uncle's frustration at not owning his own land as it was the promise of a piece of land that attracted many to get on the boat to America in the first place. He brooded over the fact that owning land was at least achievable in the States.

As Cara finished reading, a twig snapped in the fire and immediately Ma began to mutter under her breath.

"God protect and guide him, Amen," she said and clasped her fingers together in prayer.

Declan smiled at his sister and suggested she write a letter back to him.

"Will ye help me with it, Declan?"

"Of course but ye can write just as well as me these days."

Cara beamed.

A small voice piped up. "Is that it? I prefer stories about the fairies and goblins – are there any in this Am-amer-eeka place?"

They all laughed at Bridgeen but the gloom descended on Declan again as he thought of Adair. Was Bridgeen right to be scared? Should they all be? Surely all they could do was avoid any trouble with the landlord and steer clear of the Sweeneys.

They huddled around the fire until late into the evening. Alex soothed them with some tunes on his violin, before their thoughts turned to the next day's toil which sent them scurrying to bed.

Chapter 7

"Murray's been murdered."

The words hung like fumes in the air, suspended in the visible puff of Sergeant McSherry's hot breath.

"Sir," he added respectfully and to fill the stunned silence.

Even though Adair had been expecting the worst, he stood staring blankly at the sergeant for several seconds. His fears had risen when Murray's loyal sheepdog returned without his master. It was then that Adair had called the police and they agreed the blood soaked on the animal's black and white fur was not the dog's own. He had joined the band of police on the third day of the search for his land steward. Now he took in the news standing on the hillside overlooking Glenveagh valley. He followed Sergeant McSherry to the scene below a precipice where the police had just discovered the body. There, lying on his back on the stony slope, his leg bent under him and one of his arms stretched out, was the frozen corpse and mangled face of James Murray.

"Looks like he died from a blow to the head, his skull's fractured," said the sergeant.

"Could he have fallen?" asked Adair, staring up at the cliff, his tone betraying his own scepticism.

The police had surrounded the body, furiously scribbling notes. Murray's tweed cap lay scrunched up nearby on a clump of heather and his pistol lay broken in three parts. Adair crouched down and removed his own hat, staring at the lifeless body, the face barely recognisable. He had been angry with Murray for not securing any arrests of his tenants but he had recognised Murray's loyalty and although it manifested itself in a somewhat twisted way, all things considered, he had decided to keep him on. He sighed and slowly got to his feet.

Adair observed the ledges of rock and tried to piece together what could have happened. He shivered. The police were prodding at the grass and measuring distances with yard sticks. He recalled the misty day he and Murray had been taunted by the band of villagers and shook his head. *I could have been with him*, he thought. *That could have been me lying there dead and horribly disfigured. What an ignominious end! Who would remember me? I'd just be another poor bastard landlord snuffed out by his merciless tenants. Ha, they'd regale in stories about me in their cabins and at their harvest celebrations. I might even warrant a song!* He shook his head.

A shout made him jump and Adair squinted to see an

officer with some of his shepherds in the search party. They were examining a large stone that had been picked up not far from the body. Sergeant McSherry had gone to the officer and now waved him over. On the underside of the piece of granite was a large red stain and stuck to it was a clump of human hair.

"A crack from this piece of rock could have fractured his skull," said the sergeant examining the find.

Adair replaced his hat and stabbed the frozen ground with his walking stick.

"I want this whole area searched thoroughly, every blade of grass – do you hear me? I want as much evidence as possible on this – this murder!" Adair realised his hand was shaking.

"Of course sir, that's exactly what my men are doing sir. We will leave no stone… We will gather all that we can from the scene of this terrible crime. I know this is a terrible shock for you sir. You have my deepest sympathy. It is a tragic day for you and all of us in Glenveagh."

Adair regarded the sergeant's sympathy as hollow. *Didn't he lecture me on the peace-loving nature of my tenants? How would he explain this murder then?* But Adair's legs felt like jelly. All he wanted to do was get off the cursed mountain. Words and events of recent weeks filled his head as he went back down to Glenveagh Lodge. A walk he would never do again with Murray. Poor bugger, his face had really taken a pounding. He realised whoever had attacked Murray had done so out of a deep, deep rage. He recalled a piece of advice his Uncle Trench had once given him and decided if he didn't want the same fate as Murray, he would have to respond by showing no mercy.

It was of some small comfort to learn the next day that the Sweeney brothers had been brought in for questioning but Adair felt he could not rest easy until the culprits were prosecuted. He visited the police station in Church Hill where he arranged for a fifty-pound reward notice to be printed and distributed across Donegal.

'Everybody knows everything around here', he recalled the discussion with one of his tenants. *What was his name? Cavanagh, Conway, something like that.* Well, fifty pounds might loosen some of their tongues, he thought. As the inquest was scheduled for a number of days in Church Hill, he decided to accept an invitation from the Reverend Maturin to stay at the rectory for the duration. Adair was impressed with Glebe House, a fine regency-style house on a raised bank overlooking the still waters of Lough Gartan. The view wasn't as panoramic as Glenveagh Lodge but it was nonetheless picturesque.

"These are dismal circumstances that I extend this hospitality to you sir but know that the people of Church Hill and indeed the whole of Derryveagh are much aggrieved by this murder," said the Reverend Maturin, as the two gentlemen sat in his study.

Adair stared at the rotund little man facing him, with his earnest expression and sweating brow. He replied, shaking his head.

"It is terrible business – the cold-blooded murder of a man on my property. I expect every effort to be made to affect a prosecution, though I have my misgivings about the competence of this police force. They have been found wanting on several occasions since I came to Donegal – but a murder – why, it has to be solved. I will not tolerate a murderer loose in my midst."

The grandfather clock suddenly chimed the hour causing Adair to jump.

"Indeed, Mr Adair. 'Tis dreadful business. I am astonished that it should happen in our midst," the minister said, a trickle of sweat slipping down the side of his fat cheek. "I myself have lived here thirty years and I cannot recall such devilment. I cannot imagine any of your tenants that would strike a man so…"

"You cannot? Well, *I* certainly can and I probably don't know them as well as you. Why, I was threatened myself on that very mountain with Murray just some weeks ago! Who's to say the assailant wouldn't have taken my life if I had been with Murray?"

Adair peered out the window as the light began to fade.

"Oh you must settle yourself sir. Perhaps a brandy for the nerves?"

Adair agreed and turned away from the window.

"It is a terrible ordeal for us all … b-but, of course, more for you to contend with." The reverend passed him a thick-rimmed glass of the golden-brown liquor.

Adair shuffled in his armchair and reached for *The Londonderry Journal* that lay folded on the table.

"Well perhaps I shall read, take my mind off things," he said, unfolding the broadsheet. The minister was about to seize this cue to leave the study when Adair exclaimed at the headlines.

"*The Alleged Murder at Glenveagh* – did you ever?" He began jabbing the paper with his forefinger. "*Alleged*? Of course it was murder, what sort of journalism is this?"

He rustled the pages in rage.

"I can't get any peace from this, it's all over the papers. I don't want to read whatever they've made up."

"Then don't sir, don't upset yourself."

"Yes, well, let's see what's happening abroad instead…"

The clergyman sunk back into his seat.

"Ah, Lincoln has succeeded in the United States presidential contest, hmmm," Adair hummed as he scanned further down the column. "The elections throughout the Republic passed off without disorder and resulted beyond doubt in the election of Abraham Lincoln to the Presidency."

The minister creaked forward in his seat causing Adair to look up from his reading.

"An interesting result, don't you think?" asked the reverend. "I read that Lincoln was a very impressive candidate. Do you have an interest in American affairs, Mr Adair?"

"I have considered some investments in the States, land acquisitions, you know. New York is currently a very profitable place to do business, quite the up-and-coming city," said Adair. "You know I would consider myself more a businessman than a landowner. I'm sure this Mr Lincoln, a lawman, will make a good president."

"Perhaps, but there are fears his stance over slavery may cause a rift, some even say the southern states could break away from the Union."

"Well, that would not be good for business," said Adair, frowning.

"Indeed Mr Adair, but slavery is a terrible injustice. The Negro, after all, is a human being and the way they are treated by some plantation owners, not all I hasten to add … well, I think we live in a more civilised part of the world."

"Ha! Civilised – and we've just had a murder on my estate," Adair scoffed. "My father, indeed my friends, had urged me to invest in land in America but I was concerned by rumours of instability there and chose instead to purchase here in quiet Donegal. I try to improve the estate and this is how the tenantry repay me, by murdering my land steward."

The reverend shook his head.

"I urge you not to jump to conclusions and accuse your tenants Mr Adair. There are bad rogues passing through the county all the time. Mr Murray could have been very unfortunate and happened upon one of them. It could have been a robbery that turned nasty."

Adair's eyes narrowed. He decided not to waste his breath on discussing the matter further with this clearly simple man of God. He engrossed himself with reading the newspaper, until the minister piped up with a nervous cough.

"If you don't mind Mr Adair, I think I shall retire for the

evening. It has been rather a long day. I trust you will be very comfortable here tonight."

"Certainly, of course," said Adair without looking up as the door closed softly behind him. He found the minister rather tiresome and his joviality irritating given the grave circumstances.

By the early hours of the morning the wind, which had picked up after dark, had died down, and everything around Glebe House was deathly still. The grandfather clock had just chimed the third hour of the new day when the hens housed next door to the cowshed became restless and suddenly the rooster crowed. Adair woke with a start and was just pondering how short the night had been, when he heard voices roaring from downstairs.

"Fire! Fire! Everyone up! Reverend, come quickly…"

Adair rushed to the window and could see flames leaping in the air from one of the outhouses. He quickly dressed and bumped into the minister, who appeared stunned and dishevelled on the landing. Forgetting the niceties of gentlemen's manners, they both hurried downstairs and joined the gang of men, the reverend's staff and neighbours, who were tackling the fire. A terrible cacophony of animal sounds assaulted their ears. The cows were stamping their hooves in terror and cowering at one end of the shed. The hens' shrieking had drowned out the proud cock who was taking running pecks at the would-be firefighters. The fire had consumed the thatched roof of the henhouse next door and flames were licking around two ricks of hay nearby.

Adair assumed the position of fire chief. In a half-buttoned shirt, he stood on top of the gable end of the burning building, shouting directions at the men, who had gathered from all around to keep the fire from spreading. A number of police, who had been summoned from the barracks, had filled buckets of water from the well. They formed a chain with some of the neighbours to pass the buckets along to quench the fire. Adair noticed two young men, their faces covered in soot, diving into the burning shed and hauling the minister's cows out one by one with a rope around their necks. He peered at them in the dark. They looked like his tenants. Yes, wasn't that the fellow Conway, no Conaghan, he'd recently met? And the skinnier one looked familiar too. Where had he seen him? The blackened face. Amidst the shouts and animals baying, he suddenly remembered the taunting crowd on the mountain that day with Murray. That's where he'd seen him before! He felt a rage rush up inside him but the situation was frantic and the streaked face dashed back into the burning shed.

The reverend and his wife rushed to find more ropes to help with the cattle. But the flames had taken hold and within hours had devoured the entire cowshed and henhouse. As daylight broke, wisps of smoke furled up from the blackened shells that remained of the structures. Adair stood surveying the damage with the motley crew of helpers. Thanks to the quick efforts of the rescuers most of the livestock had been saved. The cows quivered a few yards away and some, unfazed by the night's drama, had begun to graze on the rectory lawn. The reverend thanked everyone for their efforts just as the young soot-covered lad appeared again carrying a frightened hen in his arms.

"That'd be them all accounted for, reverend, sir," he said, handing over the hen. "My brother and I best be getting home. We smelt the smoke from over in Gartan and thought there was some trouble."

The minister thanked him and insisted he take the hen with him.

"A token of my gratitude, Michael – your calmness and bravery saved my cattle. I am indebted."

Adair glared at the scrawny youth and was about to challenge him when Sergeant McSherry came hurrying up the path. He stared in astonishment at all the filthy faces and blinked in disbelief at the sight of John Adair in their midst. The sergeant took out his notebook and began directing the constables to search the dying embers for any clues as to the cause of the fire. Just as the minister's wife was ushering the bedraggled crowd into the rectory for cups of tea, Adair addressed the police sergeant.

"You may start with me, sergeant," he said.

"Sir?"

"As a motive, I mean. This fire was obviously started deliberately because I was staying here. Or do you think that just a coincidence?" Adair snapped. With black streaks of soot highlighting his eyes and his sleeves rolled up, he had the appearance of a bare-knuckle fighter.

"That will certainly be one line of inquiry Mr Adair. We shall examine the scene and file a report as soon as possible."

The reverend nodded at the police and then ushered the landlord away from the smoking remains.

"Perhaps something stronger than a cup of tea for you, sir?" asked Mrs Maturin in her blackened apron.

"Tea? That's all you people care about is tea!" he blustered as she placed a brandy glass in his hand. Adair muttered a half-hearted apology and turned to look back at the smoking skeleton that remained of the sheds. Their collapse had cleared a view across the rolling meadows, which had been obscured before. Adair scanned the horizon and looked back towards the lough. The water sparkled in the weak morning sunshine and a flock of birds flew across the water, their feathered breasts just skimming the still surface. As the wisps of smoke cleared and the brandy reached his limbs, Adair's temper softened, and he managed a smile.

"Ah, I see the brandy has helped a little," said the minister.

"A little, yes," said Adair. "You know, you have a much better view without those sheds. I'm just remembering the reason I bought Glenveagh was for the views."

The reverend followed his gaze.

"You do have magnificent views…"

"But interrupted by cabins all over the hillsides and fields."

"The tenants' homes, you mean." The minister gave a little cough as if to assert himself before a short sermon. "You saw how the Conaghans came to our aid. If it wasn't for their alertness my livestock could all be dead. Indeed, the fire could have spread to the house. They're your tenants.

Perhaps this is the proof you needed that they are not all bad."

Adair turned and looked coldly at the minister.

"Ah, the Conaghans – my tenants. I'm afraid, reverend, I saw the devil tonight and I will not rest until I rid my estate of all the devils."

Chapter 8

Particles of dust danced in the shafts of morning sun that poured through the windows of Church Hill Magistrates' Court. The musty courtroom had seen little use in years but was now the setting for Murray's inquest, which was the talk for miles around. It was next door to the police barracks where the murder suspects were being held. The Sweeney brothers and three of Adair's tenants had been rounded up in the days after the body was found and rumours about the suspects rustled like the wind through the rushes on Lough Gartan. Declan's ma had become so vexed by the situation she insisted on attending the last day of the hearing. Declan protested that he didn't think it proper for his ma and sister to hear all the gruesome details but Mairead gave him her steely glare and hurriedly fixed her shawl around her thin shoulders.

"Haven't ye see me skinning rabbits? And our Cara – can't she wring the neck of a chicken she's raised from a chick? What makes ye think us Conaghan women can't cope with a bloody murder?"

"Aye, Ma, but ye don't need to go to court – Mickey and I can go and tell ye all later," Declan pleaded.

"Why should I hear the story second-hand when we can go ourselves? The ground's rock hard, not much we can be doin'. And I'm not sitting here churning butter, wondering what all's being said."

Cara appeared at the half-door having just fed the hens. Mairead lowered her voice and pointed her finger in the direction of Glenveagh.

"If we are being blamed for the death of that Mr Murray, I at least want to hear the evidence." She turned to Cara. "Throw down that dibber and basket, we're going to the courthouse!"

Declan looked helplessly at Michael who just shrugged. Cara beamed. "It's not every day there's a murder in our midst. Think we should all go."

They discovered most of the tenants and villagers were packed into the courthouse. The Conaghans squeezed into a pew together and nodded at the anxious faces of their neighbours. The Bradleys, the Gallaghers and the McAwards surrounded them. It seemed like a Sunday but without the Mass and, as their ma remarked to Cara in a loud whisper, the seats were a lot more comfortable than church. Across the spartan room in a separate panel sat the all-male jury who could observe the witness box opposite.

They chatted jovially among themselves as they awaited the coroner.

Mairead leaned across to Declan. "Why are there no women in the jury? There are wiser women in this district than half the drunk 'aul men."

Declan patted her arm.

"It's just the way it is, Ma."

A number of witnesses stood quietly at the back of the room, trying not to make eye contact. Among them was Adair who appeared tired and dishevelled despite wearing a suit cut from the best cloth in the room. His dark eyes surveyed the public gallery with some disdain. He cut a very lonely figure in the bustling courtroom. Nearby hovered the shepherd, Rankin, who had taken time to shave and wore a suit whose sleeves were noticeably too short. There were a number of Murray's relatives in the front row but Mrs Murray wasn't among them. Declan heard she'd returned on the boat to Scotland.

There was a sudden hush as a clerk commanded, "All rise!" The coroner, Dr Long, entered through the wood-panelled door at the top end of the room. Once he settled himself in the large oak chair on the raised platform, he waved to the room to be seated. The jury shuffled themselves into an orderly fashion and sat bolt upright like sixteen obedient schoolchildren before their teacher. Dr Long cleared his throat and opened proceedings.

"We are here today because of the sad circumstances surrounding the death of Mr James Murray, the land steward of Glenveagh Estate. As with any sudden death by law we need an inquest to establish the facts of the case." He paused and looked around the packed courtroom. "Due to the great public interest in this death, I have assembled a jury to reach its conclusion."

Several police constables were then summoned to give evidence.

"When Mr Murray's body was found, I went over and looked at it," said one constable. "I saw a number of cuts on his face and head; I believe he did not meet his death by accident but by the hands of a man or men. As well as the stone and broken pistol, we found a hazel rod about four-and-a-half feet long. Near where the stick was found the ground showed marks as if there had been a scuffle. I saw a foot track to the left of where Mr Murray may have jumped down; below, the grass was bent, as if Mr Murray had been dragged or thrown down."

The coroner interrupted. "Other witnesses have said they saw barefoot prints near the body, did you see any?"

"No sir," replied the constable. "There were many footprints but I did not see the mark of a bare foot on the ground. I saw what looked like the mark of a heel."

"Very well," the coroner said, putting down his pen. "Unless members of the jury have any further questions that concludes the police evidence in this case. I now call Mr Dugald Rankin, shepherd on the Glenveagh Estate."

Declan could feel his ma shift in her seat next to him. The tall shepherd seemed more stooped than usual as he stepped into the witness box. To Declan he seemed less cocksure than on the night he had raided the harvest celebrations.

"Mr Rankin," the coroner began slowly as if unsure

what question he was about to ask. "You were with the search party that discovered the body of the deceased?"

"Indeed I was sir, went hunting for him every day he was missing…"

"Ye-es. Can you describe to the jury what you saw, in particular the stone found near the body?"

Rankin fiddled with his loose cuffs and cleared his throat.

"Aye sir, certainly sir. I examined the stone and on the underside it had both blood and hair stuck to it, which matched Mr Murray's hair. I also found the marks of bloody fingers on the breast of the deceased's shirt. He had no blood on his own hands. I have no doubt that he was murdered, Mr Coroner, sir."

"Hmm. I believe you have some information about one of the suspects, Mr Rankin, would you care to tell the court?" The coroner peered over his glasses.

"As I told the police, Mr Murray was threatened by one Sean Sweeney, of Gartan," Rankin coughed. "About two months before his death, Mr Murray told me he was afraid of Sweeney and cautioned me to never let him near him on the mountain."

There were whispers throughout the court and a door slammed outside the room. The coroner signalled to the police inspector who duly left the room and returned with a man in cuffs, his thick neck bowed. The buzz of voices rose to a din as the burly man lifted his head to take in the many faces surrounding him.

"Do you know the prisoner?" asked the coroner, raising his voice.

"I do sir, that is Sean Sweeney, whom I referred to," Rankin replied confidently.

A penknife with a brown tag attached was produced by the police inspector from a bag and placed on the table in front of Rankin.

"Do you recognise this weapon, Mr Rankin? It belongs to the prisoner," the coroner asked, squinting through one of his lenses.

Rankin lifted it curiously and deftly pressed the mechanism that caused the small blade to spring open. He closed the blade and sprung it open a second time. The jury watched, transfixed, as if they hadn't seen a penknife before.

"Mr Rankin?" asked the coroner impatiently.

"No," Rankin replied and handed the instrument back to the police inspector. "I haven't seen it before," he added, with a hint of disappointment in his voice.

Sean Sweeney stood silently beside a constable in the dock, his bulky frame obscuring the view of spectators in the pews. A bulbous vein throbbed in his neck betraying the deep well of anger and frustration that frothed inside him. He glared at Rankin and was then bundled back out of the courtroom to the prison cell below.

"That will be all, Mr Rankin," said the coroner.

Declan felt a rustle of skirts and realised his mother was on her feet waving her fist.

"Aren't you goin' to ask him any more questions?" she cried out. "What about Mrs Murray? We know all about him and Mrs Murray. Why don't ye ask him what he's been up to with the dead man's wife?"

There were gasps around the courtroom followed by

shouts and laughter. With one index finger the coroner pushed his glasses up to the bridge of his nose and with the other he beckoned to one of the constables to deal with the disorder. Declan went to calm his mother but was distracted by the dark look on Rankin's face. He had straightened to his full height as he craned his neck to seek out the heckler. As a constable rushed from the bench towards the gallery, another woman's voice rang out.

"She's not wrong. Why is the shepherd wearing his master's suit? 'Tis the wolf himself in sheep's clothing."

It was the Widow McAward in her cryptic manner. She began to beat her walking stick on the brass railings and pointed to the shepherd. This time Rankin self-consciously pulled on the hem of his jacket as if to stretch it longer and then scurried back to the witness seats.

"That's enough! We shall have order in this inquest," shouted the coroner over the racket. The rumbling died down and the scraping of chairs ceased. "May I remind the gallery and jury for that matter that this is not a trial, this is merely establishing the facts surrounding the death of Mr Murray. We shall not be finding anyone guilty or innocent at these proceedings. Now *can* we proceed."

There was complete silence. Declan squeezed his ma's arm. Thankfully, seeing that it was merely two women who had interrupted the case the police decided they were not a sufficient threat to require ejection from the courtroom.

"I now call Mr John Adair, Esquire, proprietor of Glenveagh Estate," the coroner said, putting down his pen.

Having been sworn in, Mr Adair read from a statement which he produced from his inside pocket.

"The late Mr James Murray was my steward and land manager," he said in his polished Trinity College accent. "He had been in my service over a year and I had the most implicit confidence in his honesty." He paused and looked up as if expecting to be contradicted.

"I received two letters from him shortly before his death. He stated that he had for some time been doing the shepherd's duty on the mountains, while the shepherds were smearing the sheep in the valley. He stated that there were gatherings of people at a certain house, and he was certain that there was some bad work going on. He had never previously alluded to anything of that kind when writing to me."

Michael and Declan exchanged a quick glance and then looked back at the witness.

Adair swallowed and raised his voice. "I do not know of any cause for ill feeling against Murray on the part of the tenantry, except on the subject of trespass, which was always going on. No sheep tax was ever levied on the district. At least, none was ever applied for by me. I believe an application had been made in error by Mr Murray as compensation for sheep he believed missing, but it was corrected and withdrawn immediately after."

He stopped abruptly and set down his statement. The coroner who had been scribbling furiously looked up.

"Thank you, Mr Adair – that was very, erm, succinct. However, might I ask you to comment on previous witnesses' remarks that there is some discontent among your tenants?"

Affronted, Adair began fiddling with the pages in front of him.

"I reject any remarks that my tenants are not content,

and certainly not on account of any actions by me," he growled. "I am ready to answer any question from the jury about my estate if it helps to solve this crime. There have been no complaints made against me as landlord."

At this, several jurors nodded their heads in agreement.

"And what about Mr Sweeney, did he make any complaints to you?" the coroner asked.

"Mr Sweeney is not one of my tenants. He is a neighbouring small farmer. They are hot-headed people, the Sweeneys, but I had received no direct complaint from them."

To Declan's relief the coroner then dismissed the landlord from the witness box. He didn't imagine his ma would be so bold as to heckle Adair but after her earlier outburst he was prepared for anything. The temperature in the courtroom had risen, with several jurors mopping their brows. Declan felt the tension in the public gallery was also high as the tenants were acutely aware of what was at stake. The murder of the land steward was a heinous crime for which they all felt they would have to pay. The coroner continued to write and, without looking up, asked the jury if they required to examine any more witnesses. After a few minutes' consultation the foreman stood up and replied that what they had heard was sufficient and that "no evidence could throw any further light on the matter". The room was then cleared and after ten minutes of discussions, the jury returned with its verdict.

"We find that certain persons, to the jurors unknown, on the thirteenth day of November 1860, feloniously, wilfully, and of their malice aforethought, did kill and murder one

James Murray, against the peace of our Lady the Queen, her crown and dignity."

A loud murmuring rose from the public gallery as neighbours exchanged glances and comments. The police then ushered them all outside into the bright, frosty morning where they continued the analysis of events.

"Of course he was murdered, sure the fools and the fairies know that," muttered Michael to Declan as they joined the huddle of tenants on the gravel path.

Briege Bradley extended her arms to their mother.

"You were so brave, Mairead! I nearly swooned when I heard yer voice and then the Widow McAward. The pair of ye could have ran that inquest better."

Mairead grimaced in her embrace.

"That's exactly what I said to Declan. A few women were needed on that jury."

The conversation stopped at the sight of Sergeant McSherry approaching, his lips pursed in a tight line.

"Mrs Conaghan, we can't have outbursts like that in a courtroom," he said sternly. "The coroner has asked me to caution you."

The Widow McAward shuffled out of the crowd and tapped the sergeant's ankles with her stick.

"Ye'll be cautioning me too then, sergeant." She squinted at him through her occluded eye. "But have ye questioned yon shepherds that worked with Murray? Seems they didn't care much for him either."

She then whirled her stick around, causing the onlookers to dive out of the way, before pointing it in the direction of Rankin. The tall Scot stood in another cluster nodding at fellow shepherds, like the chief mourner at a wake.

The sergeant sighed. "Mrs McAward, I can assure you we are following all lines of enquiry. And yes, you'll not be allowed back in the courtroom either if you disrupt proceedings like that again."

Unperturbed, the widow tutted.

"Well let's hope ye do yer job and there are no more murders to attend."

Declan could see Cara trying to suppress a giggle. Only the old widow could get away with ticking off the sergeant.

The sergeant took Declan aside and lowered his voice. "I saw Mr Adair enquire about your mother and the Widow McAward. He's, let's say, mean spirited. I would keep a low profile if I were you. Avoid those shepherds. You don't want any more false accusations."

He looked sternly at Declan. Then, his back hunched, he marched hurriedly back to the police barracks.

"Murray got what was comin' to 'im," said Alex Bradley, sucking on his pipe. "I'd have taken a shot at him myself if I was younger."

"Shush now, Alex, you'll be getting arrested," his wife scolded, looking anxiously over her shoulder at the constables mingling with the crowd outside. "Any number of folks could have done him in but my money's on that Mr Rankin."

"Looks like the Sweeneys are their chief suspects, which takes the heat off us tenants," Michael chipped in.

The Widow McAward pulled her shawl tighter about her shoulders and muttered, "I don't like to see an innocent man accused but if they don't convict someone, Adair will accuse us all, mark my words."

Declan noticed the strained, helpless looks on the faces of the people he'd known all his life as they huddled closer. The widow's warning was interrupted by the sound of a horse braying loudly. Adair's carriage had just pulled up. Declan spun round to see the landlord stride from the courthouse over to his staff. Rankin extended his hand to shake Mr Adair's, the short sleeve of his suit riding up his arm to reveal his bony, white wrist. Was it the dead man's suit, he wondered. Was Rankin indeed Adair's wolf that would tear them all apart? The widow was rarely wrong.

Chapter 9

Crack!

There was a squawk and a dull thud as the dead bird dropped like a stone, its brown feathers floated afterwards to the ground. Adair smiled to himself. He was having a good hunt and it was especially pleasing in front of his uncle and cousin. He had written to invite them to Glenveagh with the aim of enlisting his cousin Townsend Trench's help to design a castle. The three men adjusted their weapons and stomped across the field towards the trophy, their tweed coats and peaked caps camouflaging them against the rising peaks of brown moorland and bog. The Trenches had their guns slung casually over their shoulders, wearing them as if they were part of their clothes. Adair preferred to keep his gun pointed ahead as he kept a vigilant eye on the sky and all around him.

"At ease, son!" commanded his Uncle Trench. "She's dead. Are you expecting a resurrection from those feathers!"

Adair grimaced at his uncle's sarcasm. He hated being

made a fool of and now father and son were both laughing at him.

"Of course not," he replied. "One has to be alert in these parts. You may laugh but I was accosted by my tenants on this hillside not so long ago. I stood in this very spot with Murray and we know what happened to him."

"Yes, dear boy. I can tell you're still nervous but you are the landlord, you *must* assert yourself."

Trench had gained a reputation as a notorious land agent often called upon to thin out an overcrowded estate at the least possible cost to the owner or subdue a rebellious tenantry. His uncle stopped walking and rested a heavy arm around his shoulder. He surveyed the valley before them with its sloping lowlands and sparkling blue lough.

"I can see this estate has suffered the scourge of so many estates across Ireland – innumerable squatters," he remarked.

"Yes," agreed Adair. "They rather spoil the view."

"Quite," Trench tutted. "You know during the Great Famine, I arrived at the final conclusion – after the most anxious deliberation – that an extensive system of voluntary emigration was the only practicable and effective means of relieving the frightful destitution across so much of the country."

"And did many emigrate?" asked Adair.

"Only those who were desirous to go but there was practically a stampede!"

Trench closed his eyes for a minute.

"Some three-and-a-half thousand paupers emigrated in little more than a year, I believe." He nodded his double-chin. "We sent a batch of two hundred each week out of Cork, mainly to America. Of course I was criticised and accused of 'exterminating the people'. I became the object of the vilest and most bitter abuse. But the people knew well that those who complained the loudest had given them no help when in the extremity of their distress. I am happy to say I only ever received favourable accounts about the emigrants. Almost all, down even to the widows and children, found employment soon after landing and escaped the pestilence of the workhouse. It was my pleasure to have been the means of sending so many miserable beings to a land far richer and more prosperous than Ireland."

Townsend shook his head. "America isn't what it was. There's a war looming and I daresay many of those emigrants will be caught up in it."

"Wars are what make men," said Trench, unable to hide his displeasure at his son's negative interruption. "I should imagine a war in America will offer many opportunities this side of the Atlantic. I say we should just plant flax wholesale like our friends in the north and make our fortunes selling linen to the Yanks."

Trench chortled but Adair continued to frown.

"This is a splendid estate, John. I can see how it charmed you, but it is time you dealt firmly with your tenants. If they are causing you the grief you say they are, then you must evict them. Simple as that."

Townsend nodded next to his father.

"I can build you a castle here, John, but not for you to hide in. Father's right, you can't let them threaten you on your own property."

"Damn it, I *am* dealing with them! I have demanded the police inspector and the resident magistrate tackle the lawlessness of the area. I have issued rewards for information and the apprehension of Murray's killer or killers, but nothing…"

"Nothing, nothing, nothing…" Adair's exasperated voice reverberated around them.

"The police released the chief suspects, those Sweeney troublemakers. Their gang even tried to assassinate me when I stayed with the local minister. I tell you it's a conspiracy, they all want me gone."

He kicked his boot into a tuft of heather whose wiry stems bounced back unharmed. His uncle grabbed his upper arm.

"You cannot rely on the police, cretinous bunch of useless idiots! You are not the first landlord to be afflicted by this scourge, nor will you be the last."

"If you are referring to Ribbonism, I have been assured by both the clergy and the police that it doesn't exist in these parts—" Adair was interrupted by another loud laugh. This time his uncle theatrically snatched Adair's cap from his head and made to hit him with it.

"Well more fool you for listening to them," Trench growled. "Of course the magistrate and the minister don't want to alarm you. They want you to stay and maintain the estate, improve the land and make some order out of the tenantry. But I daresay Ribbonism is as alive and well in these parts as in every other part of Ireland. Where there is a landlord, there will be a Ribbon Society, believe me."

He nodded for agreement from his son, who was now casually leaning against a sapling tree.

"But I haven't received any letters or warnings from any Ribbon Society," Adair said, frowning.

"Letters? My dear boy I'm sure the peasantry are as illiterate here as elsewhere. Wasn't Murray your warning, and then the fire?"

"Yes, I had considered that but I..."

"Listen, ten years ago I was threatened by Ribbonmen when I was land agent for Lord Bath in Monaghan. I was informed by various sources that I had been tried in secret at a tenant's barn with judge and jury present. Word went out that 'Trench must be put off the walk'. They planned to have me murdered."

"So what did you do?" Adair asked.

"I thwarted their every step. I armed myself to the hilt. I bought two revolvers, each with six barrels, plus two small double-barrelled pocket pistols for use at close quarters. Oh, and I also carried a pair of double-barrelled horse pistols in the holsters of my saddle."

"Ahem, you also had me and one of the farmhands on either side of you when you rode out," Townsend reminded him. "And we were well-armed too."

"True, true. For a full year I managed to thwart every attempt on my life. Their 'blood was up' that Trench was 'still upon the walk'," he said making a poor attempt at mimicking the accent.

"We caught them in the end. Caught them trying to ambush me from behind a stone wall one dark night. They had a blunderbuss with ten inches of charge in the barrel and iron nails thrust in. Oh, they meant me to have a gruesome death," he said, faking a full-body shiver.

They reached the dead bird's resting place in a clump of yellow gorse. Townsend poked at it with his rifle and held it aloft.

"Here, I think it was your shot, old boy. Not a bad weight either," he passed it to Adair by its lifeless neck.

"Yes, you're a decent shot. I'd say you could take these peasants on in any ambush."

Adair had replaced his cap on his head but couldn't quite get it to sit comfortably.

"They were tried, weren't they? I seem to remember executions."

"That they were," replied his uncle. "But look here, I am a fair and decent man. They were sent to Mountjoy for two years' hard labour, after which they were to be executed."

"So what do you suggest I do?"

His uncle tossed his gun to his son and put his arm enthusiastically again around Adair's shoulders.

"There is something called the Writ of Habere," said Trench, rolling his 'r's with great gusto. "It is an age-old principle of English law that a district is collectively responsible for the crimes in its midst. I found it a very useful law myself."

Adair's frown eased and he found himself staring into the distance across the glen. Townsend noticed his cousin's expression and suggested they sojourn for the afternoon.

"I'll have to get cracking on the plans for that castle," he said. "We've got a lot of work to do. After all you'll need somewhere to hang all this game you're hunting."

Adair's mind suddenly switched to the castle and something caught his eye.

"There yonder!" he said, pointing his finger. "See the piece of land curving into the lough? That's where I want the castle."

Townsend lifted his shotgun and began to peer through the magnifier lens.

"Ah, yes, it is very much in the centre of the glen but a terrific vantage point. You shall certainly be Lord of the Manor then."

Trench nodded.

"Lord of Glenveagh!"

He kept a firm grip on his nephew's shoulder and steered him back towards the path to Glenveagh Lodge. Adair was pleased that he had their approval. He *would* be Lord of the Manor. He would show them all.

As they walked back to the lodge, the low winter sun behind them cast long shadows, elongating their legs to the size of giants and making Adair feel tall for the first time in weeks. The depression that had seemed to engulf him started to lift.

Chapter 10

Declan was sitting astride the roof patching the thatch as he'd promised his ma. It was an uncomfortable task with the spiky straw frequently piercing through his thin trousers. His granda, whom he'd never known, had built the cottage in the 1820s. A fact his da had been very proud to tell him about over and over.

Michael was on the ground passing tools up to him and generally keeping him back with his chatter.

"Ruairi heard there were three attacked Murray," said Michael. "One walked up to him, while two others crept up from behind. One of them carried the stone, which clobbered him over the head."

"Aye, Michael, and how would he know that? Was he a witness? Twine!" shouted Declan from his perch.

Michael passed up the twine.

"He knows everything, ye know that."

Declan grunted and bit through the twine with his teeth.

He winced as it split open a blister on his hand which began to bleed. He threw the ball back to his brother.

"Ye bleedin' ol man, let me get up there, I'd do a better job than ye."

"Blood, sweat and tears, that's what we've poured into this place," muttered Declan, realising he sounded like an old man, indeed *his* old man.

Declan concentrated on working the twine through the thatch. He was tired of all the speculation that had continued for months about Murray's murder. The Sweeneys and the others accused had been released after Sergeant McSherry concluded there was no evidence against them and the brothers had insisted they were innocent to anyone who would listen. Rankin had also disappeared a few days after the inquest. There was no search party this time as rumours circulated that he was seen packing up his cabin. No one knew whether he'd been sacked or resigned, but the storytellers in the barns and inns around Derryveagh had him fleeing to be with Mrs Murray after slaying her husband. Declan heard from staff at the big house that Adair believed the tenants were harbouring Murray's killer. He worried what Adair would do next. Since the inquest and the fire at the rectory the landlord had been largely absent from the estate. Declan hoped he might have lost interest in Donegal and simply decide to sell up.

Just then he noticed his bleeding hand had begun to stain the pale-coloured straw. He sat upright on the spine of the roof and felt in his pocket for a cloth to wrap around the cut. Michael murmured something from below, which was drowned out by a growing rumble of hooves. He scanned the horizon until a horse with a gentleman rider accompanied by two policemen came into view on the lane. Declan felt his heart sink. The tall, clean-shaven man dressed in black riding breeches and top hat drew his horse up to the cottage and dismounted. Declan didn't recognise him. He threw the reins of his grey mare to one of the policemen to hold and then strutted up to the door.

"Who's the head of the household?" demanded the stranger.

"Well there's me ma but she's in the village," Michael replied.

"Wait! I'm comin'," shouted Declan. He gripped Michael's skinny arm and swung his legs over the roof so he dangled from the waist, then lowered himself to the ground.

"Are you the head of the house?"

"Aye. Who's askin'?"

The gentleman frowned and produced a scroll of paper from his pocket.

"I'm your landlord Mr Adair's agent. I've come to serve you and the surrounding tenants with a notice to quit your holdings by April. There can be no appeal of this."

Declan snatched the scroll from the agent and looked across at the two policemen. They bowed their heads, trying to avoid eye contact.

"Ye can't do this!" shouted Michael, clenching his fist. The agent motioned to the police who stepped forward and placed their hands on their holsters. Declan manoeuvred himself in front of his brother.

"What do ye mean? Just quit our home? We're good tenants. We always pay our rent. This is *our* home and our da's home – my granda built this place, ye can't just make us leave!" Declan said, his voice breaking.

The agent stared at him nonplussed.

"Mr Adair is your landlord and he has the right to evict as he pleases. You would be advised to heed this order as it will be enforced by the constabulary."

Rat-a-tat-tat, rat-a-tat-tat! Declan and Michael jumped but it was just a bunch of magpies quarrelling in the nearby bushes. The agent didn't flinch a muscle and hauled his weight back up on the mare. Declan found his voice again and ran towards the horse, shaking the scroll of paper.

"Ye can't just evict us. There has to be a reason. We haven't done nothin'. Our ma is elderly, ye can't make her homeless."

The agent stared coldly down at them.

"That's exactly it – you – haven't – done – nothing," he clearly enunciated. "If you have information on the murder of Mr Murray and can help to effect a prosecution, I'm sure Mr Adair will look more kindly on you as tenants."

Declan and Michael looked at each other in bewilderment. Michael shook his head.

"We can't help ye with that."

"Well then, so be it. Come April you'll be gone. Good day!"

The trio departed as quickly as they had arrived, leaving the brothers gaping at each other. Declan stared at the scroll, which had become splattered with blood from his burst blister. There it was, finally, in writing – the words he'd feared, the words that kept him awake at night. In that moment he wished he couldn't read. He wished he couldn't understand the cold, formal hand of the landlord's agent. 'Notice to quit'. Quit – their homes, their land, their lives. *Surely you decide yourself to quit something,* he raged, *you don't force someone to quit.* He shook his head at the ink that spelt out a fate his father had dreaded for them.

Two dreadful words came to mind: The workhouse.

He yelled and threw the scroll in anger. Michael shoved him hard.

"Why didn't ye fight them?"

"What? How? Fight them with my fists?"

"Yeah, we could have taken them on, *together,*" said Michael, his eyes bulging with fear and anger.

"They have guns, Michael. He's probably under orders to shoot anyone who resists. That'd be a fine thing for Ma and Cara to come home to, eh, our two corpses!"

"Bastards! May God and his angels reserve a place for Adair in hell!" Michael yelled at the lane, but it was empty save for the cloud of dust kicked up by the horses.

"*In ainm an Athar agus an Mhic agus an Spioraid Naoimh. Amen.*"

They all made the sign of the cross. Dressed in his best woollen jacket, which was a bit tattered around the sleeves, Declan thrust his spade into the dirt. He raised it out of the ground and, after a few seconds' pause, shook the dirt back onto the earth.

"*Amen.*"

"*Amen!*" The small gathering chorused at the edge of the potato field. Declan then passed the long-handled spade to

Alex Bradley who stamped it into the ground with the help of his muddy boot. The Conaghans and Bradleys had come together for the annual St Brigid's Day ritual, which marked the start of the farming year in February. Only after the first sod of earth had been turned did ploughing begin. It had a morbid significance this year with the notice to quit hanging over their heads. If they were forced out in April, they'd never see the fruits of their labour so why bother, but bother they did because it was all they knew and to not work the land was a death sentence too.

Mairead clasped her hands and closed her eyes tightly as the group mumbled a litany of prayers. Cara and Michael flanked her, each carrying small, newly woven St Brigid's crosses. Cara had gone to the edge of Lough Gartan to pick the rushes to make them. As they stood praying in the field, Declan recalled his mother's instructions to his sister as she left the cottage on the way to the lough.

"Get extra rushes so we can make some crosses for the big house too."

"What, for Mr Adair?" Cara had asked, astonished.

"If we give some to his housekeeper it might help change his mind about the evictions."

Cara looked at their ma, puzzled.

"Ye know, like St Brigid would have a presence in the house maybe and change his mind," said Mairead, her eyes wide with a childish hope.

"No, I don't know and I don't think that's gonna save us…"

Declan pondered the conversation as he watched Cara fiddle with the cross in her hands which had turned a purplish colour with the cold. Cara was right, he thought. *God help us if we're relying on prayer and some holy rushes to save our homes.* He glanced about at his family and neighbours, their heads all bowed in prayer, and bit his lip until it hurt. The prayers were coming to an end as Michael took his turn to dig the soil.

"To ye do we cry poor exiled children of Eve, to ye do we send up our sighs, mourning and weeping in this valley of tears…" they muttered the prayer in unison. Mairead released a deep sigh.

"And may God grant that we will still be farming this plot next St Brigid's."

"*Amen!*"

The two families returned to their own cottages. Mairead opened a small jar of holy water and sprinkled some over one of the crosses. Michael had fixed a hook above the door where he removed last year's cross and replaced it with the freshly-woven one. The Conaghans then held hands and bowed their heads as their mother led them in prayer.

"May Brigid bless this house where we dwell; every fireside door and every wall; every heart that beats beneath its roof; every hand that toils to bring it joy; every foot that walks its portals through. May Brigid bless this house that shelters ye."

Declan opened his eyes. Realising prayer and cross-plaited reeds would not save them, he grabbed his jacket.

"Where are ye hurrying to? It's late," asked his ma, puzzled. Her brow had been set in a permanent furrow since the eviction notice, he could hardly bear to look at her.

"I'm going over to see Father O'Flanigan and any other

clergy that will listen to me. We need them to argue our case against this, this…"

Michael jumped up.

"D'ye want me to come with ye?"

"I'll go too," said Cara.

Declan held out his arm in a calming way.

"No, thanks, I can do this myself. Ye two stay with Ma, keep her company."

He half-smiled in an attempt to reassure them and then took off up the lane. He felt his heart pounding, which reminded him of the time he first went to see Father O'Flanigan. Clutching Uncle Liam's letter, he'd been a quivering wreck then at just ten years old, trying to avoid looking near the ditch where he'd found his da's lukewarm corpse. A scrawny fox had found him first, but he had managed to chase it away. A decade later he felt just as nervous, anxious about the future, not from the loss of a parent but the imminent loss of their home. At the time they lost their da they thought they'd end up in the workhouse but their ma had struggled on and kept a roof over their heads. They were helped not least by the previous landlord waiving the rent that first year and American money from Uncle Liam kept them going until Declan was old enough to get work. But there was a new harsher regime in place now. Declan didn't feel optimistic about their chances. Their only hope was to appeal to the clergy – it would take men of letters to challenge someone like Adair. Perhaps they could reason with him as civilised gentlemen. Civilised, he scoffed. He felt in his bones that he didn't want to beg Father O'Flanigan but what choice did he have?

A candle was flickering through the window at the side of the chapel. Declan took a deep breath and pushed open the heavy door. He was a lot stronger than his ten-year-old self but when he stepped into the dark empty church, the same sorrowful faces of the statues made him shudder just as before. His footsteps echoed off the stone floor as he slowly walked to the sacristy door. There was a creak and as the door opened a shaft of light from the sacristy engulfed him. Father O'Flanigan was standing in the doorframe, casting a long shadow.

"Ah, it's you Declan, it's been a long time since you visited me." His lips twitched with a smile. "I think I know what you've come about. Please, come in."

The sacristy was a dark, square-shaped chamber with a few pieces of furniture and sombre, religious pictures on the walls. There were mysterious red curtains in the centre of one wall that as a child Declan had been curious to peek behind.

"The news is bad. I'd hoped it wouldn't come to this," said Father O'Flanigan.

Declan paced the floor, pulling his hands through his thick hair.

"He can't evict us, Father, surely."

The priest bowed his head.

"He can't, Father, on what grounds?"

The priest sighed. "I've spoken to the Reverend Maturin and he says it's some old English law where he can make you all collectively responsible for crimes on the estate."

"So he can evict us for Murray's murder without any evidence?"

"It appears so." He hesitated. "I'm sorry it's come to this. Didn't I appeal to you all at Mass that if anyone knew anything to come forward? Even at this late stage is there anything you know that could help the authorities catch the killer? I think that might help everyone's situation." He put his hand on Declan's arm. Declan stepped away.

"No, Father, I don't know anything. Maybe it was the Sweeneys, maybe it was that shepherd Rankin, maybe it was a curse from the Widow McAward. Who knows!" He waved his hands in frustration. "The police haven't caught anyone. How should I know?"

The priest pursed his lips and stared at him grim-faced.

"Can ye help us, Father? Can ye write to Adair for us, make him see sense?"

"I can do better than that – the reverend and I have written a joint letter to Mr Adair."

Declan brightened a little.

"And is there anyone else? Anyone who Adair might listen to?"

"We could write to the Member for Parliament and perhaps Theobald Dillon, the Resident Magistrate. Yes, I was considering writing to them if we don't get a satisfactory response from Mr Adair. Believe me, we are doing all we can. I stand to lose half my congregation with these evictions. It is a disgraceful situation."

Wringing his cap in his hands, Declan stared at the desk where he had penned many a letter to his uncle in the States.

"I'll write to Liam as well but I'm not sure what to tell him."

"Why don't you ask him to send for you and Michael? He could pay for your passage." The priest peered at him over his glasses. Declan thought he said it so coolly as if suggesting a trip to the Letterkenny market.

"What? And leave Ma and Cara? We couldn't do that. Where would they go?"

"I hate to spell it out, Declan, but if Adair evicts you, I'm afraid it's the workhouse for all of you."

Declan glanced at the red curtains that hid the door and had a sudden urge to grab the priest's bottle of poteen that he had discovered he kept there. It was the priest who'd given him his first sip as a child. He sighed and bid Father O'Flanigan goodnight.

"God bless you son. I'll do what I can. That's a good boy."

Declan shivered. He hadn't been a boy for a long time, he thought. He walked in a trance from the church and passed the little graveyard where his da's body lay. An insignificant wooden cross marked the paupers' grave where dozens of victims from those dark days had been buried. He recalled the rusty screech of the coffin doors flapping open. The sight of the sack containing his da's withered body plummeting on top of the heap of sacks below. The chorus of crows, the wailing of the women. Above all he remembered his promise to his da. As he walked home he began to doubt the clergymen's letters would have much influence. Perhaps Ma was right, all they could do was pray. In the darkness he stumbled past a small meadow near Lough Gartan that was revered by pilgrims as a place of prayer. Rising out of the ground was an ancient rock covered in cup-marks and art, called the Stone of Sorrow. He remembered his Uncle Liam had come here, like other emigrants during the Great Hunger, and lay down on the stone before they began their long journey. Centuries ago, it was believed St Columba had prayed here before he was exiled to the island of Iona off Scotland. It became a tradition for emigrants to sleep at the stone the night before they departed to make their sadness easier to bear. In utter despair, Declan lay down on the stone, the back of his head against the slab smoothed over the centuries by the weather and weary travellers. He placed his thumbs and fingers into the holes around him and clung tight to the rock. Closing his eyes, he released a long, anguished howl into the darkness.

Chapter 11

Adair was surprised by the furore over the ejectment notices. He had returned to his father's estate in Queen's County where he had decided to remain until the evictions were completed in the spring, hoping a little distance from the local clergy and all manner of do-gooders would help. The tenants' case had been pleaded by the Resident Magistrate and both clergymen – that fat fellow Maturin and the lanky priest – had written him a series of tiresome letters calling for him to reconsider. But he had taken sound advice from his Uncle Trench and given the required notice to his tenants. What more was expected of him? There could be no pleasing this unsavoury crowd. *They won't be satisfied until I too am 'put off the walk'.* The case was even brought up in the House of Commons. Against his better nature, Adair found he slightly enjoyed the newfound notoriety. He decided not to mention the situation to his father thinking he might be concerned or worse, try to dissuade him. But he learned of it anyway since it was all over the newspapers. At first his father had said very little but Adair detected a whiff of disapproval, a sadness in his eyes when he looked at him. Over the weeks Adair had kept busy visiting his other properties in the area and discussing business with his associates. The only time he spent with his father was at dinner, which had become long, silent affairs until one evening Adair was sitting opposite his father in the study pondering another letter he'd received. A joint letter this time at the eleventh hour, given the evictions were to take place that week, from the Reverend Maturin and Father O'Flanigan in which they beseeched him to show clemency to the tenants. The old man who had been quietly sipping a brandy broke the silence.

"Goodness, John, you get more post than me these days and this is my home. Are all your tenants literate and bombarding you with letters?" he asked with what Adair believed sounded like a sneer.

Adair casually waved the letter at his father.

"The letters, dear Father, are mainly from the clergy, both Catholic and Protestant, asking me to reconsider the evictions. My actions appear to have led to a post-reformation reconciliation. It seems I have unwittingly united these warring Christian factions," he laughed. "Perhaps evictions should be entertained as an ecumenical solution throughout Ireland!"

He stopped laughing when he noticed his father's grim expression and his gnarled knuckles turning white as they gripped the arms of his chair. Alarmed, Adair refolded the letter and tried to think of a topic to change the conversation. But they'd exhausted most subjects over the past month. The unusually cold spring had been discussed to death. It hadn't snowed in April for many years. The last thing Adair wanted was a confrontation with his father. He couldn't argue with him the way they used to. Now as an old man when his blood pressure was raised he took to having rather dramatic wheezing fits, which meant having to call out the doctor. Adair just wished his father was more like his uncle and understood better how to deal with difficult tenants. But George treated his tenants like neighbours and even friends, which both he and Trench had long disapproved of. *His tenants undoubtedly ran rings around him. It was no way to run a business.* Adair coughed to break the silence.

"I'll be heading over to Scotland next week with Townsend to visit Balmoral. He's very excited about seeing the estate so he can improve on the plans for my castle."

His father leaned forward to one side, straining to hear.

"Yes, you're building a castle with that mad fellow. I s'pose you'll need to live in a fortress if you ever return to Donegal. Why, you'll probably need an army of police to protect you…"

The old man began to pick balls of fluff off the blanket around his knees. Adair set down his glass, startled by his father's rare, sharp tongue.

"I don't understand, you were initially enthusiastic about me building a castle," said Adair, seething.

"Yes, but I didn't know you planned to turf out all your tenants."

"I didn't plan that – the two things are not related."

"Oh? Well that's certainly how it appears. Why are you so convinced the murder and your tenants are related? Do you have any proof your tenants murdered Mr Murray? Could, say, there have been a fight among your own staff?"

Adair shifted uncomfortably in his seat.

"Everyone knows everything in that place and yet no one has given evidence to the police. I warned all my tenants I expected their assistance and loyalty, so it has sadly come to this. How can I or my staff feel safe on such an estate? But I s'pose you think I deserve a bullet?"

The old man threw back his head and chuckled, revealing purplish gums in the gaps between his tobacco-stained teeth.

"The fear of a bullet is probably punishment enough. Of course I wouldn't want you 'done in' – who would I leave all this to?" he said, sweeping a wrinkly, gravy-spotted hand around the study. "Perhaps if I had another son or even a daughter..." The old man began to chuckle again.

Adair knocked back his drink and wiped his moustache.

"Well, you'll just have to get used to me being around a bit more. I'll be concentrating my business in Queen's and Tipperary for a while, just until things settle up north."

"That's wonderful. I'm sure your Donegal tenants – whoever are left – will be relieved." He slurred the last word and raised his glass to his son in a mock toast.

Furious, Adair decided he would give his father a wide berth and leave for Dublin at the earliest opportunity where he could also check on his investments.

"Excuse me, Father. I have some business to attend to."

He crossed to the green baize writing desk and sat with his back to the old man as he composed a reply to the clergymen's latest letter.

Bellegrove, Ballybrittas
6th April 1861

Rev and Dear Sir,

I received your letter respecting the Derryveagh evictions. I fully appreciate your motives. To you I am glad to explain my motives for the course adopted. That this course involves very large pecuniary loss, some personal risk and great popular odium, you must be as well aware as I am. All my personal interests, all my feelings are against it. You will however recollect that on these lands I was myself attacked by a large armed party, most of whom I recognised as inhabitants; that about the same spot my manager Mr Murray was murdered; that while I was a guest in the house of one of you, the offices were maliciously burned down; that large numbers of my sheep have been from time to time made away with; and that I and my servants have lived under the shadow of threats since I acquired the estate. You are also aware that in the management of my Donegal property hitherto, there has not been one single eviction amongst a very numerous tenantry, or an acre of mountain commonage taken from the people.

Considering then that almost all the crimes enumerated above were in some way connected with that part of the property called Derryveagh, that the perpetrators of many of them, must have been known to the people of that district, and that no information or assistance has ever been given for their discovery, it seemed clearly my duty to take the strongest measures in my power to put an end to a state of things which made it impossible for myself or my servants to live without arms in our hands – a state of things almost incredible in any European country.

I therefore decided on applying one of the oldest principles of

English law, now recognised in the 'Malicious Injuries Act' and, as far as in my power lay, to make the people of the district responsible for the crimes committed. With the deepest regret for what I considered a necessity, I determined to evict the inhabitants of this part of the property.

When I purchased this property I was enchanted by the surpassing beauty of the scenery; my strongest desire was to open up these remote districts and to elevate and improve the condition of the people. I cannot suffer myself to be intimidated or diverted from this by the infernal combination called the Ribbon Society, which has so fatally spread itself over this country.

I remain, gentlemen, your obedient servant,
John G. Adair

Having glanced over the letter, he put it aside to let the ink dry and gave a deep sigh. There was a gentle breathing sound from across the room. He turned in his seat and saw his father sleeping with his mouth open. Adair pursed his lips and then turned back to the desk where he carefully melted some blood-red wax in a well. When the letter had dried, he folded it and placed it in an envelope. He then swiftly poured the wax on to the envelope and sealed it tight.

Chapter 12

Spring was usually welcomed by the Conaghans but this year April was more ominous and snow was still falling. The colourful crocuses and primroses that lined the lanes were bitten by frost and shrivelled back into the ground. Declan stared in despair at the wilted flowers. If these hardy wildflowers couldn't survive the cold, he thought, how would his family without a roof over their heads? They counted each day of April that went by as a blessing and prayed Adair would have a change of heart. But just one week into the month they learned that he'd finally found his crowbar brigade.

"He's enlisted a bunch of bastards from Tyrone," Ruairi said, gasping for breath at the Conaghans' door having run all the way from Church Hill with the news. "Couldn't get anyone local. They've gathered in Letterkenny and, Declan, I'm afraid they're heading this way."

"Christ! What can we do? These are our homes!" Declan exclaimed. Ruairi kicked the stones at his feet.

"It's done. There's nothing any of us can do." His voice choked. "The Dermott boys have already left."

Michael pushed past Ruairi.

"What? I need to find Sinead. How can they just abandon their sister!"

"I'll come with ye," said Declan, half afraid of letting Michael out of his sight. They hurried up the lane, passing the worried faces of neighbours on the way.

"Have ye heard the news?"

"Aye."

"Bastard!"

"Black Adair – curse him and his offspring."

Some tenants were already gathering up their belongings. Donkeys passed them laden with pots and pans and other possessions. Some headed for the coast, others towards Letterkenny. The Conaghans arrived at Sinead's cabin, which was more dilapidated than most. Their potato patch was overgrown with weeds, this year's crop already abandoned. Inside they found Francis slumped over the table in a puddle of his own saliva. The sight left Declan in the strange state of being torn between envy and despair. At least in Francis' stupor he was oblivious to the fate that awaited them. *But my God*, Declan thought, *what will happen to him?* Sinead appeared from the back yard, her nose pink with the cold. She had a bewildered but determined look on her face.

"So you've heard? Adair's men are coming."

Michael put his arms around her. Declan noticed her shoulders slump into his embrace.

"It's gonna be alright. We're all in this together."

"Are we?" She pulled away, unable to disguise the look

of disgust on her face. "At least youse can go to the work-house. Da could never go there, not with his drinkin'."

She marched up to the table and shook her father.

"Da! Da! I need ye to be sober just one day of yer life, please." She tugged at his arm. Declan tried to help her rouse him.

"I'm sorry, Sinead," he said weakly.

She stared at him. He noticed her eyes were bloodshot from crying probably.

"What are ye sorry for?" she murmured. "All this isn't yer fault." She sighed. "The boys just took off last night. Said they'd try Derry first for work and then Belfast – said there was no point waiting to get kicked out. We might have to follow them, maybe they'll find somewhere for us to stay. How's Cara and yer ma?"

"They've been better."

Michael picked up the empty poteen jar on the table and nervously put it back down.

"What are ye gonna do now?"

She flashed her bloodshot eyes at him and whispered. "What are any of us gonna do … we just have to wait."

The Conaghans, like most of the tenants, decided they had no choice but to stay for as long as possible. It was a plan not without risks. Declan knew the reputation of crowbar brigades, brutal lads who took pleasure in destroying people's property. The sort of characters devoid of any conscience who would rob an orphan for a few coins. He worried at Michael's reaction. He was likely to lash out and things could get ugly. He'd have preferred it if Michael wasn't home the day they'd come calling, but he knew he needed him. Even if they wrecked the cabins, thought Declan, they could salvage what they could and get by for a while in some makeshift shelter. Mairead and Briege were more accepting of the reality that they'd end up in the workhouse.

"At least we'd get a meal a day Declan," said Mairead. "Don't be stubborn like yer da, if we'd gone there during the Great Hunger he might still be alive."

He'd heard her theory before and whether or not there was any truth in it, he preferred his own heroic notion of keeping his pledge to his father and saving them all from the workhouse. If it wasn't such a cold spring, he knew they could live rough for a while and avoid the damned place. His mind also turned to the possibility of taking the priest's advice and leaving for America. For the first time he seriously considered the idea, spurred on by the frustration of not being able to keep and defend the land they had lived on for generations. He wondered if his uncle really did look like his da. Everyone said they did but he could hardly remember his uncle. He stood at the door and rubbed his finger over the initials his da had carved on the post when they got married. Liam had married too. A woman called Sarah whom they'd never met. But they lived so far away. He stared down at the last notch his da had made to measure his height when he was just ten. He liked to remember, even if the memories were painful. They would have to leave all this behind, he thought, so why not go to America?

He took the *Rath Dé ort* sign from its hook over the door and added it to their small bundle of possessions. *Where was God's grace now?* To pass the time he bundled and unbundled their spades and tools, pots and spoons.

Time seemed to stand still over the next two days. Gartan was eerily quiet as everyone waited indoors, out of the cold, for the grim sight of the crowbar brigade. The Conaghans had a short reprieve as the men with cudgels went north first closer to Glenveagh Lough to carry out their dirty work. As Declan paced in the yard outside the cottage he didn't know if the waiting game was worse than their imminent fate. There were crops to tend to but they all knew there was little point. The whole valley was empty of its usual labourers. He did his best to shut out the stories that passed like gorse fire from neighbour to neighbour.

"Ol' man Doherty was put out last night – they had to haul him away, he was clinging to his doorpost," said one.

"Aye, he's been seen wandering bewildered in the fields. How could ye put a man of eighty out like that?"

"Heartless bastard!" said Michael, out of earshot of their ma, who sat rocking herself by the fire with the other women. Briege Bradley was relaying the news as she ran back and forth between the nearby cabins. When Declan ran out of odd jobs, he decided to tackle the thatch roof again. He hadn't finished fixing it after receiving the eviction notice. But now there was a point, it would keep him busy and he couldn't bear the wailing or the disappointed sideway looks Michael kept giving him. As he yanked himself up on to the roof he noticed spirals of smoke in the near distance. They became thick plumes belching fear and trepidation across the valley. He knew immediately these didn't come from turf fires but people's actual homes being set alight. He froze rigid on the thatch and realised his hands were shaking. When he looked closer to home, there was the surreal sight of Alex Bradley leaning over his half-door smoking his pipe like it was just an ordinary day. The rest of the family flapped around the yard, begging him to do something. The more they remonstrated with him, the more he was reminded of clucking hens. Declan remained on the rooftop when the dreaded dark mounds of police helmets appeared on the horizon. They'd heard two hundred police had been enlisted, a figure which Declan had scoffed at, but now he could see for himself the large number of troops marching towards them. The waiting was over.

He watched in horror as Sheriff Crookshank, who had been sent in from Letterkenny, strode up the path to the Bradleys' cabin. The sheriff unrolled the eviction notice, which was looking a bit tattered on the third day of their mission. There was a brief exchange of words which Declan strained to hear, partly drowned out by the loud sobbing below as they realised the brigade was in sight. Michael had hollered up to him, pointing across at their neighbours but Declan simply nodded, staring transfixed. Suddenly Alex's posture changed. Declan watched aghast as he gripped the wooden door with both hands until his knuckles whitened. His pipe fell from his mouth and the contents spilled onto the sheriff's polished boot. He flicked the ash off and turned to face the snarling gang that had emerged from the lines of police who packed into the small yard. Briege stood by the stone wall, holding little Bridgeen tightly, her hands carefully shielding her eyes. She watched her husband being roughly pushed from the doorway. Ruairi was gathering bits and pieces from the cottage, which he'd bundled into a wheelbarrow. From the corner of his eye Declan spotted the flick of a red bushy tail. A fox stood watching the scene, sniffing the acrid air. Another scavenger, he thought.

"Tell the aul' man to get out of the way or we'll clobber 'im!" yelled one of the gang. Declan's knuckles whitened as he gripped the hammer in his hand. He could kill at least one of the bastards before they wrecked the Bradleys' home. One blow to the back of the head, like Murray got. But the sight of a police rifle pointed at Ruairi as he shifted the wheelbarrow out on to the lane made him reconsider. *They'd kill me first*, he thought, *and then what use would I be to anyone?* The gang seemed to have a system. First, they flung out any objects or possessions with an almost gleeful disregard for anything fragile. Metal tongs, an empty saltbox and a picture frame landed in a clatter in the yard. The police simply stood by watching. Declan thought some of the officers seemed to hang their heads in shame; others watched like it was some sort of sport. Alex stood blinking in amazement as his life's possessions flew past him. The St Brigid's cross landed at the feet of one of the policemen who kicked it aside. Suddenly he saw Alex put his hand to his mouth and run towards the door. He was hit by a wooden spoon and then a much more coveted wooden instrument flew over his head and landed with a crack in the yard. From his rooftop perch Declan saw the distinctive curves of his beloved violin. There was a loud yelp, like that of a wounded creature, and the old man was upon his knees nursing his most prized possession. The willow shaft lay in two parts, drooping like the weeping version of the tree it was carved from. The strings that had entertained and soothed them all at many a céilí over the years, now lay limp and damaged. Declan tried to look away, his anger boiling but he felt helpless to do anything. Ruairi shook his fists at the gang but the police had formed a wall between the tenants and the cottage. Alex scooped up his wrecked violin, like it was an injured child, and carried it over to the wall where his wife now stood in stunned silence. *This wasn't just an eviction*, Declan thought, *this was an eradication of their lives*. Then the hammering began. They took crowbars and other blunt instruments to the stone and clay walls, which collapsed the roof making it low enough to set fire to the thatch. Declan winced at each blunt blow like he was taking body punches in a one-sided bare-knuckle fight. He couldn't watch anymore. He tried to manoeuvre his heavy legs back to the ground, his backside numb from sitting on the roof. He knew as the first flames began to lick around the Bradleys' cottage that the brigade would be heading their way next. The whole process took just half an hour with all six working at full pelt. A few snowflakes fell from the darkened clouds that loomed overhead, threatening a blizzard. Just as the strong stench of burned sticks and thatch assaulted his nose, the sheriff arrived in their yard.

"Declan Conaghan, are you the tenant?" he said through the plumes of smoke.

"Aye, t'is. What do ye want with us? We've lived here peacefully a very long time."

"That may be the case, Mr Conaghan, but we have to evict you all, this day April 10th, 1861," he read from his scroll. "Under the Malicious Injuries Act, Mr Adair has decreed the people of this district to be responsible for the crimes committed, including as you know the grave crime of murder visited upon his land steward last November. You will be aware that Mr Adair Esquire had notified you and your neighbours that you are tenants-at-will. It is the landlord's will to remove you from this piece of land and dismantle your cottage."

Declan glanced behind the sheriff at the sneers on the blackened faces of the crowbar brigade who stood brandishing their battered cudgels, itching for their next conquest. One of them spat on the ground and leered at Cara who stood hovering nearby with their mother. They were both wrapped in several shawls and a light layer of snow. Declan's eyes narrowed and he felt the blood rush to his head. It was all he could do to resist running at the gang with his single hammer. He was about to speak when their ma stepped forward and pointed a finger at the sheriff.

"You, with yer fancy words, shouting the law at us. My family didn't do no crimes in this district. What sort of law puts people out of their homes, aye, throws them out in the cold without any proof of a crime? *You* lot are the criminals!"

Declan's chest swelled with pride. He couldn't have said it better himself and as the words resonated there was a tense silence except for the crackling of the fire that was devouring the Bradleys' cabin. The sheriff glanced at Mairead, his face unchanged. Then he seemed to look beyond her to his men who were craning for a closer look at the cause of the delay.

"Get started," he ordered with a nod.

Declan cleared his throat.

"May this be on yer conscience, Sheriff. I hope ye can sleep at night, while ye leave us without a roof over our heads."

A burly man with a stained kerchief across his nose and mouth grabbed the hammer from Declan's hand.

"This'll do nicely. G'wan, scram!"

He pushed Declan to one side and slammed the hammer into the door. It immediately splintered. A roar went up from the gang who charged into the home. The wrecking began. Declan staggered backwards, just avoiding being trampled. It wasn't their home anymore.

"Declan!" Cara shouted on the verge of tears.

He hurried to where they had all huddled together for comfort. Michael and his ma stared solemnly at him.

"We're not staying to watch this," he said. "Just take what ye can carry and we'll leave them to do their worst."

Mairead nodded and reached out her hand to him. He gently squeezed her cold, bony fingers, hands that had raised and nurtured him under this roof. They gathered the few possessions they had and walked slowly away from their cabin for the last time. Behind them played the cruel chorus of the crowbar brigade. Declan couldn't bear to look back. His ma had begun to sob but he couldn't console her; he couldn't console any of them. Cara winced at each thump and shout. Ahead of them trudged Michael, his head bent, clenching and unclenching his fists. The Bradleys walked a little way in front carrying what they could in their wheelbarrow and bundles on their backs. The sad sight reminded him of his ten-year-old self wheeling his da's body home from the ditch. He blinked back tears, knowing he had to be strong for them all. They walked past the smoking ruins of the Bradleys' cottage. In the middle of the heap of rubble, wrenched from its hinges lay the half-door Alex had been leaning over just an hour earlier. For a brief moment through the grey clouds of smoke, Declan thought he could see his father amidst the rubble smiling at him as he came running home. Mairead blessed herself as she passed the ruins and turned to look back at their own cabin.

"No, Ma, don't," he said gently. They carried on looking straight ahead, their lives changed forever.

Chapter 13

They didn't travel very far. Dusk was beginning to fall and Declan told his ma there was little point arriving at the Letterkenny Workhouse in the early hours of the morning. The doors would be firmly shut and the walls were more to keep people out, rather than keep people in. It was bad enough, he thought, to have to seek shelter there, even worse to have to queue outside. As the two families stumbled through Gartan they found themselves walking into the true horror of what had just happened. Under bushes and trees the entire length of the lane, shawled figures sat huddled around stick fires whispering in the shadows. Many of them had fashioned some shelter out of the broken stones and debris of their former homes. All around them came the sound of deep anguished sobbing like wild animals in pain.

"God bless ye son," said one elderly man.

"Mister, can ye spare us a morsel?" called a woman with a baby in her arms.

Some had been evicted two days ago but Declan

couldn't believe they were already begging. He peered at them in the growing gloom and realised he knew all their faces. Ahead of him Ruairi and Michael took turns to push the wheelbarrow. The wooden sphere grunted under the unstable weight of the barrow but Michael nursed it along the lane, stretching his upper body across the goods to keep them from sliding off. On the slope ahead Declan could see small fires burning in the meadow around the Stone of Sorrow. He realised many of the evicted tenants had camped at the holy site and were desperately praying to St Columba. He hoped all their prayers were answered. God knows, his hadn't been. They zig-zagged on with the barrow until they reached a copse of trees where Mairead had slumped down on a bulging root. Briege and little Bridgeen joined her, all three huddling together for warmth. Cara pulled a couple of frayed blankets out from the heap on the wheelbarrow and tucked it around them, settling them into a more comfortable position under the tree. Declan realised they were both shivering, which he thought was partly the cold but also the shock of the day's events. He sized up the spot and called out to the others to stop.

"I think we should rest here at least for the night," he said. "We're all tired and cold. Cara, get some water from that stream we just passed. Ruairi and Alex can ye gather some wood for a fire? Michael and I will make a bit of a shelter, to keep the snow off us."

Just then Bridgeen let out a wail and buried her face in her grandmother's back. The others set about their tasks, much to Declan's relief.

"Oh, and don't stray too far. Stay in pairs," ordered

Declan. Michael looked at his brother and Declan realised it was the first time in recent days that he'd made eye contact with him. Gone were the glances of despair. Buoyed by this, Declan lifted the wooden shafts on either side of the barrow and tipped the contents close to his ma's perch. He then turned to Michael.

"Right, we're looking for any small boulders or planks of wood we can find."

"I saw a heap back there – looked abandoned to me."

"Good, show me."

Michael looked pleased but as they began to retrace their steps past the pitiful sights, his smile faded. As it grew dark, Declan could see the pale faces and whites of people's eyes lit by the flames as they passed by. Sitting at one of the makeshift shelters, chanting by the fire, was the Widow McAward, surrounded by her granddaughters. They couldn't tell if they were praying or keening but the scene of utter despair was like a wake. Declan vividly recalled the widow at his da's grave and quickly walked on into the wilderness. Their neighbour James Gallagher, clearly drunk, staggered past them singing and belching, *"Yon Black Adair, was a blaggard I swear…"* The rest of the lyrics faded into the night. Declan suddenly remembered Sinead.

"Any word about Si—?" he began but Michael interrupted.

"Thought you'd never ask. She's fine. I found out the Dermotts are staying in the Sweeneys' barn – they took a load of families in. Though I daresay they'll not be able to stay there forever."

Declan grunted.

"Glad they're helping. Them Sweeneys got us into this bloody mess," he said.

Michael put down the wheelbarrow.

"Ye don't still think that, Declan? As that drunk Gallagher said it's yon Black Adair's fault."

Declan grunted again and picked up the wheelbarrow.

"There it is!" hissed Michael, trying not to draw too much attention to themselves. He pointed at the tumbled wreck of a cabin, similar to their own. They worked through the shattered belongings, like scavengers on a rubbish dump, occasionally stopping to clutch and stare at some object that had probably once been a precious item. Declan pulled out a slightly damaged picture framing the familiar blessing '*Rath dé ort*'. His prize recovery though was a clay pipe, which he slipped into his pocket. He noticed Michael poring over something small. He peered closer and realised it was a poppet doll like Cara used to get at Christmas. Its woollen hair was singed at the ends and it had a bead eye missing. Michael held it up for Declan to see, smiled at him and then put it in his pocket. Declan shrugged and carried on filling the wheelbarrow. All the time he kept looking over his shoulder expecting the tenants to return and chase them away like common looters. The thought made him take the pipe out of his pocket and place it back on the heap. When they could fill the barrow no more, the brothers eased it back on to its rickety wheel and headed back to the trees. Declan could feel his back aching and his fingers were numb with the cold so it was a welcome sight to find they had got the fire going. Cara had placed the iron skillet over the fire and was warming some soup.

"What took ye so long? I was worried ye ran into Adair's men," she said, pouring them each a bowl.

"Adair's men? Why, have ye seen them?" asked Declan alarmed.

"Yes, they came by with some fierce dogs. Shouted they'd set the dogs on us, 'Mr Adair's orders!'"

"Bastards! They didn't hurt ye or anyone?" asked Michael.

"No, they didn't stop for long. I think it helped that they didn't see any men. I was hoping ye wouldn't run into them." She passed them both bowls of the steaming liquid.

"Can't they just leave us alone?" said Declan and reached for the hot bowl. "Ah, thanks Cara. Michael and I have gone into the scavenging business."

"Hmm, I see that – well you'll need to build something quick as there's snow starting to fall again."

Just as they looked up at the sky a figure with white hair sauntered into view. He was elderly and stooped with a faraway look in his eyes, which seemed fixed on something in the distance.

"Look! It's ol' man Doherty. What's he doing?"

Declan stared at the elderly man wandering up the lane as if it were a summer's morning. Occasionally, he would stop and stare at a tree. Once or twice he stretched out his bony arm to touch and study the lower branches. As he came closer, they could hear him mutter to himself.

"I've fed the pigs, ate all the turnips – nothin' left … yes, ate them all up. Are ye still hungry? Aye, that Adair's a fine fella', a fine fella'. The pigs have eaten, yes."

Cara looked astonished and whispered to Declan, "He's raving. Has he gone mad? We need to help him."

Declan nodded but before he could move, Michael had approached the old man and was guiding him by the arm to their campsite.

"It's me Michael, Mr Doherty. Are ye alright? Are ye hungry?"

As he drew closer, Declan could see his face was smeared with soot and a greenish purple shiner became visible around his left eye. His jacket sleeve was torn at the armpit and his trouser pocket flapped in the biting wind.

"Come warm yerself by the fire, Mr Doherty," said Cara. "I'll fix ye some soup."

Declan saw her scraping the dregs of the soup from the skillet. He quickly touched her arm and passed his own full bowl to the old man. Cara smiled.

"Are ye sure Declan? Ye need yer strength too," she asked but he shook his head. "Well, alright then but looks like he's going to need someone to feed him."

She took Declan's bowl and sat on a tree root beside the old man. He was still mumbling about the pigs as she coaxed him to sit down. The others watched as she lifted the spoon to his thin, purple lips and tipped the brown liquid gently into his mouth. Declan thought he heard him sigh and then looked away, trying to remember the last conversation he'd had with him. Something about Murray's murder. Aye, that was it. That was six months ago, he wasn't raving then.

"D'you think those thugs whacked him?" asked Michael, as they began to build a shelter against the trees. "Maybe he's raving 'cos of a knock to the head."

"Maybe, or just the fact he's been forced from the place he's lived all his life. I think the poor man is confused."

Michael pushed some broken stones up against a plank of wood.

"Confused? Yeah, maybe that's it. He *is* old."

Declan glanced back at the squalid sight behind them. They had all been sprinkled with a light dusting of snow. His ma and Briege were still slumped against the large horizontal tree root and looked ready to sleep. Alex and Ruairi stood poking the fire. Beside them, sitting upright, Cara was still helping ol' man Doherty sip his soup. Bridgeen began to sing what sounded like a lullaby with her sweet voice faltering every now and then.

"Have ye still got that doll, Michael?" Declan asked.

"Why, do ye want to cuddle up to it tonight?" Michael laughed.

"Very funny! Just thinking wee Bridgeen might like it. Cheer her up," he said, looking at the young girl. Michael turned towards the fire and frowned.

"I was keeping it for Sinead, as a gift."

"What a singed, one-eyed doll? How romantic! Sure she's a woman – dolls are for little girls."

Michael grunted but Declan noticed him feel in his pocket for the salvaged doll. They worked for another hour reassembling stones, sticks and planks of wood to create a draughty shelter, but it was better than nothing. As the snow began to fall more thickly, the two families were grateful for the humble roof over their heads. Cara helped Mr Doherty to lie down in one corner. The others all squeezed in, their body heat a good substitute for the fire, which had gone out with the snowfall. Mairead began to cough, a terrible rasping cough, which triggered some of the others to cough. Bridgeen, who was curled up in the foetal position, began to cry. Declan glanced at Michael who immediately pulled out the doll, which looked different. Somehow Michael had found a bead-headed pin and replaced its missing eye so it looked less disturbing.

"Don't cry, I need a mama," said Michael putting on a female voice while holding the doll in front of his mouth. The little girl reached her hand out for the doll and immediately stopped crying. Briege smiled at Michael and mouthed a 'thanks' in the dark. Declan shuddered from the cold as he lay down on the hard ground and tried to get some sleep. At least lying down he didn't have to look at their faces. He felt defeated. They would have to go to the workhouse tomorrow. It would take just one stormy night to rip apart their shelter and bury them alive. He pulled his blanket tight under his chin, which felt stubbly. *Good*, he thought, *I need to grow a beard to keep warm.* He felt Michael's knobbly knee dig into his back. Normally he would have kicked him away but tonight there was something comforting about the closeness of his family. They were homeless but despite the odds they'd made a home, however temporary.

None of them got much sleep that night as the weather seemed to have conspired with the cruel landlord to howl a blizzard over their makeshift dwelling. Mairead's cough continued throughout the night. Bridgeen sobbed and chattered in her sleep. Ol' man Doherty – or maybe it was Alex – snored loudly. And Declan lay awake listening to a repeated rhythm of *cough, sob, snore, cough, sob, snore*. He kept his eyes shut tight in the vain hope that he could imagine this was all just a nightmare. Eventually he drifted off and when he woke, he struggled to unstick his eyelashes. He wiped his eyes with his fists and realised they'd been glued with the cold snow that had fallen during the night. He lifted his head and looked around the hovel. The noises from the night had been replaced by a gentle slumber. He was relieved to see how peaceful they all looked. Then he realised his ma and Briege were missing. He knew his ma was an early riser but surely she wasn't well enough to have gone out. He moved his stiff body and quietly stepped over the others to go outside. The resourceful pair had started a small fire and were warming a pot over it. As he approached, Mairead's shoulders shook violently from the cough.

"Ma, ye alright? Good morning, Briege."

Mairead shook her head. Her eyes were sunken in her head and framed by dark semi-circles. He noticed for the first time, distracted by all the recent drama, that her rosebud mouth had faded to almost a grey gash, with an ugly sore above her lip the only hint of colour on her face.

"Ma, ye look terrible!" He couldn't hide his concern.

"She's going to be fine," Briege assured him. "I'm brewing some herbs to make a strong tea that will soothe that cough, you'll see."

"I don't doubt ye but what she needs is to be at home by the fire and a good rest," he replied.

His mother stared at him and croaked weakly.

"Declan, we don't have a home anymore. It's gone, destroyed. Ye know that. We've nothing."

Declan took her hand and was glad it felt warm.

"We've got each other..."

"I know that, but we can't stay here. Adair's men will be back I've no doubt. We have to go to the workhouse..."

Another torrent of coughing caught her voice. Declan looked around him. He could smell and see other fires along the lane as people woke to the frosty morning. It was a calm day. The rising sun had started to build in strength and was beginning to thaw the earth. He breathed in the cool, fresh air and found himself agreeing. Mairead put her arms around him and whispered in his ear.

"Thank ye son. Ye've done yer best but there's nothin' ye can do to fix this."

He squeezed her gently and stroked her soft grey hair. When he looked up a horse and cart had appeared on the lane. It appeared to be stopping at each group of tenants. A tall man, dressed in a long grey coat and hat, descended from the carriage carrying what looked like a book. Declan peered at him. For an awful minute he thought it was Adair. Surely he could not be so cruel as to visit his banished tenants? There was a rustling behind him and then a child's voice.

"Grandma – look I've plaited dolly's hair!"

Bridgeen was beaming and holding up the poppet with delight. Gone were the tears. The whole camp had begun to stir and appeared out of the hovel in various slovenly states. Only ol' man Doherty continued to snore. The horse and cart approached their campfire. The tall man stepped out of the cart, this time accompanied by the familiar face of Father O'Flanigan.

"Declan! Mrs Conaghan! Mrs Bradley! Girls!" He put his arms around Briege and seemed overcome with grief. "I cannot tell you how appalled and humbled I am by this terrible state of affairs. Such wickedness in our midst. Despite my prayers…"

Mairead interrupted him. "Ah Father, sure wasn't it yer prayers that kept us alive overnight and yer prayers that brought ol' man Doherty to us. The poor critter would have frozen in the woods if he hadn't stumbled upon us last night. Guided no doubt by yer prayers Father."

"Though your letters had no effect," mumbled Declan, flicking a stone with his scuffed boot. The priest frowned and tightened the scarf around his neck.

"Old man Doherty?" the tall man enquired. "Am I to understand there is one more in this party?"

Declan stared at the gentleman who had been writing figures in some sort of ledger book. He had an owl-like face with dark, bushy eyebrows that seemed out of place against his pure white sideburns.

"Let me introduce you, this is Mr Hamilton," the priest explained. "He's the Poor Law Commissioner for Donegal County. He's reporting the numbers who've been left homeless."

"What good will that do? Has he come to help us?" asked Michael, his hair sticking up wildly.

"It's a legal requirement for reporting purposes but he wants you all to register at the workhouse in Letterkenny," said Father O'Flanigan, glancing at Declan.

"I see," said Declan, then he turned to the Commissioner. "There are nine of us in total – the four Bradleys, the four Conaghans including myself, and Mr Doherty who is not a well man."

Just then his ma began to cough loudly. They all turned and stared at her. Briege had finished her brew and poured some into a cup, which she passed to her.

"Have ye come across the Dermott family?" asked Michael, trying to read the Commissioner's open book.

The Commissioner glanced down his list and murmured, "Dermotts ... no, no note of them." Then he turned again to address Declan over his spectacles.

"Can you tell me where you lived and what happened to your home?"

"We're all from Gartan, by the lough," he said. "Our homes were dismantled and the thatch set ablaze by a crowbar brigade under our landlord Mr Adair's orders. I believe Mr Doherty suffered the same fate, he too is homeless and a man of eighty."

"Yes, I see," said Mr Hamilton, taking notes. He shook his head and as he spoke his eyebrows twitched. "The sight of these levelled and burned-out homes takes me back more than ten years to the worst sights of the Great Famine. This is a terrible blight Mr Adair has inflicted on this neighbourhood, and from all accounts an unnecessary one."

Then turning to Father O'Flanigan, he added, "I make that thirteen homeless families in this district. We may have a very full workhouse tonight."

"Erm, I don't have to go – just the elderly, women and

children surely? Just until they get better?" said Declan with Michael nodding in agreement.

The priest and Mr Hamilton looked grimly at each other and after a pause Mr Hamilton closed his book.

"Mr Conaghan, I'm afraid you all must go in as a family," he said, his eyebrows raised in alarm. "If you have somewhere else to go then that of course is different but it appears to me, Mr Conaghan, that you are as homeless as the rest of them."

Chapter 14

Mr Hamilton insisted on taking them all in the cart to Letterkenny. Reluctant at first, Declan realised it was pointless resisting. His ma's cough seemed to get raspier by the hour. Then there was ol' man Doherty who woke with little change in his condition. He looked at them all with a bewildered expression and seemed unsure even of his own name. As they all bundled onto the cart, Briege discovered her husband was missing.

"I last saw him over at yon trees, thought he needed some privacy but he hasn't come back," she said, wringing her hands. "Oh where's he gone? He's been so quiet I hadn't even noticed."

"I'll find him," said Ruairi. "He can't have gone far. He was muttering something about his violin."

They all looked at each other. The violin was beyond repair. Declan had not paid much attention to Alex in all the upheaval as he was more concerned about his ma. The violin had meant so much to him, he carried it everywhere so that it almost seemed like an extra limb. The instrument had belonged to Alex's father who had taught him to play, and for decades the Bradley family had entertained Gartan's tenants. Declan frowned as he remembered how it took just seconds for the crowbar brigade to smash it to pieces.

"I've got to go back!" a voice shouted from the copse of trees.

It was a familiar voice but they'd never heard him yell before. They all looked towards the trees. It was Alex yelling at his son who had him by the arm.

"No, no I can fix it!"

Briege rushed over to them as Bridgeen began to cry. "What's wrong with Granda? Why's he shouting?"

Declan put his arm about her.

"Don't worry he's just, just a bit lost," he said but noticed Father O'Flanigan frowning.

They managed to lift Alex on to the cart, but as he was kicking and shouting so much, Declan had to tie him with a rope to prevent him leaping out. As the cart trundled up the lane, he ranted to the passing scenery a mournful lament about the wrecked fiddle. Briege tried to comfort him but he pushed her away. Ruairi held his mother's hand with Bridgeen curled up on his lap. On the other side of the cart his ma leaned her head on Cara's shoulder. Ol' man Doherty had fallen asleep. They were all exhausted. Declan and Michael perched on opposite sides of the cart's frame. Michael looking forwards, Declan backwards. They rolled into Letterkenny, past the market square where the crowbar brigade had assembled before their rampage through Glenveagh. He wondered what those thugs were doing now. Had they crawled back home to Tyrone with their blood money and tales of tyranny? Father O'Flanigan sat up front with Mr Hamilton near the driver. He wondered what was going through his head now his parish had been decimated. They eventually reached the high stone walls of Letterkenny Workhouse and slowly trundled through the gate. Declan swallowed hard. He looked at the severe stone façade and small barred windows. The building was made from a black granite that seemed to loom over those seeking shelter. He glanced around the cart at the pale, scared faces of his family and neighbours. It dawned on him that this would be the last time they'd all be together. Even Alex, who had ranted incoherently most of the way, became silent. Declan decided to untie him but sensed Mr Hamilton staring at him.

"Are you sure that's wise?"

"I don't think he'll be able to run away from here," replied Declan, frowning as the front door creaked open.

On their arrival the porter ushered them into a dark room with an earthenware floor. There was a slate sign above the door stating '*Paupers*' in case the new arrivals were in any doubt about their status. Declan recognised some of the faces in the room as his eyes adjusted to the dimness.

"More of Adair's lot," he heard the porter sigh to the priest. He couldn't hear his mumbled answer but noticed him pointing to Mairead who leaned against Michael on the stone bench. Alex's shoulders were so hunched that Ruairi had to nearly push him along into the room. Mr Hamilton was still scribbling in his book.

"The old man isn't fit for work either," Declan overheard

Father O'Flanigan say, turning towards Mr Doherty who was plucking at the loose threads from his ripped jacket. A nurse arrived to take the patients to the workhouse infirmary at the back of the yard. Cara held her mother's hand until Father O'Flanigan unclasped their fingers. Declan and Michael quickly embraced her before the priest and nurse carried both Mairead and ol' man Doherty away. Bridgeen smiled and waved her doll as Declan's ma was carried, still coughing, out the door. The rest of them sat blinking at each other in the dark. They were unnerved by sounds drifting from the next room – thuds and splashes, doors banging and voices shrieking.

What seemed like an eternity later, they were summoned by a man in a white coat who examined their hair, ears and throat and then listened to their chests. He nodded and signalled for them to move to the next room where Declan and Michael were separated from the girls. Declan went to hug Cara but she was pulled away by what he took to be a matron wearing a full-body apron over a grey tunic. Cara gasped and pursed her lips in indignation but as she disappeared through a door, she looked over her shoulder and tried to give them a reassuring smile. Declan realised she was putting on a brave face but knew she'd be strong for the little girl's sake who trailed behind her out the door. He'd noticed Bridgeen hide her doll in the folds of her shawl as they waited in the room. Declan and the other men and boys entered another room and were asked to strip and fold their clothes, which they were ordered to place to one side. They were then doused with a white powder from head to toe. Michael's nose exploded with a series of sneezes but the more he tried to cover his face, the more powder he wiped into his nostrils. Naked but for the white layer of dust, he cowered close to the other three in a corner of the dark room.

"Stand apart!" barked a stout man in his fifties wearing a starched apron, as he flung another cup of powder over Declan.

At the end of the process the inmates examined each other dressed in identical grey shirts and trousers. Michael's nose was red from rubbing and his eyes streamed. The others stared at him, unsure if he was crying or if it was simply the powder irritating his eyes. Declan tried to avoid their stares and reassured himself that the workhouse was only temporary. He thought again of the priest's suggestion to join Liam in the States. It seemed so far to go and such a foreign place but right now he would run all the way there if he could. His expectations were low for the workhouse but he felt he needed to stay at least to make sure his ma got better. As the last inmate was doused and the powder cleared, they noticed Alex wasn't among them.

"Where's Da now?" said Ruairi, a hint of panic in his voice, as he swivelled his head around in the darkness. A door slammed and a well-dressed man with a tired expression entered the room. He introduced himself as the workhouse master, Mr Penny.

"You are here on the generosity of the Poor Relief Committee," he proclaimed. "Those kind members of the community ensure you have a roof over your heads and a morsel to eat so until you can fend for yourselves, I am here to enforce the rules of the workhouse."

"Me da? He was just here? Where's he gone?" shouted Ruairi, looking distraught.

"Ahem," Mr Penny coughed and continued. "You will see we have a list of rules which we expect all inmates to abide by. However, I'm aware many of you will be unable to read so I shall as an introduction read them all out to you. Please pay attention as breaking these rules will invariably mean you go hungry…"

Declan suddenly realised his stomach was growling. He hadn't eaten since yesterday morning and it was now dark outside. He tried to prepare his stomach not to expect much as he knew the Relief Committee endeavoured to keep the workhouse food below the standards people ate outside to deter people from going there. But where *was* Alex, he wondered.

Mr Penny's voice droned on. When he finally left the room, the powder-throwing man walked up to Ruairi and grabbed him by the ear.

"Never interrupt the workhouse master when he's speaking, d'ye hear? Or yer out."

"B-but me da…" Ruairi snivelled.

"Yer da's been taken to the asylum. We don't look after mental cases in here."

Declan looked across at Michael who stood with his arms folded, glaring. The asylum. His head reeled. The asylum was even worse than the workhouse – no one ever got out of it. Ruairi might as well have been told his da was dead. Maybe it was a mistake. Maybe the man was just punishing Ruairi for interrupting the workhouse master. There was nothing he could say so they stood silently as the grey stone walls seemed to close in on them. Declan longed for the wild, open space of the Glenveagh moors. He longed for the breeze through his hair and the screech of eagles from their eyries high up in the cliffs. He longed for his spade. How he wished he was standing cutting turf with the other men and listening to his brother chirrup about some girl or other. He knew Michael was wondering about Sinead. How long could the Dermotts hide out in the Sweeneys' barn? He imagined they'd appear someday soon at the workhouse gate but Francis would resist it as long as possible. It was a dry institution. Francis wouldn't cope without a drink. He then wondered if he himself could cope in here as he looked at the pale, sunken faces of the other inmates. Michael's eyes were red from the powder, and now Ruairi was weeping. He felt himself sway, whether from tiredness or hunger, or both he thought. The next minute he found himself being pushed into a line and marched on a tour of the workhouse. They were shown around the main building, which included the workshop and schoolroom. Then the utility building, which housed the laundry, kitchen and the dining hall which also served as a chapel on Sundays. Dark room after dark room. He walked in a daze, only partially taking it in. Finally, they were shown the dorms. There were separate quarters for the men and boys. They all slept side by side on a long, raised platform with straw mattresses. Despite its spartan appearance and lack of comfort, Declan longed to put his head down and escape what seemed to be a very long nightmare. But when they finally got to turn in for the night, he lay staring at the timber latticework on the ceiling. He overheard one of the inmates whispering.

"That's where people hang themselves, ye know. Some lad kept a bit of rope back from the workshop a few months ago and they found him here one Sunday morning. Hung himself while they were all at Mass."

Michael who was lying next to Declan heard this and poked his brother.

"God help us! I don't like this place. We can't stay here, even our bed last night was better than this."

Declan tried to reassure him.

"I know, it's grim, but Ma needs to get well, it's better she's here than sleeping rough."

"I can't stop thinking about Alex," Michael whispered. "His mind must have snapped."

"Maybe they just took him somewhere else 'cause this place is bursting at the seams. Try to get some sleep. Tomorrow's going to be a long day."

Declan forced himself to keep his eyes shut but the gift of sleep seemed to evade him for hours as he lay there and thought mournfully of Alex. He had been more than a neighbour since Declan's da had passed. He'd always looked out for them and taught him skills on the land his own da hadn't had a chance to impart before his untimely death. Alex was a gentle soul. He loved that violin. No wonder his mind went when it was destroyed so cruelly in front of him. When Declan finally drifted off amidst the sighs and snores of the other men, his dreams were disturbed by visions of their ruined home, the cruel sneers of the crowbar brigade, and the whimpers around the campfires of the evicted.

The next morning the workhouse bell rang shrilly through the dark, dank dormitory at six a.m. They all scrambled out of bed to wash in buckets of cold water fetched by inmates deemed 'refactory' for some misdemeanour or other. The refactory inmates had to rise even earlier to pump the water from the well. Breakfast was carefully measured out. It didn't look much but Mrs Penny announced loudly it was six ounces of oatmeal mixed with a third of a quart of butter-milk, for which "they all had to be grateful. Amen." Declan realised this was luxury to a lot of the paupers – not the quality or the amount of food but the regularity of receiving something to eat each morning. He had hoped to catch a glimpse of Cara over breakfast, but the harsh reality sunk in that morning. The women and men really did live separate lives in the workhouse. They even had separate times for using the dining room. The only glimpse he caught of any women was a number of them working in the kitchen.

While the women were occupied in the kitchen and laundry room, the men and older boys spent long hours in the workshop oakum picking. Declan and Michael had some experience of this tedious task when they'd worked a couple of seasons at the shipyards in Belfast and Derry. They followed the other men into the workshop, which was a dusty, dimly lit room filled with tables. Michael sneezed as soon as they entered and Declan saw his eyes were still red from yesterday. In fact they seemed redder. He wondered if it was his brother he had heard sobbing during the night.

"You paying attention?" a voice boomed in his ear. It

was Mr Penny holding a large piece of rope, which he thrust into Declan's hands. "I don't want you asking questions later or wasting any of this," he barked.

He nodded to another older inmate with long grey hair who began to demonstrate how to separate the old fibres of the rope, which were then recycled for use on ships. Declan and Michael sat down at the end of a long table and between them untwisted the heavy piece of rope until it separated into corkscrew strands. They then slid the strands backwards and forwards on their knees with the palms of their hands until the meshes loosened further. The hemp from the fibres would then gradually fray and burst open like cotton wool. After the first hour of the working day the workshop was filled with a cloud of dust, which settled on the shoulders of the men.

Michael continued to sneeze, great loud whooshing sneezes that eventually attracted the attention of the grey-haired supervisor.

"Erm, we may have to move ye to another area," he said, staring at Michael's red nose and streaming eyes. "Perhaps the laundry or infirmary – they can always do with some male help."

Michael wiped his face on his dust-laden sleeve and promptly sneezed again.

"Yes, sir. I'd be happy to help in the infirmary. My ma is one of the patients."

"Hmm, well I'll have to speak with Mr Penny first but yer clearly not much use in here and yer disrupting the others."

"I know, that's true, I'm a terrible disruption," said Michael and managed a wink at Declan.

Good plan, Declan thought. If Michael got moved to either place, he would be able to get updates on Cara and their mother.

Two days later Michael was moved to duties in the infirmary as Mr Penny agreed they needed some men to do the heavy lifting around the dorm and a range of other tasks. At the end of his first day he joined Declan in the dining room and while the men around them slurped their stirabout, Declan devoured his brother's news.

"Cara is nursing in the infirmary," he said. "She's got a smart white uniform and looks the part. She gets to look after Ma who's still weak but the cough has eased a bit. They both send their love and said they miss us."

Declan swallowed hard and felt tears come to his eyes.

"Good, good news. We better eat this before they think we're not hungry and take it away," he said, looking over his shoulder. "Ye can tell me all the detail when we go out to exercise in the yard."

"Sure," Michael nodded and picked up his spoon. With his elbow he nudged Declan and pointed to his pocket where he was concealing a green apple.

"We can share this too in the yard. I pinched it from the nurse's station – made sure no one saw me."

"I bet ye did!"

They both laughed for the first time in days.

As the weeks passed Declan wondered if he had adopted the same blank expression of the other men in the workshop. His neck ached from bending over yards and yards of rope all day but when he looked up to stretch out his muscles, his view was of the latticed rafters like those in the dorm and in his ears was the voice that first night telling them the story of the suicide. He understood more the pain of the poor lad who'd hung himself. There was nothing about the workhouse that gave him any cheer or hope. Well, Michael helped. His job was more rewarding, caring for patients, but more often than not he would come to the dining hall with news of a death, usually the elderly or very young. At least their ma was getting stronger. Declan was only permitted to visit her one day a week, on a Sunday and then only for an hour. One upside to this was that the gap between his visits helped him to see the progress she was making. Michael and Cara, on the other hand, who saw her everyday constantly fretted that she might succumb to whatever illness was sweeping the workhouse that week. His Sunday visits provided a reassuring voice.

As well as visiting the sick on a Sunday, they were expected to attend Mass. Christian worship was a requirement of the Poor Relief Committee that ran the workhouse. One Sunday at the end of May, Declan and Michael rose to their feet for the entrance hymn. They looked up to see that the celebrant dressed in green vestments standing at the altar wasn't the usual priest but Father O'Flanigan. Declan wondered if he had some business with Mr Penny or if he had brought more of Adair's tenants to Letterkenny that day. He noticed Michael twisting and turning to see if he could catch sight of any Dermotts among the congregation. After Mass, the inmates filed past the priest who shook their hands and offered his blessing.

When he came to Declan, he waved him to one side and insisted he wait nearby until the end of the line. Declan's first thought was that something had happened to their mother. Michael went to wait with him but he was ushered out of the hall. He looked anxiously back at Declan who simply shrugged his shoulders. As the last inmate left the hall, Father O'Flanigan put him out of his misery. He pulled a crumpled letter from an inside pocket of his robe and handed it to him.

"This letter was redirected to me. It's from your uncle in America," he said, smiling. "Sit there and read it while I take these vestments off. I'd like to speak to you after you've read it."

Declan turned his back on the priest, not wishing to watch him undress. He carefully unfolded the letter. Just like old times, Father O'Flanigan had already read it. His eyes quickly danced over the usual address to his uncle's news.

14 Court Street
Geneseo
Livingston County
New York State
21 April 1861

Dear Mairead and family,

I write this hurriedly as I fear I might not get another chance to send a letter for some time. My heart is pounding with the excitement of recent days. Our new President, Mr Abraham Lincoln, has finally announced war on the South. You may have read in the newspapers that several of the southern states have seceded from this great Union and declared their own government. Lincoln has called for volunteers to join the Union Army in Washington D.C. My landlord Mr Wadsworth is now Major General Wadsworth, leader of the Wadsworth Guards, officially the 104th New York Volunteer Regiment. I know this may alarm you but I have signed up to join the fight and feel honoured to serve under him. Most of the labourers in Geneseo have signed up too so I'll have plenty of company. We'll get a good wage and decent food. The whole country seems to be awash with recruitment posters. They say they'll need a lot of soldiers. Sarah is not so thrilled but she has good neighbours who will be there for her. I know in the past I've encouraged Declan and Michael to emigrate but they really should consider coming out here. There's never been a better time to get a well-paid job in the States.

Some say the war is to free the slaves but Lincoln insists it is about preserving our Union. I don't see why we should go to war over the slaves. Although I know their lives are harsh, we get it hard too up north. However, I agree with the President that if the states split we will destroy this country. I, for one, think that would be a tragedy. I know this is dramatic news but don't worry for me. We don't expect the war to be more than a matter of months.

I hope the summer will arrive shortly in Donegal and things have improved with your landlord Adair. I enclose a small sum, which you could use towards the lads' passage to America but I leave that up to you. I know you'll make good use of it whatever you decide. I shall write again from the training barracks in Geneseo. I'll be based there until we are called up, which may be some time yet. Sarah, God bless her, is hoping we never get called. Remember me to all my friends in Gartan and tell them I am now an American soldier.

Yours affectionately,
Liam

Declan paused to take in the letter, impressed by his uncle's news.

"Well?" The priest's voice startled Declan who'd almost forgotten his presence in the quiet hall.

"Father, thanks for bringing the letter…"

Remembering the reference to money, Declan looked inside the envelope.

"I have the money, not on me, but it's back at the parochial house."

Declan glanced again at the letter. America was appealing but joining the Army less so. The priest seemed to read his mind.

"I think you should take up his offer," Father O'Flanigan said emphatically.

"But what about Ma and Cara – we can't just leave them here," he stammered.

"The nurse told me your mother is improving, it won't be long before she'll be well enough to leave the infirmary and just think, the money you and Michael can send back from the States will get them out of the workhouse in quicker time."

"But this war, Father, do you think we should be fighting it? Thou shalt not kill…"

Father O'Flanigan bowed his head for what seemed like some minutes and then looked up.

"From what I know I think it is an honourable decision of your uncle's to join the war effort. It's been triggered by that ghastly institution of slavery. I believe you will be fighting on God's side." He sighed. "Declan, I realise the workhouse is not a good place for you or your family and I'm concerned you should waste your days, the most valuable days of your youth, in here. I think you should accept your uncle's offer and emigrate to America where you may be afforded a better life than what has come to be in Ireland."

Declan found himself nodding; it was as if he had received a blessing to sign up.

"You just say the word and I can arrange the passage for you and Michael from Derry. I can also clear your departure from the workhouse with Mr Penny."

His final words were like music to Declan's ears. How much did he and Michael long to escape the workhouse with all its regimented rules and dull existence.

"Thank ye, Father, I shall speak to Michael, and Ma and Cara of course." He hesitated and then swiftly shook the priest's hand. Declan thought he caught a look of relief that washed over Father O'Flanigan's face.

He walked outside to the yard, found a quiet area near the wall where the sun was beating down and reread the letter. His head was spinning. "There's never been a better time to get a well-paid job in the States." He'd always wondered about emigrating, to see his uncle again and the much-venerated United States. He'd heard many stories of people making their fortune over there but then his uncle's letters, which he'd devoured every detail of over the years, often described a lifestyle of labouring similar to his own. Was it really a better place? And could he be a soldier? Enlisting in the Army wasn't just any job, he realised. There was a rustle in the branches overhanging the wall, which momentarily distracted him. He looked up at the ravens, which seemed to glare down at him with their black, beady eyes. Beyond the wall he could see the distant hills of Donegal, which he knew like the back of his hand. Could he leave behind everything that was familiar to him? He had travelled to Belfast for work and one season as far as England, but America was an ocean away. Few people ever came home. One of the ravens flapped its wings and glided from the branch to a rooftop along the road. Declan stared after it and pondered the reality of his new miserable existence within the confines of the workhouse walls. The Wadsworth Guards and a battle on the wide-open plains of Virginia sounded a lot more enticing. He rubbed his stiff neck and realised he was smiling to himself for the first time in weeks. He would find Michael and convince him to go.

He searched for him in the dining room, passing scruffy urchins who scampered around the dimly lit corridors. Ol' man Doherty, who had been discharged from the infirmary, banged his stick repeatedly on the stone floor and called for the children to 'pipe down' but they ignored him. The Widow McAward was rocking back and forth at a corner window. In the shaft of light that fell on her sunken face, he could see even she, who had always been old to him, had aged. Declan shuddered at the thought of living out his days in the workhouse. He eventually found Michael in the dorms, playing a secret game of cards with some of the other inmates. When he saw his brother, he quickly excused himself from the group.

"What did Father O'Flanigan want?"

Declan held out the letter.

"He was giving me this from Uncle Liam, don't worry, it's good news – I'll help ye read it."

His brother seemed to go through the same heap of emotions he just had. He smiled, he frowned, he scratched his head, he pulled on his earlobe. Then finally he murmured through his hand clasped across his mouth, "Tell them I am now an American soldier. An American soldier, whoa! That could be us, Declan." He beamed at his brother.

"That could be us, Michael. Father O'Flanigan said he can help arrange our passage."

"He's always liked ye … but what about Ma and Cara?" His eyes fell to the floor.

"I know. And I thought ye might not want to leave Sinead."

"Sinead too," Michael mumbled and shook his head. "But where is she? They can't still be hiding out in the Sweeneys' barn. No one seems to know where the Dermotts have gone. Meantime we're stuck in this miserable place. We've got nothing, no land, no work. What have we to lose really?"

"That's what I've come to think. At least with both our

wages we can help Cara and Ma get out of here. We should at least try to make our fortunes."

Michael nodded.

"I don't think we can pass this up. Imagine us, the Conaghan brothers, American soldiers!" He laughed. "And with the priest's blessing."

Visiting time was later in the afternoon. He and Michael finished their dormitory chores and crossed the men's yard to the back of the workhouse where the smaller stone building housed the infirmary. Most of the inmates avoided the building, which was notorious for typhoid fever and dysentery. Declan realised his ma was fortunate to have survived weeks in the place. Her cough had subsided but she remained too weak to be of any service in the workhouse. As they walked through the whitewashed walls of the sick bay, through a din of coughing and low moaning, Declan hoped their mother wasn't asleep. He wanted her blessing more than anyone's to make a final decision. They reached her bed at the far side of the ward, where they first noticed Cara sitting with Briege. Beside them sat the pale, thin figure of their mother resting on an incline of starched white pillows. Declan rushed to the bed and threw his arms around the frail woman dressed in a grey gown.

"Oh Declan, you'll have me squeezed to death," she croaked, pushing him away. Briege was first to notice the letter Michael was gripping between his forefinger and thumb.

"Is that a letter? From yer uncle?" she demanded, looking from the envelope to Michael and back at the envelope.

Declan smoothed out the blanket beside Mairead and looked around for the nurse before he perched at the end of the bed. He looked at Michael who handed him the letter and bit his lip. Cara frowned as she saw the looks exchanged between her brothers. Declan took a deep breath and began to stumble over the news. His ma sank back in her pillows and listened patiently. She then extended a hot, wrinkled hand to touch Michael's knee and rasped.

"What about Sinead?"

Michael pursed his lips.

"I haven't seen her, Ma – not since … since we left Gartan. Last I heard she and the family were staying at the Sweeneys' but no doubt they've been moved on by now."

She sighed and patted Declan's arm.

"We've lost everything and everyone, haven't we?" she murmured.

Briege, who had fallen into a depression since Alex disappeared, muttered, "Scattered – that's what we are, like a flock of sheep that has been visited by the wolf. Just as the Widow McAward had warned. Families should be together not thrown to the far corners of the world. He meant to tear us apart but we are just sheltering here a while and you'll see, Mairead, those we love will take care of us."

Their mother managed a weak smile at Briege and then she drew both her boys close. Declan felt his heart thumping as she sat forward and placed her arm around his back. He gripped her other hand.

"Ye are good sons and have made me very proud." She stopped to wheeze a little. "I know you've come to ask me if ye should go… I want ye to know that I think it is for the best. Do I want ye to lie and rot in this workhouse? No. I know yer da wouldn't have wanted ye to be here. America is a great chance for ye both. I just hope the war is short and ye can make a home there."

There was a loud sob. Declan looked up and saw his sister's face crumple.

"It's alright, Cara," he said. "We'll write and send money to get ye out of here too."

"Oh, but we'll never see ye again."

"Of course ye will," said Michael, going over and putting his arm around his twin. "When we make our fortune, we'll come back or bring ye out to us."

But her sobs grew louder, attracting the attention of one of the nurses. Briege shook her head and sighed.

"Scattered – to the far corners of the world."

Mairead put her arms around Declan and held him tight. He could feel her hot breath on his neck and the rattle in her chest as her lungs struggled to exhale.

"You've always been a soldier Declan, now go and be one for real. Just take care of Michael, won't ye. *Dia linn.*"

Then she sank back on the pillows and drifted into a deep sleep. Cara brushed some strands of hair from her mother's forehead. Declan knew she would take care of their mother but he felt a sense of guilt that they were abandoning her, like Sinead's brothers had done. He tried to think of something to say but the words failed him. Briege's eyes seemed to bore into the back of his skull. Michael folded up the letter – their ticket out of the workhouse – and slipped it quietly into his pocket. Cara slowly stood up and brushed her hands down her nurse's tunic as if preparing herself for a new set of duties.

"Cara, we won't leave..." Michael began to stutter but she shook her head.

"Ye should go, it's for the best, but ye better write."

Her blue eyes filled with tears but she managed to smile. Declan admired his sister's strength. He watched with a lump in his throat as the twins held each other tightly. Then realising this might be the last chance to see his sister, he put his arms around them both and buried his guilty face in Cara's soft brown hair.

Chapter 15

The yellow gorse gleamed a gilded passage along the lane as the sun shone a late summer spotlight on Glenveagh. Adair pressed his nose closer to the window of the carriage, enjoying the view that had first attracted him to the estate. Swallows swooped and dived over the shimmering lough, seeming to delight in their water ballet. He admired the larger fishing birds who lifted and repositioned their long, skinny legs with mechanical efficiency for fear of disturbing their prey. As the carriage followed the curve of the lough, Adair spied the promontory where his ambitions for the castle lay. He blinked a few times as his eyes seemed to conjure up the turrets and round tower of the castle of his dreams. But it was just a mirage, there was no castle – yet. He determined that one day, when he'd put together the capital, Glenveagh would be the grandest hunting estate in all Ireland. He knocked on the carriage roof, which responded by screeching to a halt. The coachman jumped down and opened the door.

"Ye want to stop here, sir?" he enquired in his Donegal lilt.

"Yes, just for a few minutes. I want to consider the view."

"Of course, sir, magnificent, isn't it? And such a beautiful day."

"Indeed."

Adair had arrived the night before with his cousin, Townsend. Under the cover of darkness seemed to be a good idea given the police had warned him of threats from Ribbonmen. It was his first visit to the estate since the evictions. Townsend was up with the lark and announced he was going to sketch the castle *in situ*. He had been very excited about the project since their recent visit to Balmoral. Adair had risen a little later and decided he would join his cousin.

Stepping down from the carriage Adair felt the warm sun on his face. Closing his eyes, he smiled and thought to himself that if Ireland had more weather like this, it would be the most perfect island. The reality was that it had been a long, cold year, most of which he'd spent in Dublin focusing on his business interests. In truth he hadn't felt welcome at his father's home. He felt his father's chilly reception, quite literally, when the fireplace wasn't lit in his bedroom and discovered from the housekeeper that his father had asked the servants not to attend to it. His father had even harangued his Uncle Trench at a family dinner party, accusing him of playing a part in his notorious decision. *As if I don't have a mind of my own*, he raged. Glenveagh didn't seem like the centre of a battleground as he now stood in the glorious sunshine. He breathed in the mountain air.

"So peaceful," he said aloud, forgetting the coachman was sitting nearby.

"'Tis, sir, and in the valley too – barely a sinner since, since…"

"Since what?" Adair snapped.

The coachman reddened and fiddled with the whip in his hand.

"I spoke out of turn, sir, I'm sorry," he stammered.

Adair glared at him. "Take me to where you left Mr Trench this morning!"

He jumped back into the coach.

"Very well, sir."

With a crack of the whip they set off along the lane and ascended a bumpy track that overlooked the valley. Adair was very familiar with the route, which had been home to most of his tenants. This time he stared out the window with a growing sense of horror. At first he noticed what looked like a collection of rubble at the side of the road but on closer inspection he realised it was a levelled cottage, now strangled with weeds and ivy. They passed another similar ruined cabin and then another. A broken skillet, which he imagined would have had some value to a poor cottier, lay abandoned near a mound of bricks. Too heavy to carry perhaps? Or they may have left in a hurry, he pondered. Where there had once been tidy stone walls and tended fields, now there was rubble and neglected patches filled with thorny bushes and wildflowers. For the first time since his decision he felt a slight pang of guilt. Mostly because the place looked so unkempt. He remembered this area bustling with people working in the fields. Tenants smoking over half-doors and women carrying water back from the wells. Had they all gone? He hadn't evicted everyone; he knew he hadn't.

He grew more agitated as he realised the scene reminded him of the famine villages he'd ridden through more than a decade ago in Tipperary. Suddenly a young girl, barefoot, appeared on the lane. She was carrying a bucket filled with water and stopped dead in her tracks as the horse and carriage trundled past. He attempted to smile at her and felt a sense of relief that there was life about the place after all. He hadn't completely snuffed it out. The girl stared back unsmiling. He began to fiddle with his gold pocket watch and closed his eyes.

It was *the right decision; I was being targeted. The community was harbouring a murderer, for Christ's sake. Trench's advice on 'writ habere' was the only course of action.* Adair's eyes shot open as the carriage jolted to a halt. The coachman leapt down from his perch and opened the door.

"Mr Trench took his easel to that clearing over there," he said, pointing with his whip. "Nice sheltered spot but with a tremendous view for his sketching. I'll wait, shall I, sir?"

Adair grunted and, wiping his brow with his handkerchief, stepped down from the carriage. He followed a trail through freshly trampled heather until he spied his cousin focused on his drawing. He watched as he tapped a few dots on the page, followed by long sweeping strokes. The artist worked with precision, using both pencil and the ball of his forefinger to smudge bricks and shape foliage. At times he craned his neck like a seabird to get a better view of the landscape. Overhead clouds rushed across the sun constantly changing the light on his subject and a playful breeze tugged at the pages of his sketchpad, both natural elements causing him to tut with disapproval.

"Such patience," he said, causing Townsend to jump. He swung around and stuffed the pencil stump tight behind his right ear.

"John, you shouldn't creep up on one like that. I wasn't expecting you!"

"Yes, well I thought you'd like some company and to check on your progress. You're coming along well with the sketch … question is, can you design me a castle as *magnificent* as Balmoral?"

Adair recalled their recent visit to Balmoral where he had been impressed by the granite structure. Despite the castle being just over five years old, it appeared as if it had always belonged there, nestling among the hills and surrounded by mature green conifers.

"I must say the Scottish Highlands have a lot in common with your patch here in Donegal. There have been so many copied versions of Balmoral but none I would hazard in such suitable surroundings as yours. A baronial-style castle at Glenveagh is exactly what this estate needs. It will be the envy of Ireland and beyond," said Townsend, sinking his teeth into an apple he'd pulled from his pocket.

"I knew you were the man for the job – I *intend* to be envied," said Adair, leaning back on both arms and crossing his ankles.

"Yes, my father greatly admires you and what you've achieved. He probably wishes I was more like you…" His voice trailed off as he twisted the apple stem between his fingers.

"Your father has been encouraging me to consider investing overseas."

"Oh?"

"Yes, across the Atlantic and I was seriously thinking about it when this damned war erupted. There is a lot of land further west that is available for a song, so much you could fit the whole of Ireland into a small corner of it."

"I can't say acquiring land really excites me as it does you. But building a castle, well, now that's a different story…"

"Hmm, the castle is essential if I'm to turn Glenveagh into a proper hunting estate. I'll have to borrow a bit to build the castle but I've no shortage of willing backers. They trust me, you see, since I haven't reneged on any loans to date. I'm also making more money from importing the sheep, certainly more than I was earning from those damn tenants. There is one snag of course."

"What's that?" Townsend swallowed the last of his apple and flicked the core over his shoulder.

"Well, all this business with the evictions." Adair sat forward and plucked a clump of grass. "I'm not too popular at the moment."

"With the tenants…?"

"No, I don't care for *their* opinion. Besides I've got rid of most of them," Adair glowered, flinging the snatched blades of grass in the air. They shuddered gently to the ground only to be lifted and scattered again on the breeze.

"It's the authorities, the clergy, they all have me

condemned as some sort of a *scoundrel*. They seem to have forgotten the small issue of a *murder*, no less, on my estate, along with all the other trials I've been put through."

Townsend had removed the pencil from his ear and began to swing it between his fingers.

"Yes, well I've seen the press coverage, you ol' cowboy." He laughed. "You were even mentioned in Parliament, what a hoot – *another* scoundrel in the family!"

But seeing Adair's frown, he composed himself. "Well, it will all die down, you'll see. A year from now they'll be condemning someone else. My father was always getting right up the noses of the authorities as a land agent. He was a right ol' devil himself and now he's venerated in most circles for his wisdom and experience."

Adair stroked his beard and nodded. "That's true. I couldn't shake that reverend from my doorstep. He was in tears the last time I spoke to him. Not sure if he was genuine or a bloody good actor. Kept going on about 'pauperising the estate' – as if they weren't paupers already. Still, I think we may work on the castle's plans but leave building it for a while yet – just 'til the dust settles."

"That's a shame. Still, you're the landlord. I've got plenty of other projects to keep me occupied."

They both breathed in the air and enjoyed the view. Adair tried to imagine how his castle would look and closed his eyes as his cousin began jabbering on about technical details of the design of Balmoral. The architecture was of little interest to him, as long as it had a grand enough appearance. He was thinking ahead to carriages of gentlemen, and perhaps their wives, trundling alongside the lough to the castle for a week's retreat. There would be days of hunting followed by fine dining and business transactions agreed over a sherry in the study. He was determined to put Glenveagh on the map – a destination for gentlemen. He smiled to himself.

Townsend continued his sketch with the odd exclamation about his subject. A while later he presented his sketch to his cousin with all the pomp and bluster that he could summon. He spun the sketchpad around and whipped off the large linen handkerchief with which he'd carefully concealed it. Adair squinted at first and then took it in both hands with a satisfied smile.

"Well?" said Townsend, stuffing the handkerchief back in his pocket.

"I would say it is almost" – he paused for effect – "perfect. A castle fit for a nobleman!"

"Oh, *the* most noble!"

They both laughed, deep hearty laughs that reverberated around the valley.

Chapter 16

They had left the workhouse as dusk fell the night before and were escorted by Father O'Flanigan in his horse and cart to Derry where they were given lodgings in the local convent. On the journey Michael had interrogated the priest about the whereabouts of the rest of the tenants, in particular Sinead and the Dermotts. Declan watched the priest fidget with the horse reins and realised he was evading the truth.

"Surely, ye must have heard where everyone ended up?" asked Michael.

"Well now some of the tenants found plots to farm on nearby estates. I'd heard Francis may have made the journey to Derry … but I can't be certain of that, you know how there's rumours," said Father O'Flanigan, scratching at his collar.

Declan pondered his story and could see Michael was puzzled.

"Ye know I always expected Francis and the rest of the

Dermotts to turn up in the workhouse," he said. "I mean obviously he wouldn't be able to drink inside but where else would he go?"

Father O'Flanigan was silent for a bit and then said, "Well, young Michael, I doubt Francis would ever have gone to the workhouse. People like him tend to head for the city, where they can beg and be more anonymous. But then Derry's a small city."

He threw a sideways look at Declan as if seeking some assistance. Michael frowned. Declan felt for him. He knew he missed Sinead. He had talked about her constantly in the workhouse. Every time new inmates arrived, he'd first look anxiously to see if any of the Dermotts were among them and then he'd sidle over to where they stood in line for dinner and enquire about Sinead. Invariably they'd shake their head or shrug their shoulders, and sometimes stare curiously at Michael as he persisted with his interrogation. In the two months they'd been at the workhouse, there was just one positive sighting of Sinead. Their former neighbour, James Gallagher, who arrived with his family about a month after them provided the only bit of news.

"The Sweeneys kicked Francis out after a couple of weeks," said James, waving his large thickset hands. The man who had once entertained them all with his melodious voice looked a pale shadow of his former self. Michael was transfixed. It was a snippet of information he'd been desperately seeking.

"They caught him boozing from their stash of poteen," said James. "In fairness they'd caught him a couple of times and warned him."

"Did Sinead go with him?"

"Yeah, sure she looks after him. He'd be lying in a ditch dead if it weren't for that lass, as ye well know, Michael."

The news that they'd left the barn only worried Michael more. He spent hours discussing with Declan where they might have gone. Where *could* they go? Derry seemed the most likely place to harbour a destitute drunk. With their boat passage leaving Derry in the morning Michael realised tonight was his last chance to find her and say goodbye, perhaps for good. Fortunately the priest had left them at the convent steps with little ceremony. As soon as the brothers jumped from the cart, Father O'Flanigan was flexing the reins to make the return journey. Declan was relieved he wasn't staying overnight at the convent.

"I should make it back to Gartan before dusk. I'll go to the Stone of Sorrow and pray for your safe voyage. Remember me in your prayers!" he hollered, and in a cloud of dust he was gone.

For a few minutes they stared after their last piece of home before trudging up the steps to the next institution. As soon as they'd dropped their bags in the dormitory, Michael urged Declan to help search for Sinead in the city.

"I want to see if I can find her. Come with me, we can ask people if anyone has seen them," he pleaded, the dilated pupils of his eyes large pools of hope and despair. Declan feared it was a fruitless endeavour but couldn't deny his brother's request on possibly their last night in Ireland. They headed into the dark, cobbled streets of Derry, stopping people to ask if they knew anyone by the name of Dermott or had just seen a drunk man matching his description. They walked along the centuries-old walls to St Columb's Cathedral where one old lady had said the homeless often gathered. They peered closely at the mounds of people buried under blankets. From what they could tell, in the dark and from the unfriendly reception, there was no one familiar to them. They stumbled down the steep slope of Shipquay Street through the old city gate to the docks area, where sailors and drunks were milling about drinking and smoking. The huge green bulk of the *Minnehaha* rose up in front of Declan. *There she is, the 'great, green yacht from Derry' and our passage to the New World.* He admired how this massive seacraft sat so graceful and still as the waters lapped and seagulls squawked around her.

"She's a real beauty – named after a princess," said an old man smoking on top of a large roll of rope. "Ye boys sailing on her tomorrow?"

"Aye," Declan replied. "Who was the princess?"

"She was an Indian princess from the famous *Song of Hiawatha*," said the old man pointing with his pipe at the figurehead on the ship's hull. "I know it's hard to see in the dark but she's a beautiful carving on the ship. She'll guide ye across the Atlantic, never fear." He smiled, revealing his tobacco-stained teeth, what was left of them.

"Was she a real princess?" asked Michael.

"Oh, I'm not sure, an Indian legend, I think. Hiawatha was an Indian warrior and she was his sweetheart but it all ended in tragedy. She died during a severe winter."

"Ye seem to know a lot about Indian legends."

"Oh, I only learned about it because I like the ship," he said, sucking again on his pipe. "There's a poem about

Hiawatha which I've heard. I like to watch her come and go. *Minnehaha* means laughing water, isn't that a great name? She seems sure to laugh at the sea, conquered that crossing, she has. One of the best and safest ships there is to sail to America, I'd say."

Michael turned to look at the ship gently rocking in the harbour. Two younger fellows nearby who said they worked on the ship were listening in.

"Where ye boys from?" one of them with a scrappy beard asked.

"Donegal."

"From Donegal to New York." The bearded young man let out a long, low whistle. "That's some difference. From the moors to the big city."

"What's it like? Is it very big?" asked Michael.

"A lot of people." The young man whistled dramatically. "Thousands of people, all rushing around. Manhattan is a massive island but full of people from all over the world. Italians, Germans, Chinese, Indians... Maybe you'll find yer own princess over there!"

He gave a chuckle. Michael's face fell. Declan changed the subject.

"Do ye get to see much when ye dock?" he asked.

"A fair bit," replied his ginger, lankier friend. "We dock for about a week before we leave again. Gives us time to do repairs. Clean the ship properly. Get stocked up. It's a long voyage, hope ye boys are ready for it."

The bearded man gave his mate a friendly punch.

"He doesn't do much work on dry land," he laughed. "Too busy chasing skirt around the port. Have to say the women in Derry are a pretty lot. Last time we were here there wasn't much to look at. Old hags mainly but we'd a great night last night, eh Pete."

Pete, the ginger one, grinned and winked at the old man who listened while puffing on his pipe. He seemed to have lost interest in the conversation.

"Young sailors, always talking themselves up," the old man chipped in. "I'd say a life at sea would be pretty dull."

The bearded sailor frowned and turned his back on the old man.

"What ye fellas gonna do in New York then?"

Michael puffed out his chest and smiled for the first time in days.

"Me and my brother are gonna be American soldiers."

Pete nodded and pulled out a bottle of poteen from his pocket.

"Yer signing up for the Army?" he said. "That's a good plan. I might sign up myself. Like the old man says, life at sea can get pretty dull."

His bearded friend protested.

"Nothing wrong with working at sea. I'd rather join the Navy than march miles carrying heavy guns and equipment. I'd say that'd be harder work."

The old man became interested again in the conversation.

"Why're ye joining the United States Army? Who are they fighting now? The English or the Indians?"

"They're fighting each other – Americans fighting Americans; North versus South," replied Pete. "I've heard it's gonna be a long war 'cos those Confederates in the South aren't for quitting. That new President Lincoln thinks they gonna roll over quick but boys I be speaking to say they're in it for the long haul."

Pete thrust his bottle of poteen at Declan.

"Ye want some?"

"Thanks," said Declan, taking a swig. He glanced at Michael who was no longer smiling about being an American soldier. He was digging his foot into the sandy clay between the cobbled stones. Declan turned to the old man.

"We came down to the quayside because we're looking for a man, about yer age, likes to drink – a lot."

"Has he got a name, son?"

"Francis, Francis Dermott – skinny fella, wispy grey hair."

"From Donegal too, one of Adair's evicted tenants I'll bet?"

Michael stopped excavating the stones and stared at him.

"You've seen him then? Was he with a young woman?" he asked.

"I've certainly seen Francis but not for a few days mind," he said. "Not sure about a young woman."

"D'ye know where he's staying?" Declan asked.

The old man slowly removed the pipe from his mouth and used it to sweep over his head at the dark night sky.

"Under the stars I guess, think he's homeless."

Declan looked at Michael who seemed agitated. *Great,* he thought, *he'll have us looking in every shady corner of the harbour and shopfronts.* He couldn't imagine Sinead sleeping under the stars, surely she'd have found a job in one of the linen mills and somewhere to stay. Declan stared back towards the smoky city. The chimney stacks of the brick factories and linen mills jostled for position in the skyline with the tower and spires of St Columb's and St Eugene's. The industrial and spiritual elements of the city commanded the attention and obedience of the lines of terrace houses which wound uphill towards the green fields beyond.

Pete and the bearded man had started making a racket from throwing coins at an empty jar. With each chink and rattle of the jar as a coin landed they roared with delight. Suddenly over the noise, a clip clop could be heard. The clip clop of heels tapping along the cobblestones. The bearded man gave a wolf whistle and looked in the direction of a woman in heels emerging from the shadows.

"Fancy myself a bird tonight," he whistled again. He shouted after her and then continued the coin game.

Michael looked in the distance where he could just make out a woman with long, dark hair cascading down her back. She picked her way carefully over the slippery stones, now and then wobbling in her heels. She wore a red, flouncy dress with frills around the edging, which she had bunched up in her hand to keep it from being soiled on the damp stones. It was close to midnight and a mist had billowed in from the sea engulfing the figures on the docks in an eerie cloak.

"Sinead?" Michael cried out. Declan grabbed his brother's arm, in an effort to restrain him.

"Sinead, it's me, Michael!"

The woman stopped as if she recognised her name or his voice. She slowly turned around but before they could see her face fully, a burly man stepped out of the shadows and put his arm roughly around her shoulders. She tottered away with the man. Declan and Michael stood paralysed, as if their feet were stuck to the stones. They stared open-mouthed after the disappearing shadows.

"That wasn't her," said Declan, shaking his head.

"Ye don't think so?" asked Michael. "Ye don't think she would ever…"

Declan remained silent. What could he say? It would break Michael's heart if this was what Sinead had become.

"Ye were asking about a woman?" the old man spoke up. They'd forgotten he was still sitting there. "Come to think of it there was a woman with him. Young enough to be his daughter. Ye related to him?"

"No," said Michael, in a voice that was barely audible.

The old man was sharp enough.

"Ah, is she yer sweetheart?"

Silence.

"Well I hope ye find them. Who will I say was looking?"

"Michael, Michael Conaghan if ye could," Michael half-stammered his own name.

"So shall I tell them, yer stopping or going to America?" asked the old man, cocking his head to one side.

Tears began to roll down Michael's face. Declan took him by the shoulder and moved him back the way they'd come towards Shipquay Street. Michael offered no resistance and rubbed his face with his sleeve. He then looked over his shoulder and shouted back to the old man.

"Tell them we've gone – the Conaghans have gone to be American soldiers!"

Part II

JUNE 1861

Chapter 17

They left the ocean and disembarked on the shores of Manhattan Island only to find themselves in a sea of people. New York was flooded with folks from all over the world, just as the sailors had described. Declan found himself gaping at the different colours of skin and the variety of faces. Michael had to nudge him to stop him staring. The bustling port made Derry seem like a quiet fishing village. The crowds, the suitcases, the street vendors, the smells. The sights were an assault to the senses as they fell off the boat and tried to find their shore legs among the babbling sounds of foreign tongues.

They only stayed a few nights in New York City as they'd very little money. It also felt dangerous so they were both relieved to move on from the city and the wide-open vista of the countryside was a welcome sight as they went shuttling past. They had taken an early morning train and couldn't believe after nearly a whole day's travel that they were still in New York State. It gave them a sense of the scale of the country they'd reached. Declan felt overawed but tried to keep those feelings to himself by remaining his usual silent self. He knew Michael was brooding about Sinead, but Declan found it hard to know what to say. Instead he said nothing. They eventually arrived in the late afternoon at the sleepy village of Geneseo. As they stepped off the train with their few possessions a large recruitment notice caught Declan's eye.

VOLUNTEERS WANTED
FOR THE
WADSWORTH GUARDS!
THE CRACK REGIMENT OF THIS STATE.
Camp Union, Geneseo, Livingston County, N.Y.
Persons enlisting can go into camp at once, be sworn in and receive pay, rations and uniforms from the date of enlistment.
PAY $13 TO $23 PER MONTH!
AND $100 BOUNTY AT CLOSE OF THE WAR!
The Regiment is commanded by Col. J Rorbach
Capt. ALFRED KENDALL,
Lieut. J.P. RUDD,
Recruiting Officers.

Declan finished reading aloud the sun-bleached poster nailed to the station's timber fence. Michael grunted and blinked in the sunlight. Declan could see over his shoulder that the platform had emptied and the guard had disappeared into his hut. He ripped the poster from the wall and rolled it into his knapsack.

"What d'ye do that for?" snapped Michael. He was tired and irritable from the hot sun and still hadn't recovered from the long sea voyage.

"Can ye remember where we're to enlist? Na, didn't think so. Besides it's good to have in writing what they're promising to pay us."

"True, wish we could just take that one-hundred-dollar bounty now. That's a lot of money isn't it, Declan?"

"I'd settle for the thirteen dollars a month; that's more money than we've ever had," said Declan as they walked through the gate on to the main street.

"Camp Union headquarters!" said Michael.

"What about it?"

"That's where we've to enlist. Ye said I wouldn't remember."

"Very good. I also want to send the poster to Ma and Cara to let them see what we're doing."

"We can't write 'til we can send them some money," said Michael, swatting away two black flies that were buzzing around his head. "Can ye imagine how disappointed they'd be to open an envelope with just that mouldy 'oul poster in it and them stuck in yon workhouse."

Declan considered their ma and sister now thousands of miles away in Letterkenny. He prayed Ma had made a full recovery and that Cara wouldn't succumb to anything working in the infirmary. Although he was glad to have escaped the whitewashed walls of the workhouse, those they'd left behind were never far from his mind. Another reason to feel guilty.

"So what now? I'm hungry," said Michael.

"It doesn't look like a big town; we'll ask someone the way to the camp. Maybe that train guard would know."

There were few people in the main street, which seemed to be mostly residential houses with just the odd horse-drawn cart trotting past. The guard pointed them east towards North Street.

"I thought you boys looked a bit lost," he said, spitting on to the railway tracks. "You'll find the barracks at the far end, newly built with a separate kitchen and mess house thanks to Colonel Rorbach. If I was ten years younger, I'd sign up myself. The Army'll be the making of you boys, I tell you. It's an honourable thing to fight for your country…"

His eyes narrowed as he looked closely at them.

"Hmm, but this ain't your country, is it boys? Pair of mercenaries, are ye?" But he didn't wait for an answer. "Well, as long as you Irish are fighting on our side I'll not say anything against ye. Good luck!"

He tipped his guard's hat and pointed in the direction of North Street. As they walked along the dusty road they passed some beautiful timber-built houses with purple blossom hanging over well-kept verandas. Michael spotted an apple tree and plucked two low-hanging red apples.

"Here, this'll keep us going," he said, passing one to Declan. "Who knows when we'll next eat?"

They sauntered on along the street, rubbernecking at the neat row of houses. In the distance they saw the United States flag on a tall pole and knew they were approaching the camp. It was a large sloping field on the edge of the town. As they came closer, they could see a number of long brick buildings that they took to be the barracks. There was smoke rising from a chimney in a nearby building and the delicious smell of cooking.

Michael looked at Declan. "Well, this must be it. D'ye really think Uncle Liam is here? It'll be strange to see him after all these years. I can honestly say I wouldn't know what he looks like."

Declan swallowed hard. He longed for a familiar face after weeks of strangers but then considered Liam had probably changed a lot since he'd last seen him. They had both been just kids when Liam had emigrated during the worst of the famine, but he had lived nearby so Declan remembered him vividly. Their da and Liam had been very close.

"Yeah, ye were really young when he left, just six or seven years old," said Declan. "I'm sure he's changed a lot. He was only a teen himself when he went."

The sound of loud voices and deep commanding tones arrested their attention. Down the slope were two lines of men in blue uniforms. The booming voice came from a lone man in front of the two line-ups whose gold buttons gleamed in the sunlight. Declan shaded his eyes from the sun and scrutinised the lines for anyone who looked like their uncle. Freckle-faced with dark, wavy hair, he remembered, nothing very distinctive in that. But it was hard to make out any of the faces from a distance. Michael looked at Declan. His brother could read his thoughts. Did they want to sign up to this? Was thirteen dollars a month worth their freedom and maybe their lives? He thought of the guard's name for them – mercenaries. In the heat of battle how loyal could you be to a country you'd just arrived in? *Do we turn around now and find some work elsewhere?*

"Well?" said Michael.

Declan wiped his brow with a linen handkerchief he'd found on the ship that had probably blown out of a gentleman's pocket.

"Well, we're here now," he finally replied. "We came out here because of our uncle and I guess we'll only get to see him if we sign up."

"Yes, but are we good enough for the US Army?" Michael frowned.

"We'll soon find out, won't we boys!" a loud American accent boomed in their ears.

They swung round to see a big, smiling man with curly red hair wearing a gleaming uniform, with tassels and gold woven threads, towering over them. He stretched out his hand and shook each of theirs vigorously.

"Captain Kendall, young sirs, pleasure to make your acquaintance. I am the recruitment sergeant for H Company. I take it you're both here to enlist?"

Declan was immediately fascinated by how his thick, reddish-brown moustache moved with each word, like a small creature attached to his face. Michael looked at his brother and then cleared his throat.

"We are, sir!" he half-shouted and raised his hand in a salute to his forehead.

Declan managed to stifle a laugh and nodded to the sergeant. His moustache stretched into a wider smile as he looked them both over.

"Irish, I hear? Have you been in America long?"

This time Declan answered.

"No, sir, we arrived in New York just last week. We've

come to Geneseo because our uncle wrote to tell us he'd signed up with the Wadsworth Guards and he said we should join the war effort – sir."

Declan cleared his throat, staring all the while at the quivering facial ferret.

"We have quite a few Irish in the camp," said Captain Kendall. He opened a large ledger book he carried under his arm. "What is your uncle's name?"

"Conaghan, Liam Conaghan, sir!" said Michael and saluted again.

The sergeant didn't seem to notice Michael's deference, possibly well used to it, Declan thought, and watched as he ran his finger along the list of names.

"Ah, yes we have a Conaghan here," he replied, shutting the book. "Let's go to the office and fill out the necessary details. Then we can find your uncle so you can be reacquainted. I sure appreciate the recruitment efforts of your family to our cause. Are there any more boys where you're from?" He laughed.

Declan understood it wasn't really meant as a question. He could tell from the sergeant's tone he already knew there was a ready supply of immigrant recruits, and not just from Ireland. The pair obediently followed Captain Kendall into the office, glancing at what they took to be the kitchen as the smell of cooking wafted more strongly. After signing some papers, which in the heat of the day all blurred before Declan's eyes, the sergeant summoned two officers to escort them to the Mess Hall.

"These boys need kitting out," ordered the captain. "I'll go find Corporal Conaghan. I want to thank him in person for his help with recruitment and if he's not occupied, I'll bring him over to the hall." He grinned again, the ferret flapping about his face.

The two officers led the way to the Mess. The heat was intense as rows of new recruits were lining up and being assigned to different duties. Many of them were still wearing their own clothes – loose-fitting labourers' overalls – and quite a few were barefoot. Declan forgot his own plight for a few minutes as he watched the bedraggled bunch being shepherded from one table to the next. They looked pale and unhealthy and he could hear thick Irish brogues among them. They joined the queue of men and waited for what seemed like an hour. Michael leaned against his brother, such was his hunger and fatigue. Eventually they reached the front and were handed their own regulation blue uniform and pair of boots.

"Fresh blood!" said one of the officers to Captain Kendall who had reappeared accompanied by another soldier who looked a bit bewildered.

"Fresh blood indeed!" said the captain and turning to his companion, pointed to Declan and Michael. "These young men claim to be *your* blood, Conaghan."

Declan's heart almost stopped beating in his chest. His pupils enlarged as they devoured the familiar-looking figure before him. The thick black hair like his own and the same watery-blue eyes, like those behind the lids he had gently pressed closed in that Donegal ditch many years ago.

"Gentlemen, this is Corporal Liam Conaghan," said the captain, as he and the officers stood searching the trio for some sign of recognition among them. But they stood silent, in almost a trance for some minutes before Michael stretched out his arm for a handshake.

"It's me, Michael – yer nephew," he said, eyeing the serious-looking soldier they had come all this way to find.

Declan's eyes welled up and a rush of blood suddenly thawed his frozen limbs. When Michael finished his handshake, Declan grasped his uncle's hand and pulled him towards him, almost winding him, as he hugged him tightly.

"My own flesh and blood," whispered Liam in his ear as his tears wetted Declan's cheek. "My brother's boys, well I'll be damned!"

They stood staring at each other for some minutes, punctuated by slaps on the arms, spontaneous hugs and loud gasps.

"God, I wrote you boys but I never expected … well, I just never." Liam kept shaking his head but those blue eyes seemed to pierce through Declan. It was like staring at a reincarnation. Liam was so like their da, as if he'd grown from a scrawny teenager into his da's shape and size. The only difference was the drawl; he appeared to have gained an American accent. Declan wiped tears from his eyes. He finally found his manners.

"Thank ye, Uncle Liam, for the letters and the money," he said. "They've been a lifesaver over the years."

Liam shrugged.

"They weren't much. No doubt you boys'll do the same for the women back home. I take it that's why you've come out here? I mean, I wrote but I never thought you'd make the journey."

He gripped Declan's shoulder like his da used to do. His

mannerisms were so familiar, Declan had to pinch himself he wasn't talking to an apparition. Beside them, Captain Kendall and the officers who had been watching the reunion like it was entertainment appeared delighted with themselves for their minor role in the drama. Captain Kendall chuckled a deep belly laugh and slapped the reacquainted men a final blow on each shoulder.

"There, Conaghan, dry your eyes, you have to set these boys here an example of how to be a tough Union soldier, eh! And what am I going to call you now?" he said, turning to the awestruck Michael. "We'll have to call you Conaghan Junior. You know, my parents hail from County Kerry," he drawled. "Stick with your uncle and you'll be a fine soldier, lad."

"Yes, sir, I will, sir!" replied Michael, saluting the captain again.

"Well, we'll leave you three to catch up on your folks' news. I'll swap your duties tonight Conaghan so you may take the lads over to the sutler and get them some whiskey or maybe they'd prefer candy, ha!" he roared and sauntered away, laughing with his fellow officers.

Declan was still gaping at his uncle who seemed both strange and familiar.

"So you've been given your uniforms," said Liam, looking at the pile of clothes at their feet. "You look like rebels in them civilian clothes. There's room in my dorm if you want to settle in there. There's about five of us at the minute. Good men, and two of 'em are about your age."

Michael nodded and lifted the clothes they'd abandoned on the floor.

"Have you eaten?" Liam asked.

"No, but I fancy the sound of that whiskey…" Michael replied with a grin.

Liam stared hard at him and laughed.

"Ye like a drop, do you? Well, you'll fit right in here."

Declan interrupted. "He needs to eat; he was practically fainting in that queue."

"Ah, and you're still the sensible one?" said Liam, smiling. "Well c'mon across the hall. Food's normally served at set times but I know the cook and I'll see if he can fix you boys something."

They sat down on benches at a long table and in no time a soldier in an apron was bringing them a plate each of chicken and rice. It was like a feast to them.

"Eat up, boys, not every day we have family reunions," said the beaming soldier as he placed the tray in front of them. With his broad shoulders and rough hands Declan thought he looked more suited to ploughing fields than working in the kitchen.

"Thanks, Eddie. Boys, this is a good friend of mine," said Liam, introducing them.

The brothers nodded but their eyes quickly turned to the food whose smell beckoned them to pick up their forks.

"I can see the family resemblance there, Liam," said Eddie, as he wiped his large hands on his apron. "Must be some shock them just showing up?"

"It's a shock alright," Liam replied. "But in a good way. I've always been jealous of you and your family. Now I've family here of my own."

Eddie laughed. "At least they're of an age to look after themselves, not like my two young 'uns."

"Let's hope they can look after themselves. They're in the Army now. Came a long way too so that's promising!"

He thanked the cook and turned to watch them eat, his blue eyes sparkling as they greedily spooned up the food. Afterwards they walked through the camp to the barracks. Michael's neck swivelled in glee as he took it all in. There were groups of men sitting on tree stumps carving pipes and other items from pieces of wood. They looked up as the trio passed. One soldier nodded at Liam and then spat on the grass. Other groups of men sat at makeshift tables playing cards. One group who appeared to be officers with their tail-coats draped over the backs of their chairs gambled in the shade of a large tent marked with a little rustic cross, known as the canvas cathedral.

"It's a big brigade – a lot of men," remarked Michael.

"It's growing, about five hundred men I'd say, could do with more still," muttered Liam. "I persuaded Eddie Thornton, the cook, to sign up. He wasn't interested at first. Then I beat him at a game of poker. Told him he could keep what he owed me if he only signed up! Don't think his wife was too pleased, at least I know she complained to my Sarah."

He grinned and gave them a wink. Declan couldn't imagine his da playing cards or gambling anything.

"How is your wife?" asked Declan politely. "It would be good to meet her too."

"She's fine. No children yet, before you ask. You'll meet her on Sunday when visitors are allowed to come to the gates. She'll be as surprised as me at you pair showing up."

When they reached Liam's dorm, he pointed out two bunks and places for them to put their things. Some soldiers lay sleeping on their bunks. They grunted and whistled in their sleep, curled up like farm cats without a care in the world. Liam explained it was siesta time.

"What's a siesta?" asked Declan.

"You never heard of a siesta! You boys have led sheltered lives," Liam laughed. "It's when you sleep in the afternoon when it's too hot to work."

Declan looked at Michael. They shrugged their shoulders.

"It's never too hot to work in the afternoon in Donegal."

They all laughed.

"I think I need that whiskey now, Liam?" said Declan.

"Sure, follow me."

They sauntered to the edge of the camp where Liam found the sutler and filled his hip flask to the brim for a few quarters. Then their uncle led them to a set of boulders that clung to the side of a river that ran along one side of the camp. They clambered to a comfortable resting place that overlooked the babbling water. A canopy of low-hanging branches provided some shade from the glaring sun.

"This is a great throne, eh!" said Michael, patting the smooth rock.

"Yeah – you're a soldier king now, Mickey!"

"I'm on top of the world, that's what I am, Uncle Liam – I can't believe we've found ye after all this time."

Michael beamed, unable to hide his delight. The afternoon was just getting better and better. Declan couldn't take in the fact he was sitting on a rock in New

York State, sipping whiskey with the uncle who'd left Ireland all those years ago. Liam took a slug from the tin flask and passed it to his nephews, all the while still staring at them. Michael felt the sharp liquid hit the back of his dry throat and he spluttered it out over his shirt sleeve.

"Thought you were a whiskey drinker!" Liam chided him.

Michael coughed and his face flushed pink.

"Blow yer head that stuff and I thought poteen was strong."

He returned the flask.

"Poteen! Now what wouldn't I give for a swig of some Donegal moonshine. Are the Sweeneys still makin' the stuff? They were barely full-grown before their father had them distilling."

Declan's eyes widened.

"Ye remember the Sweeneys?"

"Aye, 'course I do – they're bout my age. Nearly persuaded Sean to come away with me to the States but he took cold feet," revealed Liam.

Over the next hour as the whiskey and the pleasant sound of running water relaxed them, they discussed the distant folks of Derryveagh. The brothers exclaimed at the people Liam still remembered and their uncle laughed and howled at the antics of his old friends.

"Francis Dermott," said Liam, shaking his head. "How

that old crow is still living is beyond me! Sure he was having poteen for breakfast nearly twenty years ago!"

Declan laughed and then became silent as he recalled the back of Francis' head when he was chained to him on the long walk to Letterkenny courthouse. Michael stopped laughing too. Declan imagined he was remembering Sinead and the sight of the woman picking her way across the cobbles on their last night in Ireland.

"Ah Francis – he's some boy!" Liam reminisced.

"It's all changed," said Michael sombrely staring at the granite at his feet. "Most of the folks have been moved on, their homes wrecked … there's nothing left but burned-out cottages."

Liam frowned and searched Michael's pale face for an explanation. Michael's hands were trembling. Slowly the brothers explained the evictions and their last few months before they'd taken the ship from Derry.

"You left them in the workhouse – yer ma and Cara, that's where they are, the workhouse?"

Liam suddenly lunged at Declan and grabbed him by the scruff of his open shirt pulling him to his feet.

Startled, Declan found himself stammering, "I know it sounds bad but we couldn't stay there … we weren't even with them … we were in separate quarters for men and women… Then yer letter arrived and Father O'Flanigan, well, he arranged our passage out here. We're going to get them out of there. Don't ye see, that's why we came!"

Liam's rage subsided but Declan still felt the full force of his uncle's blue eyes pierce through him. Just like his da, Liam couldn't stand the idea of the workhouse. Declan took a step backwards and slipped on the flask, which had been lying on the rock. He wobbled and Liam reached out to grab him but the pair went headlong into the river below with a loud splash. Declan yelped from the shock of the cold water on his hot skin. He wiped his wet hair from his eyes and treaded the water, twisting and turning all the while in an attempt to find his uncle. He suddenly spied Liam's head bobbing nearby, those eyes watching him cautiously like a crocodile across the surface of the water.

"I'm sorry!" shouted Liam over the noise of the rushing water. "I shouldn't have lost it with you."

Declan's head went under the water and after what seemed like several minutes he bounced back up, beaming, with the hip flask in his raised arm.

"I'm sorry too," he said, swimming to the bank, where Michael helped drag him out. "Ye don't know how sorry I am, about a lot of things."

He threw the flask onto the grass and eased himself in his soggy clothes out of the water. Then he turned and they both stretched their arms to help Liam onto the bank where they lay panting on the scorched grass.

"Well, the fightin' Irish have arrived," sighed Liam. "We'll be getting a reputation, boys. Think you've come to the right place."

Chapter 18

The sun had dropped but the fields around them still simmered with the day's heat. Men and boys in various states of uniform milled about the camp. Some were carrying out duties fetching buckets of water or sweeping the yard around the mess house. Others were lounging on walls or sitting in packs under the shade of the trees that formed the perimeter of the main yard. From the nearby woods whippoorwill cried out and cicadas chirruped their constant beat. They were fascinating sounds to Declan and Michael who thrilled at the richness of this exotic fauna in their new home. Declan also enjoyed the pleasure of the warm evenings, a welcome contrast to the damp chill that usually accompanied dusk dropping in Donegal. They sat on a couple of tree stumps that served as seats around a table. The bunch of men were other new recruits, mostly from New York State and a few other immigrants recently landed on the East Coast.

"You in? Yeah, you paleface!"

Michael blinked and looked again at his hand. He shook his head.

"Who you callin' paleface? Least I'm no redneck," he shot back.

The men laughed. Liam slapped Michael on the shoulder.

"That's my lad, don't take no lip from that sonofabitch."

Declan played his hand and grinned to himself. He scanned the men around the table and compared to the others, Michael's pale skin shone like the full moon.

"We'll be needing extra camouflage in battle – full mud streaks if we don't want to be targets for the rebs, eh, Michael!" said Declan in an attempt to offer his brother some support.

"Huh! That's if they let you girls near the frontline," drawled one New Yorker. There was a roar around the table, followed by a chorus of spitting and coughing. The commotion attracted the attention of Captain Kendall who was strolling past.

"Keep it down over there or I'll withdraw privileges!"

The soldiers nodded and bent their heads back down to look at their cards.

"Jeez we'll never make it to the front if you lot continue fightin' among yerselves," said Eddie the cook who'd managed to escape the kitchen for one night. "Besides, once I've those two fattened up they'll be more than fit for fightin'."

He was a short, stocky man who always seemed to be wheezing. As well as working in the kitchen, Eddie joined them in training for battle. Declan wondered how fit he was but he'd noticed there were many recruits who seemed unhealthy.

"No better man to fatten up my nephews," said Liam, beaming. "His food's good fellas, don't you think? You'll get more than spuds and cabbage over here."

Declan smiled. They had taken some stick for weeks in the camp for being pale and skinny but it was all good-spirited. Declan could handle himself and felt the Army had given them an instant entry into a community. He shuddered at the thought of how he and Michael would have fared alone in the big city if they'd stayed in New York. Liam had helped them to settle in quicker than most. Having spent ten years in Geneseo, he was regarded more as a local boy. He'd known and worked with many of the soldiers on the Wadsworth estate for years. Being Liam's nephew was a swift pass into a circle of his friends. Their uncle was also a practical support. Declan recalled their first day of drills when they were handed wooden guns.

"Have they given us toy guns?" Michael whispered.

Declan shrugged but checked down the line only to see that all the new recruits had been provided with wooden rifles. Liam noticed their puzzled expressions and laughed.

"We haven't seen a gun since we got here," he said. "Don't worry it's not a joke on the Irish. We'll be trusting you with our lives soon enough. This is just for drills. By the end of the week you'll be sick of marching up and down like a toy soldier!"

As Liam predicted, they fell into a relentless routine of drills and training. The siestas in the afternoon were a welcome relief and also gave them time to catch up properly with their uncle. Most of the men retired to the dorms, which had thick brick walls that kept them cool. Liam preferred to relax in the shade of a beech tree near the river. One day they were sitting there chatting while Michael snored on the grass. Liam began to recount how their father had wanted to emigrate with the whole family during the Great Hunger.

"You know he talked to me a lot about emigrating," Liam confided. "We'd survived the worst years in the late forties but things didn't seem to be getting any better so I took my chances on my own. Dan was worried about crossing the ocean. All the stories about children dying on board the ships with little food or water. It would've been a struggle to pay for you all too, so in the end he stayed. But his other big worry was yon workhouse. He hated the place, said it would kill him to go there."

"I know," said Declan, and his face fell. "He made me promise I'd look after them all so we'd not end up in the workhouse."

"But you haven't ended up in there Declan, you're here now, aren't ye!"

Liam had got over his initial shock of them leaving Mairead and Cara behind in the workhouse. He put his hand on Declan's shoulder.

"You've told me the story, I understand and you know what, Dan would too. You took care of them all these years when you were just a boy. I've no doubt your da would be very proud of you. Proud of you both."

He paused.

"Did you know your da helped build that workhouse?"

"Did he?"

"Sure, he was one of the labourers that cut the stone and transported it to Letterkenny. It was good work but he always felt ashamed about it, like he had some hand in building a prison. He'd good hands, your da. I think in another life he'd have been an artist or craftsman. But he had mouths to feed, so he took the work when it came."

Declan realised he was biting his nails.

"Aye it was breaking stones for Portnablagh harbour that killed him. He wasn't strong enough for that work but he refused to take handouts – not that there was much charity then."

Liam stared at him with his da's same, pale blue eyes.

"Yer ma has a strong spirit, she'll be fine. We'll have them out of that workhouse in no time. You did the right thing. I think I'd have murdered that landlord with my own two hands if I'd still been in Donegal."

"Murder has crossed my mind," Declan sighed. "With any luck someone will do it before I go back."

"D'ye think you'll go back?" Liam scratched his stubble. "You boys could have a fine life here."

Declan shrugged his shoulders.

"I'd like to see Ma and Cara again, make sure they're alright. Michael's still pining over his girl, Sinead. I'd say we'd both like to go back – after we make some money of course."

Liam released a deep breath that unsettled the tassels dangling from his cotton shirt.

"That's what they all say – we'll make our fortunes and then go home. Listen to me son, there's not many that make a fortune here. You'll probably just make enough to get by, be comfortable. A labouring man is a labouring man wherever he is in the world. I'm not sayin' there ain't some that get lucky. There's talk of gold in the mountains out west but you be doing well to make the fare back home. You hear what I'm saying?"

"I hear ye," Declan frowned. "Don't ye ever want to go home?"

Liam's eyes widened and he faked a bit of a shudder.

"No harm to you son. I'm fond of our family and I sure missed y'all in the first years but…"

"But what?"

"Donegal was hell when I left – people starvin' … absent landlords … nobody caring a damn. When I think of home, I think of the skeletons of people crowding on to them boats in Derry, with nothing but rags on their backs. I swore when my ship sailed out of that harbour that I'd never go back."

Declan thought about his own recent journey across the Atlantic. At least he had his brother's company even if he was in sullen form most of the time. He admired his uncle.

"So how'd ye end up in this town?'

"It's a pretty valley, ain't it? Well, I worked on the railroads with gangs of other men just off the boat. There was plenty of work, hard mind you, but wages were reliable. The work took me further and further upstate. Our camp was pitched close to Geneseo. Some of the boys and me went into a saloon in the town one day and I saw the prettiest girl I'd ever clapped eyes on. She was blonde, with the neatest wee waist, and, boy, could she dance. I was smitten."

Michael rolled over on the grass and gave a loud yawn.

"Ye pair talkin' about girls? Huh, waste of time."

"Private Slumber awakes!" Declan poked him. "Ach, don't listen to him, he's just had his heart broken."

Liam laughed.

"Aye well this dame broke my heart too. I followed her around like a lapdog for months. Left the railroad and found labouring work on the Wadsworth estate. She led me up the garden path, then went off with another lad, but I didn't regret stopping in Geneseo. Eventually I met Sarah. I got steady work, a comfortable cabin and the landlord has been very generous."

"Ye said that in yer letters. How has he been generous, this Mr Wadsworth?"

Liam stuffed some tobacco into his pipe and considered his answer.

"Well, it's the whole family really. They're kind people, look out for their tenants and staff if you know what I mean."

Declan shrugged.

"I wish I did know what that meant. None of the landlords we've known have ever really been around, let alone been kind and generous."

"Well, he pays good wages, certainly better than the railroad. Cabin's included and anything needs doing there's always help. Sure he even looks after our, what they say – spiritual needs – didn't he build the Catholic church in Geneseo? When I heard Mr Wadsworth had joined the Army and was looking for recruits for his own brigade, I'm sure I was one of the first to sign up."

Michael sat up on his elbows.

"So yer saying yer fighting for General Wadsworth rather than the United States?" he asked.

Liam paused to suck on his pipe.

"I guess the two are related. I owe a lot to Mr Wadsworth – 'scuse me, the general – so I'm loyal to him and his whole family – they've been good to me and the Irish that came to this town."

"Has he much of a family?" asked Declan.

"He has a beautiful wife, comes from Philadelphia, that's a big city way south of here, and six children – three boys and three girls. I've watched them grow up. The eldest girl Cornelia is almost as beautiful as her mother. When she turned eighteen, she married a Boston gentleman and Mr Wadsworth threw the greatest fete the town ever saw – balloons and taffeta everywhere!"

"Sounds like a generous man," said Declan. "I'd like to meet him, see who I'm fighting for."

"Well, you'll not get to shake his hand – he's still a gentleman. Come to think of it, I haven't seen him at the camp for some months."

Michael slumped back down on the grass and closed his eyes.

"Huh, they're all the same – landlords."

They lay for a while listening to the cicadas, Liam sucking on his pipe. When Michael began to snore again, Declan turned again to his uncle.

"Say Liam, did ye mean what ye said earlier about killing Adair? Ye think I oughta' have done it before I left Ireland?"

Liam fixed his blue eyes on him and he realised for the first time there was a hardness in his stare.

"A bastard like that, turning women and children out into the cold, takin' the land they worked on for years – he doesn't deserve to live."

Declan began to wring his hands.

"Damn. I shoulda' done him in before takin' that boat." He considered this for a minute, then shook his head. "Na, he wasn't in Donegal. The cowardly bastard disappeared around the evictions; wasn't seen for months. But then what would I have killed him with? He's the one with the guns. I can't even shoot one."

"Don't torture yourself, son. He'll get what's comin' to him. By the time you leave the Army you'll know how to handle a gun. Starting with this pistol here."

His uncle pulled up his loose cotton trouser leg to reveal the smooth metal handle of a handgun, a real one, tucked snugly into his sock.

Chapter 19

Camp Union

Geneseo

New York State

24 Aug 1861

Dear Ma and Cara,

I hope this letter finds you both well and that you, Ma, have fully recovered. I ought to have written sooner, only I was waiting to send you some dollars with this letter. We finally got paid this week for twenty days service in July and I fear we will not see any more wages for some time. It's strange because we did little service in July, bar drills. Despite the war being underway we have not yet seen any fighting.

You'll be pleased to know we found Uncle Liam and have joined him in the Wadsworth Guards in Geneseo. He is so like Da, it's hard to believe my eyes sometimes but then he opens his mouth and he sounds American. You know he has that strong accent and is quite loud…

"Declan!"

He dropped his pen and jumped to his feet. Seconds later, his uncle appeared, slightly out of breath, at the entrance to the dorm.

"I've been looking all over for you. C'mon, we've been summoned!"

Declan folded the half-written letter. He put on his jacket and kepi hat; if there was an inspection he had to be in full uniform.

"What is it? I was in the middle of writing home."

"Plenty of time for that. C'mon, there's ladies in the camp."

"Ladies?"

"The Wadsworths. Mrs Wadsworth and her daughter Cornelia. Remember I was telling you about them? The big wedding? We've been asked to line up in the parade ground."

Declan hurried his step to keep up with his uncle. Ladies weren't normally permitted in the grounds of the camp. Some of the wives and mothers would bring food to the gates once a week but they wouldn't be allowed past the entrance. It was clearly a different story for the wealthy ladies, especially those related to the general. He had heard how women were helping with the war effort. Women's aid societies rolled bandages, knitted socks and gloves, sewed uniforms and scraped lint to use for packing wounds. As the Wadsworth Guards sat about for months, the soldiers joked about the fact their women were more engaged in the war effort than they were. By the time they crossed the camp to the parade ground, Declan felt a frisson of excitement.

"So why are they here?"

Liam shrugged his large shoulders.

"What about Michael, where is he?"

"He was sent on an errand into town. Fix your collar. That's better, and your hair's sticking out. You have to look respectable especially in front of the ladies," he commanded, pointing at his ear.

Declan spat on his hand and smoothed out his unkempt hair. They joined the end of a line of dishevelled soldiers who had hurried to the parade ground, which was baking in the midday sun. Declan squinted in the distance at a moving flash of yellow. There were two women carrying white parasols escorted down the line by Captain Kendall who plucked nervously at his large moustache. As the footsteps came towards him, Declan tore his gaze away from the women to look straight ahead as was Army protocol.

"Yes, ma'am; yes ma'am…" The words floated down the line.

Declan noticed the shadow of his uncle swaying a little and began to worry that he might faint. He knew his uncle would be mortified to collapse but especially in front of the ladies. A petite, young woman stopped nearby. She wore a bright lemon dress with a tight bodice as if she'd stepped out of a garden party. An older lady who wore a stern expression stood next to her inspecting the soldiers.

"Some very scrawny-looking soldiers," she remarked.

"I was thinking the very same, Mama. Do they get fed well?"

Captain Kendall seemed to stutter over his words. Declan couldn't tell whether he was astonished or offended.

"Er, yes ma'am. There's plenty of food in the camp. The men have great appetites."

"Well, I imagine they do, but is it good, wholesome food?" the woman in lemon enquired.

The older lady interrupted. "Your father loves his food so I've no doubt he'd ensure his troops were well fed. At the same time, you don't want them becoming so fat they can't move."

The captain mumbled and the party moved closer.

A trickle of sweat rolled down Declan's face and splashed onto his sleeve. It caught the eye of Captain Kendall who had stopped before him.

"Heat getting to you, Irish?"

"No, sir, I mean, yes, sir."

The young woman nodded and smiled. "You're Irish. Born in Ireland or descended?"

Declan looked to the captain who nodded his permission to speak.

"I'm from Ireland, ma'am."

The way she carried herself she had the haughty air of an aristocrat but she smiled with eyes that sparkled like blue sapphires. She turned to address Captain Kendall.

"Are there many Irish in the ranks?"

"Yes, ma'am, quite a few. In fact, this soldier, Private Conaghan, came straight off the boat with his brother to join the Wadsworth Guards. His uncle next to him has lived in Geneseo for years. He recruited his two nephews. Saved me a job finding young men to sign up."

"Bravo! I'm glad to see the Irish gainfully employed. We have such trouble with mobs in New York City." Her blue eyes seemed to bore right into Declan and he couldn't believe a lady would even know of the existence of Irish mobs in New York or any city.

"Still, I hear the Irish are great fighters – fiery blood! And I suppose we have something in common, standing up to the English colonialists, yes?"

Declan realised she was addressing him and, dumbfounded, looked again to Captain Kendall. The captain looked back at the Conaghans standing wilting in the heat and puffed out his chest.

"Indeed, Mrs Wadsworth Ritchie. The Irish are great fighters – my own family hail from County Kerry."

"Is that so, Captain Kendall? I should have known from the red hair." She chuckled, unbothered at whether she had offended anyone.

Declan tried to stop his lips twitching. Her laughter was infectious.

"That's another thing we have in common with the Irish. You like our potatoes," she said with a note of glee. "Well, they come from South America actually. The great explorer Sir Walter Raleigh introduced them to Ireland. You were enjoying them long before the rest of Europe."

"Enjoyed them too much; relied on them too much," said Liam who had stopped swaying and was clenching his fists next to Declan.

"Don't speak until you're spoken to, Conaghan!"

The young woman waved her gloved hand at the captain.

"Oh captain, I'm glad he has a tongue." She then turned to study Liam. "I take it you mean that awful famine. Were you affected by it?"

Liam looked to Captain Kendall who nodded his permission.

"Yes, ma'am, it was the reason I emigrated. My brother died from starvation, my nephew here's father."

"I'm so sorry to hear that." Her sympathetic eyes flitted between them both.

"You know my father, General Wadsworth, sent a boat-load of wheat to Ireland at the height of the Great Famine. He was deeply moved by your plight. He couldn't understand how a country in the British Empire, and so close to the Crown, should starve the way it did."

"We are mighty grateful, ma'am, for your father's generosity," Liam replied.

"Mama, shall we ask these two to join us in the tent? We've heard from the officers, but I'd really value the opinion of some of the infantry."

"If we must." The older woman sighed. "But let's get out of this sunshine, it's giving me a frightful headache."

The inspection swiftly ended. Bewildered, Declan and Liam were ushered into the captains' tent at the edge of the parade ground. As their eyes adjusted to the indoor shade, they settled on a number of sketches laid out on the large table in the centre. There was a rustle of skirts as the younger woman swished past them to the table. To Declan's surprise, she took command of the room while Captain Kendall looked on.

"I realise I haven't introduced myself properly. I am

General Wadsworth's daughter, Cornelia – Cornelia Wadsworth Ritchie. This is my mother, Mrs Wadsworth."

Declan's gaze fixed on her bosom as she took a quick breath.

"The Ladies' Committee has been working on some plans for the brigade flag and before we invest in the silk and workmanship we thought we'd get some opinions from the soldiers. After all it will be you men that will be carrying the colours into battle."

Declan had never met a woman who spoke so confidently and eloquently before. His head felt a bit dizzy.

"Y-yes ma'am!" replied Liam, finding his voice.

Just then Eddie appeared, wheezing at the entrance to the tent carrying a tray of glasses and a jug.

"Lemonade, sir, as you requested."

Captain Kendall signalled for him to approach the table.

"Ah, wonderful," said Cornelia. "Would you men care for some lemonade? I daresay you're as thirsty as we are."

Declan certainly felt like he needed something in his hand to stop him from fidgeting. He accepted the tumbler of freshly squeezed lemonade and ice from Eddie who gave him a wink before retreating from the tent. He then tried to focus on the large paper scroll spread out on the table.

"Shall we just get on with this?" said Mrs Wadsworth who had been given a seat. "I plan to attend the debate at the Lyceum Society this evening."

"Of course, Mama." She dabbed her finger at the sketch. "Let me explain. Most brigades will fly the standard United States flag, like this one, with the thirty-four stars. Across one of the stripes the name of the brigade is embroidered. We propose to have one of these but in addition—"

"Yes, we've had lots of ideas from the ladies but none of us can agree," Mrs Wadsworth interrupted.

Cornelia fixed them with an earnest stare.

"That's where you can help us, perhaps," she said. "What would inspire *you* to carry on in the heat of battle if you looked up and saw your flag?"

Declan's first thought was that this woman, despite her petite demeanour, would inspire him to charge to the front-line. But he couldn't say that. He'd never been asked his opinion before, certainly not by the gentry. He took a quick slug of the lemonade and enjoyed the coolness of the ice slipping down his throat. Liam was looking between him and the sketch on the table.

"I know that colour is important 'cos that's maybe all you'll see across a battlefield," he replied.

"What about words?" asked Cornelia, "I know my father is keen to have some Latin." She prodded the captain to produce another scroll. As Captain Kendall unfurled it, Liam rubbed his chin in contemplation. Declan wondered if he was often asked for his opinion as he seemed a dab hand at it.

"Now Latin, that would be an educated man's language – some of the men, well, they can't even read English," Liam said.

The captain placed a couple of paperweights to hold open the new sketch, which revealed a coat of arms.

"He's right," Captain Kendall piped up. "Many of the men could barely sign their names when they enlisted."

"But we're proposing just the one Latin word, see here," said Cornelia. "*Excelsior*."

Declan stared at the word and heard himself blurt, "Higher, elevated – like we're an elite force."

As Declan stared back down at his feet, he could hear the ladies' skirts shuffling as they craned their necks to look at him.

"Bravo!" Cornelia clapped her hands. "I'm surprised, Private Conaghan. Did you study Latin?"

Declan looked up, blushing. "It's only a little I learned from the Mass and some schooling with the local priest. It's just one word."

Cornelia beamed at him and in that instance he thought she was the most beautiful woman he'd ever seen. He felt himself glow.

"Just one word – see, that's all we need and the men will easily learn what it means and it will inspire them," Cornelia said. "I think that's agreed then, don't you?"

Mrs Wadsworth eased herself up from the chair and placed her finished glass on the tray.

"Good!" she said. "I'm glad that's settled, such a lot of fuss about a flag that may only see a few months of battle."

Captain Kendall glanced at them and carried on rolling up the sketches.

"I wouldn't be so sure, ma'am, some of the generals are predicting this war could last for years."

Cornelia turned to Liam and Declan. "I'm sure you'll be glad to return to your families after this is all over? They must be so worried about you."

She said it with such maternal warmth that Declan felt

himself longing to see his mother. He felt a pang of homesickness.

"Yes, ma'am," he muttered.

"You know I've been to Europe several times – mostly visiting London and Paris but I've always been curious about Ireland. I suppose with there being so many Irish in New York. Perhaps when this war is over, I shall take my family for a tour. I hear the climate is very agreeable."

The way she spoke to him, for a moment Declan imagined there was no one else in the tent.

"It doesn't get as hot as here, that's for sure," he replied, mopping his forehead with the back of his sleeve.

Captain Kendall stepped forward.

"Will that be all, ladies?"

"Oh yes, of course, they will need to be getting back to duties," said Cornelia, lifting her parasol. "I don't want to take up any more of your time. Sincere thanks."

The captain, Declan and Liam simultaneously raised their hands in a salute as the ladies swished out of the tent to their waiting carriage.

Captain Kendall appeared in a bit of a daze and confided his thoughts aloud.

"If that young woman was in uniform, I'd follow her into battle. A Wadsworth through and through," he said, staring at the empty lemonade glasses. "Thanks for your assistance. You're dismissed!"

As the soldiers walked back into the sunshine, Liam gave a long whistle.

"A fine-looking dame. You impressed her with your Latin, you dark horse!"

Declan grinned.

"I picked that up from Father O'Flanigan while learning to write to ye."

"What goes around, comes around! Michael will be sorry he missed seeing that piece of skirt."

"Ye can't call her that! She was a real lady, a genuine, good sort. Did ye know that about the general sending wheat to Ireland?

"I'd heard it said, way back when I first came to Geneseo. Mind you, they could well afford it – you should see the harvests in this valley."

"Still, he didn't have to send anything," he replied. "It's good to know they're not all the same – the gentry I mean. I don't think I've ever met a lady like her before, or ever will again."

He stared after the figure in lemon who had stepped up into her carriage and then disappeared from view.

Chapter 20

He didn't clap eyes on her again until the following spring. The day the Wadsworth Guards would finally leave Geneseo to join hundreds of other companies in Washington D.C. The men had drilled long and hard at the training camp through the hottest summer and harshest winter Declan had ever experienced. Some of the troops had begun to despair that they'd ever see battle. But on a fresh spring morning the boots of the brigade stomped out through the gates and with great purpose along Main Street towards the train station.

Declan, carrying a real rifle, was more excited than the day he'd first enlisted in the Army. The parade passed the entrance to Hartford House where a group of Geneseo's finest ladies clutched parasols and waved to their husbands, fathers and brothers. Declan turned to stare at the women wearing long, grey dresses who stood so still like an ornate sculpture of freshly poured cement. All bar one of them. He recognised Cornelia Wadsworth Ritchie, who appeared more agitated than the others as she twisted and turned to catch a glimpse of all those she held dearest heading to the warfront. Her two young sons stood close to her, dressed in striped jackets and shorts with their white socks pulled fully up. The Wadsworths were well-represented in the brigade with Cornelia's two brothers, her husband and of course the brigadier general himself leading at the front. It was one of the few times the brigade got to see him. He was a tall, broad-shouldered man with extravagant white sideburns that decorated a proud face. He was well-respected by the troops and known for his rousing speeches. There was a rumour that he would be a better politician than military man but either way, Liam argued, he had the qualities of a leader whom people would follow into battle. As Declan observed Cornelia's pained expression, he felt a twinge of jealousy that there was no one to see them off. Their folks were so far away in Donegal. Of course he and Michael had written to them and described their training but he wondered, with the distance, if anyone at home would know what this war was actually about? Did they really understand it themselves?

He was comforted by their latest letters, which revealed they had finally left the workhouse. Cara had written that the Reverend Maturin's housekeeper had passed away suddenly, leaving a vacancy. It hadn't proved easy to fill as so many people had emigrated or moved away after the evictions. Remembering the Conaghan brothers' help during the fire at the rectory, the reverend had contacted Mr Penny at the workhouse and secured her service. The job came with a cottage on the estate at Glebe House so Cara and Mairead had moved in that March. Cara's letter finished with a plea for them to return, saying they now had a home to go to. But it now seemed impossible to leave the Army and they couldn't let their uncle down. Liam had managed to sneak out of the camp to spend his last night with Sarah before their departure. Wearing her best dress, she stood at the side of the road, waving a handkerchief at the troops. Next to her were Eddie's wife and young girls who began jumping excitedly and waved their dolls as their da paraded past. Declan couldn't detect any sadness in Sarah's face, just pure pride and joy from her broad smile. He smiled back at her. She was family, he supposed, someone to wave them off. They had got to know her a little from her Sunday visits to the camp. She brought them homemade bread and cakes, and any other little tokens they requested from the village. But Liam mostly kept her visits to himself, given there was precious little time allocated those afternoons.

"You boys need to get your own wives," he would say with a wink. "I can't be sharing my Sarah."

Michael rolled his eyes at these remarks. He rarely mentioned Sinead anymore as if he'd resigned himself to never seeing her again. But one night as they sat up playing cards when most of the dorm had gone to sleep, Michael confided in him that he felt homesick. *The war won't last long*, Declan had assured him.

"We'll get back on that green yacht as soon as we defeat these rebels and we'll be paid handsomely for our service. Just think, we'll return to Ireland wearing the best of clothes and money in our pockets so no Adair or any landlord like him can evict us again," Declan declared. Michael unfurled his sleeves and blew on invisible cufflinks in mock pretence at dressing up.

"Sure we will, and all the lasses will be chasing us from Donegal to Belfast, aye!" He laughed. But Declan could see a sadness in his eyes. Sinead had surely broken his heart and he just hoped he would find someone else to love in the future, wherever it would be.

The parade stopped just past Hartford House and as Declan strained his neck to see what the holdup was, he saw Cornelia being led firmly by her mother back to the side of the road. It was mumbled down the line that she had rushed into the troops to give her husband one last embrace. Ahead of them Captain Montgomery Ritchie looked over his shoulder, his face beaming under his black felt Hardee hat with the left brim pinned up by a metallic eagle. He had a handsome face with a neat black moustache and ample sideburns.

"Och, true love eh!" said Michael with a wink. Declan nodded and berated himself for the pang of jealousy that gripped him. On a simple level he realised he was jealous because she was beautiful but it was so much more than that. As he scanned the families, wives and parents that waved from the grass verge he envied Cornelia for her whole family's commitment to this war. They were all here. He and Michael on the other hand were blow-ins. Just as the first person they'd met in Geneseo had said, they were mercenaries. Soldiers of fortune with no wives or parents to proudly wave them off.

The men assembled at the end of the lawn where General Wadsworth stepped up on to a makeshift wooden podium. He cleared his throat and the rustling and chatter of voices immediately subsided.

"Guards and the good people of Geneseo. I stand before you to decree that the day has finally come. H Company has been mustered into United States service for three years as part of the 104th New York Infantry. The hard work and training of these past months will now be put to the test. We have been summoned to our great capital in Washington to join the war effort. Some of you were just boys when you signed up; some of you I know personally from working for me on the estate. I know from my captains and my own personal inspection of the troops that you leave Geneseo today as men – a fighting machine that will go into battle to preserve and strengthen the Union of this great nation." The general paused to allow the loud clapping to interrupt his speech.

"There is a peculiar institution in the South, which I have made no secret of my disdain for. The institution of slavery has torn this nation asunder and has made chattel from human beings… We cannot stand for this, we *will* not stand for this. I believe God is on our side in this civil war and will see our cause vindicated. But this would not be possible without the support and sacrifices of our families. I know my own daughters and wife have rolled up their sleeves to assist in the war effort, as have many women of this town. I ask you all to join me in thanking them for their efforts…"

The troops stamped their feet in a roar of approval and were joined by applause from the large assembly of townspeople. General Wadsworth beamed at his audience, exuding confidence in his words. Declan thought his eyes seemed to sparkle, perhaps there was even a tear. He raised his gloved hands and immediately silenced the audience again.

"I ought to finish as these fine men have a train to catch and the President, no less, is waiting for them." He flashed his wide smile again and was met with a ripple of laughter. "Let us join together and give these brave men the traditional send-off they deserve. Hip hip…"

The crowd roared a deafening 'hooray' three times in response. It was a rousing send-off, after which the troops continued their march to the station. Declan looked back towards the town. Through the swirling dust kicked up by the soldiers he spied one of the recruitment posters that had first caught their eye when they arrived in Geneseo. It read 'A Few Good Men Wanted'. He guessed that's all the Army wanted and consoled himself that being a good man in his own right would please his da, wherever he was.

A long train with a yellow engine and large smokestack stood waiting at the depot. The bugle was sounded and the troops boarded the train southbound for the capital. There was a mad scramble for a window view but Michael shrugged his shoulders and made way for one of the local boys to press his head out the window.

"Makes no difference to me," he said. "Got no one out there to wave to."

But Declan strained to keep sight of Cornelia and the group of Geneseo women for as long as he could. Eventually the dust billowed up and obscured his view of the town that had been their home these past nine months.

After the cramped train journey Declan was pleased to stretch his legs when they reached Washington. The normally thronging city was bursting at the seams with newly arrived volunteers and soldiers from across the northern states. The chattering brigades mingled with squealing pigs in the muddy streets which were lined with stalls, hawkers and filthy shanties. He breathed in the spicy air and took in the sights. The hovels of Washington fought for space beside many elegant homes with large verandas – some virtual palaces next door to squalor. He watched the Negro men and women scurrying to open barouches carrying gentlemen in top hats or sweeping brooms across some of the impressive entrances. The sudden arrival of troops had surprised the government, which had not planned where to put everybody. As a result, the various regiments camped around the city and in the Capitol itself. Declan was reminded of the bustling melting pot of New York but he felt safer somehow being with his brigade than when they landed, just the two of them, from the boat last year. He observed some of the young soldiers – mere boys from Pennsylvania and New England farms – who stared bewildered at the swirling crowds of foreign faces and voices around them and realised this was all new to them too. They were finally in the thick of it, or so Declan thought. But soon the excited anticipation of arriving in Washington dissipated as their company was billeted to the city's defences and as Michael put it, the 'dreary days of drills' continued.

The one highlight of those long months was a parade

past the president who was doing an inspection of troops. Each brigade and regiment filed into the city and marched up Pennsylvania Avenue waving their coloured banners as they passed the White House, creating a spectacular military show. Liam was delighted to be assigned as one of the flag bearers for the Wadsworth Guards and marched proudly. Declan grinned at the beautifully woven silk motif, bearing the golden letters '*Excelsior*'. It instantly brought him back to a vision of Cornelia on that sultry afternoon. He marched behind the flag, only shifting his gaze like all the troops to catch a glimpse of the tall, lanky figure who stood on the white balcony draped in US flags. 'Old Abe' as they affectionately called him, towered from above with a hawk-like eye fixed on the parading soldiers. The band crashed its cymbals louder as they saluted the Commander-in-Chief. Later that night, Liam remarked that he was glad to see who he was fighting for, which sparked a raucous debate among the boys and men in the camp.

"We're fighting for the Union, not one man," said Eddie.

"Aye, this ain't a kingdom like England," roared another with an Irish accent.

Declan listened to the men sparring and then added his own tuppence worth. "Does anyone know what we're fighting for? I might have fought for the South if I'd happened to land there."

"You sound like a mercenary, Dec," said Liam.

"Sure aren't most of us?"

The men shrugged and the row subsided. Some rolled tobacco and lit pipes, others began games of cards. Declan thought of writing home again but after his last letter, so charged with anticipation of going into battle, he didn't want his next to be an anti-climax.

Liam tapped his lower leg and hissed, "You boys wanna practise your shot?" Michael jumped up eagerly in contrast to Declan's sigh.

"Och, we've been handling weapons all day, Liam. Captain Kendall let us use the new Enfields today. Michael nearly shot Eddie in the foot with his, so maybe he needs the practice."

Michael threw him a punch on the arm.

"Hey, that wasn't my fault. We were just lining up to shoot at the target when Kendall shouted 'fire'. I was just obeying orders!"

Eddie overheard the conversation.

"There's obeying orders and shooting your own men." His face creased with laughter. He was so laid back, even Michael's wild shooting didn't unnerve him. "Good job they were blanks we were firing or you'd have some explaining to do to my wife and kids."

Liam pulled out the shiny Colt Pocket revolver from his sock and poked Declan with it.

"C'mon, you boys need the practice. I'll make killers outta ye yet."

Michael and Declan followed him to the far end of the camp where they set up some wooden crosses in the soil. Liam filled the barrel with some blanks from his pockets, which always seemed to bulge with all sorts of useful items, from twine and coins to pocketknives and paper. He was like a walking cupboard.

"Now you see this Colt, it's popular with the officers. I

traded in my last pistol for this. Much easier to handle. And like all these pistols it's got about a twenty-five-yard range."

"That's not much use," said Michael scornfully. "The breech-loading artillery we were using can blast a row of soldiers hundreds of feet away. Think that'd be my weapon of choice."

"Is that so, young Mickey? And how're you lugging that thing around? It's all very well in a long-distance battle, but if you wanna weapon for self-defence, when you're on your own, or face-to-face with the enemy, this piece of steel is your best buddy."

Liam caressed the nuzzle of the gun with his forefinger, then ran it along the shaft until he curled it around the trigger. He pulled the catch back with his thumb, raised his forearm and fired. Declan and Michael watched, mesmerised, as the wooden cross exploded into splinters.

"You have a go, Declan."

Michael huffed.

"Aw let me go first, he's not even interested."

Declan shoved him.

"I'll show ye who's not interested. At least I can point a weapon at the right target, not someone's bloody foot!"

Liam laughed.

"That's it, Declan. Just keep your hand steady. Focus on that cross. Think of those rebs."

"Yes imagine that stick's wearing a grey cap..." Michael chipped in.

Bang!

The right arm of the cross snapped off.

"Not bad," said Liam, peering at the damage. "You

didn't miss at least. It helps, doesn't it, to think of the enemy?"

Declan frowned.

"It does, but I'm not thinking of the rebels. I'm thinking of that devil Adair."

Liam grinned.

"Hell yeah, that's my boy. Have another go and this time get the bastard!"

Chapter 21

The summer of 1862 proved to be long and hot, and the assembling troops grew lazy, lounging in their camps. When they weren't doing drills, they idled days away listening to the military bands. They waited and waited for a call to action. It finally came in the fierce heat of early August. The New York Infantry had been moved South joining the Army of Virginia under a new general, John Pope. They marched into Culpeper County in northern Virginia with the objective of capturing the rail junction at Gordonsville. The Wadsworth Guards had been marching all day. Even though it was pretty countryside, with miles of corn and wheatfields, Declan couldn't enjoy the views and longed to escape the blinding sun. He turned to Michael whose face was peeling from sunburn.

"I could do with a drink right now – bloomin' heat has me parched," he said smacking his dry lips. Michael nodded, wiping his face.

"Keep in line!" the commanding officer hollered down

from his saddle. Declan cursed him under his breath. He cursed all the bloody horses that had drank much of the stream they'd just crossed and then pissed in it, just as they were trying to fill up their flasks. Ahead of their company was a string of horses pulling heavy artillery, which had been ordered to a battleline near a place called Cedar Mountain where they were all headed. As he heard the horses panting and wheezing, he felt a twinge of sympathy for them. It was a hot day for such heavy work. The men trudged on along the dusty track but the officers were fighting a losing battle. Many of the soldiers were floundering in the heat. The brigade ahead had discovered a hedgerow of blackberries and had fallen out of line to fill their pockets. The soldiers had stripped the hedge bare and as Declan marched past, he spied groups of men lounging in the shade of trees with dark red juice trickling from their mouths. Their brigade broke from the lines and rushed to join the other soldiers in an impromptu break, ignoring the protests of the cavalry officers. Declan was arrested by the sight of one young soldier lying in the field. His eyes were closed and his hands, just visible behind his head, were stained a dark red. Despite the searing heat, Declan shuddered.

"We *are* going into battle, aren't we?" Declan asked Liam who had thrown down his knapsack and lay stretched out on the grass.

"I daresay that's where we're headed." He yawned, cradling his head in his large palms.

Michael, sitting next to them, had pulled out his belt from the loops at the top of his trousers. He continued his latest project, scratching out his name on the soft metal buckle with his penknife.

"But relax son, we'll get there in due course," Liam added. "You spoilin' for a fight, are ye?"

"'Course not." Declan plucked a lonely blackberry from the hedge. "Just all feels a bit surreal, not what I imagined going into battle would be like."

"Aye, 'tis maybe the calm before the storm."

"Still, at least we're being led by a pope and not a king!" said Michael, grinning through his sore red face. Liam laughed and slapped him on the shoulder.

"Young Mickey, you're a hoot, I'll have to remember that one."

"You'll only remember it if the pope wins," said Declan. He bit into the sour berry and allowed the juice to cool his mouth before he swallowed it. He then saw his thumb and forefinger had been bleached by the berry. He sucked and sucked at each digit but to no avail, he would have to live with the stain. When several colonels arrived upon the blackberry picnic, the troops were rounded up and driven back into line. Michael pulled his belt back through his trousers, his carving incomplete.

"Ye may get yer first initial on that since there's at least three Conaghans in this Company," said Declan, scratching his head. The lice had been driving him mad.

"Don't ye worry about my corpse. Some reb bastard is likely to steal my belt in the spoils of the battlefield anyway."

"Aye, ye still got the medal Ma gave us? I'd know ye from that."

Michael pulled open his collar where his Agnus Dei

medal hung round his neck.

"My lamb to the slaughter medal, sure have." He laughed.

They were just back on the road when the mood changed dramatically. Long, low rumbling sounds seemed to come from underfoot. Union artillery guns had been fired and were answered by Confederate cannon. The officers were barking orders and steering the infantry towards a hillside where brigades of men and supply wagons had gathered. Their cries became more urgent as the first wounded soldiers were stretchered past them to the medical tents. Some stumbled back leaning on spent-looking colleagues. Declan noticed one blond-haired boy being dragged away by two soldiers. He was clutching the middle of his face with his blood-soaked cap and as he passed their line, Declan realised the boy's nose was completely gone. Michael yelped beside him. Still marching, Declan swung round thinking his brother had been hit by a stray bullet but his shoulder had just been drenched in vomit from a passing officer on horseback. There was no time to mop it up. The men had been ordered to advance. They would just have to live with the smell, which proved to be the least offensive sight of the day as the Battle of Cedar Mountain erupted.

The Wadsworth Guards were ordered to spread out across a line behind the large artillery guns that were smoking in the distance and for the first time Declan caught sight of the grey uniforms of the rebels and the unfamiliar flag of the Confederate states limply flapping in the occasional gust of air. As he lay flat on the ground, he realised how close to the front they were. The smoke and heat seemed to suffocate him and his ears ached with the constant explosions and whirring of gunfire. His nose was pressed close to the dusty earth and his stomach gurgled with nausea. He would have something to write about if he ever made it out of this.

The fighting went on for hours as the Union troops pushed forward and fell back all afternoon. In the chaos and heat, Declan and Michael had no idea if they were making any progress. They didn't speak to each other but there were nods and gestures and passing of cartridge boxes. Declan began to hallucinate about blackberry juice and in one break in the gunfire turned his head to see if he could spy any berries on the nearby hedges. Instead all he could see were rows of bent blue heads covered in dust stretching for miles to his left.

Late that afternoon the guns fell silent on both sides. Declan could still hear a ringing in his ears but the ground had stopped shuddering, which meant a break in the fighting. Then just as his tired bones began to relax an almighty blood-curdling shriek echoed all around them. It came from beyond the Union artillery and triggered bewildered stares from the blackened faces of the prostrate soldiers. Declan was reminded of the Widow McAward's wail along with the chorus of women keening at his father's burial. He stumbled to his feet as a rumble of boots of Union soldiers emerged through the smoke. In seconds their line uncocked their rifles and scrambled to their feet.

"What is it?" shouted Declan

"I don't know but it's coming to get us!" Michael yelled back.

Frenzied soldiers with terror etched on their faces piled past, pushing and shoving to get away. The horrific shriek continued to rattle in their heads. Soldiers from every brigade – Maine, Pennsylvania and New York – pushed past them, all with one goal: to get the hell out of hell. Declan hauled Michael to his feet after he was nearly stamped on in the rush.

"What the Christ?"

"Our line's been broken!" Declan shouted over the cacophony of boots, shots and piercing shrieks. "Run!"

Confused officers on horseback were frantically waving their arms and weapons at the stampede.

"Stop, I command you! It's just the rebels' battle cry. Stay and fight!" shouted one officer. With flaring nostrils, his horse bucked from under him and threw him to the ground. The brothers ran past him and continued to run until they could no longer hear the shrieking. Shots were fired at the retreating soldiers and some order was eventually restored but Declan realised the battle had been lost. Their first altercation with the rebels had been a defeat. He lay in the dust and longed for a drink. He thought of the clean, clear waterfall at Glenveagh and imagined standing in it, the cold water splashing over his sunburnt cheeks and cleaning the dust out of his eyes and ears. He imagined being able to gulp mouthfuls of the crystal-clear water to quench his dry throat. He realised that while his thirst was overwhelming, that long awaited first battle had sated his hunger for combat.

Chapter 22

"Conaghan? Letter for you."

A boy's voice croaked through the tent. Declan looked up from the wooden lap desk where he'd been scribbling in his diary. The young lad whose voice was beginning to break, grinned, revealing missing teeth, and presented the letter. The drummer boy also doubled as the mail boy.

"Might be your girlfriend!" He winked at Declan who ruffled his blonde hair and shooed him away.

"I wish! More likely my sister."

"Wouldn't put that past you Irish – keep it in the family!" the boy yelled, running off to his next delivery.

Declan shook his head and closed his diary. He had begun a journal to keep up his handwriting but mostly for something to do. Between battles they had so much time on their hands in the camp. He wasn't used to just hanging around but that seemed to be the order of the day. When they weren't doing drills, Michael played cards, Liam smoked and Declan wrote. That was their routine.

As long as their wages came through, the brothers continued to send dollars home to Derryveagh. But Declan's letters were short. Mainly he didn't want to alarm them with the ugliness of war. So he put it in his diary, for his eyes only.

His regiment had marched into villages and commandeered supplies and property for 'the Union cause' in a manner that reminded him of the evictions. He was no better than that crowbar brigade, he thought. So they weren't wrecking people's homes but they were officially looting them. They were under orders of course but he felt uncomfortable raiding the food stores of farmers and widows, knowing they would have little to keep them going through the winter. He recalled one time when he and Michael had been sent into a farmhouse where the woman bore an uncanny resemblance to Cara. When he opened a hatch in the floor, Declan could see a crate of green apples below. He looked about to call for Michael to help him hoist it up but caught the pleading look in the woman's eyes. She didn't speak, she didn't have to. She could have been his sister, so he quickly dropped the hatch and kicked a straw mat back over to conceal it. They moved on to the next farmhouse.

He sliced the letter open with his penknife, then used it to swipe a black fly away from his face. Flies plagued the camp and even though the heat of summer was fading there still seemed to be great black swarms of them. His eyes danced across the page, devouring the letter. It began with the usual effusive greetings and concern over their health. Then he stopped at the first piece of news – Francis

Dermott had been killed in Derry. He read the sentences a few times to take it in.

All we heard was he was struck by a cart in the town, cracked his skull. Ma thinks he was probably drunk and wandered into its path.

Declan took a moment. He closed his eyes and murmured a prayer, holding tight the holy medal around his neck. His thoughts turned to Sinead and her brothers. They must have all gone to the city after the evictions as they originally thought. There hadn't been any other news of the Dermott family since they'd left home. He pondered whether the accident was a better death for Francis, a quick death, rather than slowly dying from the effects of poteen on his gut. Just then Michael burst into the tent.

"Young scrapper tells me we got a letter? Did ye go ahead and open it, ye did, ye bastard!" He playfully threw his kepi hat at Declan and then stared as he saw his brother's sombre face.

"What is it? Are they alright?"

"Aw, sit down. Ma and Cara are fine," he said quickly. "Well, it's Francis, Francis Dermott – he was knocked down by a cart in Derry and killed."

Michael frowned and for a few seconds he appeared as if he was somewhere else. Declan wondered if he was thinking less about Francis and more remembering Derry and their last night in Ireland hunting for Sinead.

"Och no! He didn't deserve that." And after a minute.

"She didn't say anything about, about Sinead – any news of her?"

Declan shook his head and patted his brother's shoulder. They had spent the past week building a fortification around the camp as the enemy was pitched nearby. Hauling logs, earth and dirt under the watchful eye of an officer was harder work than even they'd experienced labouring on the stony soils of Donegal and Michael had bulked out a bit from all the heavy lifting.

"So, go on, read it to me."

Declan turned back to the letter, as Cara revealed another bombshell – this time about Adair. The sight of his name on the page made him grip the letter, crumpling it. His brow furrowed as he read how she'd served him tea in the rectory and that she had overheard him discuss plans to set up a business in New York. He read her words over and over again, slowly taking them in. Adair was coming out to America, not to fight, but to make money out of the war. His face reddened and he threw the letter at Michael.

"Look at that! Black Adair's coming out to the States. The devious bastard has sniffed out a business opportunity amidst this carnage, can ye believe it?" Declan was shaking with rage.

Michael grabbed the letter. He tried to read it slowly using his finger.

"Come out here during a war? Is he mad?" asked Michael.

"There must be money to be made, land speculation, whatever it is he does. He's just repeating what he and those filthy landlords did after the famine – buying the land cheap. He's an opportunist – a brutal one at that!"

Michael passed the letter back to his brother.

"If we ever get finished with this war, now we know how to handle a gun, we should go find him, ye know." He made a pistol shape of his hand and pointed it at Declan's temple. "I'd empty those cartridges with great pleasure."

"Aye, the thought of him sipping tea across the lough from where he evicted us all. Why, he's the devil himself."

"And being hosted by a man of God!"

Declan muttered, "Well, I don't think much of so-called men of God…"

"Did someone mention God?"

It was Liam whose head suddenly appeared through the tent flaps. He still bore scars from their first battle. He insisted the gashes on his forehead were from enemy fire but Declan and Michael knew he'd simply fallen in the mad scramble to get away from the rebel cry.

"What about God?" asked Declan.

"I've come to drag you two to Mass – the chaplain is going to celebrate it in about ten minutes. Thinks we need to have the Lord on our side to win the next battle."

Declan decided to forget about Adair. He might be in New York, but they were in northern Virginia, hundreds of miles away. He might as well have been in a different country. One blessing, he thought, was he wouldn't be in Donegal to bother their mother and Cara.

They shuffled into the large tent past the cross made from sticks over the entrance and squeezed onto a bench with dozens of other soldiers. The smell of incense burning at the wooden bench that served as an altar instantly reached Michael's nose. He sneezed. Some of the men whose heads had been bent in prayer looked up. No one wanted to get sick but as the days grew colder that autumn their fellow soldiers seemed to drop like flies with coughs and infections. There were as many soldiers filling the hospital tent suffering from pneumonia and dysentery as war wounds.

Declan blessed himself. He closed his eyes and tried to feel close to God, pushing out all other thoughts. In his head he ran through his usual list of intentions, which always opened his prayers.

God bless Ma and Cara … Michael and Liam … God bless our brigade … God bless our leaders … God bless the Bradleys and all the folks at… He paused as his thoughts returned to the letter.

God bless Francis – may you forgive his sins, may he be at peace. And God bless Sinead and all the family…

He shut his eyes tighter, trying to focus but his mind drifted away. He imagined Adair in a suit and top hat arriving at the docks in New York, followed off the boat by servants carrying his cases. He could picture him hailing a carriage and knocking the dust and grime off his polished shoes before ascending the steps out of the chaos of new arrivals. His thoughts grew darker until he was jolted back to reality by the congregation rising.

After Mass he sat down to reply to Cara. He thanked her for the news and praised her elegant handwriting. But beyond a brief update on camp life, Liam and Michael's health, he found his words were limited. Instead he poured his thoughts of revenge and frustration into his diary.

Three months passed. It was nearly Christmas but there was no Christmas spirit in the camp. The Union Army had assembled in mid-November at Falmouth across the Rappahannock River from the town of Fredericksburg in Virginia. The Wadsworth Guards waited with the rest of their regiment. The plan, they were told, was to place pontoons across the expansive river to lead the troops across but they didn't arrive until well into December, by which time heavy snowfall delayed military operations for a further week.

Declan's hands burned like two balls of fire as he looked out across the camp, which was under a thick sheet of snow. He glared at his red knuckles that were being gnawed away by the cold. He blew on them repeatedly, but they remained numb. He'd tried wrapping them with some old bandages he'd found lying around the tent but these rendered his hands even more useless. He gave up and put the bandages back in the first aid box. *There'll be others more in need of them than me.* Michael lay fast asleep in the back of the tent. He reached in and pulled out Michael's hip flask, taking a few swigs of whiskey. He'd just returned the flask when he stirred. His eyes flickered and then he screamed, "Ma! Ma!"

Michael sat bolt upright, his hair messy, his dark eyelashes wet with tears.

"Shush," Declan tried to calm him. "Ma's alright. Ye just had a bad dream." He took Michael's thin blanket with his raw, red hands and pulled it back over his brother. He gradually lay back down but held on tightly to Declan's arm.

"Are we fighting tomorrow?"

"It seems so. Today, in fact. Try to get back to sleep, you'll need it."

"What about ye? Can't ye sleep?"

"Too cold. I tried to write but can't move my hands."

Michael wiped his tear-stained face. "Stay close to me, will ye? We can keep each other warm, like those nights in the Sweeneys' barn back home."

"Aye, there was a bit more poteen to keep us warm then too. Never felt cold like this. I'm sure you'd prefer to be curled up with Sinead."

"Aye, but no doubt she's curled up with someone else."

"Och, ye don't know that Michael…"

"'Course she is. Now we know Francis was killed in Derry, I've no doubt she went there too. The woman at the docks that night, that was her."

"Shush, don't believe that. Sure we couldn't see in the dark."

Declan shuddered and cradled his brother in his arms. When dawn broke both their beards were stuck together with icicles.

It was the last rest they had for a week as the Battle of Fredericksburg burst into action and the rebels pounded the Union Army with heavy artillery and gunfire. The rebels had the higher ground and although they were outnumbered, they cut down the bluecoats like they were mere corn to their scythes. Men they'd fought and trained with over the past two years were just blown away beside them. Still, the captains sent them forward – "March on!" – until the fighting ceased on that fifth and final day. They bivouacked that night under the glistening stars, beside the gaseous dead. Some of the men made pillows of the dead bodies and lay like that until dawn. Declan slept out of pure exhaustion and woke to the stench of the swollen, blackened corpses all around them. Through sleepy eyes Declan peered across and could see Liam and Michael lying close by.

As he stretched his own stiff limbs, he heard a rustling followed by a moan coming from behind him. He quickly rolled over. It was a soldier, one of their own, desperately trying to slither towards him. As he sat up blinking in the morning light, he realised it was Eddie the cook. Liam's friend from Geneseo. The man who'd given them their first meal in the Army. Half of his leg was gone and his ear was missing. Declan poked Michael awake with his foot. They watched as Eddie made his slow, torturous crawl towards them, dragging his mutilated leg and stopping every few minutes to cry out with the pain. Declan looked at Michael helplessly.

"We can't risk going over to him," he hissed. "The rebels across the wall could have a sharpshooter trained on us."

Michael scrambled in his knapsack for some water.

"We gotta give him some water."

"What for? He's gonna die soon enough," Declan hissed again.

"Jesus, Declan, at least make his struggle to get to us worthwhile."

Declan decided not to argue with him. If it made him feel better to give Eddie their precious water then so be it. They waited, scarcely able to breathe, until Eddie slumped down beside them. Blood and mud were caked to the side of his face where his ear had once been. He was done in. His face was etched with pain and he brought with him a terrible smell, a mixture of gangrene from his seeping wounds and where he had soiled himself. After a few minutes' rest he found the strength to point at his severed leg and panted hoarsely to Michael, "I can't live without my leg. I don't wanna be a cripple."

Michael pressed his canteen of water to the dying man's lips.

"Drink some of this, you'll feel better. We'll make a tourniquet and save the rest of yer leg."

At this Eddie gave a loud moan. He seemed to summon up all his energy and pulled open his tattered jacket revealing another oozing wound in his stomach. He pointed weakly at the wooden handle of a small knife poking out of his inside pocket.

"Please Mickey, please, I can't…" He began to cry.

Michael just stared open-mouthed at him and then began to sob too. Eddie dragged his broken body closer to Declan and held out the knife to him.

"Please don't make me beg anymore." He dropped the blade beside Declan in the dirt.

Declan looked across at the battlefield strewn with lumps of bodies and bewildered survivors. Liam was in a deep sleep some yards away. Amidst the cries of pain, they could hear him snoring. Declan was relieved he didn't have to witness his friend's agony or what was to follow. The sun was nearly risen, yet it gave off no warmth. It was just another day of the war with no end in sight. Eddie pulled a crumpled envelope from his pocket and pressed it into Declan's hand.

"Give this to Liam to send to my wife, won't you?" His eyes were wide, pleading.

Declan looked at Michael who nodded and turned his head away. Declan quickly took the knife and plunged it into Eddie's neck. As the gushing blood slowed to a trickle, Declan brushed his hand over Eddie's eyelids. He then turned to Michael who was clutching his holy medal to his lips and whispering a prayer.

Declan sighed deeply. "At least his pain's over. We have another day to get through."

When the dust had settled on the Battle of Fredericksburg and the normal tedium of camp life resumed, Declan picked up his diary again. He needed to record what had happened. It reminded him of what he'd done. Above all he needed to figure out who he'd become – a man of mercy or a cold killer.

Chapter 23

A year and a half later, May 1864

Another winter had passed. Declan couldn't feel the cold anymore. His face was a thick carpet of hair and any patches of skin felt rough like the bark of a tree. Michael was like a mirror to him. He could see he'd lost weight. Their brigade, what was left of the Wadsworth Guards, had been reassigned into the V Corps following the slaughter at Chancellorsville, Gettysburg and other battles that had passed Declan by in a blur. A year on they were back at Chancellorsville, which seemed to sum up the whole damn war to Declan. They were preparing for a new offensive against the Confederates but to Declan and many of the soldiers it felt like déjà-vu – they had fought and lost here before. The stories of the Battle of Chancellorsville were among the grisliest of the war. As if they needed a reminder, the skeletons of the previous year's campaign appeared to greet them as they pitched camp near the Wilderness Tavern that would lend its name to the next battle. The heavy rains of the winter had washed the layer of soil from their shallow graves, unearthing the dead soldiers. Michael jumped back as his boot kicked a rotting blue rag that revealed an arm bone.

"Jesus," he hissed to Declan who was using his ramrod to clean his gun. "If this isn't the dead tryin' to tell us something I don't know what is. We're camping on a mass grave here."

Declan looked with indifference at the skeletal remains and carried on cleaning his weapon.

"Small frame, probably a boy."

"Shit, Declan, is that all ye can say? I hope the generals have seen some of these skeletons – maybe reconsider ye know. Some fellas are saying this campaign is suicide."

"Well then, consider this yer last supper!" Declan sighed as he took out some pickled beef and hardtack from his haversack. They'd noticed how the rations had become smaller over the past three years. General Wadsworth was known for his concern for the welfare of his brigade and more than most generals ensured they had enough to eat. Despite his efforts, Declan thought their stomachs had shrunk. Michael scrunched up his face, which had lost some of its boyish freshness, and threw his heavy body down inside the tent. With his battered boots still on his feet, he was soon snoring. Declan pinched his last biscuit crumbs between his thumb and forefinger and swallowed them watching the stars twinkle against the dark, velvet sky. He took some tobacco out of a dented sardine tin and began to smoke. Before the war it wasn't something he enjoyed but the long days and nights in the Army had drawn him into the habit. He thought of writing home – it had been a while, and paper had been hard to come by. Cara had seemed more content in her last letter and satisfied with her position at the rectory. Michael and Declan talked less and less about the folks back home. The only person Michael mentioned frequently was Sinead and usually when the men had had a few drinks and the subject of women came up.

"The finest in all Ireland," he would pine, slurring his words from the effects of porter. "If I could clap eyes on her lovely, long hair once more..."

"So why did you leave her back home, Mickey?" one of the soldiers asked.

"Cos I heard the ladies were even better-lookin' over here!" he'd reply and they'd fall around laughing. Michael had arrived in New York a boy, Declan thought, and had become not just a man, but an old man.

In the distance he could just make out the tangle of brambles and outline of the dense pine and cedar trees lit by the moonlight. He could hear the mumble of men in prayer as a priest said Mass in the nearby church tent but he'd given up on prayer. He often thought of Father O'Flanigan and his sermons 'Thou shalt not kill'. *How ironic*, he thought, *given he sent us into this slaughter.* Liam sat nearby with some of the other men using the light of the moon to sew their names into their uniforms. It was a familiar sight on the eve of many a battle as the men were almost as concerned about their bodies not being identified as dying itself. Declan ran his fingers across the label now faded on his own blue jacket and heard himself talking to the boy skeleton.

"Nobody came for ye son, eh? They didn't even give ye a decent grave. Ah sure, who'd be looking for me anyway?"

He frowned and scrambled into the tent, taking care not to wake his brother, and settled down for the short night's rest.

Dawn was just breaking when the troops began to move at five a.m. into the dense thicket that had claimed the lives of so many of their comrades. The recent grim history heightened the usual pre-battle tension. When a dry twig snapped under foot, one nervous soldier fired his pistol by accident. This sent a flock of whippoorwills screeching from the trees.

"Sonofabitch!" hissed Michael to Declan. "I don't like this place."

Declan clasped his gun tighter. "I feel there are eyes all around watching us through the trees."

Word came down the line that skirmishes had broken out deeper in the woods between Union troops and rebels. The colonels looked surprised and began conferring with each other as more news broke that Confederate infantry lay ahead. Riding into the mix was the tall, distinctive figure of General Wadsworth himself, which astonished Declan.

"He's right in the thick of it," he whispered to Liam.

"I wouldn't doubt him. That's our leader."

As he replied Declan noticed Liam puff out his chest and the troops around them seemed buoyed by the general's arrival.

By noon their brigade had pushed through the dense woodland and reformed their lines, which had been broken up through the trees at one of the few open spaces at Saunders Field. The troops emerged, blinking, into the daylight from the darkness of the heavy tree canopy. Like giant caterpillars, the brigades surged out of the undergrowth, bulking up until the front lines shifted forward and then bulking up again. A pattern that was repeated until all had assembled in long lines. Bugles sounded and the Union troops advanced. Shooting rang out all around them with the added ping of bullets ricocheting off tree trunks. Declan and Michael knelt as low as possible in the thick brushwood.

"I can't see what I'm shooting at," yelled Michael.

"Then don't waste yer rounds. Keep near me!"

Scrabbling in his knapsack, Declan pulled out a hand grenade, lit it, yelled to the men near him and lobbed it high over the trees. They waited for the boom but it didn't come. Minutes later the same steel cylinder was pitched back and landed at Michael's feet. He kicked it as gently and firmly as he could and dived in the opposite direction.

"Bloody rebs – don't have yer own firepower!" roared Declan over the din. This time the grenade exploded and flames began licking the thicket of vines and low-hanging branches around them.

"Move, move!" shouted a captain spotting the fire.

The brigade moved even deeper into the woods, which were now convulsed with the ferocious sound of warfare. Pistols cracked, artillery boomed, bullets pinged, bones exploded, trees crashed, men yelled and whimpered and the burning undergrowth crackled all around them. Billows of dark smoke obscured the troops' already poor vision and for most of the afternoon, both sides fought a terrifying blind battle. Casualties were dragged screaming out of danger before the fires engulfed them. Many weren't so lucky. Declan saw a soldier whose leg had been blown off squeal as he desperately rolled himself on the ground to beat out flames that had spread to his jacket. But the ground itself was a carpet of ash smouldering under their feet. He watched as Michael clambered over the underbrush to his aid, emptying his canteen of water over the burning man who looked not much older than twenty. The fire went out but the soldier seemed to take a fit and collapsed at Michael's feet.

"Leave 'em!" yelled Declan. "Anyway he's not one of ours. We gotta' keep movin'."

Michael brushed his hand over the dead rebel's eyelids and then searched on his body for the soldier's canteen to replace his own. He tugged the strap tight around his body and followed Declan who, looking back, could just distinguish the faint outline of his brother through the fug of smoke. The fighting went on for hours in what was a scrappy contest where the stakes were raised by the smoke, ricocheting bullets and fast-spreading bush fires. Thirsty and exhausted, the blackened faces of the Wadsworth Guards regrouped at Saunders Field to await further orders.

Michael got down on his haunches and swigged from his newly acquired canteen, pouring some of the water over his head. The bewildered looks on the men's faces were mirrored by the officers and colonels buzzing back and forth through the dishevelled lines. The whizzing and popping of bullets and distant boom of cannon drowned out any conversation among the troops but the men were too anxious and exhausted to speak. Declan looked up as General Wadsworth trotted into view on a dappled mare. He dismounted and with a stern expression gathered his captains and officers in a corner of the field. Declan nudged Michael and pointed out the meeting.

"Something's going on. I hope they're calling it a day."

Michael was less optimistic.

"I doubt it. There's pretty fierce fightin' going on in them woods still. Feels like this day'll never end."

The officers broke away from the meeting and summoned the brigade to its feet. The infantry was given a new mission.

"Rebs have captured two cannon from the First New York Light Artillery. They are in a clearing west of here. Our task is to recapture them."

The troops responded with a clamour of groans and muffled comments. The officer was Captain Kendall, the recruitment officer they had first met in Geneseo, a shadow of the man he had been at the start of the war. Declan noticed his vibrant red locks had faded to a wispy grey and the broken veins on his nose betrayed his whiskey habit. He raised a hoarse voice above the noise.

"They have decorated *our* cannon with the Confederate flag. Are we gonna let that pass?" He paused for effect. "Are we gonna show these bastards who made them cannon? Not these soft southern cotton pickers! No!"

The men roared. Michael raised his gun above his wet hair and yelled. Declan sighed and checked his cartridge box. The Wadsworth Guards fell into line and were directed by the officers through even more dense woodland to the scene of this great outrage. There, in a small clearing surrounded by a jungle of poplars, creepers and vines were the steel cannon, bedecked in the familiar blue cross and stars on a blood-red flag – the rebel colours that haunted Declan's dreams and damned them to this seemingly endless war. The banner flapped as a gust of wind caught the ends almost taunting the watching bluecoats. Some of the men made to dash into the clearing but were held back by hisses from the officers. As they stood observing the stolen weaponry, which looked like exhibits in an open-air museum, an unfamiliar peace settled on the scene and muffled the distant rumbling of artillery. Flattened tracks of grass led from the cannon, branded with the Union flag, from where they had been pushed into the clearing from the woods. Declan scrutinised the trees beyond the tracks.

"I hope someone's checked the woods yonder," he said, turning to Liam who also looked anxious.

"You'd like to think that's been thought of," he replied, heaving his big shoulders. "But I don't like the look of this."

Michael stood motionless, his lips pursed in the determined expression Declan had noticed on his brother's face so often before going into battle together. A lone bugle blasted the stillness to oblivion. Captain Kendall raised his arm and bellowed.

"Advance. *Charge*!"

With a blood-curdling yell the first lines of the brigade

crashed through the undergrowth and into the glaring sunlight. They had only advanced a few strides towards the cannon when a hail of bullets came raining down from the trees opposite them. Chaos ensued. Almost the entire first line of men dropped like stones. The lines immediately behind fell over the writhing bodies of the injured. Some soldiers turned around and crashed into the troops that followed. Captain Kendall had ridden into the middle of the mayhem but realised too late that it was a trap. He signalled to the officers to get the men to retreat. But in the maelstrom of mangled men and blind panic, he struggled to rally any order. The cannon were quickly forgotten as the troops fled in all directions and crawled over bodies to escape the slaughter. Declan ducked his head under branches and was jumping over vines before realising he was deep in the woods again. Liam came panting up behind him and then grabbed his shoulders spinning him round. In a state of panic, Declan half pushed his uncle away as he lay gasping for air against a blackened tree trunk. But Liam gripped his upper arms tighter, with a grim expression on his face. No words were needed. He turned back the way he'd come and running through the blinding smoke, screeched his brother's name.

After what seemed like an age they found Michael curled in the foetal position between the gnarled roots of a charred red cedar. The bed of ashes was soaked with his blood and a peculiar gurgling sound was coming from his mouth. Declan froze in horror. He'd seen enough dying men to know his brother's fate. The hardened shell he'd cultivated through each battle immediately shattered. He fell to his knees and gently held Michael in his arms. As he cradled him, he could see the blood oozing from the back of his neck where the bullet had struck. The tears streamed down Declan's face and all he could think to say was, "There, there, yer gonna be fine, Michael."

Liam stood nearby with one eye on the woods and hissed, "Declan we have to move him. We can't stay here, place is crawling with the enemy."

Declan shook his head. "*You* go, I need to stay with my brother. He's not got long."

Michael's blue eyes blinked open and stared at him.

"Ye don't think I'll make it," he said in a defiant whisper. "Ye never had much faith in me. I'm stronger than ye think."

Declan spoke in a gentle voice he'd only ever used with his sister.

"Shush, I know yer strong. Yer the strongest man I know. I couldn't have got by these years without ye. The workhouse, coming to America and this bloody war..." He felt himself choking. "But it's time, ye know, yer lucky really, yer gonna see Da this day..."

Michael suddenly winced and squeezed his brother's hand.

"You'll take care of Ma and Cara, and tell Sinead I..."

His body jerked and the smile slowly faded from his face.

"I know," Declan whispered in his ear. He felt a massive lump sting his throat but Liam quickly grabbed Michael's legs.

"C'mon, I'm so sorry Declan but we gotta get outta here!" he shouted with an urgency that injected Declan with the adrenalin he needed. He hoisted Michael's upper half, with his head pressed against his right arm and they staggered into another clearing. They looked about for the best escape route, hearing the crackling of the bush fire all around them.

"We're lost," shouted Liam. "Where the Jaysus is our camp?"

Declan's head began to spin. Suddenly a familiar horse galloped into view. General Wadsworth squinted through the smoke and pointed down at them with his rifle. His normally immaculate uniform was dishevelled, his sleeve torn and two brass buttons missing.

"You boys, follow me!" he shouted with authority but his face could not hide his terror. "There's a skirmish in that direction so we should head back this way."

He then spotted Michael and leaned down towards Declan.

"Here!" He shook his head. "Throw him over the back of my saddle, he must be weighing you down."

"Aye, but careful with him, he's my brother," said Declan. He and Liam reluctantly placed Michael's lifeless but still warm body on to the horse.

"I'm sorry for your loss," the general replied, touching Michael's blood-spattered shoulder with his gloved hand. "He's my loss too."

For a moment Declan forgot his rank and they were just two men grieving. Amidst the swirling smoke everything seemed hazy and in slow motion to Declan. He felt numb. Suddenly bullets whistled past them, shaking him out of his paralysis. A bullet whizzed past his shoulder and the horse bucked from under the general, as another shot met its target. Blood spurted from the general's head as he slumped over the reins.

"Christ!" Declan screamed and dragged the horse still carrying the wounded general and Michael's body away from the clearing.

"He's had it, we best leave 'em," yelled Liam as he rushed over to where Declan was examining Wadsworth's injury.

"He's still conscious. Rip Michael's jacket for me!"

"What? We should go!"

"I'll do it myself!" Declan tore off Michael's sleeve, which he used to stem the blood gushing from the general's head.

"There's no time to be heroes Dec. We'll have to leave them."

A stampede of hooves arrived, bringing some of the captains who looked horrified at the scene.

"Is that General Wadsworth?" shouted one. "Can't see a damn thing in here."

"Aye, it's his horse," replied another.

"He's looking pretty bad," said Declan, now covered in blood having tightened the makeshift bandage around the general's head.

"Thank you, boys, what are your names?"

Liam answered for them. "Both Conaghan, sir! He was my general and my landlord sir."

Declan stared at his uncle whose eyes were glassy and he realised he looked like a man in deep shock.

"I see, loyal to the end," replied the captain who then

noticed Michael's lifeless body and felt for a pulse on his sleeveless arm. "I see this lad didn't make it. We need to go, there are rebs right on our tail."

They heard gunfire nearby and shrieks from the bushes. Wadsworth's horse bolted at the sound. With a yelp, the captains dug their spurs and galloped after the terrified horse and its precious cargo. Liam waved his hands and yelled at Declan.

"We gotta move! Have you any grenades left?"

Declan reached in his pocket. A bullet ricocheted off a nearby tree, followed by another. Declan dived to the ground and pulled the pin on the grenade. There was a loud bang and then everything went dark.

Chapter 24

The relentless rattle of artillery and howls of men had ceased. In their place was a low mumble of groans and intermittent blood-curdling screams. Declan opened his eyes where he lay and observed for the first time in weeks his toes, sockless, and tinged a deep shade of purple. He tried to swallow but his throat and mouth felt dry as if he'd swallowed hot sand. He realised his head was throbbing but there was a sharper pain that came in waves that his sleepy brain couldn't locate. There were blurry figures gathered around a bed across from his as he became conscious of their low voices. They were muttering and shaking their heads at the patient who was completely obscured by their grey backs. A terrifying thought sliced through his tired brain like the cold steel of a dagger and made him sit up. Grey! The figures dressed in grey uniforms were rebel soldiers. Where was he? Was he dreaming and what was that agonising pain in his left arm? He yelled in shock as he noticed the blood-soaked bandage where his hand had once been and then blacked out again.

Hours later he woke up to the same mumbling – like the tone of voices at a funeral – but this time he lay very still. The pain was worse in his left arm but he didn't dare look again. He lay with his head turned to the right and watched streams of rebel soldiers coming and going from the bed of the patient opposite. It helped take his mind off the dreadful mutilation he hoped he'd imagined. There were rows of makeshift wooden beds in the field hospital but none were receiving as much attention as the bed near Declan. He caught a quick glimpse of the patient as some soldiers departed leaving a gap. He didn't look in great shape. An older man, perhaps fifty-something, with white sideburns and a prominent nose and chin. He lay very still and Declan wondered if he'd actually passed away. He strained to decipher the murmuring and heard whispers about "the general" and "no hope for him". Such was their deference for the patient that Declan assumed he was a Confederate general who had been mortally injured. The moment of truth came sometime later when a doctor approached him to dress his wounds.

"I'm afraid we couldn't save your hand," he said. "Looks like a grenade injury, so probably self-inflicted."

Declan asked for some water.

"Certainly," replied the doctor, checking his eyes. "We'll have you up in no time. Not that you'll be going anywhere.

You realise you're a prisoner? You might wish you'd died at Wilderness, like your leader over there."

Declan found his voice. "My leader? Christ, who *is* that?"

"Who? Don't you recognise him? Hmm, I guess it's hard to get a good view with all these visitors. Getting in my way too," the doctor grumbled. "Why, it's General Wadsworth, from New York. He was shot in the back of the head and taken here. He was never going to make it with that wound but he's sure been getting some attention from our boys. Fascinated they are!"

The doctor whose eyes were ringed with dark, grey bags leaned his face closer to Declan and whispered, "They say he's worth more than the Confederate's entire treasury." He shook his head. "Why he didn't pay someone to fight in his place like most wealthy folk, I'll never know. Now just you rest and count yourself lucky you didn't get a bullet in the head."

Declan finished gulping his water and sneaked a glance at the fresh bandage. Then he tried to forget the pain and the scene unfolding in front of him. Losing his hand was bad but he considered it far worse to have a parade of gawking rebel soldiers around his cold, dead body. He fell into a deep sleep but still recovering from the morphine administered during the amputation, it was not a peaceful sleep. He could hear cries and yelps and the popping of artillery, a constant noise ringing in his ears. He found himself shooting at an army of skeletons that kept rising up from amidst the trees and running towards him. Some of them collapsed in a heap of bones before him but most drifted through him, like ghosts. The skeleton of the boy in the woods stood up and handed him his tobacco tin. As he reached out to take it, the boy's skull grew a face. It was Michael's face. He called his name, but he didn't – couldn't – hear him so he called again and again.

"Michael, Michael, Mickeee!"

Something wet touched his forehead and he woke up. Two concerned faces were staring down at him. One was the doctor dabbing a cold cloth on his head; the other he didn't recognise at first but was instantly comforted by the sight of the blue uniform. The stranger looked at the doctor.

"Is there nothing you can give him? This soldier's clearly disturbed," he demanded.

"It's just a nightmare – they all have them. His temperature's a bit raised but he's over the worst, I think. He came in with your father-in-law. Do you know him?"

"No. I hear he tried to save the General's life, so the other captains tell me. That's why I wanted to see him. Battle of the Wilderness, bloody disaster."

"Well, you've only got a minute to see him. Our captain only agreed for you to retrieve your father-in-law's body. They're watching you," the doctor whispered, looking over his shoulder. "He's lost his hand, but he can't remember a thing. Keeps raving about someone called Michael."

The stranger noticed Declan's eyes had opened and that he had heard the conversation.

"Good morning, Private Conaghan," he said with a salute. "My name is Ritchie, Captain Montgomery Ritchie… I'm sorry for your injury. It was a terrible battle and to have survived at all is little short of a miracle."

Declan moved his lips but no sound came out. His throat was raw again.

"Get him some water!" Captain Ritchie commanded, which seemed all the more peculiar in the rebel field hospital. But the doctor obeyed and immediately poured some water from an earthenware jug and helped it to Declan's pale lips.

"I want to thank you for your bravery. The other captains told me about you and your uncle. You tried to save my father-in-law. I'm afraid he couldn't survive his wound. He passed away last night." Captain Ritchie paused and stared at him.

"You've been calling for Michael. Is that your brother?"

The ringing in his ears reached a new sharper decibel and Declan felt himself gasping. The doctor leaned over him.

"It's alright, you're alright. You don't have to talk." The doctor looked reproachfully at Captain Ritchie. But Declan reached out his good arm to the captain and croaked.

"Ye-es – my brother – we, I lost him – in the battle." He winced. "I remember General Wadsworth. He was in the woods. He took Michael's body on his horse. He was trying … to save us. What, what happened?"

Captain Ritchie closed his eyes for a moment revealing the strain across his forehead. His sideburns were now flecked with silver. He appeared a much older man than the enthusiastic soldier who left Geneseo three years ago. He touched Declan's shoulder.

"All I know is there was an ambush by an Alabama

brigade. The general was shot and then you were all captured. My wife is inconsolable."

"All of us? Did-did Liam not make it?" He looked around the tent longing to hear his familiar loud laugh.

The captain hesitated. "I don't think anyone could have escaped that inferno. I think you can assume he's gone."

Declan slumped back on his pillow reeling at the news. He'd lost them both. He stared in numb disbelief at his bandaged arm and wished the rest of him was gone too. Captain Ritchie turned again to the doctor and hissed in a low voice.

"I should take this patient with me – he's shocked and mutilated – a one-armed man is hardly a candidate to return to the Army."

The doctor grimaced and gave a helpless shrug of his shoulders. Captain Ritchie glanced across the hospital floor at the Confederate officers who shifted their feet impatiently near the door. They now looked with increasing suspicion at the discussion around Declan's bed. At the sound of boots stamping across the room, Captain Ritchie bade him a hasty farewell. He leaned close to Declan's ear and whispered, "Stay strong. We will win this war. It won't be long. I'll try to get you exchanged. *Excelsior*!"

His words and warm embrace lifted Declan enough for him to find his voice again. "Thank you, captain. I'm sorry for the general. His men thought very highly of him."

The captain nodded and hurried back to his father-in-law's bedside where two other Union officers waited. They turned to the great bulk of General Wadsworth who had been wrapped in sheeting tied at the feet, waist and head.

Declan stared at the solemn scene just yards from his bed as Captain Ritchie and the other men heaved the dead general on to a stretcher. They carefully wove past the maze of beds and gawking soldiers out into the sunshine.

Declan found himself whispering a prayer in Irish and reaching for the medal that miraculously still hung around his neck. He thought of his ma and Cara, they were all he had left in the world. Would he ever see them again? And how could he look them in the eye and tell them about Michael? His mind lurched between rage and grief leaving his head throbbing so much that the stinging in his arm felt like a secondary pain. He twisted and turned on the bed, occasionally releasing a moan. Eventually he curled himself into a ball and buried his face in the pillow to try to shut everything out. He couldn't bear to be reminded of being in a Confederate hospital. He couldn't bear to know that he was still alive. He lay like that for some time until he was disturbed by a rebel soldier who came clinking over to his bed. He opened his eyes and through bleary tears saw a soldier about his own age carrying a thick metal chain. He grunted at him and then wrapped the chain roughly around Declan's ankles.

"What the—?" Declan tried to sit up, levering himself with his right elbow.

"Just lie back there," drawled the soldier. "Any resistance, I'll have to shoot you. You're a prisoner. Prisoners are kept in chains."

It was on the tip of his tongue to ask him to go ahead and shoot him but instead Declan slumped back, defeated. He stared with dead eyes at the grey-white canvas of the tent roof and suddenly recalled the workhouse and the timber rafters they lay under. He muttered to himself, "Oh Da, now I know there are worse places than the workhouse."

The soldier finished chaining him and came closer to Declan's face, his breath smelling of stale smoke.

"Conaghan's your name then? You Irish?"

Declan continued to stare at the ceiling and made no reply.

"No tongue then, that's not like an Irishman," the soldier persisted. "'A fought alongside a lotta Irish. 'Am from Louisiana, brave lotta bastards they were too. 'A ran away from a crazy-assed battle – like lambs to the slaughter we were – but they caught me and made me work here, so 'am sorta' a prisoner too. But look, this ain't the worst prison." His voice then dropped to a whisper. "Your lot are whipping our asses so 'a don't think this war will go on much longer. It's all arithmetic, your side simply got more lambs. Chin up, you've only lost a hand."

Declan turned his head on the pillow and stared at the rebel runaway, willing him to go away. He had never felt so alone.

Chapter 25

Time seemed to pass slowly in the field hospital. Declan wasn't sure if he had lain there for days or weeks. In his morphine-induced haze he had all sorts of hallucinations that both amused and terrified him. The doctor advised that he ought to mobilise, get his legs moving again, but the clunky chain around his ankles didn't really help his movement. Besides, the Louisiana guard, who went by the name Winky, preferred to keep him chained to his bedposts.

"'A ken keep a better eye on ye, Irish," he drawled. Declan was too weak and depressed to ask him to remove the shackles or indeed to ask him to stop talking. The rebel guard had taken a shine to him, as his ma would say, and spent hours perched at the end of Declan's bed discussing the war and his life back home.

As Declan became more alert he realised he had other injuries aside from losing his hand. Pieces of shrapnel had pierced his side and thigh – probably from his own grenade – and though the doctor assured him the wounds were superficial, he did warn that they could be a problem if they became infected. Declan had been a patient in the hospital long enough to see what happened to infected limbs. As he lay that night listening to the long, low moans of the patients around him, he wished he was back in Donegal but how could he go home without Michael? What would he tell them? He agonised for the umpteenth time over their decision to go to America in the first place.

The dawn was streaming in through the dusty ward and his eyes lighted on a squad of busy greyshirts who were pointing at various patients and giving orders to unlock them. He rubbed his face awake and looked around for the few possessions he had. If this was his departure day, he didn't want to forget anything.

"Conaghan, Declan – Wadsworth Guards!" A stern-looking officer appeared at his bed. He scrutinised him more closely. "Ah, you came in with the general. That was a mighty fine scalp for us. You'll be wishin' you'd taken a bullet in the head too when you get to prison."

Declan shrugged at the irony of his threat when he was already lying in chains. He knew their little power games. He gave a cough and pointed at the shackle.

"Ah right," the officer muttered. "Winky, is this your patient? Unlock him, he's going to the station!"

Winky scuttled across the floor, faster than Declan had ever seen him move, and began to grapple with the padlock. When the officer was out of earshot, Winky hissed, "Train's going south, of course. Say it's stopping at Salisbury, North Carolina. Ye better pray it does – worse places than that. All these camps have filled up since they stopped the prisoner exchanges."

"They've stopped them?"

"You ain't noticed they haven't swapped prisoners since Lincoln's Proclamation? He mighta' liberated the slaves but didn't help liberate his own troops from these Godforsaken prisons."

Declan's blood ran cold. From his conversation with Captain Ritchie his hopes had been raised that he would find a way to exchange him but that now seemed unlikely.

"What goes on in these camps, Winky? Do-do they torture prisoners?"

"Hell no!" Winky stared at him, seeming affronted. "Besides they don't need to. The places are so overcrowded, yer fella inmates will torture you enough. I hear the rations are poor so you'll have to barter to survive. Keep yer wits about ye!"

Winky helped him roll his clothes and other items into a sheet, which he tied into a makeshift bag. The guard then glanced over his shoulder and handed Declan a folded blanket.

"Take this too, ye'll need it at night. So long, Irish!" He clapped him on his good shoulder and shuffled back to his duties as Declan joined a line-up of patients outside the hospital, some in better shape than others. They were handcuffed to one long chain and led to a boxcar train that was waiting for them. The men quipped they were going "cattle class" to the great South as the officers poked and prodded them on to the train. Declan settled himself on the dusty floor, hugging his knees to his chest, as they all squeezed in. He didn't know the other men. They were all Union soldiers but from so many different brigades, some with accents he could barely understand. It was hard to believe they had all been fighting on the same side. The wooden doors were pulled shut and they began their journey blinking in the darkness. The train rattled along for several hours without stopping. It wasn't the longest train journey and might have been quite pleasant, Declan thought, if he could have seen out and his arse wasn't rubbed raw by the hard floor. He sat for a time on his rolled-up clothes and blanket but eventually he could feel the slats again from the floor.

He pulled the blanket out from under him to discover some hardtack wrapped in parchment paper within its folds. It must have been half Winky's ration that day. He considered how, if it was ever possible, he could repay Winky's kindness. The thought and the imagined reunion raised the corners of his mouth into a smile, buoying him, despite the heat and stench of the rest of the journey until they screeched to a halt at a railroad intersection. They had arrived in Salisbury.

"*Get out! Move, Move*!"

The men's nervous whispering was silenced by a simultaneous assault on their ears and eyes as the wooden door was flung open, flooding the boxcar with brilliant sunlight and the bustling noise of the station platform. Declan raised his stump to shield his eyes and found himself roughly hauled out of the carriage. He scrambled to grab his blanket and makeshift bag as the prisoners staggered forward into the afternoon sun. The greyshirts on the platform shouted orders and just as before chained them together to begin the short journey to the prison. Declan quickly noticed the prisoners outnumbered the rebel soldiers and puzzled at the lack of energy or will to resist their capture.

It was the summer of 1864. His fourth summer in America and as a soldier. They were all weary, tired of this war. No wonder there was no fight left in them. Thankfully they didn't have far to walk as Salisbury prison was a large stockade next to the railroad. An eight-foot-high fence rose before them with a parapet half that height on which guards were patrolling between portholes filled with cannon. There was a crowd of civilians, including women, huddled near the entrance, shouting and waving their fists at the prisoners.

"We don't want ya here. Vermin!"

Some of the prisoners replied by pointing to their chains but the angry crowd simply heckled them more. They passed through the entrance beside what looked like a blacksmith's shop where they suddenly stopped. An officer yelled an order up ahead and the bundle of prisoners were shunted aside as a wagon wobbled its way out past them. Declan had been staring down at his feet when the rebel soldier nearby elbowed him.

"Look up, Yankee! That's how you'll be transported outta here."

Declan squinted at the wagon and then noticed arms and legs of corpses jutting through the shafts. He glared back at the guard who seemed amused.

"Gone for burial in the cornfield yonder. We had to dig a new burial pit, the last five have filled up that fast." He chortled and then spat on the hot ground. Declan could have sworn it sizzled. They marched on through the gates, past the original four-storey brick prison shaded by oak trees.

"That place, along with those cottages over there, once housed all our prisoners but we've been capturing too many of ye," sneered the guard. "The place is overcrowded, it's every man for himself."

As he finished these words they shuffled into the large open space of the stockade that must have once been a place for exercise. Now it buzzed with the noise of prisoners and flies. Declan had seen some shocking scenes in all the battles he'd fought but he grimaced at the sight before him. It was a honeycomb of holes as far as the eye could see. Prisoners had burrowed into the ground to make their own cells. They had used sticks to hoist whatever material or clothes they could stretch across for shelter. They were living, if you could call it that, like animals. Over the din the lead officer shouted to the new arrivals who were being unchained.

"Line up to get registered over there." He pointed to a table under a tree on the eastern side of the compound. "When you're done, find yourself a spot on this side, the western side, that's reserved for enlisted troops. Eastern side's for officers only. If you're lucky there might be some cowpea soup tonight. Hope I'm whetting your appetites, fellas!"

A mumbling rose among the new inmates. Declan overheard the pair beside him who sounded like New Yorkers.

"What? We just camp with that feral lot?"

"Ye heard 'im. We may be digging a hole too."

"Might as well dig ma own grave."

At the last remark the spitting guard cuffed the prisoner around the head.

"G'wan get in the line! Just need ye to register yer name before ye die."

It wasn't the strongest punch but the young prisoner, weak from his hospital stay, fell to the ground. Declan extended his good arm and hauled him to his feet.

"Obliged. You Irish? Am Scott, that's ma name. I'm not Scottish."

Declan smiled. "How d'ye know me?"

"*Get in line*!"

They all shuffled towards the registration table.

"The whole hospital knew ye as the Irish fella that tried to save General Wadsworth. They say ye'll get a reward – if ye ever get out of here that is," the man next to Scott replied.

"Aye, would be reward enough just to get my freedom from this hole. Ye boys fight together?" Declan asked.

"Yeah, we're from the 49th New York Infantry. Got wounded at Spotsylvania. We're old schoolfriends. I'm Tom."

"Tom, I'm Declan, that's my real name, not Irish. I was captured at Wilderness – lost my brother and uncle there."

They fell silent as they neared the front of the queue. A fight had broken out beside a well where inmates had been scrambling to get water. Buckets were hurled, along with insults, which then descended into bare-knuckle fighting. The initial five fighters swelled to ten until a mob of emaciated, ragged creatures slugged it out on the scorched ground. Declan noticed the greyshirt guards made no attempt to intervene. This was dog eat dog. He had thought Wilderness was hell. He realised he'd descended a few steps lower.

The officer at the registration table barked at the young New York soldier, "Number three hundred! That's how many prisoners we've taken in this week and we're only mid-week." He shook his head. "You may find a spot and dig in. Stay clear of the gangs." He gestured with his chin towards the fight. "We've our own civil war goin' on in here."

The spitty guard threw a spade to Scott who looked bewildered.

"You'll need this. Head back over western side and make yourself at home."

Scott nodded, evidently unsure whether to thank him or throw it back at him. The young New York soldier with his floppy black hair and clear blue eyes reminded Declan of his brother.

"Come with us, Irish – sorry, Declan. Can't be easy for ya to dig with one hand. We might need to stick together in this place."

With that invitation Declan joined the small band of New York soldiers who dug their own 'Manhattan' as they named it. Declan shared the digging, proving his stump wasn't the worst handicap. Scott was very feeble and after a few hours in the hot sun fell asleep. They learned between the three of them to always have one man on guard, to stop the thieving that was rampant and general attacks from the other inmates. When the cowpea soup didn't arrive on the first night, Declan dug into his coat and pulled out the hard-tack from Winky.

"A gift from Louisiana!" Declan declared.

Tom and Scott stared at him with wide, hungry eyes before getting stuck in. Their prison bond was sealed.

"Ye got any family here?" asked Scott, looking dubiously at the water after they'd eaten. "I mean, pardon me, ye said yer brother and uncle were killed but have ye any folks left?"

Declan stared at the small fire they'd lit and thought of the warm inglenook in the wrecked cabin in Donegal. He shook his head.

"Not in the States, no. Well, there is my aunt in Geneseo. My sister and ma are back home in Ireland."

"If ye make it out of this hole, will ye stay or go back?"

Declan frowned. "I'd like to but I'm … I'm afraid to go home."

He surprised himself talking to strangers so openly but he had quickly warmed to the New Yorkers. Tom poked a stick into the embers.

"What ye afraid of?" he asked. "I can't wait to see my family again."

Scott turned back to Declan.

"Ye afraid to go home without yer brother?"

"There's that yeah, and I'm afraid of myself … what I might do." He hesitated.

Scott stared at him with his piercing blue eyes. "Yer afraid ye've become a killer? That haunts us all." He began to cough, long and hard, until he was so red in the face Declan thought he'd pass out.

To his relief, the coughing fit ended the conversation and they all found a spot in the burrow for the night. Declan lay in the dirt, grateful for Winky's blanket as he stared up at the

Carolina stars. Despite the heat of the day, it became chilly at night. He lay so close to Scott, he could feel him shivering. After a while he unfolded the blanket and spread it over the shaking soldier.

"Yer a gent, not a killer," whispered Scott, the outline of his face just visible in the silvery light.

"Sure, now maybe we'll both get some sleep," Declan hissed back.

Before he was captured there were long periods when the troops just sat about. Long days of just waiting. Declan looked back to those times as blissful now. He berated himself for ever complaining about boredom in the past. Yes, they were confined to the camp but there were characters, card games, a sense of camaraderie. Often the officers gave them instructions, mainly to keep them occupied – drills, building breastworks or general maintenance of the camp. Salisbury prison had none of that, it was just a cesspit. Union and Confederate prisoners were thrown in together, itself a recipe for conflict since they'd been sworn enemies since '61. Declan looked around at the vista of burrows and thought of a plague of meerkats. He realised he'd arrived in a disease-ridden waiting room and he'd be there 'til the end of the war. Later that first week two more New Yorkers who arrived off the train joined their burrow. Scott recognised one of the boys as an old neighbour from back home and invited them to join 'Manhattan'. Space was more cramped but they all agreed there was strength in numbers as fights broke out day and night as inmates squabbled over food rations, water and even spitting too close to someone. The few officers there just looked idly on.

A month passed and as the prison grew more crowded the rations shrunk. Scott went to sleep one night curled in his usual ball, the crown of his head touching Declan's head and his feet at Tom's back. He didn't wake up.

"If he'd eaten properly, he could have survived," said Tom, staring mournfully at the curled-up corpse. Declan couldn't find any words to comfort him. He stared at the dark, tousled hair that had reminded him so much of his brother, haunted by his last memories of Michael's hair mottled with blood as it spilled out over those tree roots in the Wilderness.

One of the soldiers began to mutter a prayer that Declan recognised but he stepped out of the burrow. He needed some air. A guard came past, nearly as skinny as the inmates, doing his cursory check.

"You look like you've seen a ghost," he quipped. "Any dead? You know the drill, throw them up to the blacksmith's shop."

Declan clenched his only fist and wished he had the strength to punch him.

Chapter 26

Three months later Declan was summoned to the registration table. The same tired-looking officer sat at the desk, which had been moved into a tent as it had been pouring for days. Declan wobbled in front of him in his now ragged uniform. The only food he'd had for days was scraps of squirrel meat that they'd foraged for.

"Declan Conaghan?" said the officer, tapping his pen.

"Yes, sir!"

The officer got up from the table and began inspecting Declan. He was surprisingly tall to Declan who had never seen him not seated before.

"You lost your hand in the Battle of the Wilderness, is that correct?"

"I-I did sir."

"You're not really fit for service again by the looks of you."

"Er, no sir," replied Declan, puzzled.

"You seem to be regarded as a bit of a hero by the

Yankees. Wounded in the same battle as General Wadsworth of Geneseo…" The officer had retaken his seat and was reading from a letter.

"Well, it seems you have a guardian angel. I have papers here signed by a Captain Ritchie asking for your release. The letter was sent some time ago but has only just got here. There are too many of you stinkin' Yankees here so it's my great pleasure to get rid of you…"

Declan's head began to spin as the officer explained the details of his transfer up north. He was getting out. Out of Salisbury. Out of the South. Out of the war. God bless Captain Ritchie.

"They keep sending us bags of bones, not patients," quipped one of the doctors whose black sense of humour shielded his own horror at the constant stream of half-dead men that arrived on his ward. Declan was one of them, arriving at the military hospital in Washington after being transferred across enemy lines.

His bed might have smelt of dried blood and worse but Declan rejoiced at having a bed to lie on after months curled on top of his things with his nose in the dirt. One day a photographer was allowed in to record the state of the patients and Declan was helped from his bed to lean practically naked on a stool as bulbs flashed from the box on a tripod.

"Sorry for the intrusion," said the newspaper man. "We need to show how them damn rebel bastards treat their prisoners. The war might be nearly over but the propaganda war sure ain't."

"I'm lucky," muttered Declan. "Least I survived."

The newspaper man shook his head, his face full of pity and disgust.

Declan often thought of his fellow prisoners. He hoped Tom would make it to see his family again. The rations had got fewer towards the end of '64 and the wagon stacked higher with corpses from the diseases that swept the prison. As he gradually got his strength back, he realised he still had a life to lead. His first plan was to visit Geneseo where he had a number of duties to attend to. He might have left the Army, but he still thought like a soldier.

After the Union victory in the spring of 1865, Declan finally felt well enough to travel to Geneseo. When he arrived at the station, he could still see the tattered traces of army recruitment posters. This is where it all began, he thought, and could almost feel Michael at his side walking towards North Street to the Army barracks. He walked slowly past the same timber houses with the large verandas. There must have been stormy weather as the pink and white blossom petals filled the dusty streets. The only people he saw were elderly, sitting in the shade, watching him watching them. One old man saluted him. He returned the gesture by tipping his hat. He stopped dead at the sight of the apple tree where they had picked apples all those years ago. In his mind's eye he could see Michael reaching up and furtively picking two, then pitching one to him. A lump formed in his throat. He carried on up the street and licked the salty stream from his upper lip. His mouth filled with the bitter taste.

His first stop was with Liam's widow, Sarah, who had accepted by then that her husband wasn't coming home. Her hair was tied back in a bun and she was dressed all in black like many of the widows he'd seen throughout the war. She listened, her face blank, as he described her husband's valiant efforts during the Battle of the Wilderness. When he used the word 'hero', he realised how hollow it sounded.

"And there's no body? He's never been found?" she enquired, her face much more lined than Declan remembered.

"No," he whispered. He carefully repeated what Captain Ritchie had told him in the field hospital. She listened but there were no tears. She clutched at a small cross around her neck which Declan thought must have brought her comfort.

"It belonged to Liam," she said, noticing him looking. "He gave it to me before he left Geneseo." She sighed. "You are a miracle, Declan. So many men didn't return. Geneseo is full of widows. In a strange way that sustains me knowing I'm not the only one to have suffered loss. You know the captain died, too?"

Declan gasped.

"No, I didn't. I wanted to thank him. When did he die? What happened?"

"They say he got sick last summer. It was just weeks after the general was killed. Mrs Ritchie at the big house was just devastated – to lose both her father and her husband so close together."

Declan pondered this. One of the last things the captain must have done was try to get his release. His death perhaps explained the delay in sending the letter. He considered how easily he might have been left to languish in Salisbury prison. He then thought of Mrs Ritchie – Cornelia – and her two young sons, left without a father. He determined to go to Hartford House and leave a message of condolence and thanks. If it helped at all, he wanted them to know what a good man their father was.

"What are you going to do now, Declan? There's no shortage of labouring work here, given the lack of men. You just have to ask at the big house." She offered him lodgings so he decided to stay a while.

He asked Sarah about Eddie Thornton's family, the cook killed at Fredericksburg. That's how he referred to his death, preferring not to share the gruesome details of his last minutes in that body-strewn field.

"You mean Martha? She lives in the next street. We've become close. I help her out sometimes. She can't work in a shop like me because of her children so she does some needlework instead at home. I've always felt terrible that Liam persuaded her Eddie to sign up. He was one of the few men round here that didn't want to join the war effort."

Declan wondered what his aunt would think if he told her how Eddie really died.

A few days later she brought him to Martha's small wooden cabin. Eddie's two girls were playing on the front grass.

Martha appeared red-faced in the doorway, her hands covered in flour. She noticed Sarah at the gate and her jaw dropped open.

"Sarah! I thought for a second Liam had come home. You must be one of his nephews, you look so like him." She beamed and invited them inside.

Martha had been baking bread and the delicious smell filled the cabin. She swiftly moved piles of clothes to make room for them to sit and for the next hour they chatted about Eddie, the girls, the other lost men of Geneseo and eventually the battle that had claimed her husband's life. Declan apologised that many of the battles were now blurred in his memory.

"Did you see my Eddie after, after…?" asked Martha, checking the girls were out of earshot.

"I did. We did – Liam, Michael and I. He got a burial and a good send-off, I can assure you. Did the envelope reach you? I know Liam sent it on."

Martha nodded and pointed to the framed lithograph of the four of them.

"He carried that with him to all the battles. He wrote that he hoped it would get back to me. He said the picture had given him strength to keep going and he wanted it to give me strength should he not return. He'd written the letter just before his final battle."

Declan stared at the picture.

"He was a brave soldier. He talked about ye and the girls all the time. I-I just hope ye don't hold it against my Uncle Liam for persuading him to sign up. He could never have known the extent of the war. I'm so sorry."

Martha glanced at Sarah and back again at Declan.

"Oh Declan, please don't think that. My Eddie was a grown man. He made his own decisions and I know he enjoyed being part of the Wadsworth Guards. Sure if he hadn't signed up everyone would have been talking about him. This is a small place. We've all lost loved ones but I'm fortunate I have my girls. I see Eddie in them every day."

There was a shy giggle from the doorway that made them all look up. The younger girl who was around six years old was twirling one of her plaits. She stared at Declan.

"Did you know my papa, sir?"

Declan smiled and nodded.

"I remember my papa used to swing me. Can you give me a swing?"

Martha and Sarah both looked dubiously at his stump. Her mother scolded her. "Bethany, leave our guest alone. Haven't you got your sister to play with?"

Declan stood up and walked over to where she stood in the door. He beckoned her to take his good arm.

"I think I can give you a swing. Anything for Eddie's girls."

She shrieked in delight, an innocent sound that filled the empty chasm of Declan's heavy body. They stepped outside on to the patch of grass where he swung her round and round until they were both dizzy.

Just as Sarah had predicted, his stump didn't prevent him finding employment. Hartford House gave him some labouring work. The head groundsman was sympathetic to Declan's situation. As he merrily informed him, "I've seen a lot worse. At least the rest of you is intact."

He mostly worked in the gardens, pruning hedges and shrubs, which was gentle work compared to digging breast-works. The house was just as he remembered. Ornate gates opened on to a long avenue of trees whose branches seemed to bow as you walked towards the colonnaded portico of the white house. Its beauty, however, was now veiled in a deep sense of sadness. Declan often saw Mrs Wadsworth, all in black, strolling through the gardens or sitting on the swing. He had only been there a week when he was summoned to see her in the drawing room. He scrunched up the cap in his hand and hovered by the door. Thankfully it was first thing in the morning so his clothes weren't grubby yet.

"Oh do come closer," she beckoned him. "Come near the window so I can see you. It's a very dull morning and my eyesight is not what it was."

He followed her instructions and stood awkwardly as she gazed at him. He had a flashback to the photographer in the hospital in Washington but at least he had his clothes on and a bit more flesh on him this time. Mrs Wadsworth remained seated.

"We met before, didn't we? At the barracks. You were the Latin Irish scholar, am I right?"

Declan reddened, not knowing what to say.

"You have a very serious face … for a young man…" Her voice drifted away. "I can see you've suffered a lot. May I ask how and when did you lose your hand?"

"It was a grenade took it; at Wilderness." He looked down at the polished wooden floor. He could hear her sip her tea. The grandfather clock in a corner of the room chimed the half hour.

"Another casualty of Wilderness." She shook her head. "What a disaster that was! What a disaster the whole war was! I had begged James – sorry, the general to you – not to continue with the war, especially when it dragged on. You know he was one of the oldest generals in the Army? He could easily have retired before '64 but he was a stubborn man... Now he's left me a widow and his grandchildren without their grandfather. My dear daughter Cornelia was also widowed. She couldn't stand it here; she took the children away to Paris. Said she didn't want them seeing or reading any more about the bloodshed."

"Mrs Wadsworth don't be upsetting yourself."

Declan swung round, startled by the voice that came from a woman wearing an apron and bonnet who had been sitting quietly at the far side of the room.

"I know, Daisy, but it's still so raw. I'm sorry, I don't wish to embarrass myself or you, Private Conaghan." She wiped her nose. "I just wanted to thank you personally for the effort you and your uncle made to try to save my husband. I know it was in vain but I want you to know the Wadsworth family's gratitude. Thank you."

The drawing room was of course much larger than his aunt's or Martha's with its beautifully crafted high ceilings and satin-draped windows but Declan realised the pain felt by all three widows was the same. Mrs Wadsworth nodded to the maid who swished across the floor. She presented an envelope to Declan and gave what he thought was almost a curtsey.

He became flustered and was lost for words for a moment. Finally he mumbled, "Thank you Mrs Wadsworth. I-I wish I could have saved your husband. He was a great general. You should know he was also trying to save us. He tried to guide us out of the wilderness."

Mrs Wadsworth put her cup down firmly on the saucer and stared at him.

"Guide us out of the wilderness," she echoed. "I knew it, playing God right to the end."

The maid pressed her hand on Declan's arm and he found himself guided out of the drawing room.

When he checked the envelope later that evening, he discovered a generous wad of dollars. Aunt Sarah beamed at him.

"Well, it won't replace your hand but there's enough there for your ship back home."

Declan's face fell.

"D'ye want me to leave? Am I in yer way?"

"Of course not," she reassured him. "It's lovely to have your company after so long on my own but I think one day you'll want to return to Ireland, to see your mother and sister. Don't you want to see your home again?"

Declan grimaced.

"My home was destroyed by that landlord Adair. If I go back, I have a very big score to settle."

He decided to stay. He didn't have the strength to face the journey home. The war had taken its toll on his health and although he wasn't yet thirty, he felt his whole body had aged. He felt slower at everything. It was as if the weight of all his experiences had come crushing down on him. So he finally wrote to Cara and broke the news of Michael's death, and all that had happened. He imagined they'd have assumed they'd all died given the lack of letters. And as he finished writing, taking care not to spoil the ink with his tears, he promised he'd return, some day.

Chapter 27

September 1866, Manhattan

Dusk had begun to settle over the city, casting shadows across the broken cobbled streets and making the alleyways seem more threatening. Red streaks that had stained the sky faded as the sun made its final descent behind the hundreds of tenement blocks that obscured the magnificent view of the sunset. John Adair enjoyed this time of day and made a point of stopping his work to take in the spectacle from an upstairs window of his office on Pine Street. It was of course a very different view from the wilderness of Glenveagh but he enjoyed the raw beauty of the heaving city. The blocks of buildings stretched for miles and seemed to expand in numbers every week. There were still plenty of people about for that time of the evening in downtown Manhattan. Men in tailcoats and beaver top hats clutched briefcases and hurried along the sidewalk, avoiding eye contact with the crouched gypsy women who stretched out their hands to beg as they passed. Small boys in grey caps shrieked as they struck hoops along the road and dodged between barouches and carts of damaged fruit and vegetables returning from the market. The gas lighter plodded along first one side of the street and then the other, seemingly unfazed by the bustling commuters returning home while he began his day's work.

Two office clerks entered the room and said goodnight as they reached for their coats and hats from the wooden stand.

"Have you any plans this evening, Mr Adair?" one of the young men asked, emphasising the 'r' at the end of his name. He turned from the window and waved a small card with a gold inscription at the enquirer.

"Indeed. As a matter of fact I'm attending a reception tonight. A Republican Party ball at Congressman Hughes' house," he replied.

"Very good. Is he seeking your support in the forthcoming Congressional elections?"

"Well now. It's my money he'll be after, given I can't vote in this country – yet," Adair replied. "Probably a good thing though as I haven't got my head around your political system. It's a lot simpler in the United Kingdom."

"Yes, but then you don't even vote for your head of state. Is Victoria still on the throne?" the wide-eyed young man asked, securing the belt on his coat.

"Last time I checked Her Majesty was," replied Adair with a curtness that hinted the conversation was over.

"Well, good evening to you, sir." The clerk and his colleague both raised their hats and scurried out of the dark, wood-panelled office.

Adair turned again to the window and watched the men disappear into the sidewalk of thronging people bustling to the station or port to catch the steamer home. He was relieved he wouldn't have to join the crowd this evening. He had had his tuxedo cleaned, pressed and delivered to the office so he could go straight to the reception. There was a shuffling on the stairs outside the door. The brass knob turned and the charwoman entered.

"Oh I'm sorry, sir," she said in an unmistakable Irish accent. "I thought all ye gentlemen had left for the day."

Adair smiled. He was somewhat comforted by the familiar accent in the sea of strange voices and clipped New York drawls.

"I'm sorry to alarm you, Mrs Keenan. I'll be using the bathroom for a little while to change into my tuxedo, and then I'll be on my way."

Mrs Keenan put down the heavy pail of soapy water and wiped her red hands on her apron. He noticed she eyed him curiously and realised he hadn't said more than two words to her before. He felt in a good mood, buoyed by the invitation to an important event in New York's social calendar. In many ways he realised it was easier to climb the social ladder in America. All you really needed was money.

"Well, I'll just start in here then and letcha' get on." She nodded and shuffled to the far corner of the office.

Twenty minutes later, Adair emerged from the bathroom in his fresh suit and velvet bow tie. He was fixing the chain of his gold pocket watch to his suit and glanced at the time.

"I shall be off then, Mrs Keenan. I think I'll walk there as it's a pleasant evening."

"Are ye sure ye won't take a carriage sir? You'll ruin that good suit and there be pickpockets about – and worse..." she warned, placing her wet, raw hands on her hips.

"I'll take the risk and I'd like to think there won't be any thieves near the address I'm going to."

Adair lifted his top hat and swept out of the office. He stepped on to the sidewalk and immediately smelt the rancid mix of horse manure, baking chestnuts and raw sewage. He placed his hand to his nose as he passed the sweating chestnut seller who was raking an open grill on a stand just a block away from his office. He was heading uptown to Madison Square, which by his calculations would be a half-hour stroll. A gaggle of women dandered past clutching bunches of flowers on their way downtown to sell to romantic couples. He lifted his tall frame and tried to sidle past but the chattering women pounced on him.

"Ooh! Goin' somewhere nice, sir?" said one pressing close to his arm. Another one stroked his left sleeve.

"Lovely suit, sir. Will ya buy a bunch for your good lady?"

Adair brushed them aside, muttering under his breath about vermin. They chased after him for a few yards until a police officer appeared and took his truncheon to their billowing skirts. Two empty carriages trundled past and Adair thought of hailing one but then decided to continue his walk along Broadway. He chose his route carefully to avoid Tompkins Square on the east side, which was the sort of place where Mrs Keenan's warning could be realised. The tenement blocks rose tall around the square and teemed with new and second-generation migrants speaking a host of different languages. The streets were dirty and badly drained in this area and the air stank of a revolting cocktail. Many an unsuspecting visitor that strayed into the area was known to retch from the smells alone. But even on Broadway the drainage was poor and the afternoon's downpours had left a stream of deep brown mud which Adair crossed the road to avoid. He marched on, only slowing his pace when the streets became broader and more residential, featuring pseudo-Georgian façades and marble awnings. He had caught up with the gas lighter who was criss-crossing the street with his short ladder over his shoulder. Adair studied him and wondered how many miles he walked each evening, lighting the city, and then later making it dark. *The God of the Light*, he mused. The sound of a tinkling piano drifted to his ears. Looking ahead, he could see a large mansion with all its windows illuminated. There were a number of figures and what looked like a butler standing on the entrance veranda. As he moved closer, he could hear men's voices and women's laughter. A number of barouches were just pulling away from the sidewalk to reveal a woman in a fur throw escorted by an older man in a tuxedo. He puzzled at the age difference. The woman was certainly not a debutante. He couldn't see her face very well in the dark but there was something about her gait or manner that spoke of a maturity. A second woman joined them on the steps and the fur-coated lady held out her gloved hand.

"Ah, Mrs Van Lynden so glad you could come," said the woman in fur.

Confidence, Adair thought, *that's what she has*. Yes, being wealthy was vital to climb the social ladder in the States, but Adair was aware of an established circle of high society that he remained outside of. He suddenly realised he was staring at the women from just a few feet away and began to fidget with the invitation in his pocket. The smart-suited butler approached him. "Can I help you, sir? This is invitation only."

Adair quickly produced the card from his pocket and adopted a haughty tone.

"And I have an invitation from the Congressman himself."

The butler nodded and escorted him into the hallway where he urged a young pageboy to take the gentleman's coat. A large stars and stripes banner hung on one wall, while opposite, a red, white and blue garland decorated the curved staircase. Adair found himself wincing at the garish taste and tried to imagine the balls he had been to in London and Dublin indulging in such vulgar decor.

"Congressman Hughes is greeting guests first in the drawing room, then there will be a buffet in the main hall followed by the ball," the butler said robotically. Adair made his way to the drawing room where he was instantly struck by the number of women filling armchairs and standing in various groups around the room. Not recognising anyone, he headed for the open French doors, which led on to the balcony. There were a number of men having a heated discussion at one end. He reached for the silver cigar box inside his jacket, snapped open the clasp, selected one and lit it. More carriages had stopped outside the house and a number of pageboys were busy escorting guests to the cloakroom. The lights burning from the house put the rest of the street in the shade even though the lamp lighter had finished his business and passed into the next neighbourhood.

"Jack!" A New York accent boomed behind him and before he could turn round a heavy hand slammed onto his shoulder.

"Why it *is* you. Great that you could come!"

"Franklyn. Good to see you and thanks for arranging the invitation," Adair said holding out his hand. But the businessman, who was slightly smaller than Adair although a lot wider, had overridden his handshake by putting his arm around his back.

"Frank, Jack, you can call me Frank! Now let me introduce you to some of the boys…"

Adair found himself being ushered over to the debate in the corner. He was introduced to the four men in the overly enthusiastic way he was finding hard to get used to in New York. Two of the men were in business, the other two in law – the usual profile of New York's high society – and they were all keen Republicans. Adair was puzzled then by the raging debate, given they all supported the same political party.

"Jack has opened a brokerage firm near Wall Street," Frank explained. "We've done some business together. He's got a lot of real estate back in Ireland, ain't that right, Jack?"

Adair nodded and took a glass of wine from a passing waiter's tray.

"Are you looking to buy land here?" asked one of the lawyers wearing spectacles.

"I've already bought land here," Adair replied. "I'm exploring a sizeable ranch out west in Texas."

"Is that so? Beautiful state, have you been there?"

"No, not yet but I plan to make a trip. I have a lot of land to occupy me at home. I'm working on a project to establish a hunting estate similar to Balmoral."

"What's that?"

"You haven't heard of Balmoral?" The spectacled lawyer laughed. "It belongs to the Queen of England, you buffoon. I think it's in Scotland. Is your estate in Scotland then?"

Adair suddenly wished he'd never divulged any of his business, but he had wanted to impress them.

"No, my estate is in the northwest of Ireland. A place called Donegal."

"Dun-e-gaal!" the men drawled in unison.

"Gee the Irish have some beautiful place names. I mean, look at this city, you think someone could have come up with something more original than New – York," Frank said.

Desperate to change the subject, Adair asked about the political debate.

"Aren't you all Republicans? What is the disagreement, I couldn't help but overhear," he asked, sipping his Chianti.

"Sure we're all Republicans but there are some more radical than others," the lawyer piped up. "The Civil Rights Bill has finally been passed and that should end the Negro question once and for all."

"You know that bill's meaningless if Negroes can't vote – how can they protect those rights?" said Frank, his voice quivering. "God damn it, Mannering, you're a lawyer, you know it's not enough."

"The war's over, Frank – we've got to build bridges with the South and if that means resting the black suffrage issue, so be it."

The heads of some ladies in the drawing room turned at the commotion and Frank raised his glass in a meek apology. He turned to the other men. "I apologise. I was forgetting myself and that there are ladies present."

Adair, who had been silent throughout the argument, cleared his throat.

"Yes, I noticed there are quite a number of ladies here tonight and they don't all seem to have escorts."

The lawyer peered at him over his spectacles. "I'm sure they all have escorts, but each gentleman is probably accompanying several women. Most of them are widows." He lowered his voice. "From the war. No doubt news of our little rebellion reached Ireland?"

Adair flushed a little and tried not to glare at the lawman. Frank seemed to notice his discomfort and interrupted.

"Of course, Mannering. Why do you think Jack's here? He's got a sharp eye for business and heard this place was booming post-war. I daresay he's also got an eye for the ladies. There's plenty here would make a nice little investment." Frank winked and with his arm about Adair excused them from the other gentlemen.

"Come inside and meet the Congressman," he said,

pulling Adair's arm. "I said I'd introduce you. The captain, as most of us know him, is a bit of a war hero. He was in the Sixty-Seventh New York Volunteer Infantry and was promoted up the ranks. Fought at Cold Harbor and was wounded but he stayed fighting 'til the bitter end."

Inside the drawing room the air was heavy with expensive perfume and cigarette smoke. There was a medley of conversations, mostly female voices, and in the midst of these was a stocky man leaning on a stick with a red, white and blue rosette adorning his suit. He caught sight of Frank approaching and excused himself from the circle. He limped towards them, then leaning on his good leg, opened his arms wide to embrace the New York businessman.

"Frank, Frank. Good to see you," he said with a surprisingly high-pitched voice. "I never thought I'd say this, but it's good to see some gents. Us boys are a bit thin on it tonight."

"We were just saying the very thing," said Frank, gesturing to Adair, and then he lowered his voice. "So many broads, so little time!"

The pair began to cackle and Adair looked around a little uneasily. As he surveyed the room his eyes settled on a serious-looking woman perched on a straight-backed chair near the door. She was listening to some of the older ladies who were thronged about her. One of them was the Van Lynden woman he had seen at the front entrance. She had a beak-like face and her continual nodding reminded him of a chicken. Her stiff red collar simply added to the effect. The serious woman took a delicate sip from her wine glass and the corners of her lips curled as she attempted to smile when two gentlemen were introduced to her. As she got up from the chair and stretched out her hand, Adair realised she was the woman in the fur he'd seen outside.

"Ah, I see you've spotted one of our most eligible widows," said Frank, following Adair's gaze across the room. Adair looked away and realised the Congressman had been accosted by other party supporters who had whisked him away. He turned back again and saw the men were scribbling their names on the woman's dance card.

"Yes, she seems popular," Adair turned to Frank. "She's a widow? She does appear rather sad-looking."

Frank replaced his empty glass on a tray and grabbed a new one.

"I guess she does have a sad expression," he observed. "Well she did lose her husband and father in the war – within weeks of each other in fact. Left with two boys to raise herself. Although she's from one of the wealthiest families in the entire state so I'm sure she's got plenty of help. Her father was General Wadsworth. You may have heard of him; he was killed in battle about a year before the war ended. Brave soldier I believe…"

Frank lifted his chubby hand to his mouth as much for effect than necessity and whispered, "Damn fool too if you ask me. He didn't need to fight, could have paid a hundred soldiers to serve in his place. Story goes that when the rebs captured him, they gathered round his bed just to catch a glimpse of a man worth more than the entire Confederate treasury."

Adair raised his eyebrows and glanced back at the widow whose hand was being embraced again. He then surveyed the room and realised several of the women were watching them. As he caught their eye, they smiled and lowered their gaze. He had not expected to find so many ladies at what he had originally thought would be a dry political gathering with speeches and anthem-playing. At his age the pool of available women in society circles in Dublin had shrunk and he had never entertained taking on a silly debutante who would just drain his finances. But as he studied the various bodices and frilly busts around him, he found his eyes went back to the serious widow in the corner.

"She must be worth a fortune and she is rather pretty," he confided in Frank who had moved on to explaining the machinations of New York politics.

"Who? Jack, I can see you're distracted. Shall I introduce you?"

Before Adair could protest, Frank's familiar arm was steering him across the room through the labyrinth of ladies until they stood looking down on the ornate tresses piled high on her bent head.

"Mrs Wadsworth Ritchie," Frank said in his most charming manner and put out his hand to take hers. "How are you and the boys?"

"Oh, Franklyn." She looked up and grasped his hand almost tenderly. "I did wonder when you were going to visit my little corner. It seems you've been around them all."

"Just saving the best for last." He beamed.

"And Mrs Parker, how is she doing?" the widow asked, her eyes darting sideways to Adair.

"The very best. I will tell her you were asking after her. You know how she despises politics of all shades. How I wish she was as enthusiastic as you about the party."

"Well, I do my bit. My father would've been appalled if I hadn't. You know how passionate he was about the party. I'm just glad he was spared the loss of Lincoln, it would have broken his heart," she said. Adair took a sip of his wine and gave a slight cough.

"Oh I apologise," said Frank. "Let me introduce my business associate, Jack Adair, all the way from Ireland. This is Mrs Cornelia Wadsworth Ritchie from upstate New York."

The petite woman peered at him for a few seconds and they both then tried to speak at once.

"Ireland!"

"Cornelia!"

Adair took her tiny, outstretched hand and brushed it with his whiskered face.

"I'm sorry. You were about to say? It's just such a lovely, might I add, unusual, name."

"Latin," she replied. Adair looked puzzled.

"It's Latin," she repeated and then laughed. "I guess when your parents have lots of children they have to look further for distinctive names – even to dead languages!"

"I see." Adair found himself speechless and slightly in awe of this beautiful, articulate American woman.

"Well, are either of you going to ask me to dance?" she said, holding out her dance card packed with signatures. "It's filling up fast and I've never danced with an Irishman before."

Her smile was almost coquettish and melted away her serious expression. Adair felt his head grow dizzy but he reached for her dance card and signed his name.

"I look forward to it," Cornelia said as she retrieved the little card and tucked it into her handbag. But her response ended the conversation and disappointed, Adair nodded and stepped away from the corner. Frank had lifted two glasses of champagne and thrust one at Adair.

"She's a charming lady and seems rather taken by you," said Frank, uncomfortably for Adair within earshot of the lady in question. Still somewhat dizzy, Adair declined the champagne.

"Ah but you must," Frank insisted. "The captain is about to speak and he always ends with a toast!"

Adair acquiesced and held the glass of golden liquid up to the light from the chandelier. He spied Mrs Wadsworth Ritchie through the flute. The shape of the glass elongated her pale, thin neck, which seemed to miraculously hold up her voluminous hair scraped into such an intricate style on top of her head. She wore a simple gold chain with a locket attached. Adair wondered about its contents. Was it a picture of her dead husband perhaps, or a lock of his hair? She was greeting another suitor but was shaking her head apologetically this time. He was pleased to see her dance card remained in her bag. She caught his gaze and he lowered the glass only to raise it again in an awkward gesture of recognition. Her eyes narrowed as if working out who he was and then she lifted her chin in acknowledgement and smiled with pursed lips this time. It was a look, Adair thought, of a proud woman, that only a woman of means would be capable of. Adair took a gulp of his champagne and looked back to the stage. The Congressman was shuffling some papers and began a lengthy speech in which he paid tribute to those who had fought in the war, glossing over his own war record with fake modesty.

"We should not forget, of course, those who fought bravely and did not return," the Congressman said, dropping his voice to a solemn growl. "More than 600,000 men paid the ultimate price and it is through their sacrifice that we have preserved this mighty Union. Under the leadership of our late, great President Abraham Lincoln this incredible nation survived and has been made stronger. He was our first Republican President and by your efforts we will ensure his legacy will live on and Republicans will continue to lead this great country."

Adair fidgeted with his pocket watch and tried to stifle a yawn as the speech dragged on. He was impatient for the ball to begin and scanned the room for a glimpse again of Mrs Wadsworth Ritchie who sat transfixed as if listening to a powerful church sermon. Adair knew little about the war but cynically believed a country the size of the United States could not hope to remain united forever. He was excited however by the opportunities, especially for purchasing land in the aftermath of the war, and regarded New York as a city of infinite possibilities.

As the speech ended, the room erupted with cheers and clapping. In the ballroom the band began to play and the dancing began in earnest. A brisk five-step waltz saw the dancefloor fill and every available man was snapped up, leaving numerous ladies to watch around the perimeter. As Adair obliged a woman wearing an ornate feathered plume in her hair, he considered the grim reality of the war's consumption of men. Ducking around the flapping feather, he noticed the faces of couples spinning past and how most of the men were generally grey or balding. This became starker with the next dance, the polka. Adair was relieved to make his escape from the irritating feather and took his place in the line of men facing the ladies. He watched couple after couple skip down the centre and then return to their places, leaving some of the older men puffing for breath. As the night wore on, Adair felt his own energy begin to flag when the time finally came for his dance with the intriguing widow. She approached waving her dance card and pointed at where his name had been entered as 'Mr Adair' which seemed all the more formal next to the other entries simply ascribed a Christian name.

"Mrs Wadsworth Ritchie," he said, feeling a bit nervous, and took her gloved hand. She gave a tight little smile and then turned her back to him to assume her position with the ladies in a line facing the centre of the room.

"The night would not be complete without the Union Dance," boomed the compère, as Adair found himself close to the back of the widow's slender neck. He looked puzzled until he realised the dance began back-to-back. It was a swift gallop-style dance that left Adair flustered and disappointed at its lack of intimacy. As the music came to an end, he was relieved that she appeared to be taking a break and they moved to the side of the dancefloor.

"I'd have thought you'd have been familiar with that dance, Mr Adair? It was a schottische sequence – isn't your name Scottish?" she said, her bodice still heaving with the exertion. Adair reddened, surprised at her insight, and found himself panting.

"I am, I was, I mean I am Scots Irish but I…"

"Don't go ballroom dancing a lot?" She laughed.

Adair surrendered to her humour and joined in her infectious laughter, shaking his head.

"I'm much better at the waltz. You got a raw deal, as they say in New York City."

"And how do you find New York City?" she asked waving, her fan.

"I find it very, well, very agreeable," Adair replied, rubbing his nose.

"Ha! You can't deceive me…"

Taken aback, Adair opened his mouth to protest and insist on the beauty of the city when he noticed her wink, slow and deliberate, slightly shielded by her outstretched fan. Adair found himself flummoxed and surrendered again.

"Well there are the smells…" he conceded, scrunching up his nose.

"Hideous odours, yes, and the filth, the noise, the thieves and the desperate abject poverty," she rhymed off, drawling out all the horrors of the city.

Adair nodded in agreement.

"So why are you here, Mr Adair?" she said, snapping shut her fan.

"Well, I'm here for business, as Frank said. I'm interested in acquiring some land." He was flustered by her directness but his last words seemed to pique her interest.

"Ahh, land – now that is a worthy business." She began to poke in her bag and produced an ambrotype, which showed a landscape with some farmhands in the foreground. "This is my family home in upstate New York. My parents and grandparents before them farmed huge swathes of the country and built up quite an estate. I hope it will always remain in our family."

When she looked back up her face was shining and her sapphire-blue eyes gleamed. In that moment Adair thought she was the most beautiful creature he had ever clapped eyes on.

"I have some fine estates myself back home," he declared. "I am planning to transform one of them in a very remote part of the north into a hunting estate. It has truly spectacular scenery."

"Magnificent, I'm sure. I've never been to Ireland but I've heard wonderful descriptions of how incredibly green it all is. That's my favourite colour you know. I love Europe, simply adore Paris. I took my boys there straight after the war." She dropped her voice to a flat tone. "Well, when I knew their father wasn't coming home. They have the finest tutors in Paris. I think the boys missed home though."

Cornelia had returned the picture to her bag and took out a cigarette case.

"Care for one?"

Adair had never smoked with a lady before, never mind been offered a cigarette by one.

"Oh do indulge me. One doesn't have so many pleasures these days Mr Adair," she said, leaning forward to light his cigarette. He exhaled, taking care to direct the smoke away from Cornelia even though she was lighting one herself.

"So Paris? Did you not find *that* city offensive? Isn't there filth and poverty there too?"

"Oh Mr Adair you misunderstand me," she said with a

slight cough. "I don't find poverty offensive. Why, it's a very human condition. I guess we are all born with nothing. Some of us just find ourselves in more fortunate circumstances."

Adair laughed.

"Or work hard. My father will leave me his estate but I have more than tripled my assets through land speculation."

Her eyes narrowed and she seemed to study him a while, taking several swift draws of her cigarette.

"Yes, Mr Adair, but the reality is you could not have achieved all that without initially being *born* into fortunate circumstances."

Adair was stunned by this retort.

"John, you can call me John."

"Oh, I thought it was Jack," she said, distracted by one of the ladies who was waving her goodnight. "Well, Mr Adair, I'm not sure what religious denomination you belong to but when I'm in New York I spend a great deal of time at Trinity Church, which does a lot of relief work in the tenements. Given there are so many of your fellow Irishmen living in such squalor here, I'm sure you will be keen to offer some assistance."

Adair gaped at her, his cigarette burning a long cylinder of ash that scattered dust over the polished side table. Somehow, he found himself agreeing.

"Certainly, I'd be happy to make a donation."

"Oh a donation would be splendid but what of your time? Or are you afraid to get your hands dirty?"

There was that laugh again, mischievous and bewitching. He felt hypnotised by her.

"Afraid? Me? Certainly not, I can roll up my sleeves and assist in any way required," he replied, tugging on his bowtie, which seemed to be constricting his neck.

"Good." She beamed. "We need some volunteers to help in the soup kitchen next Thursday."

She rummaged in her bag again and this time pulled out a flyer. Lost for words, Adair took the flyer and stubbed out his cigarette in a carved buffalo bone ashtray that sat majestically on the table. The band began playing the familiar first notes of the national anthem and suddenly the room erupted with the scraping of chairs as seated guests rose to their feet in patriotic unison. Cornelia joined with her fellow Americans in song, placing her hand on her heaving bosom. Adair stood in awkward silence next to her. His mind raced as he considered her invitation. The poor and soup kitchens did not inspire him but to spend more time in Cornelia's company, well, he would relish that. As the band finished the anthem he reached for her hand.

"Mrs Wadsworth Ritchie, it has been a pleasure making your acquaintance. I look forward to seeing you at Trinity Church."

Chapter 28

Adair trotted to his office that week with an extra spring in his step. The streets seemed less dirty, the odours less pungent. He lifted his gaze from the gutter and looked at the skyline around him. The rows of tenements and office blocks had acquired a wonderful uniformity, a neatness, as if they were all in their rightful place. Even the lines of bedraggled clothes and bedding hanging between the tenements seemed to jerk cheerfully in the breeze. Usually he glared in disdain at the sight of other people's washing but that morning he didn't even bark at the scruffy children running past with their hoops.

"Watch out, mister!" they shrieked as the hoop wobbled towards him, but he simply sidestepped it and carried on towards Pine Street. He even managed to smile at the gypsy women selling their posies, although he knew his grin was safely hidden behind his moustache. He suddenly remembered his whiskers and that they probably needed a tidy up. He put his hand to his beard and tugged at it self-consciously. He made a mental note to call in at the barbers at lunchtime.

When he arrived at his block, he scraped the mud off his shoes at the entrance. In the hallway a thick glass door led through to a law firm and beyond it a beautiful mahogany banister and staircase, which led to his office above. Normally he stomped up the stairs but today he ascended lightly on the balls of his feet, so softly that his arrival surprised his clerk who jumped up to greet him.

"Good morning, Mr Adair! Sorry, I was just sorting your post. It will be on your desk in a minute." His voice had a note of panic and his face had reddened as he shuffled through a pile of envelopes.

"I'm in no hurry, Mr McCann, take your time," Adair replied, hanging his hat on the coat-stand. He paused, considered the hat and repositioned it at a slight angle. He went over to his desk, lifted a copy of the newspaper and casually flicked through it.

"Huh, all politics, elections, yawn, yawn. Ah, what's this? Something from Paris." Adair looked up as the red-faced clerk approached his desk with his post. "Tell me, Mr McCann, have you ever been to Paris?"

The clerk looked even more flustered and shook his head.

"I've never been outside New York, sir. I wasn't old enough to enlist so never got outside the state."

Adair looked up from his paper and studied the young man who seemed older than his years.

"You weren't old enough for the Army? I thought by the end they were taking anyone, boys, old men..." He didn't wait for an answer. "Fortunately for you then, Mr McCann. If it wasn't for chance of birth, you could've been cannon fodder."

Mr McCann coughed.

"Indeed, sir, although I would have liked to have served my country."

"You *will* serve your country now by being one of the few young men left to rebuild it. Are you married, Mr McCann?"

The clerk's face went a deeper shade of red.

"N-no sir, but I hope to, sir, one day."

"Well, I'd say you'll have no problem finding a bride thanks to that ghastly war. There seems to be no shortage of women and widows – another fortunate chance of birth for you."

The clerk was silent before quietly admitting, "My mother was widowed in the war."

Adair looked up from his newspaper, suddenly regretting that his good form had led him to converse with his clerk rather than maintain their usual library-like atmosphere.

"Ah, I'm sorry if I was flippant. I didn't realise you'd lost your father."

The clerk shook his head and smiled.

"No sir, he wasn't my father. I never knew my father; he died when I was quite young. My mother remarried when I was a lot older so he was sort of my step-father. He was a good man. It's been a real struggle for her since he was killed."

Adair studied his face, framed by a furrowed brow, and wondered if the tragedies of his short life had made him look older. He also realised that despite being in his employment nearly two years, he knew so little about him. He crossed the office and laid his hand on Mr McCann's shoulder.

"I think it is fortunate you were spared the war so you could look after your mother. That is an honourable thing," said Adair and noticed his clerk's eyes had begun to water. Suddenly the door burst open and another one of his staff appeared, flushed and out of breath.

"Oh, Mr Adair, I am so sorry for my lateness," the man gushed, his eyes bulging so large that Adair thought he detected fear. "There was a terrible accident with a horse and cart on my way in and some ladies were injured and, well, I had to stop and assist them."

Adair raised his hand in a bid to silence him.

"Of course, accidents happen. We've just been having a little chat. Go tidy yourself up and we can then meet about that paperwork."

Adair strode back to his desk and as he turned to sit down on the leather chair, he caught the two clerks exchanging a surprised glance. Mr McCann shrugged his shoulders and bowed his head.

Silence resumed and Adair let his mind wander back to the night of the ball.

The clock ticked slowly all day as Adair anticipated his meeting with Cornelia. He wasn't exactly sure what the soup kitchen involved only that it provided an opportunity to speak again with Mrs Wadsworth Ritchie. After a short stop for a shoeshine he headed to Trinity Episcopal Church, which was just a stone's throw away on Wall Street. He passed it most days of the week but had never looked inside, assuming it would be just like any other church. It was a striking building made of brown stone, in the Gothic Revival style, and with a decent amount of history, at least by American standards. None of that piqued his curiosity so much as knowing Cornelia was a parishioner. He'd also never noticed the queues of people waiting near the gates for the soup kitchen to open. As he walked through the cemetery past the line of scruffy, half-starved-looking creatures, he began to doubt for the first time his purpose in going.

"Doors ain't open yet, mister," said one man leaning on a crutch.

"Ye lost, mister? He don't look like he needs fed," said an elderly woman wrapped in a shawl who pointed and laughed with a group of women.

Adair brushed past them and peered through the plain glass in the door. He thought he could see figures moving in a corridor and tapped the glass. After what seemed like an age, the door opened and a rotund woman in an apron peeked out. She frowned and then gestured for him to come through.

"You must be Mr Adair?"

"Yes, I came to volunteer at Mrs Wadsworth Ritchie's request."

"Indeed, of course, she's in a room along the corridor in a committee meeting."

"Oh good, if you could show me the way?" Adair asked,

looking down the corridor, which was filled with the smell of cooking.

"Ah no, Mr Adair, I'm afraid it's a closed meeting of the Trinity Relief Committee. Just you come with me. We have a lot of vegetables that need peeling. The extra hands are a blessing."

Adair coughed with indignation but before he could protest the woman had escorted him into the small, steamy hall from where the smell was wafting. The room was filled with long wooden tables and benches with earthenware bowls stacked at each end. On the far wall was a stone counter covered in piles of vegetables in various states of preparedness, and three women and a man were stirring bubbling soup in two large iron skillets at the end of the counter.

"You see, we're very short of volunteers at the moment," said the aproned woman. "Thank you for joining us. Mrs Wadsworth Ritchie spoke very highly of you."

"She did?" asked Adair, forgetting his indignation.

"Oh, very highly indeed, sir. Said it did her 'heart good to meet an Irish gentleman willing to help the plight of his own impoverished people'."

Adair tried to imagine her saying this and felt his cheeks flush slightly. He stared at the woman who was wiping her hands on her apron and then handed him a paring knife.

"You can help me prepare the veg. Just peel the carrots lightly mind. I've washed them well and we want to stretch them as far as we can. We had a volunteer once who peeled them away to nothing. My name's Annie by the way."

She introduced the other volunteers who smiled politely and continued stirring the steaming vats.

"So, Annie, why do we need to prepare more veg given the soup looks ready?" asked Adair, puzzled.

The woman chortled.

"Oh, my dear that soup is just for tonight – we are preparing for tomorrow."

Adair eyed the large pots with alarm.

"Goodness, there's enough there to feed an army."

"Oh believe me, we will be. You saw the queue outside before we've even opened the doors. There are so many hungry mouths in Manhattan. They come here with high hopes of a new life from Ireland, Russia, Italy, all over. And yes, there *is* work but it just takes them to have an accident or get sick and they can't work anymore, so how do they feed themselves?"

Adair looked up from his peeling.

"I'm sure many of them are drinkers, that's why they don't work."

Annie frowned.

"Yes, many of them are, but they hit the bottle for lots of reasons – loneliness, homesickness, losing their job, eviction – then it becomes a vicious circle into destitution," she sighed.

Adair scraped harder on the carrot at the mention of the word 'eviction'. It stung every nerve in his body. In his mind's eye flashed the sight of the tumbled cottages over-grown with weeds on his last visit to Glenveagh.

Thankfully, his thoughts were interrupted by a commo-tion near the doors as two of the volunteers had crossed the hall and were organising a queue to enter. Then they began to stream in. Adair found himself staring. They were all manner of folk, men and women, young and old. A lot of very elderly and some on crutches. Many of them looked like they hadn't washed in weeks and at times the stench of dried urine and stale body odour almost overwhelmed the smell of the leek and potato soup. Most of them trooped in silently, their heads bowed. Adair wondered if this was from a sense of shame or reverence for being on church property. A group of women entered whom he recognised from outside, some with distinctive Irish accents. They were directed to lift their bowls and carry them to the volunteers who were pouring generous portions. Adair watched two old men with greasy, long hair and sunken cheeks, expecting them to quickly devour their meal. Instead they sat patiently at the long tables, waiting until everyone was seated, then they bowed their heads as Annie raised her hands and said grace. As soon as she finished, the spoons began to rattle in the bowls and the hall filled with a loud slurping and humming. Adair stared intrigued at the transformation from the gaunt faces that silently entered the hall to the smiling people who chatted and laughed.

"Heart-warming, isn't it?" said Annie who had appeared beside him. He looked down at his hands and realised he'd been peeling the same carrot for the past ten minutes. He blinked a few times.

"Quite a sight," he mumbled and felt moved to add. "You do good work here."

From behind him a familiar voice replied, "I like to think so."

He swung round to see Cornelia dressed a lot more demurely than at the ball but with her long hair swept up in the same ornate style at the back of her pretty head. She held out a white gloved hand to Adair who quickly grasped it with his free hand.

"So you came? And I see Annie here has wasted no time putting you to work." She laughed and her blue eyes sparkled. Adair felt a bit speechless and realised he'd touched her glove with his wet hand.

"Yes, she has." He looked away. "Can't say I've peeled too many carrots in my time. Possibly the last time was at boys' camp at school."

"I'm sure you never forget how to peel a carrot," said Cornelia, smiling and looking around the hall. "You can see how busy we are. A lot of them are Irish as you've probably realised. Both my late husband and father had only high praise for the Irish during the war. They fought valiantly and helped save our Union. We are indebted to your fellow countrymen."

"No doubt, but isn't it true there were many Irish fighting on the other side too?"

"Yes, of course. There are many Irish immigrants, and they've settled all over the US. I guess they signed up to whichever side they were living in when the war broke out."

After a pause, she frowned and confided, "When my dear father was shot at the Battle of the Wilderness it was two Irishmen who tried to help him – one of them happened to be one of his own tenants. Tragically, his tenant was killed and the other man captured by the enemy. I am so grateful to them, for their sacrifice."

Adair frowned. He understood now why she engaged so passionately in this charitable work. She felt as though she was repaying some kind of debt. He found himself even more intrigued and enchanted by her. She was both beautiful and passionate. The babble of sound rose suddenly and above the din a man's voice could be heard mid-ballad.

Farewell dear Erin, fare thee well, that once
was call'd the Isle of Saints,
For here no longer I can dwell, I'm going
to cross the stormy sea.
For to live here I can't endure, there's
nothing but slavery,
My heart's oppress'd, I can find no rest, I
will try the land of liberty.

His voice had a fragile edge that lilted across the room causing those who were still eating to stop and listen. Adair caught Cornelia's smiling face and joined with her in the brief round of applause, which seemed to encourage the singer who got to his feet and began another ballad.

On Irish soil my father dwelt since the time
of Brian Boru,
He paid his rent and lived content,
convenient to Carrockonsure.
The landlord's agent into our cabin went,
and moved my poor father and me,
But we must leave our home far away to
roam in the fields of Americee.

Voices from across the hall rose up in unison for the chorus.

So farewell, I can no longer dwell at home acushla asthore machree
Oh sad is my fate I must emigrate to the shores of Americee.

Adair dropped the peeled carrot and placed the knife on the counter. The lyrics of the last song had left him ruffled and he struggled to be heard over the repeated chorus.

"How was your committee meeting, Mrs Wadsworth Ritchie?" he shouted.

"Oh you must call me Cornelia."

"If you insist, Cornelia," he said, drying his hands on a cloth.

"The meeting went as well as could be expected. Trinity Church does a lot of relief work in the tenements. We are hopeful that the Metropolitan Board of Health will start to make some progress in improving the most stricken parts of the city. But there is always enough work for relief societies as well."

The lament seemed to grow louder, drowning out Cornelia's soft voice. Adair strained to hear her but along with the heat and smell, he felt his head begin to spin.

"I didn't catch that last…" he said, loosening his collar.

"I said perhaps you'd like to join the Committee…"

Suddenly the room went black and Adair felt a rushing sound about his head.

When he opened his eyes minutes later, he was lying on the stone floor staring up into Cornelia's concerned face.

"You're back! That was a dramatic way of getting out of peeling vegetables."

"I'm so sorry, reverend, what have I done…" he muttered, confused.

"Reverend? It's Cornelia. Oh dear, I think you might be concussed."

He closed his eyes and hoped when he opened them again he'd still see her pretty face.

Part III

APRIL 1867

Chapter 29

Declan had forgotten what it was like not to have a feeling of nausea in his stomach. He had been at sea just over two weeks and it didn't agree with him. He comforted himself that he was not in steerage class and scoffed at the fact that he had 'made something' of himself, as he could at least afford a cabin home. But it was a tiny cabin, which he shared with another returning Irishman. Again, he reminded himself how much worse it had been six years ago when he and Michael had been bunked up with a dormitory full of exiles, crawling with lice and coughing a chorus of phlegm all night. His cabin-mate was from a different era of emigrants. Gerard O'Reilly was a twenty-one-year-old carpenter who had travelled to New York after the civil war looking to make his fortune. But he was an impatient man and after a year had decided he would be better off at home.

"Wasn't how I thought it would be, Mr Conaghan," he said, perched on a bench in the cabin, his legs stretched across to the lower bunk where his stockinged feet were resting. "Plenty of carpenters in New York from all over the world. Half of them don't speak English. Just wasn't my cuppa tea, if ye know whatta' mean?"

Declan lay on the top bunk and nodded, his hand gripping his stomach to steady it from the lurching motion of the ship. He listened to the young carpenter gibber away, half-irritated by his constant babble and half-relieved as it took his mind off the journey.

"I take it ye weren't a sailor in the war?" asked Gerard, with a half-mocking tone, picking up a newspaper.

"I'd never have made it," he growled. Declan scratched at his long, dark sideburns and beard that he'd grown until it was quite bushy. It was partly an attempt to hide the long, thin scar that ran down his cheek close to his earlobe but the skinny, white line was still visible.

"So is this ye home for good, Mr Conaghan? Will ye stay and live in Donegal?"

He had one reason for coming home and once done his life would be over, Declan thought. He moved slowly from the bunk, carefully easing himself up with his stump. Despite his obvious disability, he'd stubbornly insisted on sleeping on the top bunk. Declan peered through splashes of water, salt and dirt that dripped down the port-hole window and grunted his reply.

"Hmm, maybe."

Gerard shuffled his toes and returned to his newspaper. Declan reached in his pocket for his watch. It was a fine solid silver one on a chain that he'd found on a rebel soldier's body. He couldn't remember from which battle. Without a word, he left the cabin. It was time for his twice daily stroll of the upper deck. That was another consequence of the Army. He found he couldn't live without order, a routine. He even felt he missed the incessant drills. As the cabin door clicked shut behind him, he heard Gerard mutter, 'Military men', and sigh.

As it was a gusty day Declan struggled to move as easily along the boat. He gulped in the fresh air and felt the splashes of salt carried on the breeze sting his eyes like a shower of needles. The ship's captain, a bullish Dutchman, approached and saluted him.

"Shan't be long 'til ve reach land. Vis zis vind pushing us along, I'd say if you stay on deck, ve should sight Arland," he announced.

Declan nodded and continued to move towards the ship's bow as the wind buffeted his great coat. He grimaced at the respect he commanded as a war veteran, which was in stark contrast to the anonymity and worthlessness he'd felt during service.

He stared out to sea and its distant horizon, which seemed to offer little prospect of dry land. While he longed to get off the ship and stand on stable ground, he feared what lay ahead. Would Ma and Cara want to see him? Would they be angry about him losing Michael? He vividly recalled Cara's tears in the workhouse when she held her twin and prophesied that she'd never see him again. Would she forgive him? And what use was he to them with one hand? He intended to complete his mission as quickly as possible and then he would be out of their lives. He realised he was trembling. It wasn't that cold on deck but he recognised the trembling as the same nerves that took over him as the bugle blasted the start of a battle. He told himself he didn't care ultimately what happened to him. If they rejected him maybe it was what he deserved.

As he pondered these fears, he stared out at the ocean and blinked as an object appeared to grow. At first it was just a dim line then it appeared to widen and lengthen as the ship pulled ever closer. He pulled a handkerchief from his pocket and wiped his watery eyes, but no sooner had he done this than they filled up again. Dozens of passengers had appeared on deck and were pointing and exclaiming at the vision of land.

"We're home!"

"There she is!"

"Ireland, it's Ireland!"

Some of the men took off their hats and waved them wildly in the air as if imagining someone could see them from the distant island. Declan screwed up his face and squinted at the land mass, which as they came closer, broke into pieces of rock and jutting headlands. He tried to recall the shape of the Donegal coastline and pondered if he was staring at Fanad or Malin Head. Places the men used to fish from before they'd sold their nets to buy oats and milk during the hunger years. He shuddered at the sight of the jagged rock looming in the distance and questioned for the millionth time why he had returned. Beyond the rugged coastline, he was startled by the bright green meadows that undulated as far as the eye could see. It looked like fertile countryside, which offered some reassurance that he wouldn't starve in this land again.

The passengers stood pointing and talking excitedly on deck for at least another hour before the ship entered the mouth of the channel to dock in Derry. The ship was now moving at what seemed like a snail's pace on the calm waters. But there was anything but calm on deck as the crew rushed about, hauling ropes and other equipment, dodging the excited passengers who flitted from side to side pointing sights out to each other. The chatter was finally silenced momentarily by the boom of the ship's horn declaring they had docked.

Declan was one of the first to disembark. He grabbed his canvas knapsack, which contained all his worldly possessions, and placed the leather strap across his shoulder. The bag was stencilled with the name 'the 104th New York' but he turned this inward against his coat to avoid drawing attention to himself. He stepped gingerly on to the pier and was immediately lost in the throng of greeting relatives, hawkers and other passengers.

As he shuffled through the jostling people, he felt he had stepped back in time. It was the same cobbled pier that he had left from but there was a shabby, worn appearance to the place. Looming in the distance his view was dominated by the great granite walls that completely surrounded the hill-top city, their battlements as rigid as the days of the famous siege nearly 200 years ago. He stopped for a few minutes to admire the structure, which he had a deeper appreciation for since his own battle experience and the many hastily constructed breastworks his brigade had built.

He looked back to the docks where they'd spent that last night in Ireland searching in vain for Sinead. The heart-stopping moment when that woman stepped out of the shadows on the pier. Was that really her? They'd probably never know. Derry had certainly changed, he thought. He noticed the old wooden bridge that crossed the River Foyle had been replaced by a new two-tier structure, with the lower deck a railway line.

He nodded at a woman with a familiar-looking face who was fiercely brushing the steps of a Georgian terrace house in Shipquay Street. She stared hard at him but carried on with her chores. He had planned to make his way to Gartan immediately and find his family but he decided he needed some more time and courage. It began to pour, great sheets of driving rain, which provided the excuse he sought to delay his journey. He dived into a pub and shook the water off his coat like a dog. He hadn't walked very far from the docks but his legs still felt wobbly from the long voyage. He fell into a snug near an empty grate and tried to adjust his eyes to the dark interior. There were a few sailors on stools at the bar and a couple of old men smoking pipes in a far corner. The barman excused himself from conversation with the sailors and strode over to Declan.

"Just off the boat, sir?" he asked.

"I am."

"Ah, American?" The barman nodded.

"Naw, am from Donegal actually. Just lived some time in the States. Could I get a whiskey please?"

The barman pulled a bottle from the deep pocket of his long coat and lifted a glass from a shelf behind his customer.

He slapped the glass on the table and poured a measure from a great height without spilling a drop.

"Great service!" Declan smiled.

"Aw thanks. The name's Joe," the barman replied. "So yer a Donegal man. Home for good? We've had plenty of exiles return in recent years. Seems that war ended the fairy-tale of the New World, eh! We got plenty of everything here these days – jobs, food, women … ye name it! I take boarders if ye need to stay a night or two."

Declan knocked back the whiskey then nudged his glass to be filled again. He was beginning to relax. This was how he remembered home, falling into conversation with complete strangers.

An hour or two passed and after four pints of stout Declan began to feel drowsy.

"Ye said ye have some rooms?" he asked as the barman passed his table. "I might need to rest the night."

Joe nodded with a grin and poured him another whiskey. Suddenly the doors swung open and three cackling women in garish dresses burst into the dark saloon. The sailors looked up from the bar as the women made a beeline for them.

"Afternoon, gents," said the fattest woman, her short elasticated sleeves revealing rolls of dimpled flesh. "Who's gonna buy a lady a drink?"

One of the sailors placed an arm about her waist and signalled to the barman who had barely given them a second glance. A second woman began to stroke her fingers playfully on another sailor's collar. Declan realised the smallest of the three was staring over at him. She had dark brown hair, which fell down her back and covered the excessive frills and bows of her deep green dress. Declan noticed she wore blusher on her cheeks and deep red lipstick like the women he and the fellas had met when off-duty in the seedier districts of Washington and Philadelphia. They look the same the world over, he thought. Suddenly he found himself staring at her voluptuous bosom as she'd scurried from the bar and was leaning across his table.

"Just off the ship from America, mister?" she spoke, imitating an American drawl.

Declan smiled into her pretty face, his vision a bit blurry from the drink, and tried to imagine her without the pink streaks that made her seem clown-like.

"I am indeed and just finding my land legs," he quipped and slapped his hand in an inviting gesture on the top of his thigh. He was feeling more mellow than he'd felt in a month. In a flash, the young woman was perched on his knee and stretched her arm around his neck where she began caressing his hairline. He watched the top of her breasts move slowly up and down and then lifted his eyes to her face. She wasn't looking at him but signalled to the barman. This time he came across with a pint of stout.

"See, we've got the best girls in the world," Joe said, setting the pint in front of him. "No need to go to America – am I right, Mary?"

She squeezed Declan's shoulders tighter to her small frame.

"Mary? Is that yer name?" Declan took a sip of his pint and placed his good hand on her knee.

"Might be," she teased. "I usually charge men who want to know my name…"

"Is that so? Well since I got yer name for free, what can I pay ye for?"

He slid his hand under her dress and was startled to discover the warm flesh of her leg. Most of the women he'd paid for in the States wore stockings and bloomers under their dresses. But the sudden softness of her skin on the rough palm of his hand sent his blood racing. He could feel himself swell in his pants. He took another gulp of his stout. She began to nuzzle her face into his neck and reached for his other hand, which he'd kept firmly in his pocket.

"Hope that hand's not up to mischief in there … oh!" She suddenly jumped from his knee, sending the table and Declan's pint flying to the stone floor.

The sailors and women at the bar stopped chatting and turned to stare at the racket. Declan raised his stump to his sweating forehead and standing tall saluted his new audience.

"Victory to the Union Army of the United States of America. At ease, everyone!" He clicked his heels together for effect.

There was silence as they all stared at the black-clothed stump. Then the sailors at the bar began to clap and were joined by the old men in the corner. The woman in the green dress recovered herself and helped Joe put the table upright again. He whispered something to her and slipped a key into her hand. Declan sat down again, like a man both bemused and bored of the reaction.

"I'm sorry 'bout that mister," she said softly in his ear and planted a tender kiss on his scarred cheek. He shrugged his shoulders as if unbothered by the commotion. For the first time Declan registered a familiar tone to her voice as she had stopped mocking his American accent. He wondered if she was from Donegal.

"I'd like to make it up to ye if I can." She slipped her hand into his good hand and slowly led him through the bar to a door at the back. They climbed a steep set of stairs and arrived in a narrow corridor with several doors on the street side. Stopping at one door, the young woman placed the key in the lock and they entered a small room with a sloping ceiling that almost touched one end of the iron bed that filled the room.

"Here we are," she said as she took his bag and set it behind the closed door. Declan puzzled again at her voice but he dismissed his curiosity and suddenly dropped his passiveness in the privacy of the room. He took her in both his arms and pulled her close. His face filled hers and his lips and tongue sucked on her mouth. Almost immediately he could taste the thick, wax lipstick and drew back repulsed. The red lipstick had become smudged into a circle around her open mouth as she gasped for breath. Declan looked around the room and spied an earthenware bowl and jug of water.

"Just a minute." He moved her gently aside. He opened his knapsack and produced a cloth, which he dipped in the cold water.

"What ye at?" she said, the pink stains on her face making her appearance even more clown-like. He took her wrist and with the cloth gently wiped her face until the red smear and the blusher were gone and he could see faint freckles emerge on her cheekbones.

"Gee, for a soldier and someone whose been on a ship all these weeks yer in no hurry," she said, staring at him.

"That's better," he said and then used the cloth to wipe his own face clean of the ghastly lipstick. "I can see ye better now."

Mary stepped closer to him and began to unbutton his trousers.

"Well, let's see ye," she said, grinning slyly.

They were soon lying naked in the damp little room with just the thin blanket covering them. Declan forgot his worries and wore himself out until he fell into a deep sleep. He woke up as dawn was breaking through the threadbare curtains to the smell of cigarette smoke and a throbbing headache. Mary was sitting up in the bed with her shawl covering her thin shoulders and a cigarette between her fingers. Declan watched her smoke through sleepy eyes. She drew deeply on the cigarette and let the smoke slowly filter from her nostrils and a tiny gap in her pale pursed lips. She'd put her underwear back on as if preparing to leave and tucked the blanket tight to her midriff.

"Ye awake, soldier?" she said, her face cracking into a smile as she caught him looking at her. Refreshed from his sleep and now sober, it dawned on him that she really did have a Donegal accent. He bolted upright in the bed causing the squeaky frame to rattle and the floor to creak.

"Where are ye from?" he asked, peering closely at her.

"Am from Derry," she said, the smoke curling from her pouted lips that seemed more familiar in the dawn light.

"Yeah, but originally? You're from Donegal, aren't ye?"

"Good guess for someone who's been away so long. I'm from a wee place called Gartan in the Derryveagh hills."

Declan gasped and let out a long, low cry, which startled the woman. He grabbed her wrist causing the ash from her cigarette to fall on the floor.

"M-Mary," he stuttered. "That isn't yer real name?"

"No, my real name's Queen Victoria – I've nothin' to hide." She shrugged, pulling away from him. "Oldest profession in the world, as my da would've said. I won't bother ye with my tale of woe." She sighed and then continued in a defensive tone. "I ended up on the game ye know. We were evicted some years ago. Hadn't done nothin' wrong. Bastard landlord put us out one cold spring. It was either this or the workhouse. What's the matter? Ye look like you've seen a ghost."

"Sinead? Sinead Dermott? Don't ye remember me? I'm Declan Conaghan – M-Michael's brother."

Her jaw dropped and she stared at him for what seemed like an age. There was a stillness in the little attic that was filled with the sobering morning gloom. Declan shivered and grabbed his shirt from the iron headboard. The sound of a ship's horn blasted in the distance, making her jump. She stubbed out her cigarette and stretched out her arm to touch him.

"Declan, it *is* you? I didn't recognise ye at all," she said, shaking her head, a bewildered look in her eyes.

"Perhaps I should shave?" He smiled, rubbing his face.

"Yes, there's the beard … but ye look so different, bigger and older… Ye and Michael were just boys when I last…" She shook her head, still staring at him as he buttoned his shirt.

She began to laugh, that infectious laugh he remembered Michael so easily triggered by pulling a face or telling her a funny story. It rang in his ears and suddenly he could see them sitting all those years ago in their cabin in Gartan, eating together and telling stories.

"Michael mentioned ye had an uncle in America and that you'd thought of going out there. So ye went in the end. D-did Michael go with ye?" she asked and he noticed she was trembling.

Declan stopped dressing and sat down on the bed beside her, pulling her shawl across her shoulders.

"After Adair evicted us, we all ended up in Letterkenny Workhouse – me, Ma, Michael and Cara," he said, bowing his head. "My uncle sent us money for our passage to the States. The civil war had just started when we arrived, so we joined my uncle's brigade. I thought our biggest battle was against Adair, but I was wrong."

Sinead smiled and seemed to have a faraway look in her eyes.

"I bet Michael was a great soldier, he would have loved that," she said. "Sooo … did he meet someone over there? Is that why ye came back on yer own?"

Declan took a deep breath, shook his head and tapped his stump with his good hand.

"I didn't just lose my hand in the war, Sinead." He

paused. "I'm sorry but Michael … I'm afraid he's never coming home."

Birds began to twitter on the eaves outside and the sound of hooves began to fill the street below, but in the tiny attic room on Shipquay Street there was a deathly silence. Sinead stared at him aghast.

"Never?"

Declan looked down at his feet.

"He was killed in battle. I should never have…"

"I can't believe…" Sinead shook her head.

In a vain attempt to change the subject he remembered Francis.

"We heard about yer da. Poor Francis, I'm sorry for yer loss."

"Don't be," she snapped, looking away.

"What?"

"Don't be sorry about *him*." Her voice had taken on a hard edge. "What sort of da lets his daughter become a whore – aye, just to keep him in money for booze. I should never have gone with him to Derry. I'd have been better in the workhouse with yer family." She began to sob. "I might have said goodbye properly to Michael."

She sunk down on the pillow where she curled into the foetal position. She turned her face away from Declan's and he heard her whisper, "My Michael."

Declan touched her bare shoulder peeping above the blanket and stood.

"Ye know he looked for ye in Derry, the night before we boarded the ship? He … he loved ye."

She began to sob, quietly at first, then deep mournful cries that shook her whole body.

"I loved him too. So it *was* ye that night at the docks. I thought it was but I-I was too ashamed … I didn't want Michael to see me like that." She hugged her arms tighter around her knees where she lay on her side.

"There was a man with ye."

"That was Joe."

"Joe?"

She sat up and rubbed her tear-stained face.

"The barman downstairs. Well, back then he didn't have a bar. He looked after a lot of girls, like me. Then when he got a bit of money together, he took over this place. Paid Da with drink too so he didn't complain."

She bowed her head and her beautiful long hair that he had lusted after last night spilled over her shoulders. At that moment he didn't have feelings of lust but wanted to scoop her into his arms and take care of her.

"Ye don't have to lead this life, Sinead," he whispered. "I'm going back to Gartan, why don't ye come with me?"

"And do what? Anyway Joe wouldn't let me go, I owe him a lot of money."

There was an awkward silence. The room had gone cold and Declan's head throbbed. What was he thinking? He was back for one reason and it didn't involve women.

"Just go!" she said matter-of-factly. "Joe said that was on the house."

Declan stared for a while at the back of her head. Then he splashed some cold water from the bowl about his face, lifted his knapsack and closed the door gently behind him.

Chapter 30

He hitched a ride on the back of a cart from Derry to Letterkenny and walked the rest of the way towards the Derryveagh range. In the distance he could see the spire at Church Hill and suddenly his stomach churned with fears of how Ma and Cara would react to him. It was a beautiful, sunny afternoon and the golden yellow gorse along the hedgerows seemed to light up his path home. Home. He couldn't believe he was really back. The many dark hours he'd spent lying face-down in muddy ditches and woods with bullets flying overhead, thinking he'd never get out of this alive. Home, for all its hardships and history, was far from the hell of the battlefield and yet it was because of home he'd ended up there. He had to pinch himself to believe the familiar sights were really there again in front of his eyes. The sun shining on the green hillside and the swooping swallows celebrating summer and their freedom. He strolled through Church Hill down to the valley where the rectory was nestled beside Lough Gartan. There were very few people about but the village itself hadn't changed. The police station, St Columba's Church and Donnelly's Inn. He was tempted to make a diversion for a drink but the events of last night made him reconsider. Besides, he wanted to be completely sober for greeting Ma and Cara. He really had no idea how they would react to his arrival out of the blue. Horror, when they saw his arm. Grief, that he was alone. He steeled himself for all eventualities. Hadn't he rehearsed every possible scenario when he made the decision to come home?

He stood staring for some minutes at the glistening black door of the rectory with its lion-faced brass knocker. It was the middle of the afternoon and chances were that Cara was working and might answer the door. He swallowed hard and slowly banged the knocker. Within seconds the reverend's wife appeared. She stared at him.

"Can I help you?" There was a note of hesitancy in her voice.

Declan cleared his throat.

"Good afternoon, ma'am, I'm looking for my sister, Cara Conaghan, I believe she is on yer staff?"

The woman peered even closer at him.

"Mr Conaghan, I see. Could you wait here a moment please?"

She disappeared behind the black door, which she closed tight, and Declan felt his heart sink.

A few moments later he heard heavy footsteps coming closer and loud whispering.

"There's something peculiar about him. He's wearing this great coat, the like I haven't seen in these parts. I'm concerned the way he has his arm … stuffed in his pocket as if he's hiding something. And then there's the accent…"

The door swung open and the Reverend Maturin stood filling the doorframe.

"Ahh, it's the American soldier!" He beamed. "Welcome, welcome, you must have had a very long journey."

His wife stared wide-eyed over his shoulder.

"It's Declan Conaghan, sir, Cara's oldest brother. I've come to see her if I may?" he stammered.

"Of course, of course. You've been apart a very long time; since the workhouse, I imagine." He turned to his wife. "Please dear could you fetch Cara and dismiss her from duties for the day?"

She nodded and disappeared into the dark hallway. Declan stood swaying slightly on the doorstep from fatigue and the heat of the day.

"They were dark days, terrible times those evictions. Not many have come back. I'm surprised you have, Mr Conaghan."

"Surprised myself to be honest, reverend, sir, but I guess blood is thicker than water, even the Atlantic Ocean."

"Ha!" laughed the minister.

Then she appeared. A female version of Michael with her dark hair and bright blue eyes. Her face was pale and quivering and he noticed she was clenching and unclenching her fists – the way Michael did.

"Cara, I – it's me, Declan."

Suddenly her arms were around his neck, her wet face buried in his coat. He held her tightly, taking care not to touch her body with the stump of his arm. They stood like that for a long time. He could hear her mumbling faint sounds into his sleeve but couldn't decipher them. A painful lump formed in his throat. He had not known such affection in all his adult life and her warmth seemed to filter through him, filling every capillary and nerve ending.

"Shall we go find Ma?" he said, gently coaxing her out from his thick coat. Her tear-stained face peered up at him and she nodded, smiling. They had both forgotten about the minister and his wife who stood, astonished and delighted by the reunion.

"We'll see you in the morning then, Cara," said Mrs Maturin.

"Yes, of course, thank you, thank you both."

Declan also thanked the couple and they walked along the gravel path towards the servants' cottages at the back of the rectory. When they were out of earshot of the minister, Cara stopped and stared at him.

"My God, Declan. I can't believe it's *you*!"

She touched his beard and then caught sight of his stump. Declan became flustered.

"The rest of me is still here."

"Oh, I'm sorry. I didn't mean to stare. I just can't believe it. Ye should have written, told us ye were coming."

Declan nodded, afraid to tell her that he had struggled with the decision to come home at all. She smiled.

"I'm sure yer exhausted. We have so much to talk about." She squeezed his good arm. He walked with her, finding a fresh source of energy from her beaming face and warm reception as they approached the little stone cottage tucked off the road.

Cara led him around to the back entrance where Ma was churning butter in the kitchen.

"Is that ye, Cara? I didn't realise it was so late in the day."

"No, Ma. I left early. We have a visitor who I think you'll be pleased to see..."

Declan smoothed his hair and peered through the doorway where he saw the back of an old woman wearing a headscarf.

"It's me, Ma, d' ye remember me?"

She stopped swinging the urn and turned around, rubbing her hands clean on her apron. There was a moment's silence except for the scratching of hens in the yard before Mairead ran to Declan, burying her face in his chest.

"Ye came home, ye came home! Declan, my son."

He felt her thin frame heave with deep sobs as he held her closely. The tears streamed down all their faces and as Mairead gathered herself, Cara kneeled before Declan and gently removed his boots stained with sea-salt and earth. He stared at her in disbelief but allowed her to remove them, leaning back against the rough stone wall of the cottage. He noticed she glanced at his left arm and her hands began to tremble. He wondered if she was concerned his boots might reveal some other ghastly injury but she carried on, loosening the battered leather and then easing his feet out on to the cold, kitchen floor. She removed his worn socks and Declan felt his hot feet sting against the coolness of the stone. He wriggled his toes and sighed in relief.

"You've come a long way," said Ma, not taking her eyes

off him. Every few minutes she reached across and stroked his cheek with her rough fingers.

"Aye, 'twas far. The journey on the ship was the worst part, made me very sick. I stayed a night in Derry and then jumped on a cart to Letterkenny. I walked from there."

"We could have met ye at the docks in Derry, if we'd known…"

"I know. I'm sorry I didn't write and tell ye I was comin'…" Declan dropped his head and rubbed it with his good hand. "I'm sorry for a lot of things…"

Cara and Ma looked at each other and then at the sad figure hunched in front of them. They both rushed to comfort him and the three of them huddled together and wept. When it began to grow dark, they built a turf fire and made some supper of fried bread, bacon and cabbage. Declan filled his lungs with the smells and smiled, causing the scar to crease on his cheek.

"This smells of home. I missed the old turf fires."

"I'm sure there are lots of things you've missed. How could ye stay away so long? And just that one letter after the war about Michael … we began to think we'd lost ye too," said Ma, sitting opposite him her arms now folded.

"Ma!"

"It's alright, Cara. I'm sure you've lots of questions, I've many too."

"Well, yer not going anywhere in a hurry, are ye?"

"If it's alright with ye, Ma, I'd like to stay, at least until I sort myself out," he said, his eyes darting to each of them.

"Of course!" said Cara. "It's more than alright. Yer

family and we stick… Ye can stay as long as ye please." She touched his shoulder.

"Does it hurt – yer hand?" she asked, nodding at the black-clothed stump.

Declan hesitated. He was about to give his usual sarcastic reply along the lines of not having a hand to be sore.

"I've got used to it. Hurt like hell when I woke in the prison hospital but the morphine and whiskey helped." He shook his arm as if his hand might miraculously reappear from his sleeve. "To be honest my wound seemed small compared to a lot of the other soldiers – some had both legs amputated or their whole arm blown off – and it's my left hand so it could have been worse."

"Or ye could have lost yer life, like Michael," said Ma.

Declan noticed her hands trembling.

"How did he die, Declan? Did he suffer?" she asked in almost a whisper.

"Ma, don't do this now. I'm sure Declan's tired." Cara took Ma's hand gently, but she persisted.

"It's just ye didn't say much in yer letter, just-just that he'd been, what were those words? Cara had to check it with Father O'Flanigan…"

"Fatally wounded," said Declan, clearing his throat as he recalled how long he had spent writing and rewriting that letter.

"That's right – how exactly did he die? Were ye with him?"

"Yes, Ma. Me and Liam were with him at the end. He

was shot in the neck so it was quick. He died in my arms in the Battle of the Wilderness."

Ma and Cara stared at him transfixed.

"The Battle of the Wilderness," Ma echoed him. "Why would ye fight for a wilderness? I don't understand."

"No, Ma, that's just the name of the place. There were so many battles in so many places. They just got named after the place. Like Bull Run or Gettysburg?"

They both looked at him blankly. He could only guess their thoughts but hoped to reassure them. He went on to describe how brave a soldier Michael had been, his acts of kindness even to enemy soldiers.

"I watched him empty his own canteen of water over a rebel soldier whose clothes had caught fire in the fighting."

"Michael was always kind," said Ma, rocking back and forth. "For that act alone I'm sure he's in heaven."

"'Course Ma and I'd say he watched over me the rest of the war. Don't know how else I survived it."

"And he brought ye home safely to us," Cara added with a beam.

"And we mustn't forget Liam. He didn't make it either…" Ma's voice tailed off.

Declan frowned. A weariness had descended on him.

"No Ma, he didn't make it. I'm afraid I don't know what happened to him. We were ambushed, I threw a grenade and then everything went dark. He was counted as missing, presumed dead."

The fire crackled in the grate but otherwise the room was silent, their thoughts occupied with the horrors of the war. Declan got up from his seat and peered out the window at Lough Gartan in the distance. It was a still night with a full moon that bathed the valley in a silver light.

"This is a great cottage – some improvement on the old one," he said, thinking he should change the subject from the war.

Ma grunted and began poking the fire.

"Yes, it is," Cara said. "Though it's only mine while I work for the reverend, sort of on a lease to me. Ma misses our old cabin. I guess it was our home for so many years—"

"Until that savage destroyed it, destroyed everything," snapped Ma. She poked more vigorously at the fire and began to sob.

"Ma, settle yourself. We're alright now."

Cara took the poker from her and coaxed her to sit again, but she started pacing the floor.

"If it wasn't for Adair, ye and Michael wouldn't have left for that stupid war!"

"Ma!" cried Cara.

Declan's face froze. He didn't flinch a muscle but stared out the window.

"The Great Hunger didn't ruin this place quite like that bastard did," Ma continued, her chest heaving. "Tis a disgrace what happened here. We did nobody any harm. Always paid our rent and then he threw us out of our homes like dogs on the street. The shame of it, ending up in yon workhouse. But we were the lucky ones. Aye, some ended their days there. God bless 'em. When Alex Bradley ended up in the asylum it broke Briege's heart. You know she died in the bed next to me in the workhouse? Ol' man Doherty, he didn't last long either. Then ye heard about Francis Dermott?"

Declan nodded but she carried on.

"He took to begging on the streets for a bottle and was run over by a cart, probably drunk. Poor Sinead." Declan reddened and turned to Cara whose eyes were filled with tears.

"Have … have ye seen Sinead?" he asked Cara. "Michael always talked about her. He wanted to pay for her passage to the States after the war and he would've done if, ye know…"

Cara pursed her lips.

"No, I haven't seen nor heard of her all these years but no doubt she'll have some other sweetheart now. She's probably forgotten all about Michael."

"I'll never forget my son, bless his soul," said Ma, still pacing the floor.

"Aye Ma, none of us will forget him, he gave his life for a great country," Declan replied. "At least he was on the winning side of the war."

"What did he win? What did *you* win?"

Declan realised she was staring at his stump, and he glanced down at the floor.

"Yer right, Ma. Adair should be made to pay for what he did. I saw for myself walking here today how empty the hillside is – dozens and dozens of empty cottages. Families, friends just uprooted overnight."

Ma stomped over to the window and pointed out across the lough.

"Ye know why he evicted us? His staff said we were

spoiling his view. His view! Ye couldn't even see us from Glenveagh Lodge. All he cares about are his sheep and creating his fancy notion of a grand estate. Tell 'im about the castle, Cara!"

Declan's eyes narrowed as he absorbed her anger.

"What castle?"

"Ma, please don't be getting yourself worked up," said Cara, settling her mother back beside the fire. "Remember yer supposed to be taking things easy."

"Tell 'im!"

Cara sighed.

"He's building a castle at Glenveagh. Right on the lough. The foundations were dug a few years ago. It's got turrets and everything."

For several seconds Declan stared at her, stunned.

"A castle," he said, stroking his scarred cheek. "Well I look forward to seeing this, this, King John…"

"Oh, you'll not see him, he's never here. That's one blessing. He spends a lot of his time in the States. He only really comes back in the warmer months."

"He's due a visit then," said Declan as he took the hot poker from her and jabbed it deep into the flames. Ma reached for her rosary beads.

"Aw, try not to mind him, I pray every day not to let him blacken my heart. And isn't this a great day? You've returned, my first-born."

She reached up to hug him and he felt a pang of guilt for staying away so long.

"I'm tired, think I'll go to bed," said Ma. "Isn't it great

we've two rooms now – so you'll not be disturbing me if ye want to sit up."

Cara smiled. "Aye, we'll sit up, just 'til the fire goes out, and Declan can sleep in here."

"I've slept in rougher places and out under the stars so this is luxury." He laughed.

Ma shuffled out of the room, stopping to stare at Declan's face. She brushed his cheek with her hand as if he might disappear again and then left them alone. Cara remembered they had some porter and suggested they have a jar each.

"It's not every day yer brother returns home – and from a bloody war! Sláinte," she said, holding out her jar to him.

"Sláinte! And to the brother that didn't return."

"To Michael, God rest him."

Cara's smile faded. Declan took a slug and stared at her.

"To John Adair, may the devil catch him and avenge Michael and all the evicted."

Cara's eyes widened but Declan was pleased to see she raised her jar again to his toast.

News quickly spread of Declan's return and for days after his arrival there was a stream of well-wishers calling at the Conaghans' cabin. Declan heard all sorts of rumours as the story of his war wound got passed from neighbour to neighbour – as far-fetched as he'd lost a leg – and some came just to stare at the stump where his hand had once been. Being a spectacle didn't irk him as much as he thought it would though. He was just pleased to see the community hadn't been completely wiped out by the evictions as he'd feared. He sat in Ma's rocking chair like a man on his throne as well-wishers came to pay their respects. While visitors kept Declan occupied, Ma and Cara busied themselves preparing a feast to celebrate his return. The atmosphere in the village was akin to Christmas but as Ma told the priest in confession, "it's like we've been reborn".

To Declan's surprise, Father O'Flanigan came to see him a few days after he arrived home. He wondered if he was simply curious to see a ghost returned. Ma hustled him into the tiny room, clearly so delighted with their guest that Declan decided not to walk out. The tall figure in black stooped as he entered the doorway and then proclaimed with an overloud confidence, "Declan, my son!"

He was met with a frosty silence, which Ma filled by clucking around the priest, making sure he had a comfortable seat next to the hearth.

"Well, I'll leave you two alone," she said and turned to Declan. "Father O'Flanigan always remembered you in his prayers."

Declan responded with a stony smile. He stayed seated, allowing the priest to bless him as he sat in his chair. He bowed his head and remembered all the battles they'd fought where the chaplain would ride on horseback along the frontline, giving them absolution for the mass murder they were about to commit. For Liam, it was important to be clutching a set of rosary beads together with his bayonet when they charged. He looked up startled as he felt droplets on his head. Father O'Flanigan had sprinkled him with holy water from a little glass bottle and was whispering a prayer. His hair had receded a bit but generally he looked the same. Declan thought there was something about priests that they looked either old or ageless.

"It was a brave thing for you to come home," said the priest after he finished his prayer. "I'm sure you were worried about the sort of reception you'd get, but you can see we are overjoyed you came back."

"Overjoyed, are you, father? I am humbled at their forgiveness for my returning without Michael."

"But you cannot blame yourself for his death. You might as well blame me for encouraging you to go." The priest hung his head.

"Well, maybe I do." The words tumbled from Declan's mouth. "Why did you insist we go? Why didn't you leave us in the workhouse? Michael might still be with us."

Father O'Flanigan looked up, shocked. After a minute the priest cleared his throat. "I understand your anger and who knows, Michael might still have been alive today or, as I feared, both of you could have caught fever in that workhouse and died. I thought sending you away was for the best."

"Best for who?"

The priest began to wring his hands but ignored the question.

"I had no idea how brutal that civil war would be."

"Should I blame God then?"

"It was men who went to war; men are responsible for their actions." Father O'Flanigan frowned.

"Yes, grown men *are* responsible for their actions, aren't

they, father?" growled Declan.

The priest shifted uncomfortably in his seat but continued as if he was mid-sermon.

"I can't imagine what you've been through, Declan, especially losing your only brother. It's understandable that your faith could be shaken."

"Shaken is putting it mildly…"

"You survived, Declan, does that not renew your faith? Your mother is fortunate that one of you returned at least. War has little mercy."

"Like God and John Adair – they both have little mercy," said Declan through gritted teeth. "Should I blame Adair for all this?"

The priest stared hard at him but gave no answer.

"I hear Adair is building a castle." Declan's growl grew louder.

"'Tis easier for a camel to pass through the eye of a needle than for a rich man to enter into the kingdom of heaven…"

"D'ye think he cares about the kingdom of heaven when he has his kingdom and castle on this earth? Lording over us all and destroying the homes and livelihoods of good people." Declan slammed his fist on the hearth, causing the priest to jump.

"We have lived through cruel times," he offered, in an attempt to pacify him. "You have clearly been to hell. Tell me son, do you sleep at night?"

Declan hesitated, not expecting the question.

"For a long time no, I didn't. But I sleep better now."

"Good."

"But every night I see Michael dying in my arms, struggling for his last breath."

Father O'Flanigan looked mournful and muttered another prayer. After a while he stood and patted Declan's shoulder.

"I know war can change people but I'm-I'm glad you've come back to us."

Declan gave a half-hearted nod but his eyes failed to meet the priest's.

Chapter 31

The merry-making began in earnest on the Saturday evening as the tenants and small farmers of Gartan and Church Hill gathered for the welcoming party. The festivities were to take place in the Sweeneys' barn, which had been decorated with wildflowers, and they even managed to find a star-spangled banner to drape from the rafters. The women had provided a magnificent spread of barmbrack, cakes and oat-tatties, though not as good, Declan thought as Briege Bradley's fare. Still, they helped fuel the céilí-dancing until the early hours. There were faces Declan had hoped to see but he learned that many of them had emigrated or moved to other counties. The barn was not bursting at the seams as he recalled during Harvest Home celebrations. Ruairi Bradley had acquired a new fiddle and took the place of his absent father, with a friend accompanying him on the bodhrán. The women skipped around the room, through each other's arched arms, then grabbing the waists of the moving line of dancers. He noticed Cara seemed to have as much energy as he remembered she had as a young girl and Ma was tapping her thigh to the beat of the drum next to the Widow McAward. To think she survived the workhouse and there was Michael, gone. He looked back to the dancefloor and recognised one of the young girls. Was that wee Bridgeen, now a teenager? He remembered her tears the night of the evictions and Michael giving her the doll he found. She was laughing as she danced, which made him smile.

The Sweeney brothers sauntered over to him and Sean produced a bottle of poteen. Despite their years of friendship, they had sat eyeing each other like complete strangers for the early part of the evening.

"I bet ye missed this stuff," said Sean, filling several beakers on the table. "Nothing quite like Sweeney's Surprise!"

His brother Owen laughed and clinked his cup against Declan's.

"Ye've been gone a long time. Never thought I'd clap eyes on ye again."

Declan grinned and tasted the bitter warm liquid as it slithered down his throat. He gasped and the group of men around the table laughed.

"Jeeze, can't say I missed this stuff at all Sean," said Declan, his throat on fire.

"So what do they drink in America – *coffee*?" replied Sean, mocking the accent while wiping his mouth with the back of his large hand. The brothers roared with laughter.

"The Germans brew some amazing wheat beers, as do the Dutch and the Danes. But the Poles and the Russians make yer poteen taste like piss." On his last word Declan turned and spat his second mouthful onto the ground.

Sean stared at Declan's feet where the trail of liquid was soaking into the sawdust and Owen then came to defend his brother's pride. "No one's forcing ye to drink it."

"It's alright," interrupted Sean, raising his hand to silence his brother and then pronounced to his stunned audience, "It *is* piss!"

He laughed his familiar loud laugh that made his belly shake, the cue for the rest to join in. They slapped and thumped Sean and Declan on the back. A freckle-faced girl approached the group and grabbed Owen's hand leading him to join the frenetic dancing at the other end of the barn. Some of the other men drifted away to join wives and children, leaving Sean and Declan glaring over the rim of their beakers.

"Something botherin' ye, Declan?"

"Ye know I haven't set eyes on ye since before we were evicted."

"Aye, they were dark days – you've come through them now. It's been quiet for some time."

"Sure anywhere would be quiet if the place was emptied."

Sean's face reddened.

"True, and Black Adair vanished too. Went to America. We hoped he wouldn't come back but he's built a castle. Did you hear about that? Flamin' turrets an' all, next he'll be hoisting a flag up over people's graves." Sean spat in the sawdust.

"Is that why ye boys didn't deal with Adair, 'cos he wasn't around?" asked Declan, his eyes narrowing.

"Whatcha mean? Murder 'im?"

"Yeah murder the bastard, like ye did Murray."

Sean wiped his mouth again so Declan couldn't tell his expression. He could just see his eyes, which didn't blink.

"Don't deny it, Sean. After all this time, it was yer fault we were all evicted."

The violin stopped but the bodhrán continued to beat out a rhythm like a countdown to something dramatic. Sean put down his beaker and turned full-square to Declan.

"Told ye before, Declan. It wasn't us. It had to have been his mate, Rankin. Funny how he vanished back to Scotland not long after the funeral. Anyway, he got what he deserved. So, what exactly happened to Michael?"

Declan's foot stopped tapping.

"I said, what happened to Michael? Have ye lost yer hearing as well as yer hand?" Sean's voice boomed into his ear and Declan swung round on the form and with his good hand grabbed him by the shirt-collar. In a split second he had pinned Sean's head to the wooden seat in a vice-like grip with his arms flailing close to the floor.

"See what I can do with one hand, ye ginger bastard!" hissed Declan at his victim's earlobe.

The bodhrán rumbled to a halt as the revellers began to notice the commotion. Cara rushed over to the two men with the sort of stern look she reserved for young children.

"What's going on? I thought ye two were friends?"

Sean tried to speak but his cheeks were splayed out on the rough wood.

"Let him go, Declan! This is meant to be a celebration not some shebeen," she beseeched him.

Declan released his grip and stepped aside, shoving his gloved stump back into his pocket. Sean raised his beef-like neck and rubbed the circulation back into his pressed cheeks. They both nodded at Cara but kept their eyes to the ground. The Widow McAward, who had hobbled over for a closer look, decided to enter the fray.

"Fighting among yerselves, are ye? We're all kin here. This is a celebration. T'would have served us all better if you'd fought that landlord Adair off this land before he ruined it, Sean Sweeney," she said, pointing in the direction of Glenveagh.

"Aye, true," said Declan, grinning at the old lady.

"And what ye smirking at, Declan Conaghan?" She waggled her stick in his face. "Ye go off and fight some other people's war and come back to us lame. Shame on ye!"

Declan stiffened.

"I'm not lame."

Cara went to intervene, but Sean had stood and gently lowered the old lady's stick.

"Come on, dear," said Sean to the widow. "I think it's time I walked ye home." He turned his marked cheek briefly to Declan. "I'll be seein' ye."

He then took the widow's arm and led her out the barn door passing under the now-drooping stars and stripes flag. There were whispers among the revellers and the musicians took up their instruments again. Gradually the dancing resumed leaving the Conaghans at one end of the barn, unsure whether to console or cajole the party's special guest.

Finally, Ma spoke. "I'm not sure what Sean said to ye but he can be a bit hot-headed. The Widow McAward may have her strange ways but what she said about us all being kin is true, Declan. Ye may have forgotten, living in America, but this is a small community and we can't be fighting among ourselves."

Declan swirled the remains of the poteen in his beaker. "I know, Ma, I'm sorry. I don't know what came over me."

"Probably just the poteen," said Cara, sitting down next to him.

"Yeah, rotten stuff."

Declan poured the remains of his cup on the ground and kicked sawdust over the damp patch. Owen Sweeney approached Declan and pointed to where the US flag was hanging. "Sean wanted ye to have this," he said. "Sort of a gift, a homecoming gift. Ye might prefer it to the poteen."

Declan looked up at the slightly tattered flag.

"Thanks, Owen, and 'am sorry for my outburst."

Owen patted his shoulder.

"Aye, well, Michael's spirit clearly lives on in ye 'cos I seem to remember it was him that was hot-headed; ye were the sensible, quiet brother."

Declan raised his stump in a mock salute.

"Aye, look where that got me," he said. "The widow's right, what use am I with one hand?"

Owen raised his eyebrows.

"Ye fool, we could do with some help, looking after the livestock say, or cutting the turf like ye did before. Sean was going to ask ye but then … It'll be fine, ye'll be fine."

Declan looked across to where Cara was helping Ma

clear away plates and tidy up as the party was ending. Following his gaze, Owen said, "I'm sure ye want to take care of yer ma and Cara but they've managed well without ye, so while the American money helped, they've done well on their own."

"Aye, I know."

Declan wasn't thinking about a future in Gartan. He didn't want to work for the Sweeneys again. He couldn't picture going back to the peat bogs without his brother. It was too painful. He shoved his stump back into his pocket, and muttered, "There's somebody else I'd like to take care of and I can still do that with one hand."

When Ma finally let him out of her sight the next day, Declan went for a wander along the wooded lane at the side of Lough Gartan where they used to live. He hoped he might find remnants of the old cottage and in some way pay his respects to the family home. On the day of the evictions he'd refused to look back at the damage the crowbar brigade had done and he imagined there wouldn't be much left to see. But as he walked further along the lane, he came across one tumbled cottage after another, still standing amidst the weeds and overgrowth like tombs in a neglected graveyard. At each one he paused to remember the tenants he knew had once lived there.

First, he came to ol' man Doherty's place, pausing to stare at the dilapidated doorpost it was rumoured he kissed before his eviction. He imagined the old man thought he'd finish his days in his own home. He walked on through the long grass and nettles. There was the Gallaghers' cottage. They'd moved to Belfast where there was work in the mills. The Bradleys. He sighed and thought of Alex and Briege. Their tiny home that always smelt of cooking and rosin wax, now a warren for rabbits.

Eventually, he came to their own pile of rubble beside their tiny plot of land. It was a bed of pretty wildflowers and stinging nettles. He took his cap off and reminisced about the long hours the family had tended their patch. The stone wall, which he and Michael frequently mended, was now just scattered stones around the cottage ruins. A gentle breeze rustled the trees that had invaded the plots of land since that fateful night more than six years ago. Declan closed his eyes, remembering the shouts and cries of the tenants mixed with the cold, threatening commands of the crowbar brigade. It was hard to believe all that had taken place in this now serene corner of Donegal.

"A sorry sight, man!"

Declan jumped. Sean was standing a few yards away holding a stick.

"Sean! D'ye normally creep up like that, scared the shite outta me."

"Sorry, Declan. I didn't mean to. God, when are we gonna stop apologising to each other, eh?" He fidgeted with the crook in his hands. Declan looked around, it was a lonely lane with few passers-by.

"How did ye know I was here?"

"Yer ma told me I'd find ye here. Look, I didn't come to

disturb yer peace. I came to ask if yer looking for work. There's plenty with us."

Declan relaxed a little.

"Thanks, appreciate that." He paused. "If, that is, ye have work for a one-armed man?"

"The way ye floored me last night, I've no doubt yer as capable as any man with two arms."

Sean came closer and sat down on the broken wall, pulling some tobacco out of a pouch from his pocket. He indicated to Declan to join him as he started filling a pipe. Declan perched beside him, crushing the clumps of wildflowers underfoot.

"We've a lot of cattle now that need looking after – here, this is for ye," he said, handing him the crook. Declan took it and rubbed the palm of his hand over the smoothly carved handle.

"Nice bit of wood … thought you'd brought it to beat me up."

"What, to get ye back for last night?

"That, I s'pose, and what I said about Murray."

"Look, I'm sorry about the evictions." He sighed deeply. "I know we caused some bother with Adair but I swear we didn't murder his land steward."

"No, he'd a lot of enemies. I shouldn't have accused ye."

Sean frowned. "But yer right, ye and the Widow McAward – we shoulda dealt with Adair years ago."

Declan kicked a piece of rubble with his boot. It bounced off a stone and split in two.

"I've come back to kill him," he announced and turned to gauge Sean's reaction. The other man's eyes narrowed as he began to suck on his pipe and then slowly blew out the smoke.

"Ye didn't come over on that Erin's Hope ship with the rest of them useless Fenians, did ye?"

Declan laughed at the thought of his own passage home.

"Hell, no! I haven't returned to lead any rebellion. I just plan to put Adair off the walk," said Declan, breathing hard.

"Simple as that. So yer not in the Brotherhood, yer a lone wolf – is that what yer saying?"

"The only brother I had is dead, no thanks to Adair. We wouldn't have been fighting in that bloody war if he hadn't evicted us. Ye asked what happened to Michael? Well, I'll tell ye. He was shot in the back of the neck in the middle of some wilderness we knew nothing about, nor cared for. But we had a pact that if we made it out alive, we'd come back and get Adair. So that's what I plan to do." He paused and stared hard at Sean. "Yer my only brothers now. Ye could help me. If not, I can be a lone wolf, hell a cunning fox – I'll rip him apart."

Declan could feel the blood pulsing in his temples. He steadied himself against the broken wall, feeling some of the tension across his chest ease having divulged his plan. Sean's bull-like neck had begun to redden and Declan could tell he was warming to the idea.

After a few minutes' silence, Sean spoke. "We'll need some guns – I know some people…"

"I know ye do, that'll help. I have one shotgun I managed to smuggle back," said Declan and pointed to his stump. "Easy to hide it up this sleeve, not many people keen to search an old, mutilated soldier on the boat back here."

Sean laughed.

"Och, it's great to have ye home."

"I'm not kidding about killing Adair."

Sean raised his large hands in an attempt to calm him.

"Sure, I know yer dead serious. But we need to plan it properly. Find out his whereabouts and do it cleanly."

"Cara says he spends summers at Glenveagh and now he's built this castle…"

Sean spat on the ground.

"Aye, a bloody castle," he said. "Have ye seen it yet? No! Well, come with me now. I'll show ye what's risen out of the ashes of these homes."

He kicked the rubble at his feet as he led Declan past the remains of the village. They climbed a trail to a viewpoint high up on the hill. Declan could feel the anger rise inside him, the task more urgent. A flash of blue glistened before them as they came over the ridge into the Glenveagh valley: Lough Veagh snaking into the distance, dotted with tiny islands. Declan tried to figure out which one was the home of the illicit still where they'd evaded the police that moonlit night before the evictions.

"See it? Just on the edge of the lough." Sean jabbed his fat fingers in the air.

And there it was. The sky had turned to a grey cotton and rising up to meet it were the granite walls of a castle in the middle of the wilderness. Declan stopped dead. There were turrets alright – he counted four – with a taller turret to crown them all.

"We can't stop here. Adair's shepherds are always

combing the hillside for poachers and strays. There's a sheltered spot up ahead with a good view."

Declan followed him, feeling magnetised by the fortress that rose large before them. It was a four-storey rectangular keep with corner turrets, narrow slit windows and a kind of watchtower looking out at the lough. Declan found himself struggling not to admire the structure. He'd known Glenveagh since he was a boy – it was a quiet, lonely valley; even the wildlife were shy. To find a castle here was incongruous to his memories of the place, but the more he stared, he had to admit the majestic scenery was fitting for a castle.

The entrance was a busy thoroughfare with carts ferrying supplies and men in and out of the work site. They watched the hive of activity. Men in flat-caps and boots, their sleeves rolled up. Some were levering large pieces of stone from wagons and lifting other pieces on pulleys to get to higher sections. Declan could see they were finishing a low wall, shaped like a battlement, which seemed to form an outer perimeter wall around the castle. The team effort of the builders reminded him of his army days. He had cursed his lot then and the demands made of them by senior officers but at least back then he had full use of both his limbs. He watched as the workmen hauled heavy wheelbarrows laden with bricks back and forth. They seemed focused and happy with their labour and again, Declan felt a twinge of envy. He then remembered the crowbar brigade and the pleasure they took in wrecking his home. All their homes. He felt the smooth stone in his pocket that he'd picked up earlier from the ruins of their cabin. He began to wonder if any of these labourers were the cudgel men from Tyrone.

"They can build with stones and destroy with just the same," he muttered to himself.

"What's that?" Sean interrupted his thoughts. "We'll have to ambush him on his way in or out. We'll never shoot him inside that fortress."

Declan grunted.

"Yer Cara will know when he's back 'cos he usually calls at Church Hill to visit the minister."

Declan raised the staff and rested it horizontally across his stump, then lowered his chin and squinted one eye as if taking aim.

"I was a good shooter in the war," he said. "God knows we drilled enough. Never used a gun in my life before the Army."

"I daresay yer a good shot and a man with a cause is less likely to miss."

Just then a magpie landed in a nearby tree and cocked its sleek black head at them, fixing Declan with its shiny eye.

"Oh, I don't intend to miss," he replied. "I want to see his fear as I snuff out his life. Point blank range."

Chapter 32

L'Hotel Meurice
Rue de Rivoli
Paris
25 June 1867

Dear Father,

I trust you are in good health and are enjoying a pleasant summer. I have some news which may surprise you. I got married in New York last month and am now on honeymoon in Europe. I know I should have mentioned this before but New York is a busy place and events simply overtook me. I was introduced to my wife Cornelia at a congressman's ball last year and she is a lady of the highest reputation and standing in New York society, as well as a great benefactor to many excellent causes. She is some fifteen years younger than I, but we enjoy each other's company and I must admit she has enriched my life.

Sadly, she has known some tragedy. She was widowed during the civil war and her father was also killed in battle. Her father was

General James Wadsworth, a highly regarded leader of Union troops, whose family own a lot of land in upstate New York. We were married in her hometown of Geneseo, which is a splendid little place, not far from the magnificent Niagara Falls, which you must have heard about. As well as gaining a wife, I have gained two sons as Cornelia has two young boys from her first marriage. Their names are Arthur and Montgomery. They are fine children and have suffered much from the loss of their young father. We have left them in the capable hands of Cornelia's mother and a governess while we take our tour of Europe. As you can see, we are currently in Paris, which is Cornelia's favourite city. She brought the boys here for two years after their father died and tells me the city has the best tutors in the world. It is a fine place but I am looking forward to showing her Ireland and, of course, introducing her to you. It was Cornelia who made me sit down to pen this letter so that we wouldn't give you a fright simply arriving at Bellegrove as a married couple. Clearly, she is much more considerate than I am.

And so, Father, we shall be making a stop-off in Ireland next month, July. By then hopefully you will have had time to take all this in and I look forward to you welcoming us both.

Sincerely,

Your son, John

The temperature had begun to soar in their last few days in Paris so they were relieved to escape the sultry heat for the mild Irish summer. Adair admitted to himself that he was nervous about introducing his wife to his father. He hadn't left him on the best of terms but he was pleased to find the news had sunk in by the time the newly-weds arrived at Bellegrove and his father gave them a more welcoming reception than he'd received in recent years. He was always a ladies' man and was keen to impress his new daughter-in-law. Then again it was hard to resist Cornelia's charm; there was a confidence and tenderness about her that he noticed people instantly warmed to.

"The climate is most agreeable here. The air is so fresh." She took a deep breath as if to savour it. "Yes, very comfortable indeed."

"I'm glad you find it so. I really hope we can make Ireland our second home. The boys could come during vacations in the summer and I'm really looking forward to showing you my estate at Glenveagh and the new castle."

Cornelia laughed, revealing little creases around her eyes, which he found very pretty.

"The boys think you're some sort of knight from a fairy tale with your talk of castles and lakes. Arthur has been telling his cousins about the adventures he's going to have at this castle. I must check it out for him first so I know you're not making it up!"

This time Adair laughed and hugged her close. He was very fond of the two boys even though he'd spent little time with them. They were very well-behaved and called him 'sir'. He pinched himself sometimes that this was now his life as he'd never expected to marry and least of all acquire two sons overnight. He imagined this was what they called contentment.

They had been watching wild ducks congregate on the pond when a familiar bald head appeared on the far side accompanied by his father leaning on a brass-topped cane.

"Look! It's my cousin, Townsend – the castle architect

himself." Adair gave a wave and escorted Cornelia around to the terrace by the pond for more introductions.

"Delighted to meet you. Townsend, that's an unusual name," she said, allowing him to kiss her hand.

"Suits an unusual person," replied Adair, elbowing his cousin.

"We've just been talking about Glenveagh Castle – it sounds so charming." Cornelia beamed at him. "I'm really excited to see it."

"Ah yes, the castle, well it's coming along nicely, in fact it's nearly completed," said Townsend.

"Shall we take a stroll, old boy, while we discuss the project?" Adair suggested and looked at his father. "I trust you will keep my wife company, Father?"

George grinned and put the crook of his arm out for Cornelia to take.

"Come, my dear, we can have more fun than those two dullards." He cackled and they trotted over to the wrought iron bench.

Minutes later John looked across the duck pond to see the pair deep in conversation.

"Can't take your eyes off her, you rascal!" Townsend laughed.

"Would you?"

"You certainly picked a beauty, not the sort of widow I was expecting."

"No, she's quite a find. Beautiful, smart and very wealthy too."

"Ha! I knew there'd be some business angle to this latest venture."

"Whatever do you mean? I haven't married her for her money, that's … that's just a bonus. She's from a very good family."

"Ah, it's a status thing – a wonder you didn't fall for one of the society ladies in Dublin."

"Well, there were plenty, I just didn't marry any."

"And what makes this one different?" asked Townsend, pushing the boundaries of inquisitiveness much to Adair's irritation.

"She's just different," he replied, his face reddening. "Anyway I thought we were discussing Glenveagh Castle."

He knew he was overreacting to Townsend's questions. The real reason he felt tetchy was the sudden realisation that his father was alone with Cornelia for the first time since their arrival and he feared what stories he might be telling her. Adair half-listened while Townsend talked about snagging and pipework. After a short while he steered them back to the terrace where his father and Cornelia sat hunched conspiratorially.

"Fantastic flock of geese on the pond today, Father," said Adair as the shadows of the two men fell across the bench.

George looked up, startled.

"Damn nuisance, those birds – disturb all my year-round residents. Blow in, make a racket and then fly off again!" he said, winking at Townsend.

"Sounds a bit like your son."

"Very witty! And I thought you were charming my lovely wife, not comparing us to a couple of geese."

"So when do you lovebirds fly off again?" asked Townsend.

"Day after tomorrow. We'll head up to Donegal. You've been looking forward to seeing Glenveagh, haven't you, my dear?"

This time Cornelia looked startled and quickly glanced at George who had now left the bench and was waggling his cane in the direction of the geese.

"Yes of course..." She hesitated and sucked in a deep breath. "Your father has just been telling me about the recent history of Glenveagh. Why didn't you mention the murder or the evictions before?"

Adair's face glowed hot under his beard and his hands gripped the iron frame of the bench. Townsend kicked a piece of gravel with his shoe and let out a long, low whistle.

"Well done, Uncle George! Have you been frightening the lady?"

George now pointed his stick at his son and nephew.

"I have done no such thing. The lady was interested in Glenveagh, and I thought I'd fill her in, properly."

Cornelia waved her hand at George to lower his stick.

"Come, gentlemen! Let's not argue," she said. "I was just astonished to hear about these terrible deeds on your land, John, especially when you have spoken so highly of the estate."

"Terrible deeds? By whom? Father, what exactly have you been telling my wife?"

"The truth," replied George. "There was a murder, no one was caught, so you evicted the tenants."

Adair glanced bewildered between his father and Cornelia.

"It isn't *quite* that simple," he said, trying not to glare at his father. "Cornelia, I-I just hadn't got around to the subject." He then composed himself and slumped down on the bench next to his wife. "I didn't want to concern you with events that happened a long time ago. It was before your Arthur was even born."

He took her hand in his and glared at his cousin who stood watching them with an amused expression. She began twisting the ring on her finger. It was the diamond engagement ring from her first husband. She wore it next to the sapphire Adair had bought her. When he proposed, he told her he picked it to match her sparkling blue eyes. He didn't mind that she still wore the other ring. Besides, he thought it was too expensive to languish in a drawer.

George had begun to totter off back to the house and Townsend took the hint and scrambled after his uncle, taking care to join the side not assisted by his menacing stick. Cornelia was silent.

"My dear, I simply did not want to alarm you with such matters. A lady should not be vexed by unpleasant stories."

"You should know I am tougher than most ladies," she replied, but he detected a note of irritation in her voice. "Don't try to shelter me, John. I can handle the unpleasant as well as any man."

He cleared his throat. "I do not doubt your strengths, but I assure you what … what happened at Glenveagh is all in the past."

Cornelia frowned and after a pause turned to him.

"Do you think there's still a murderer loose in Glenveagh?"

Adair hesitated and then feigned a casual laugh.

"I like to think my decision to clear the tenants dealt with that problem."

"But no one was ever actually caught?"

"Oh, there were arrests and strong suspicions but no, I'm afraid the police and the judiciary are not very effective in that part of the country. So you see, my dear, I had no choice but to take the law into my own hands. It was Townsend and his father who advised me on the evictions."

"And your own father? What did he advise?"

Adair felt his head begin to swim with all the questions.

"I didn't really seek his advice." He paused. "My uncle is a very accomplished land agent so I trusted his opinion. You really shouldn't concern yourself, Cornelia. It's all in the past and when we complete the castle, we shall begin a new chapter there."

She smiled up at him. "Very well."

She rested her head against his shoulder and Adair breathed an inward sigh of relief. He had been away from Glenveagh for a long time, he could only hope that terrible chapter of his life was closed.

They sat silently together for some time and watched the flocks of birds swim in their V-shaped formations back and forth gracefully across the pond.

Chapter 33

The Adairs had travelled on to Donegal, which greeted the newly-weds with several days of heavy rain. When the rain eventually stopped and the sun rose one morning spectacularly over the valley, Adair announced it was the perfect day to view the castle.

He swiftly organised the carriage and the couple were driven along the lough path to the castle grounds. Between the trees they enjoyed flashes of the navy lough reflecting the cloudless sky above and as they rounded a bend in the lane, the grey, castellated mansion rose up before them. Cornelia gave an excited gasp and pointed through the open window. Adair simply smiled, straining his neck for a better view. There it was. Glenveagh Castle. His dream realised. It had a lonesome aspect to it, which he relished. There wasn't another inhabited building, and certainly none as spectacular for miles, just the tumbled ruins of cottages dotted across the hillside. He had noticed Cornelia stare curiously at them and was prepared to explain them as famine cottages but thankfully she hadn't asked.

"What a splendid day for your first visit to the castle!"

"It's breath-taking. I-I'm almost speechless, John. Oh, the lodge is very pretty by the waterfall but only a castle is fitting for such a majestic fjord as this."

She slipped her arm through his as they took in the view together. The carriage sailed through a narrow gateway guarded by two stone stags' heads and shortly afterwards they came to a halt outside the low battlement wall that surrounded the castle. Adair noticed the workmen milling about in overalls staring at Cornelia in her long skirts as she descended from the carriage – the first woman to have visited the castle. She peered up at the tall granite tower that obscured the sun from where she stood. Jagged gables lined the parapets of the battlements and roughly hewn arrow-loops decorated the turrets.

"It's like something medieval and yet it's brand new," she said, pointing to the stepped structure of the battlements. Adair slapped his large hand on the wall.

"It is a fine piece of masonry, isn't it? It's difficult to carve much decoration in granite – as materials go it's fairly plain – but the important thing is granite is plentiful in Donegal and it certainly makes for a sturdy castle that can withstand the harsh weather here."

The foreman of the site approached Adair, removing his cap and nodding to Cornelia.

"Good morning, Mr Adair, sir! We weren't expecting ye but ye've certainly picked a good day."

"Yes, a beautiful summer's day. I was afraid the only

picture my wife would have of Ireland would be the incessant rain."

Glancing at Cornelia, the foreman hesitated.

"Aye the weather *is* fine today sir, but I was meaning we're just finishing carving yer coat of arms above the doorway, as ye requested. The men are nearly done so may I ask ye to go in through the back door? It will be ready in about an hour and ye'll be the first to see it."

"Very well! Does the lady mind going in through the servants' quarters?" he said, turning to his wife.

"Of course not," she said, nudging him affectionately with her elbow. "I'm impressed by how close to completion the castle is. From what you told me I was expecting more of a building site." She laughed and nodded at the foreman who took a step away from the couple.

"If ye'll follow me then," he said and still clutching his cap at his belt, led them through the stable-yard and into the large kitchen space at the rear of the castle. It was bare except for some exposed pipes, which several men were working at. They hurried through a door into what was announced as the dining room and Adair watched Cornelia as she examined the window frames and mused aloud about the colour of drapes to hang against the view of the glistening lough.

"This will be perfect for entertaining, John – what a marvellous view our guests will have over dinner."

Adair carefully inspected the wood as they proceeded into the main reception, a large drawing room that also overlooked the lough. The room took up most of the downstairs area of the keep and was partially furnished with sofas and tables. At one end was a large fireplace with a white marble mantelpiece, which drew all their gazes. Cornelia hastened straight over to it and ran her gloved fingers gently along the top.

"Is this antique?" she asked.

"It's last century, m'lady," said the foreman before Adair could respond. "A fine piece of work. Ye'll not see fireplaces like that in many homes around here."

"Oh, I can just picture little Rex curling up in front of a big roaring fire in the hearth, snuggled on a rug…"

"Rex?" asked the foreman, puzzled.

"Yes, my Scottish terrier. I've left him behind of course, with the children in New York. He will love it here, I've no doubt."

"I'm glad you like the marble, my dear," interrupted Adair. "You'll find several similar mantelpieces throughout the house."

He indicated to the foreman to continue the tour and they passed through a number of other ground-floor rooms in which Adair proudly announced their purpose.

"The billiards room – for the gentlemen, of course!"

"A fine study, don't you think, will make a great schoolroom for the boys…"

"And no hunting estate would be complete without a gun room."

Then they returned along the corridor into a rectangular hallway and stopped at the foot of the staircase to admire the light cascading through the two long arched windows.

"Heavenly!" exclaimed Cornelia, placing a hand on the dark-stained banister. Adair smiled and took her other hand.

"Shall we ascend?" he said with a wry smile.

Cornelia picked her way up the stairs, lifting her long skirts slightly to avoid them trailing on the uncarpeted stairwell. Fortunately, the foreman had manoeuvred in front of them to avoid the embarrassment of glimpsing her ankles and Adair allowed him to continue to lead the way through the numerous upstairs bedrooms and library.

Cornelia exclaimed at the view from the library, which looked up the valley to where the lough weaved and narrowed until it was hidden by the bulbous hump of Dooish Mountain. She tapped her finger on the windowpane.

"That patch of land just beyond the battlements, do you see it, John? That would make a perfect garden. It's already quite sheltered but we could plant some trees and landscape it to create a lawn. It's a delightful view as it is but a garden would just complete it."

Adair nodded with equal enthusiasm.

"My dear, you can landscape the whole grounds to your liking. Every castle should have gardens and pleasure grounds. It is a blank canvas for you to put your mark on."

"I shall quite enjoy 'putting my mark' on Glenveagh." She smiled at the foreman.

He returned her smile, and looking relieved that the tour appeared to have been a success, he cleared his throat.

"On the subject of putting yer mark on Glenveagh, shall we take a look at yer family's coat of arms now, Mr Adair? I imagine it'll be ready for inspection."

"If we've finished up here?" asked Adair.

Cornelia was still gazing at her imagined garden and

gave a distracted nod of approval. They arrived back at the entrance hallway where a number of workmen stood to attention at the open doorway. With the foreman leading the way they stepped out into the fresh air and turned to inspect the grey slab above the doorframe. There were two sets of motifs carved side-by-side in the slab – three hands with palms outward-facing, as if raised in salute, next to three feathers – and below them an inscription in French. Cornelia peered through the shade of the tower and read the inscription aloud in a peculiar French-American drawl.

"*Loyal au mort*," she read slowly. "Au mort? Ah, loyal unto death… Well, I hope to spend many more years with you than I got to spend with my first husband before that happens!"

Adair squeezed her hand and stood back to admire the coat of arms. As he stood blinking in the sun, he felt his chest swell with pride for both the castle and his wife. Just in that moment he couldn't decide which was more precious.

The Adairs returned to Glenveagh Lodge where they prepared to go to dinner that evening at the rectory. It was still bright but a northerly wind had swept through the valley, turning the air chilly. Cornelia puzzled over her attire in the long mirror in the hallway as Adair waited. She finally summoned the housekeeper to bring her coat.

"I hate to have to wear it during the summer, but I guess your summer is more like my fall."

"I beg yer pardon, ma'am?" said the housekeeper,

opening Cornelia's fur-lined coat and helping her to slip one slim arm through at a time.

"Fall? Oh, that's autumn to you. Goodness I was probably better understood in Paris!" She laughed as Adair took her arm and she clicked down the steps to the waiting carriage. Dressed in a smart suit he'd bought in Paris, he jumped in behind her and rapped sharply on the roof with his cane. The carriage crunched over the stony courtyard and the horses fell into a fast trot along the lough-side track. Adair felt another glow of pride as Cornelia squeezed his arm and peered through the window past him.

"Look at those magnificent geese!" She pointed to a flock that flew overhead in the distance.

"Yes, marvellous. Would make a fine supper too," said Adair, squinting out the window. "I wonder what's on the menu at the minister's. I don't know about you, but I'm famished."

"Oh John, are all creatures just game to you?" She laughed and squeezed him tighter. The coach-driver pulled on the reins as a group of black-faced sheep spilled across the lane in front of them. He stood up and cracked his whip above his head. "G'wan!" The startled sheep scattered to either side and the coach continued. Cornelia stared at their bedraggled coats and stubby tails as they waddled out of the way.

"Are the sheep slaughtered for their meat or is it mainly their wool that's valuable?" she asked.

"The main market is for their wool. It's quite a tough yarn, which the factories in Londonderry buy up to make coats. We have such a large flock now that we also export a lot of the wool."

"Is it really such a large flock? I've seen huge ranches of sheep in the States – they go on for miles and miles."

"True," Adair conceded. "But for Ireland this would count as a large flock. Actually, funny you should mention ranches in the States. I received a letter from my associates in New York about some land in the state of Texas. I hear there are some lucrative swathes of land around the Texas Panhandle and when we go back to New York I'm planning to take a trip out to see it for myself – lots of investment possibilities."

"Goodness. Texas is a long way from New York but that sounds interesting," she said, giving her husband an admiring glance. He smiled and stroked her hand.

"We could have our own *huge ranch* if you want to invest with me," he said, leaving the intonation vague so it appeared as neither a statement nor a question, and hoping she wouldn't pick up on the nervous tension in his voice. It was a business proposition because he knew he couldn't do it without his wife's investment. Cornelia leaned her head to one side as if pondering the idea.

"Hmm, there's an idea. Well, I'll leave you to investigate the possibilities. My father would certainly have been impressed with me owning a ranch," she said.

They reached Church Hill village and passed the little stone church at the top of the hill whose spire could be seen for miles around before reaching the rectory, nestled at the bottom of the village.

The carriage came to a halt in front of the Georgian

house which Adair always thought appeared as if it had been transplanted from Dublin. Reverend Maturin filled the door-frame as he came out to greet them.

"What a charming house and grounds!" Cornelia drawled through the window. Adair had jumped out, nodded briefly at the minister and turned to assist his wife down the steps of the carriage.

The minister ushered them both straight to the dining room where the table had been set for dinner. From the minute she arrived in the hallway Cornelia showered the rectory with a string of compliments, which slightly irritated Adair.

"I adore this crockery – is it local? Yes? Goodness, John, we really ought to buy some of this for Glenveagh Castle. I do love the delicate pastel colours. So much you see these days is so garish."

After a while Adair conceded inwardly that her chatter helped to break the ice.

"Well, I must first congratulate you Mr Adair on your marriage," said the reverend, shaking Adair's hand vigorously. "It came as a surprise to us all."

"Us all? And who might that be?" asked Adair.

"Oh you know, my wife and family," the reverend continued. "I have five sons, Mrs Adair." He beamed in her direction.

"Oh will they be joining us?" asked Cornelia.

"My wife will be along shortly but the boys won't be. Two of my sons are studying at Trinity College in Dublin. One has a law practice in Londonderry and the other two are busy on the farm."

"Goodness, they are all suitably employed. You must be very proud of them, reverend," said Cornelia.

"Yes, yes we are – very proud. Although pride is a sin so we try to remain humble in the eyes of God." The reverend blushed and took a sip of water. Adair shook his napkin out across his lap and then scraped his chair closer to the table.

"I have two sons myself," Cornelia stated.

The minister swallowed the water quickly and tried to conceal a puzzled expression.

"They're not my children, reverend," added Adair. "My wife was widowed in the American Civil War when her first husband was tragically killed in battle."

The minister paused and signalled to a young maid to pour the wine.

"That's dreadful. You seem so young to have suffered such tragedy and the boys, they must miss their father?" he asked, wide-eyed. Cornelia began twisting the rings on her finger.

"Of course they do, although they were very young when he passed. My husband actually succumbed to disease from the terrible conditions of the camps." She glanced across at Adair. "It was my father who died in battle."

"Your father too! How terrible! War is such a waste of life," murmured the minister. "My dear, I shall think of you in my prayers – you have come through a lot."

At that, Cornelia stretched her hand across the table and gripped the minister's arm before he had time to react.

"Thank you, reverend. That means a lot to me."

Reverend Maturin gave Adair a helpless, almost apologetic look while Adair took a sip of red wine. The door burst open then and Mrs Maturin entered carrying a tray with two soup bowls.

"Good evening, good evening! I thought I'd assist the kitchen so that the food doesn't get cold," she said, setting the bowls down in front of their guests.

All three stood from the table to greet the lady of the house.

"Delighted to meet you," said Cornelia. "You have such a charming home."

"Why thank you. Pleased to meet you too, Mrs Wadsworth Ritchie Adair. We do love it here. It is so peaceful and the community is a joy to minister to."

The maid followed behind her with the other soups and there was silence for a time as they all sat down to savour the cream of vegetable broth. Finishing her last drop, Mrs Maturin smiled at Cornelia as she placed her spoon in the empty bowl.

"It is delightful for us to have a caller all the way from New York." She chuckled. "You know I think you're our most exotic guest, isn't that right, reverend?"

Cornelia smiled back and looked at the minister as if to confirm her exoticness. He was still slurping his soup.

"Hmmm, probably. Although there *was* Mr O'Leary from Melbourne…" he started. Mrs Maturin's smile faded and she threw her husband a glance.

"Goodness, Melbourne, Australia? Now that *is* a very long way," replied Cornelia. "What was his business in these parts?"

"Oh, he was originally from these parts but is now a-a

benefactor," the reverend began to stutter. "He contributes to our Relief Fund."

"Ah, I see," said Cornelia, nodding. "It's so good that he should think of poverty despite living so far away. I believe we all have a Christian duty to assist the poor."

Adair noticed the hosts both lowered their heads to avoid eye contact but Cornelia had found a subject she was eager to discuss and continued.

"John has been contributing to a relief fund for Irish immigrants facing poverty in New York City and I'm on the committee at Trinity Church in Manhattan. It's such rewarding work. We have become quite influential in making the city authorities improve sanitation and conditions in the tenements. John is one of our most enthusiastic donors, aren't you, dear?"

She looked warmly across at her husband and missed the look of bewilderment that passed between their hosts. The corners of Adair's lips twitched into a slight smile and he hesitated before replying, "As the Bible says, charity vaunteth not itself."

"Oh you're too modest," said Cornelia, still beaming. "It's actually what brought us together. We met at a Republican Party ball and we got chatting about the work of the committee."

There was a sudden rattle from the side of the room as the young maid emerged out of the shadows with a tray to remove the empty soup bowls. Adair thought the Maturins looked at her with a relief fuelled by more than just interest in the next course.

"Thank you, Cara," said the reverend. Turning back to

his guests, he said, "For our next course we are having roasted lamb with all the trimmings."

"Excellent," said Adair, smiling properly for the first time that evening.

Cornelia sipped delicately from her glass of wine and turned her attention to the minister again. "What sort of relief work does your committee do?" she asked. The minister looked helplessly at Adair again and took a deep breath.

"The work of that committee has all been wrapped up now," he said. "We had a situation some years ago which, let's say, encouraged a number of our young people to emigrate. Our committee, sponsored by the kindly Melbourne benefactor, assisted them with their passage to Australia. There was a lot of poverty you see and then of course there were the evictions in '61."

Adair slammed down his glass and the minister's face flushed red. Cornelia looked concerned.

"Ah yes, the evictions…" Her voice drifted away as the maid began clattering crockery on the sideboard. Mrs Maturin smiled and invited their guests to begin the main course, which had arrived steaming on their plates. The conversation again stopped as the two couples filled their forks with slices of the delicate meat, mashed potato and boiled cabbage.

"Might I ask about your interest in Irish immigrants, aside from the fact that you've just married one?" asked the reverend, daring to make a joke. Adair spluttered on his wine but Cornelia had already begun to answer.

"Of course, reverend. Well, the village where I'm from

in upstate New York always had a steady influx of Irish," she said. "The Geneseo valley is very fertile and they come for the labouring work. My father employed them. Many second-generation Irish and new arrivals fought in the civil war alongside my father and husband. They were among the bravest fighters. Indeed some Irish soldiers tried to save my father when he was wounded. Sadly, one of them was captured, the other killed. I guess I have a soft spot for them because of their courage and the obvious hardships they suffered."

Suddenly the minister's eyes lit up and he swung round in his chair.

"Cara!" he called and beckoned to the maid who stepped forward, her hands clenched tightly in front of her apron.

"I've just remembered Cara's brother recently returned from America where he fought on the Union side in the war. He arrived back in the spring, didn't he, Mrs Maturin? Cara, when did your brother come home?"

The young maid's eyes were as large as saucers and her face seemed to grow paler in the fast-diminishing light. She opened her mouth but no words came out.

"Oh reverend, the girl isn't used to being addressed at the table," Mrs Maturin scolded her husband as she beckoned her to approach. The maid bent down and whispered in Mrs Maturin's ear.

"I see," she said and looked up. "She says her brother has been home four months."

Adair took another mouthful of his dinner fearing it

would go cold and hoped this little drama would end. But his wife was getting as excited as the minister at this news.

"My goodness, you go halfway across the world and still find people who fought in that God-forsaken war!" said Cornelia, staring at the maid. "Tell me, what's your name again?"

The maid looked from Cornelia to Mrs Maturin and back at Cornelia. She finally found her voice.

"I-it's Cara, Cara Conaghan, ma'am," she almost whispered.

Adair scraped his plate clean and noticed Cornelia had barely touched her lamb.

"Miss Conaghan, why did your brother come back home? Did the war sicken him of America?"

Cara looked again at Mrs Maturin. She slowly unclenched her fingers and looking at Mrs Maturin, pointed to her arm.

"Ah yes, of course, well Mrs Adair, Cara's poor brother lost his hand in the war," said Mrs Maturin, shaking her head. "In fact she had two brothers who fought but one was killed. Her older brother Declan was so badly maimed he decided it would be better for him to come home and be with his family."

Adair coughed and pointed with his fork at his wife's plate.

"Hmm, brave soldier. Cornelia, your food will go cold."

"Yes dear," Cornelia replied but didn't take her eyes off the maid. "I am so sorry for your family's loss."

Cornelia put down her cutlery.

"I should like to meet your brother sometime. Does he live nearby?"

The maid nodded and Mrs Maturin replied, looking rather pleased with the connection. "Yes, he lives with Cara and her mother on the grounds."

"Good, we should like to make his acquaintance," said Cornelia, raising a reaffirming eyebrow at Adair who tried to look interested. Mrs Maturin gave an appreciative nod to Cara who began to busy herself clearing plates from the table.

Reverend Maturin, who had sat quietly marvelling at the conversation, finally chipped in. "As you say, Mrs Adair, such a devastating war and with such far-reaching effects. To think of two local boys from Donegal being caught up in a battle so far away."

"When did they emigrate?" Cornelia addressed the minister who slowly reddened and glanced at Adair.

"It was that spring of '61…" His voice faltered.

Adair glared at the reverend and announced, "Yes, there was a lot of emigration that year – for lots of reasons. Now I must say that was a delicious meal." He took another swig of his wine.

"I will be sure to inform cook," said the reverend. "Praise, where praise is due."

Adair hoped that would change the subject but as the maid was refilling Cornelia's glass, she asked, "One last question, my dear, do you know which brigade your brothers fought with?"

The maid held the bottle tightly almost as if she was

protecting herself with it and whispered, "Yer brigade, ma'am."

"*My* brigade? Whatever do you mean?" asked Cornelia, looking across at Mrs Maturin as if seeking a translation.

"I mean the name ye said earlier," said the girl and then turned to Mrs Maturin. "Didn't ma'am say the lady's name was Mrs Wadsworth Ritchie Adair?"

"Yes Cara, that *is* our guest's name but what do you mean? The lady is asking the name of your brothers' brigade in the Army," she pronounced the words slowly. "Oh perhaps you don't know…"

"Oh but I do Mrs Maturin. My brothers fought in the Wadsworth Guards."

Adair heard his wife's sudden intake of breath, which seemed to suck the life out of the room. They all stared at the maid in astonishment.

Chapter 34

"The poor woman. Better she didn't marry again than end up with that wicked scoundrel!"

"Well, ye've always told me not to be fussy about husbands…" said Cara to Ma with a giggle.

Declan overheard their conversation as he walked into the yard of the cottage.

"What poor woman?" he asked, appearing at the door, his clothes dirty from labouring at the Sweeneys. His dark hair was tousled and laden with husks of straw. Cara pointed out the half-empty pail of water for him to wash in.

"Ye'll need to go to the well and fill that up when it's finished," she said. "I was talkin' about John Adair's new wife. She's hardly poor, a real lady in fact. She's very pretty. Met her this evenin'. They ate with the minister."

Declan frowned.

"I just heard he's back. Didn't know he got married. Who would have him?"

"We were just sayin' that. But ye won't believe this, she wants to meet ye."

Hearing that Adair's wife wanted to meet him sent a cold shiver down his spine. He'd just been talking to the Sweeney brothers about setting up an ambush on the road to Glenveagh. As the weeks had passed into late July both brothers had been getting more excited about their plans and frustrated there had been no sign of Adair's return. It was only that day they had heard from workmen at the castle that Adair was back in Donegal.

"Why would Adair's wife want to meet me? Whatever for?" he asked, puzzled. The thought occurred to him that their plan had been leaked, but how could it? No one but the Sweeneys knew anything.

"She's American," said Cara, handing him a rag to wash with. "Adair met her in New York. She was widowed in the Civil War. They were talkin' bout it over dinner when the reverend mentioned about ye being a soldier over there."

Declan stared intrigued at his sister but carried on washing. He wrung out the wet rag between his teeth and his good hand.

"So why does she want to meet me? I'm sure she's met a lot of soldiers from the war."

Ma raised her voice. "Why wouldn't she want to meet ye? Did your bit, didn't ye, for her country. Lost your brother, didn't ye, for *her* country."

Declan hung his head, and shrugging his bare shoulders, continued to rub his neck and oxters clean with the wet rag.

"That's true, Ma. She got really excited when I said ye fought in the Wadsworth Guards," Cara continued, her eyes sparkling. "I remembered because that was her name when she was introduced."

Declan dropped the rag into the pail.

"What d'ye mean that was her name?"

"I'd never heard such a grand name, so many names in fact." Cara smiled. "Her name's Cornelia Wadsworth Ritchie…" As she paused Declan's mouth fell open. "Adair. That's it. Cornelia Wadsworth Ritchie Adair. I knew I'd heard the name Wadsworth before."

Declan stared at the ground and muttered to himself, "Wadsworth Ritchie! General Wadsworth's daughter married *John … Adair…?*"

Cara and Ma exchanged puzzled glances. For some minutes Declan seemed to forget they were there. He stood in a trance, dripping wet in the yard.

"Why? D'ye know her?" asked Cara. Then her brow furrowed. "Ahh, is she related to Uncle Liam's landlord, the one he used to write about?"

Still appearing stunned, Declan replaced his galluses over his bare shoulders.

"Will ye not be putting yer shirt on first, Declan?" asked Ma, handing him a clean, folded one.

"Aye, sorry," said Declan, removing the galluses so they dangled again at his waist. Cara stepped in to help him as he struggled with his stump to put on the clean shirt. He then noticed her concerned expression.

"Wadsworth was my general. Yes, yer right, he was Uncle Liam's landlord." His face fell. "But he was killed, like Michael, in the Battle of the Wilderness. Are ye sure that's her name? And … and that she's married to Adair?"

Cara nodded, her eyes widening.

"As sure as fate, Declan. I heard the whole conversation. She said her husband died from disease in the war and her father was killed in battle. Oh, where ye goin' now?"

Without a word, Declan began walking out of the yard.

"But ye haven't eaten…?" Ma called after him.

He waved his good arm in the air and continued down the lane leaving the two women to gape at the wet patches forming on the back of his shirt. Declan mumbled the name Wadsworth Ritchie over and over as he pondered the news of Adair's bride. He marched all the way to Glenveagh Lough and stared across at the outline of the castle. He threw stones into the deep blue water and watched them sink in a mass of rings to the bottom. He wondered what he had come here for. As far as he knew, the Adairs weren't living in the castle and he couldn't go to Glenveagh Lodge and simply ask to speak to her. He needed to see her to believe she was here – a piece of that world, those tumultuous years, he thought he'd left behind. He leaned against a rock and relived the scene in the rebel hospital where he had last met Captain Ritchie. The sight of his blue uniform had been comforting enough and when he spoke to him, it took all of his willpower not to cry on his shoulder. The captain had appeared to him like an angel and, in Declan's morphine-induced haze, he could well have been. He brought him the news that his uncle had died. Although painful, Declan was grateful not to have been left in the dark in those final months of the war as a prisoner in the Confederate camp.

As Declan looked across the lough, he shuddered at the

thought of the captain's widow being married to the man whom he blamed for so much. How the hell had Adair married her? He threw another stone into the water and watched the ripples span out in perfect circles. Of course, he realised Adair would have moved in similar circles to her in New York society. It was a fairly small group of wealthy folk and Adair was probably a sought-after bachelor given there were so many widowed by the war.

"Damn!" he yelled, his voice echoing through the quiet valley. Why did she marry him? Why did she have to remarry at all? He then remembered the brigade's send-off from Geneseo and Captain Ritchie's young sons standing at the side of the road with their mother waving him off to war. She'd have wanted a father for her boys. He shook his head and sighed. He put his hand into his pocket and pulled out the Agnus Dei medal that had belonged to Michael. The proud lamb's face on the cheap tin had worn away over the years. Still, it was the only possession Declan had of his brother's and he prized it far more than his army medal for bravery.

"What would ye do, Mickey? I won't let ye down," he whispered, turning it over between his fingers.

He still lay slumped against a boulder staring over the valley when he realised it was beginning to grow dark. Glenveagh had given him no answers, so he slowly made his way back home. By the time he got there he was tired and prayed he wouldn't get an interrogation from Ma about where he'd gone and "the American woman". Better still, he hoped they'd both turned in for the night. But when he reached the cabin, candles were flickering in the window and he could see a number of shadows cast on the wall. They were waiting up for him. Damn.

"He's back," called Cara as he entered the cosy room, which smelt of a pungent mix of turf and cabbage soup. Cara stood clutching a shawl about her night-dress, her hair tangled in a sleepy mess around her shoulders.

"Hope ye didn't wait up for me?"

"Well, we'd gone to bed but then we had an unexpected visitor – a woman," she replied, staring at him with an odd expression on her face that he couldn't work out. Declan scratched his beard and looked around the cabin.

"Who? Not Mrs Wadsworth Ritchie?" he asked, almost hopeful and unable to add Adair's name.

"No, no, of course not, but *she* might have been less of a surprise."

Just then Ma appeared from the back room also dressed for bed.

"I'm sorry, Ma. We didn't mean to wake ye," he said, throwing a glare at Cara. "Just go on back to bed…"

But Ma resisted his attempts to move her and reached out a hand to his shoulder.

"I'm up now, Declan," she said. "Don't fuss. I guess Cara has told ye then?"

It was Declan's turn to look puzzled. Cara nodded solemnly towards a figure that slowly emerged from the back room. He stared in disbelief at the long-haired girl whose silhouette against the wall was dominated by her lightly rounded stomach. An awkward silence engulfed the cabin.

"Sinead…?" he half-whispered.

Ma looked from her son to the young woman.

"Ah, so ye remember her. She says she's having yer baby…"

Sinead's face was pale and she appeared to have been crying.

"I know it's a shock me turning up like this, Declan, but I didn't know what else to do," she began to sob.

Declan shook his head.

"Yer havin a baby but…"

She shook her head.

"I know it's yours."

Ma and Cara seemed to shrink into the shadows, watching the exchange with bated breath. Declan felt like the walls were caving in on him. He couldn't believe Sinead had appeared in the state she was in. He couldn't have this conversation in front of his Ma and sister.

"Shall we walk down to the lough, Sinead?" he found himself pleading. "It's mild out and, well, I don't like to keep Ma and Cara up."

Ma suddenly stuck out her chin and with arms folded, half-scolded him.

"Ye got to do the right thing by her, son. Sinead's practically family and it seems she's got no one now."

Large tears rolled down Sinead's cheeks as she tried to stifle another sob. Cara put her arm about her long-lost friend and seemed to almost glare at him.

"I know, Ma, but I need to talk to Sinead – alone," he

replied and turning to her said more gently, "Shall we go for a walk? I don't think I can sleep with this news."

She nodded and took the shawl Cara had handed to her. With slight relief, Declan escaped the cramped cabin and led Sinead along the gravel path behind the rectory towards Lough Gartan. There was a bright moon, which lit their path and in other circumstances, Declan thought, this could have been a romantic stroll. But his head was racing. Sinead was Michael's girl. He shouldn't have been with her and now she was pregnant. He couldn't take it all in. They walked silently with just the crunch of the stony path underfoot and came to a large log at the edge of the water.

"Would you like to sit, Sinead?" he asked, placing his coat on the log. She looked a bit dubious but half-sat, half-leaned against the wood.

"I'm sorry I came, I should just have the baby and give it up to the nuns, like the other women do." She sighed.

"Don't be sorry, I'm glad ye came here and if it's my child…"

"He *is*…"

"He?"

"Well, the baby, I just know it has to be yours. That night was the first I'd worked in two months. I'd caught a bad fever at the end of the winter and couldn't work for ages. That's why I was wearing so much make-up. I still looked pretty sickly," she hung her head. "After that night I couldn't continue working for Joe. I always thought Michael would find me and rescue me from that life in the city. When ye told me he was dead I realised of course he'd never come for me and, even worse, that he could probably see me, see everything…" She turned her large, sad eyes to him and shook her head. "I got a job in the mill after that and paid Joe back what I owed. Then I realised last month that I was pregnant."

"So ye stopped whoring after that night?"

She winced slightly at his words and he could see her beautiful cheekbones gleaming in the moonlight. She clutched her shawl defensively about her shoulders.

"I don't expect ye to understand – I had to look after Da but we couldn't go to the workhouse, not with his boozin', and my brothers had left us, took off to England after the evictions. I thought I'd get a job in a factory in Derry but then I met these women in the boarding house… One night all our money was stolen and they made it sound, well, alright. Da didn't care as long as I kept him in poteen."

She began to cry, long, deep sobs. Declan moved closer to her and brought her head to his shoulder.

"There, husshh, I didn't mean to upset ye. We've all suffered at the hands of that bastard, Adair," he hissed and looked across the lough in the direction of Glenveagh.

"Who?" she sniffled.

"The landlord, John Adair."

"Oh, I'd almost forgotten him. Is he still here? I'd heard he'd been threatened, that he'd gone to America."

"Yes, well he's back unfortunately but…" He hesitated. He couldn't tell her their plans. She might try to change his mind or tell someone. She'd gone quiet and he realised her eyes were closed where she lay with her head nestled into his shoulder. He could smell her hair and skin. He realised it felt good and he let himself relax.

"I should take ye back home," he said softly in her ear.

She bolted upright.

"Home? To Derry?"

"No, just up the path, home. I guess it's yer home now – if ye'll let me take care of ye both."

She smiled and he felt himself drawn to her lips. He kissed her gently and felt his head go into an even deeper spin. The lough lapped loudly in his ears.

Chapter 35

Declan pushed open the church door and held it for Sinead to enter. It was mid-week and empty of parishioners. Inside was dark and smelt dusty. Sinead tip-toed slightly behind him and appeared to cower from the row of watching saints at the side.

"It's fine," he tried to reassure her. "Look, Ma thinks the priest will understand."

She looked down doubtfully at her stomach and placed her hand over the slight swell. He took Sinead's hand and squeezed it attempting to reassure her.

"The priest will want us wed and ye know Ma and Cara won't let us stay under their roof unless we marry."

"And is it what ye want, Declan?" She peered at him.

He didn't want to go cap-in-hand to the priest again – Father O'Flanigan of all priests – but he couldn't abandon her. Michael would want him to take care of her.

"I-I want to do the right thing."

They walked together to the sacristy door beside the altar and knocked.

A voice cried out, "I'm not doing confessions this morning, come back tomorrow!"

Declan smiled a bit sheepishly at Sinead who looked even more terrified. Then he turned the door handle and put his head around the door.

"Hello, father, it's not about confession. Can we talk with ye?"

The priest swung around in his wooden chair and at the sight of Sinead jumped to his feet.

"Why Sinead, how are you? Where did you spring from? It's been such a long time."

He opened his arms and embraced her warmly. Immediately she started to cry. The priest looked at Declan with concern and stepped back. He searched in his cassock for his handkerchief and handed it to her.

"Come, my dear, what troubles you? Please, take a seat."

He offered Sinead his chair and they all sat down around the table where a large leather-bound copy of the catechism lay open. Declan began to pour out the story of Sinead's return, the pregnancy and their wish to get married.

Father O'Flanigan listened intently, taking occasional sips of water from a tin cup. At the end he said with a laugh which broke the tense atmosphere, "I did say no confessions today. And that was quite a confession – from both of you."

He then extended his hand to Sinead and held it loosely.

"My dear, I think God has punished you enough for it wasn't an easy road you chose after the evictions."

"She hardly chose it, father. None of us have many choices when we're destitute," Declan snapped.

The priest frowned and let go of Sinead's hand.

"I'm not denying you've both had a very difficult time, but we always have choices, Declan."

"Yes, we do," Declan muttered. Sinead caught both of them scowling at each other and stood up.

"I'm sorry father, I shouldn't have come." She started to cry again. "I should just give the baby up to the nuns."

Father O'Flanigan took her wrist and bade her to sit again.

"This baby is a gift from God, and I think it has come to rescue you both."

The priest then closed his eyes and held one hand in the air as he began the act of absolution. Declan ground his teeth and started scuffing the tiled floor with his shoe the way he did as a child when he got frustrated or annoyed during the priest's lessons. When Sinead touched his arm he realised he was making quite a din with his shoe. As the priest finished his prayer, she asked quietly, "So will ye marry us then, father?"

"Of course I will. I think it is best for you both and the child certainly."

"Thank ye, father," Declan said and looked around the old sacristy, trying to digest what was happening. Planning a wedding and a family was the last thing on his mind just days ago. All three stood and a sense of relief washed over Declan. Father O'Flanigan smiled and placed his hands on Declan's shoulders.

"I'm happy for you both," he said and then looking

closely at Declan he added, "I was a bit concerned when you returned from America and were spending time with those Sweeneys that you might, well, get involved in trouble. But this – these circumstances – give you a whole new start, don't you think? A new reason for living."

Declan's heart pounded in his chest. He felt like the priest could peer right into his soul. He took Sinead's hand and stammered, "Thank ye, we'll be in touch about arrangements. As soon as possible."

Sinead settled into the cottage as if she'd always lived there. It was a tight squeeze, four adults in the tiny two-room cabin, but they were all used to having little space. Despite that, Declan knew he would have to find their own home. He had a lot to think about. This hadn't been his plan when he returned to Donegal. He'd come to settle scores and say goodbye, dramatic though the end might be. But now there was this new life to consider. And Sinead.

She was more beautiful than he remembered her as a girl, especially now as Ma said with her "in full bloom" and she fired his blood with an energy he believed had died at Wilderness. But when his thoughts turned to marriage, it seemed tainted by the revelation that Glenveagh's cruel landlord had wed the beautiful heiress of Geneseo.

One afternoon, despite the heat, he put on his long overcoat. It helped conceal his shotgun. He mumbled to Sinead about working at the Sweeneys' and instead headed to the Glenveagh Estate. He climbed the hill to the vantage point and lay between the boulders, shuffling forward on his belly and resting his shotgun on his stump. He carefully wiped the sight-glass of the gun and adjusted the barrel for a closer look at the construction site. Immediately the little brown ants that he'd spied scurrying about below took shape. They were of course all workmen. He was disappointed there was no sign of a lady among them. As time passed, he considered approaching the lodge but was afraid he'd be apprehended by one of Adair's shepherds if he went there.

He became aware of a tingling in his stump and realised he'd been leaning the gun on his arm for a long time. He moved to adjust it and saw a pair of black boots, the toes pointed towards him. He quickly wriggled to a standing position, but the muzzle of a pistol was jabbed firmly into his shoulder.

"What's your business?" a voice growled. Declan dropped his gun to the ground and raised his good hand in a salute.

"New York 104th Regiment, sir!"

The gamekeeper looked startled by his response. His expression turned to unconcealed horror when he spied Declan's grass-stained stump but he recovered himself quickly.

"Well, it seems you've lost your way, soldier."

For what seemed like several minutes they stared at each other as if trying to work out what should happen next. Then the gamekeeper kicked Declan's gun aside with his foot.

"What were you after with that? There's no wildfowl around here."

Declan tuned in to his pronunciation of wildfowl and realised he was facing one of Adair's notorious Scotsmen.

"Seems yer lost too. It's a long way from the Highlands here."

"Never you mind what *I'm* doing here. This is my job. I work for the landlord, and you are trespassing."

He repeated his question, bending slowly to lift Declan's gun without taking his eyes off him. Declan pointed to the construction site below.

"I was just looking at the work. I'm interested, ye know, in castles."

"So what was the gun for? Are you one of those Ribbonmen or did they hire you for a job? I know people round here are still itching to put Adair off the walk. Is that what you've come for? This is very bad business. I'm going to have to bring you in…"

"I was just using the sight-glass of the gun – ye know, to get a better view." Declan stepped back as the gamekeeper prodded him with his own gun.

"Just you save your confessions for the landlord. He'll be keen to hear your story. Just so happens he be at home with his good lady wife, but reckon you knew that already."

Declan winced as the muzzle dug into his flesh. He dropped his head and trudged towards Glenveagh Lodge.

The gamekeeper marched him down the hill along a trail familiar to Declan as the same one the tenants used to trudge to pay their rent. The sullen pair entered the servants' quarters where another shepherd was scraping mud from his boots.

"Wait here," said the gamekeeper. "Watch him!" he added, throwing his gun to the puzzled shepherd.

"Yes, Mr Grierson!"

Grierson disappeared into the cottage, leaving Declan leaning slovenly against the scullery wall, his arms folded. The nervous-looking shepherd stood wearing just one boot and pointing his gun at the scar-faced captive. Declan considered how easy it would be to overpower the scrawny, half-booted man in front of him, but he was eager to meet the Adairs.

He wasn't kept waiting long.

There was a commotion beyond the scullery door and suddenly two men burst in. He instantly recognised the tall figure of Adair in a sombre suit followed by Grierson, grinning from ear-to-ear. Adair looked no different from the last time he'd seen him at the courthouse before the evictions. His dark beard was just peppered with more grey.

"Who are you?"

Declan straightened to his full height and stood square to Adair. They glowered at each other. Grierson stepped forward and shoved Declan's bad arm.

"Go on. Tell the gentleman what you told me, soldier!"

Declan glared at the gamekeeper and then turned back to Adair whose dark eyes seemed to bore right through him.

"My name is Conaghan, Declan Conaghan. I am from Gartan … sir."

Declan raised his chin as he had learned to do when responding to questions in the military. Adair stared with a puzzled expression at the crumpled, yet proud creature before him and pondered the name aloud.

"I found him with that shotgun, sir, high on the hill observing the castle," said Grierson, snatching the firearm from the wide-eyed shepherd.

"What were you doing on my estate with such a weapon? Were you planning to kill me?" Adair spat out the words as he examined the weapon.

Declan bristled. "No. I wasn't. I was just watching the castle being built. If I wanted to kill ye, wouldn't I have come here?"

Declan didn't see the fist before it connected to his jaw. Grierson then grabbed his collars.

"Enough of your cheek! Address the gentleman with respect."

"Hold it!" Adair commanded, raising his hand to Grierson. "Your name. I heard it recently, you said you were a soldier. You're not the young rectory maid's brother who fought in America?"

"Yes, I did, me and my brother," replied Declan, glaring at the landlord. "We were yer tenants. We paid ye rent and then ye destroyed our home. We ended up in the workhouse and then fled for a new life in America. My brother was killed fighting for a country we barely knew."

"You must be Private Conaghan from the Wadsworth Guards," a woman's voice interrupted from behind Adair and Grierson. "I am so pleased you came. I am Mrs Wadsworth Ritchie Adair but you may call me Cornelia."

She stood in the doorway, her face ashen. Declan stared

at the beautiful, petite woman in an elegant cream gown that seemed so out of place in the lodge scullery.

Declan slowly raised his good arm and saluted the lady.

"The Wadsworth Guards ma'am, until '64. The Battle of the Wilderness was my last rout before I was captured."

Cornelia managed a weak smile and cleared her throat.

"Yes, it was my father's, too. Such terrible carnage. Your sister told me you lost your brother in that same battle. I am so sorry for your loss."

Pressing her hands to her mouth, she crossed the scullery to stand next to him. Declan felt unnerved as she looked up into his face for what seemed like minutes.

"But you, you were one of the soldiers who tried to help my father. When I met your sister, I knew your name was familiar. I checked the last letter I received from my late husband. He described seeing you in the prison hospital. He didn't seem too hopeful for you in his letter and yet you survived and are now back home..." She swallowed hard. "I can't tell you how delighted I am to make your acquaintance, in Ireland of all places."

Her eyes began to water and she turned to Adair.

"Why are we having this conversation in the kitchen? We must bring this young man into the house. We have so much to discuss."

Declan could now feel Adair and Grierson's eyes boring into him.

"I met yer mother too, ma'am, after the war, in Geneseo. She was very good to me and gave me a job."

"She did, that's right, she told me..." Her voice drifted off as if she was miles away.

"Mrs Adair, this wasn't a social visit, I caught him near the castle with a gun," Grierson exclaimed and held up the rifle. Adair looked helplessly at his wife and back to Grierson.

"I meant no harm, ma'am," said Declan, appealing to Cornelia.

"Of course," she replied and frowning at Grierson. "What soldier doesn't carry a gun? John, you remember I told his sister I wished to meet him. This man was awarded for bravery, in relation to my father, the least we can do is offer him a seat."

She glanced across at Adair whose face had reddened. Declan felt the tension in the air and for one sweet moment enjoyed it. In that brief exchange Declan watched as the man he most despised in the world appeared to submit passively to his wife's request.

"Very well, if you wish to discuss that bloody war you may take him through to the lounge. I have some business to attend to, my dear. Grierson will chaperone you."

Adair pursed his lips and nodded to his land steward. Declan felt a wave of dizziness sweep across his head and stepped back against the wall.

"Ma'am, that is very kind of ye but I also have some business and must be on my way." He hesitated. "I apologise if … if I alarmed the gentlemen with my gun."

Cornelia smiled.

"Well, I was about to retire for the evening anyway. Hopefully we can meet again at a better hour. But I am glad we have met and, as I said, I am so *very* sorry for your loss. The United States will always be indebted to your service."

Declan felt his heart beat faster. Her words brought tears to his eyes more than the vicious punch from Grierson minutes earlier.

"Are you able to work still?" she asked, looking directly at his stump.

"I manage. I'm the best one-handed turf-cutter in Donegal!" He grinned and she smiled back, her face tired and flushed.

"We'll be needing staff to work in the castle grounds, won't we, John? I have plans to create some gardens. I daresay it won't be as strenuous as labour in the fields. If you're interested, Mr Conaghan, I'm sure my husband can make the arrangements."

She glanced across at Adair and then, without waiting for an answer, she departed with a rustle of her skirts. Adair was speechless for a few minutes, clenching and unclenching his fist, but once his wife was out of earshot he snapped at his land steward. "Escort him off the estate!" Turning to Declan, he added, "Don't let any of my staff find you trespassing again."

Declan threw him a parting glare.

"Trespassing? It seems I had an invitation, Mr Adair."

Chaper 36

Adair checked the living room first but there was no sign of Cornelia. Perhaps she really had gone to bed. He placed his hand on the wooden banister at the foot of the stairs and realised he was still trembling. The soldier had unnerved him in so many ways. The fact he was a trespasser with a gun was worrying enough, never mind the fact that the man had a clear motive for killing him. Those blasted evictees would forever haunt him. But most alarming was the connection to his wife. Not only had he fought in that bloody American war but he'd tried to save her father. In their short exchange he witnessed the soldier's gruff demeanour fall away and, in response, Cornelia spoke to him with what he could only describe as tenderness. He was confused and vexed by the whole episode. His usual recourse would be to pour himself a whiskey and fume but he knew he couldn't leave this to the morning. The bedroom was empty. Where was she?

"My wife? Have you seen her?" he asked one of the servants.

"Mrs Adair is in the study, sir."

Adair tugged on his beard and proceeded to the study. The door creaked as he opened it and Cornelia swung round from where she was standing at the window. He noticed she had a glass of some liquor in her hand.

"Ah, so you haven't gone to bed?"

"No, I'm not sure I'd sleep. Did you get rid of him?"

Adair frowned and pondered at the sudden hardness in her tone.

"He's gone if that's what you mean. Did you want me to get rid of him?"

"Why are we talking in riddles? I simply meant is he gone." She sighed and turned back to stare out at the lough.

"Yes, Grierson is seeing to that." Adair poured himself a drink. "My dear, I can see his arrival has shaken you, brought back memories of the war and all that... I appreciate he fought in your father's brigade but you must understand I cannot countenance him trespassing on my estate, especially armed with a gun. Not in light of everything..."

"In light of everything." As she echoed him he realised there was a hard edge to her voice. "If it wasn't for your father, I may never have known anything of that murky episode."

"Murky, why you make it seem sordid! These people detest me, they detest all landlords in this country." His voice rose as he jabbed his finger at the window. "They would happily see me float face down in that lough, you understand?"

"We don't know that he planned to shoot you. You heard him, he said he meant no harm."

Adair let out a half grunt, half laugh and gripped her upper arms. Cornelia wriggled free from him and pushed against his chest with her open hand.

"How many did you evict from their homes John? Fifty, a hundred? Tell me!" she demanded, her glistening eyes narrowing to slits.

"What difference would it make if I evicted two hundred and fifty?" he raged. "This is *my* land!"

Cornelia's voice dropped to a whisper. "You made that boy and his brother homeless. They took a boat to America seeking a better life. One of them was killed and the other is horribly maimed. Don't you feel any responsibility?"

"I didn't force them on to a boat or make them take up arms. I didn't take his brother's life. He is nothing to me, or us."

"He is to me – he fought with my father and then tried to save his life!"

She took a breath.

"There is something else I've just remembered. I met him and another relative briefly at the camp in Geneseo."

"What? You remember meeting him, that particular soldier? Do they not all look the same in their uniforms?" said Adair unable to hide his irritation.

Cornelia sipped delicately from the crystal glass and replied with a faraway look on her face, "Yes I remember now. Conaghan was the name, definitely. He and his uncle came to see the regimental colours while they were all still in training camp. I remember him because he understood the Latin inscription, which impressed us all."

Adair snorted. "That peasant would never understand Latin."

Cornelia's eyes widened.

"Is that how you saw them? Merely as ignorant peasants?"

Adair poured himself another whiskey.

"I'm sorry if you don't like my opinion of my tenants but I tried my best as their landlord and have had nothing but trouble from them. When I bought Glenveagh I was enchanted by the beauty of the landscape, this view of the lough," he said, pointing with his glass. "I knew immediately it would be the perfect hunting estate. I brought in herds of Scottish sheep, hardy animals best equipped for this terrain, in order to make some profit from the land. But the tenants jumped to their own conclusions and spread rumours that I planned to evict them all."

"And did you?"

"I did no such thing! What do you take me for, a monster?"

Adair swigged his whiskey and shook his head.

"There were dozens and dozens of pathetic potato plots on every hillock. How they could eke out a living from them I will never know. I merely followed my uncle's example. He advised me to improve the land by re-arranging tenants' plots, which would improve their situation." He felt his face flush.

Cornelia sat unblinking by the window.

"It all got out of hand," he continued. "The rumours

grew and the tenants became practically hysterical. My staff were threatened and in these parts there was a history of landlords being murdered over land disputes. I appealed to the authorities to calm the situation, but it was too late. Just before Christmas 1860, my good and loyal estate manager, Murray, was murdered."

Adair walked away from the window and flopped into an armchair.

"I gave the tenants an ultimatum – give up the killer or be evicted. They chose to harbour a criminal, a cold-blooded murderer. I had no choice but to throw them off my land."

Adair swallowed the last of his whiskey and tried to avoid his wife's gaze. The clock chimed violently in its case and seemed to cause the whole room to tremble. Cornelia unclasped her fan and began waving it.

"Collective responsibility," she muttered.

Adair stared at her with a puzzled expression.

"You heard me. You held all the tenants responsible for your land steward's murder and yet you resist the idea that this soldier might hold you responsible for his brother's death."

"You can't blame me for that boy's death; he was on the other side of the Atlantic!"

The door creaked open and the housekeeper appeared in the flickering light from the hallway.

"Is everything alright, sir, madam?" she asked, looking between the pair nervously. "Sorry, I was knocking but you mustn't have heard me..."

"We're fine. Thank you!" replied Cornelia with her back to the door. The housekeeper nodded and closed the door.

"Are we fine?" Adair asked, fidgeting with his pocket-watch.

"We, my dear? That all depends on you making amends with those peasants, as you call them. But don't worry. I'm an Adair now – *loyal au mort.*"

Adair frowned and with a rustle of her skirts she left him alone in the room with his view of the lough.

Chapter 37

"Ye always had the fastest boat," said Sinead with a pout of feigned annoyance and then her face creased into a huge smile. Declan picked up another stick. Holding it up, he pared away bits of twigs and knots from it and then held it out to her as she leaned back against the low wall over the brook.

"The trick is to choose the lightest stick and one that's not going to catch on rocks or in the reeds. See, try this one."

She snatched it from him and waited while he scrabbled in the dirt for another stick. He deliberately picked a weighty stick, which they set a yard apart on the wall.

"Alright, on the count of three," said Sinead, laughing. "One, two, three!"

They launched their boats off the wall and into the fast-moving stream below. It had been a favourite haunt of their childhoods. Michael had liked to paddle in the stream and Declan remembered one hot summer the girls stole their clothes and they'd had to find ferns near the lough to cover their modesty to get home. He wondered what Michael would think now, seeing Declan with his girl. He'd talked this over with Sinead and even his sister, and they both thought Michael would only want the best for them.

"What's the alternative, Declan?" Cara had said quite sharply. "Give the baby up to the nuns to raise in an institution like yon workhouse?"

When she put it in that stark light, he knew he was doing the right thing. But what of his pledge to his brother? He couldn't let him down.

"Mine's winning!" shrieked Sinead from across the lane. Declan hurried across and peered over the wall as Sinead's stick triumphantly sailed ahead of the heavier stick, which had hit a rock.

"Well done! See, it's not just luck but a little bit of skill," he said with a wink and put his arm about her waist. She grabbed his hand and placed it on her small bump.

"I'm glad ye came back, Declan," she said softly. Declan turned her round to look at her.

"I'm not worthy of ye," he whispered in her ear as they held one another.

As the brook babbled underneath them, he thought of all the water that had passed under the little bridge since they were kids. Through the innocent times, the hungry times, the painful times. He thought of how the evictions had scattered them so far apart. Michael to his grave in a distant war and Sinead to a whore's life on the streets of Derry. He swallowed a lump in his throat. Sinead lifted her head and he felt her bump brush against him.

"Are ye crying?" she asked.

He blinked several times and shook his head.

"Naw, my eyes sometimes water." He quickly wiped his face. "Look, I have to head over to the Sweeneys this evening – they need some help in the barn – so tell Ma I'll not be needing any dinner."

He was relieved she didn't ask any questions. Cara and Ma were both a lot more suspicious. They had quizzed him when he came home with a shiner on his jaw and his jacket ripped thanks to that Grierson fella at Glenveagh Lodge. He had made up a story about tripping on a spade at the Sweeneys but of course he couldn't tell that one to Sean or Owen. They were annoyed at first that he'd got caught by Grierson and especially the fact he'd confiscated the shotgun but it had resolved them all to hasten their mission to get rid of Adair. But when the Sweeneys learned about the baby they had given him the option then to back out.

"Ye have a kid to think about now, Declan. What if we get caught? That kid'll have no da. What'll Sinead do then?" said Sean.

"Aye ye can leave it to us, we'll finish the job," said Owen. "Ye helped us get the guns. Mind ye, ye did just lose one. Maybe it's a sign we're better off without ye."

Declan had glared at Owen for that remark.

"Look! I came back to do this. I promised Michael I'd kill Adair. Ye boys have had five, six years to have a go and ye done nothin'. So I'm still in this plot."

"And what about Adair's wife? Ye seemed concerned about her in the mix," asked Sean who was always so astute. He was right, Declan had been having doubts since setting eyes on her again at Glenveagh but knew that she'd be better off without Adair in her life. They would be doing her a favour, and he owed that to the Wadsworths, surely?

"She was a fool to marry him," snapped Declan. "Anyway we'll ambush him alone. She won't see it. All she'll know is he's dead and she'll get the first boat back to the States where she ought to have stayed."

Owen laughed. "She'll be wishing you stayed in the States too when we see to her husband."

"Right, that's that then," said Sean. "We have to do it before they really do head back to America. I'm told they've been packing cases so we have to get him on his return from Derry tomorrow night. That's probably our last chance."

Declan pondered all this as he left Sinead on the laneway and turned towards Glenveagh where he'd arranged to meet the Sweeneys. He stared up at the streaks of red and deep pink that shimmered on the skyline over Glenveagh Lough. The promise of another bright dawn in Donegal, he thought, although maybe not for some. He came to a small flock of sheep near the copse of trees where they had agreed to meet. There was a rustle and then a familiar hiss.

"So ye came after all," said Owen, rising out of the leafy hedge.

Declan grunted. "We got time yet and it's still bright."

"We brought ye a mask but rub some of that mud into yer face in case it gets pulled off," growled Sean, getting up from his crouched position. "It'll not be long if I've judged that train right. We brought some helpers," he said, nodding at the sheep.

Declan waded through the gorse bushes and scooped a dollop of moist dirt from the roots. He streaked his face, especially around his eyes, which were more visible through the sack holes. While Owen moved through the hedgerow further down the lane to keep a lookout Sean handed Declan a pistol, which he began to fidget with. A week had passed since his confrontation with the Adairs. A week in which he had wrestled even more with his conscience. He didn't want to cause Cornelia more pain, especially given how much he had revered her father and first husband, but there were other louder voices in his head. His pledge to Michael and his own desire for justice and indeed revenge. A half hour passed and the sun sank lower in the sky. Declan unclasped the pistol cap again.

"Are ye still not happy with that pistol?" said Sean, spitting at a nosy sheep. "Ye'll break it snapping it open and shut like that. I've gotta give it back in one piece."

Declan thrust the pistol into his belt, snatched up the sack mask and shoved it over his head. Then he squared up to Sean and spoke through the mask, which gave his speech a muffled, sinister tone.

"Are ye sayin' I can't handle a gun? Got more experience than the pair of ye put together. And ye'll not be handing it back to your pal, it's goin' in the lough straight after this! Got it?"

Sean backed away. A sharp-pitched hoot of an owl rang out and the two men looked to see Owen waving wildly at them from his viewpoint down the lane. Sean flapped at the flock of sheep who spilled out across the narrow road and began munching hungrily at the grass verge as Owen hurried back towards them. He was followed by the thumping hooves and trundle of carriage wheels, which were still a speck in the distance. Declan patted Sean on the back and got a grunt in return before he made a dash to the treeline on the other side of the lane. He crouched against the rough bark and felt his breath hot inside the sack mask. He was close to the roadside but hidden by the knotted birches whose shadows loomed around him. For a few seconds he thought he could hear the crackle of burning wood and splintering trees, and as he put his hands to his ears the sounds grew louder. Sounds that haunted him. The low boom of shelling and the faint moans of men yelling, then crying.

Declan shook his head as the cold dampness of the soil crept through his trousers where he knelt and he could feel his whole body shiver. He held his breath and tried to focus on the task at hand but he started to feel the moisture in the ground become warm next to his body and imagined he was kneeling in a pool of freshly-spilled blood. His heart raced as he mumbled his brother's name and shook his head again to block out the demons that seemed to come out of the woods' shadows. He snapped back to reality when the two-horse carriage came speeding around the corner heading straight for the woolly bundle in the lane. It came to an abrupt halt in front of him. The coach-driver was flailing his whip at the hapless sheep who stubbornly refused to move. Declan strained to see who was in the carriage. He could just see the outline of a beaver top-hat. It was definitely Adair and then a woman's face appeared at the window.

"Perhaps you could jump down and move them," the distinctive American accent called to the driver.

Declan felt his good hand grow numb as he clutched the pistol tighter. He thought Adair had gone to Derry alone. Hadn't he seen Cornelia in Church Hill that afternoon? She must have waited to meet her husband at the train. Damn, it was too late! All those gnawing doubts brought a wave of nausea to his stomach. The coach-driver had no sooner jumped down among the sheep than a hooded figure lunged at the driver from out of the shadows and hauled him to the ground with a yelp. Sean's burly weight kept the driver pinned to the ground as he grabbed the man's whip and pressed it tightly against his throat. Declan felt his body move mechanically out of the woods as if he was following orders again in the Army. As soon as the driver was felled, he and Owen sprang on to the carriage and pulled open both doors to the shrieks of the occupants. Adair struggled to get to his feet and knocked his hat off against the low ceiling of the carriage. Owen shoved Adair roughly back on to the seat beside Cornelia who hit their assailant with her silk parasol until he snatched it roughly from her. Adair threw the back of his arm around his wife as he attempted to shield her. The few strands of wispy dark hair on his balding head stood unkempt where his hat had once been.

"What the … Leave my wife alone, I beg you … Is it money you're after?"

"Aye, empty yer pockets!" growled Owen, spying the lady's handbag.

Declan peered silently at Adair from his perch on the carriage step where he hovered in the dark to disguise his missing limb. He suddenly produced the pistol and leaned half his body into the carriage. Cornelia screamed and lunged against her husband's arm but he held her back firmly. Adair slowly raised his other hand above his head and whimpered.

"No please, don't do this. We-we're just married. We have children…"

Declan stared out through the sack holes, unblinking, and raised the pistol to Adair's right temple. Seconds passed that seemed like minutes as the carriage reverberated with the wails and moans of its two passengers.

"Go on – finish him!" shouted Owen as he stuffed notes from Cornelia's handbag into his pockets.

Declan jammed the pistol tighter against Adair's head causing him to jerk open his eyes revealing the full fear of his dilating pupils. His bulging eyes brought to mind the fish-like stare of dead soldiers lying misshapen on the battlefield. He tried to imagine Adair in a kepi hat and the grey uniform of the enemy and nudged the butt of the gun harder against his skull. He hated the landlord more than any rebel but his finger had frozen on the trigger. Adair winced and shut his eyes tight again.

"C'mon, shoot him!" urged Owen who had begun to pull the sparkling rings from Cornelia's fingers as she sobbed. Declan wondered if she still wore Captain Ritchie's wedding ring. His head raced with words and blinding images. *Excelsior … be the best. Adair, the enemy. Shoot him! Grey-coat. Parasite landlord.* He saw Michael beat out the flames on the body of that rebel soldier. *Show mercy … Bloody battles of the wilderness*. He released a yell, a blood-curdling scream akin to the rebel shriek.

"Leave her alone!" he commanded, then he pulled the trigger.

A shot rang out but was muffled as the bullet lodged in the cushioned ceiling, filling the carriage with a cloud of feathers and dust. Coughing, Declan leapt down and motioned frantically for the Sweeneys to follow him. Sean had beaten the coach-driver unconscious and had been sitting on the driver's back waiting for the deed to be completed. He staggered through the trees after the pair, fleeing from the sounds of Cornelia screaming.

"What happened? Is he dead?"

"Keep running. We'll talk later," snapped Declan stuffing his sack mask into his jacket.

They staggered through the woods and ascended the hillside that overlooked the lough, leaping over boulders and falling into ditches in their haste to escape the scene of the ambush. They had passed a bend in the lough, out of sight from the lane, when Owen stubbed his foot on some loose stones and cried out. Declan and Sean stopped in their tracks at the sound of his gulder. Welcoming the break, Sean bent double, his hands on his knees, to catch his breath while Declan inspected the injured party.

"We can't stop here," said Declan, his neck swivelling feverishly around. "Adair's shepherds are all over this moor. C'mon, keep movin'."

Declan had barely broken a sweat.

"What the hell happened?" demanded Sean, glaring at Declan.

"He croaked it," panted Owen. "Fuckin' soldier and he couldn't shoot a sitting duck!"

"The gun jammed."

Declan felt a hand at his belt as Sean seized the pistol.

"Told ye ye'd break it – playing with it ye were before they pulled up."

Sean knocked the cap of the gun in his large rough palm. He examined it closely, inspecting the bullets and then slipped the cap back into place.

"One bullet, that's all ye used, huh?" he said, waving the gun menacingly in Declan's direction. "If this piece of steel had been in my hands, I wouldn't have left without emptying the whole lot into his skull."

Declan stared as if in a trance past Sean's bulging shape towards Glenveagh Castle. The valley was silent, except for the occasional hoot from a bird or lonely bleat echoing from the hillside. The lough itself was still, like a long wavy streak from a painter's brush that separated the mountain scenery in a picture. He remembered the night he'd saved the Sweeney brothers from being caught by Adair making poteen. His head rushed with thoughts about loyalty and brotherhood. The bonds you were born into and those created in the Army and by life events. A cool breeze danced into the clearing and briefly whipped around the three men who stood trembling in the shadow of an over-hanging rock.

Bang. Crack. Bang. Bang. The silence was shattered by several gun shots in quick succession. Declan dived to the ground for cover.

"Nothin' wrong with this gun."

Declan peered up at Sean who was idly pointing the

pistol in the air. Owen who lay beside him jumped to his feet.

"We better get the hell outta' here. Adair's men will have heard that," said Owen. "We're all done for now."

Declan rubbed his forehead and gave a huge sigh.

"I'm done for. They'll come after me, I know that but I'll say nothin'."

"They can't prove nothin'. We'll say we were home all night. Yer ma will say the same."

Sean shook his head. He then stretched his arm behind him and flung the pistol far out into the lough. They waited to hear the distant splash, then Sean stepped towards Declan and with a look of puzzled resignation slapped his shoulder. He nodded to Owen and they fled their separate ways.

Declan staggered home, dejected. He reached Cara's cottage and bristled at the sight of a flickering candle in the front window. He slipped through the back door into the parlour and began to strip off his shirt and undo his belt in a hurry. Cara appeared in the doorway, her arms folded tightly about her grey nightshirt.

"What's going on?"

Declan had begun to bundle his clothes together.

"I need to hide these, destroy them even, in case there's any sign of gun-powder."

"Ye killed him, ye've killed Adair," said Cara in a quiet, steely voice.

Declan stuffed the bundle into the smouldering fire and

then beckoned her to sit with him.

"Adair's not dead – he's very much alive. I did not kill him, just gave him a fright that's all."

"A *fright*? Oh, what have ye done, Declan?" she said, her pupils dilating from both the dark and fear.

"Listen, hush, listen. I'm a fool, I should never have gone with the Sweeneys. We ambushed the Adairs on the road to Glenveagh. I was to pull the trigger, blow 'em to bits but I didn't. I couldn't."

"But why, what happened?"

"She was with him and I just couldn't, I don't know…"

"Oh sweet Jesus, Mrs Adair was in the carriage? Was she hurt?" Cara had jumped to her feet and began pulling her hands through her hair.

"No one was hurt, I tell ye, believe me. I fired a shot but no one was hit. Then we ran away." Declan stared in despair at the clay floor.

"Such big, brave men ye are!" said Cara in a mocking tone that surprised Declan. "What did ye expect to achieve, huh? Put Adair off the walk and then what? The last murder in these parts saw most of us evicted, turned out into the cold, our homes burned down. Ye know that!"

Declan gazed up at her through hollow eyes but let her continue her speech.

"I despise Adair as much as anyone in this valley but murdering him makes ye as bad as him," she said, pacing the floor. Then she turned and stared hard at him again. "Didn't ye spill enough blood in America? Did ye have to come back here and spill more?"

Declan found his voice, as a rage welled up inside him.

"Adair declared war when he flooded the hills with his sheep and then evicted us all. I didn't start this war. I came to finish it!"

Tears filled Cara's eyes and began to spill down her red cheeks.

"And … and I thought ye came home to see us again, to be with yer family. B-but ye came home to kill…"

"I came home for Michael, it's what he wanted…"

"Yes, to come home to us, to be a family again but not to kill Adair."

"He wanted Adair dead too," said Declan in a low growl. "He'd have done it himself if he'd come home. I owed him."

"Then why didn't ye just kill him?" Cara raised her voice.

"Kill? Kill who, what's going on, at this ungodly hour?"

It was Ma clutching a shawl about her night-dress. Behind her stood Sinead. Declan jumped to his feet and tried to usher them back to bed.

"I'm sorry Ma, Sinead. We didn't mean to wake ye," he said, glaring at Cara.

"Are ye alright, Declan, ye look like ye've seen a ghost?" said Sinead, rubbing her sleepy eyes.

Before anything more could be said there was a low rumble outside followed by the thunderous arrival of horses' hooves. Declan looked helplessly around him, transfixed to the spot where the three women encircled him. There was a banging at the door and a voice boomed, "Declan Conaghan – are you in there? You are under arrest for the attempted murder of John Adair and his wife, Cornelia!"

Chapter 38

"I'm quite certain the snarling, scar-faced creature who was caught on my land with a shotgun was the same man under that mask last night," Adair said, his voice quivering with rage.

"But you didn't see his face?" asked Sergeant McSherry.

"No, but…"

"Well, we *are* questioning him sir. But he's denied everything and he has alibis who swear he was at home in Gartan all last night."

The police barracks in Church Hill were buzzing about the night's drama when Adair arrived accompanied by his wife, despite his protestations. He had hoped she'd stay in bed the next morning while he dealt with the police but she insisted she wasn't tired, despite the dark rings under her eyes.

His head was thumping from his own lack of sleep and the bruise on his temple from the muzzle of the pistol. He realised he was fortunate he only had a headache. His mind had raced all through the night when they eventually got back to Glenveagh Lodge. He'd tried to persuade her to leave at first light for Londonderry where they could take an earlier boat back to America, but she had refused.

"I'm not letting you out of my sight," she insisted. "I've already lost one husband; I don't intend to lose another."

Adair could hardly argue with that. So there she was, despite the very traumatic night, standing next to him at the police counter, dressed in an elegant lime-green dress.

"Who are his alibis, sergeant?" asked Cornelia in a calm voice that contrasted with her husband.

"His mother, sister, and his fiancée, a Miss Sinead Dermott," the sergeant replied reading from his notebook. "She is pregnant with his child."

"Feral heathens, the lot of them," Adair spluttered. "He'll not be much of a father locked up, will he!"

"John!" Cornelia exclaimed. "Surely he is innocent until proven guilty, that is the law of this land I presume?"

"Yes, but … but…" He turned to Sergeant McSherry. "You can't just accept their testimony at face value, they are his relatives, of course they're going to stand by him. This is a farce!"

The sergeant sighed and closed his notebook.

"We are searching for evidence and when we find it, we will nail your assailants, Mr Adair, you have my word. It is curious though, don't you think, that the gun was fired into the carriage ceiling. Was there a scuffle with the gunman?"

"I tried to protect my wife, yes…" Adair began but then he saw Cornelia look at him. "…But no, I didn't actually tackle the gunman."

"Well, if there was no scuffle and he seems to have had a working pistol then I would conclude that this ambush was a robbery or a bid to scare you rather than a serious attempt on your life, Mr Adair," said the sergeant.

"I'm telling you one of them clearly said 'go on – finish him'. We heard him clear as a bell, didn't we?"

Cornelia nodded in agreement. "Yes, and he repeated it," she said. "One of them was wrenching the rings off my fingers when he shouted 'go on – shoot him' but the gunman seemed to freeze. I saw him staring at me through the holes in his mask."

The sergeant looked at her. "Ah, did you see the colour of his eyes? Any distinguishing marks?"

Adair turned to his wife who looked down at her naked hands. She paused and then mumbled, "N-no, it was dark, I couldn't really tell."

"It would of course help if you were both able to identify him, which is the main reason I asked you here," said the sergeant.

"I'll give you your evidence. I'll identify Conaghan, my wife doesn't need to."

"Oh but John I must … I want to see Mr Conaghan," she insisted.

"My dear, I'd have preferred you stayed at home." He sighed and took her outstretched hand. "You really ought to try to forget this unpleasant business."

"Forget? How can I just *forget* being ambushed last night, having a gun pointed at us and then fired over our heads? I cannot sleep for the ringing in my ears; I *will* not sleep until this business is settled once and for all."

"Mr Adair, it would help our case if *both* of you were able to identify Conaghan as your assailant," said Sergeant McSherry.

"Very well," said Adair. "We shall both identify him and put this rat behind bars for a very long time."

The sergeant signalled for the prisoner to be brought up from the holding cell and ushered them into a room behind the counter. Two policemen joined them while Adair sat next to his wife on the wooden bench behind a table. Minutes later the prisoner was jostled into the room, handcuffed to another policeman. His hair was ruffled and a bruise darkened his left cheekbone. Adair jumped to his feet and went to lunge at the prisoner across the table but he could feel his wife's hand clutch his wrist.

"No, John, please!" she pleaded. He took a deep breath and fell back on to the bench beside her. Conaghan kept his head bowed, his eyes downcast. There he was, the same one-handed man who had spoken so defiantly to him in his kitchen. *I should have wrung his neck then, while I had the chance*, Adair thought.

"This is Declan Conaghan from Gartan, the man we arrested last night on suspicion of the ambush," announced the sergeant. He nodded at one of his men who pulled the prisoner's head back by the hair so his face could be seen. "Do you recognise this man?"

"Most definitely, that's him, that's the man who was caught skulking near Glenveagh Castle with a gun," said Adair, glaring at him.

The prisoner avoided his gaze and seemed almost drowsy the way his head lolled.

"But is he the man that ambushed your carriage last night?" enquired the sergeant.

"Yes, I'd recognise that scoundrel anywhere."

"But his face was masked, how can you be certain? Did he have any distinguishing features like this man has?" asked the sergeant pointing to the prisoner's missing hand.

"It's definitely him," Adair began.

"You're sure?" he asked, flipping open his notebook. "It's just in both your statements you said you could only partially see the second assailant, that he leaned in from the step with his gun. You made no mention of any of the assailants having just one hand."

"I may have omitted that detail," said Adair, frowning. "And now we know why he was leaning from the door frame because he was trying to conceal the fact he had just one hand."

"But if he planned to kill you, surely that wouldn't have mattered? Which goes back to my theory that this was always a robbery."

"Sergeant, my wife and I are certain this was an attempt on my life, *our* lives. Just as these men hid their faces, this one attempted to hide the fact he has only one hand."

Adair began to rap his knuckles on the table in agitation as the policeman continued to make notes. Cornelia cleared her throat and gently took his hand.

"May I speak, sergeant?" she asked.

"Of course, Mrs Adair, I was just coming to you. You've observed the prisoner and I know you met him briefly at Glenveagh Lodge. Do you believe this same man ambushed you last night?"

She took a quick breath and replied, "No, it's not him."

Adair gasped and his head swivelled from his wife to the prisoner who blinked several times before dropping his gaze again to the floor.

"I know it's not him because I didn't see anyone with a missing limb. I saw all three as they ran away. This man isn't one of them."

"Cornelia! How? What? Of course this is the man…" Adair jumped to his feet. But Cornelia calmly sipped some water that had been placed on the table.

"I'm sorry, dear, but I know what I saw. You had dust in your eyes and then you began examining the bullet hole in the roof while I watched them all flee. There were three of them and none…" She paused. "None like him."

Adair thought he detected a smile twitch on Sergeant McSherry's lips.

"Are you absolutely certain of this, Mrs Adair? It is an important piece of evidence. You've heard your husband thinks differently."

Adair's mind was racing over the aftermath in the carriage. He had indeed stared in shock for some minutes at the hole in the roof and couldn't recall what his wife was doing during that time. Cornelia gave a loud sigh.

"Yes, but I cannot be expected to perjure myself in a court of law just so my story tallies with my husband's," she said and then turned to Adair. "John, trust me, he's not one of them."

Adair's fist thumped the table making them all jump, except for Cornelia who simply raised an eyebrow. She began to roll on her silk gloves, which had been dangling over her handbag.

"Sergeant, you may not be aware but this man is a war hero," she said. "I would hate to think he received that bruise on his face while in your custody."

Sergeant McSherry looked perplexed.

"Bruise? Oh, that, yes – no, I mean no, my officers wouldn't have done that."

"Glad to hear. Mr Conaghan, I really do hope we meet in better circumstances someday. I'm sure our paths will cross again."

She stood swiftly to much scraping of chairs around her, including the prisoner who mirrored Adair's own surprised expression.

"I think we're done here, dear," she said to him.

Sergeant McSherry stood up and made to usher them out of the room.

"Mr Adair, this is a very early stage in the investigation. I assure you we will track down your assailants and we will keep you informed of our progress."

Adair could feel the rage rise inside him, only controlled by the fact his wife was nearby. He stepped as close as possible to the sergeant's ear and hissed, "You owe me sergeant, I want someone to go down for this, not like the last time…"

The sergeant stiffened.

"What? The last time when you destroyed the whole village over Murray? We would have got the culprits for that eventually, but no one was going to give them up after your actions."

Adair stepped away from the sergeant's glare. The policeman then shifted his face to smile at Cornelia.

"We have a police escort waiting in the carriage outside, just to offer you some protection and comfort, Mrs Adair."

She thanked the sergeant. Adair felt her small hand slip into his and she led him outside into the misty morning. Rising out of the mist was the steeple of St Columba's across the road from the barracks and beside it the cemetery. A shiver went down his spine as he considered what could have happened on that lonely lane to Glenveagh last night. Cornelia caught his gaze and squeezed his hand.

They sat in silence on the journey home until they were approaching Glenveagh Castle.

"Shall we stop here for one last look around the grounds?" said Cornelia.

"Certainly, my dear, perhaps it will be our last look," he replied, knocking the roof for the driver's attention. They slowed to a halt at the perimeter wall and he watched his wife lift her long skirts and breeze majestically past the builders towards the front entrance. They hurriedly dropped their barrows and doffed their caps and he smiled in sympathy with their reaction. She had turned his world upside down too. This morning's events had confounded him again. He always thought he'd find an obedient wife, and yet it was her headstrong ways that he was attracted to. His world, which had once been so grey and drab, was now colourful. A ray of sunshine filtered through one of the battlements illuminating her green dress. If Townsend had been there, he could not have drawn a better picture, he thought. He had designed the granite structure but she … she brought the castle to life. As he watched her sweep across the courtyard, he remembered his vision of a hunting estate for ladies and gentlemen. She turned around and waved him over.

"John, what are you doing standing there?"

He hastened to her side and confessed, "I was just admiring you."

"Really, not the view this time?"

"You are better than the view, my dear."

"Very charming. I know you're upset with me and I understand but I just couldn't say that man was … was involved in what happened last night."

Adair sighed.

"You're just protecting him because of his past, his war record," Adair hesitated. "And yes I-I can see why you would."

Cornelia shook her head. "That's not it. I know what I saw and what I didn't see. Besides, even if we had both identified him, I doubt it would have been enough to secure a conviction. How strong a case is the evidence of two people attacked in the dark by masked assailants? It would be thrown out immediately."

"I should never have brought you here," he said, shaking his head. "I can sell Glenveagh."

"*Sell* Glenveagh? But what about our plans, and the castle? It's nearly finished."

Adair stared blankly at his wife.

"So you want me to keep Glenveagh?" he asked, puzzled.

"Of course I do, I adore it here," she said and paused. "I trust you when you say your intention was just to improve the land, even if you went about it, well, rather clumsily. Progress, I believe, is something that cannot be halted. To me, Glenveagh has parallels with Geneseo. Just like my father, I know you have a vision for the land. You must see it through after all the efforts you've made…"

Adair nodded solemnly and revisited in his head Cornelia's family home, tastefully decorated with ribbons and balloons at their recent wedding. And the acres of land her father and forefathers had owned and cultivated out of wilderness.

She pointed her parasol to the coat of arms above the doorframe.

"I asked to stop here to reaffirm my commitment to you, darling. I am an Adair now. Just as the inscription says: '*loyal au mort*'. But I want to have a husband for many years. Goodness, if I were to lose you too, I'd get a reputation for being careless!" She laughed.

"But I can't guarantee your safety here. Last night's ambush was a shock but…"

"So you're just going to run away, after all you've done with the castle, the land?" Cornelia stared at him, wide-eyed.

"You can't reason with these people. Why my Uncle Trench—"

"Your uncle is not someone I'd be seeking advice from, John," interrupted Cornelia to Adair's astonishment. "I know you'll not want to hear this but your father told me all about Mr Trench and his land dealings. If you are so afraid of assassination, why on earth would you heed someone who has attracted death threats for years! I never knew a wiser man than the late President Lincoln who once said, 'the best way to destroy an enemy is to make him a friend'."

"Huh, his wisdom didn't save *him* from assassination!" Adair sneered.

"Well, you would have been wise to have heeded his words when murder visited this estate, for Lincoln also said, 'mercy bears richer fruits than strict justice'. You have only yourself to blame for your unease. Why do you employ only Scottish shepherds? If the local people felt some ownership of the estate and the new castle then they would come to treasure it and ultimately support you."

"I've had to bring servants in from outside the district because nobody will work for me."

Cornelia's tone softened. "I'm not saying it will be easy, John. It takes time to win people over, but we can make a start. I meant what I said about offering the soldier work in the gardens. It's the least I can do to make up for what he's been through." She sighed. "Though we should probably let the dust settle first. It is better than building a fortress where you lie in fear of being attacked. That's not somewhere I want to bring my children."

"But we have homes in London, New York and my father's estate at Bellegrove. Glenveagh is surplus to requirements."

"Nonsense!" said Cornelia, sticking out her chin defiantly. "It is a project we shall complete – together. The scenery and the castle are spectacular. Let's not give up just yet on Glenveagh."

He gazed at his wife with a mixture of admiration and relief. Then, clearing his throat, he raised his hand in a mock toast. "To us and Glenveagh!"

"To us and *Gleann Bheatha*!" she replied with a twinkle in her eye. "That's it in Gaelic, my dear."

Chapter 39

Declan stumbled up the familiar stone steps from the bowels of the police barracks, stepped outside and blinked in the daylight. There was blue sky ahead in Gartan but over him a grey cloud rained a light drizzle. He turned his face upwards and enjoyed the spray of water. It revived him. He stood at the edge of the road and considered the two directions he could go. Right would take him to Derry where he could take a boat and leave Ireland for good. Left, the shorter journey, would take him back home to Gartan where he could try to make a life for himself and Sinead. It was a shorter journey but standing there in the drizzle it seemed a steeper mountain to climb. He'd had three days in the dark cell to ponder the future. Because thanks to Cornelia Wadsworth he *had* a future.

"The Adairs have gone back to New York," Sergeant McSherry had said as he jangled the keys to his cell. "You're free to leave. Just stay away from Glenveagh, for my sake."

Now, Declan smiled. He knew in his heart he couldn't

stay away from Glenveagh and he made up his mind to go home.

He walked slowly towards Lough Gartan whose crystal-clear waters lapped gently in the breeze. A couple of fishermen doffed their caps at him but carried on their quiet pursuit as he turned up the hill to Glebe House, which appeared empty. Then he remembered it was a Sunday. The minister and his wife would be at church. He turned up the lane towards Cara's cottage and just as he wondered if they would be at home or at Mass, he heard a woman's voice.

"Look! It's Declan!" Sinead shouted from the half-door. She pushed it open and hurried down the path to greet him. He held her tight for some minutes, feeling the warmth of her neck pulsate against his own. When he looked up from their embrace, he could see a line of severe faces standing in the doorway. Ma with her hands on her hips; Cara, a younger version of Ma with her arms folded; and the Widow McAward bent nearly double over her stick.

"So they released you?" Ma said with a frown but her hand gently brushed his face. He nodded, afraid to meet her gaze.

"It would have been a hero's welcome had ye done Adair in good and proper but at least ye sent him scurrying back to the States," the Widow McAward cackled.

"Hussshhh!" said Cara, her eyes wide. "I'm on thin ground as it is after his heroics. We can't have any more trouble or I'll lose my position and this cottage. D'ye understand?"

It felt strange to be scolded by his sister but Declan accepted it.

"I'm sorry," he mumbled. Fearing another interrogation, he changed the subject. "I thought you'd all be at Mass – praying for my soul."

"We did go," said Ma, shrugging her shoulders. "But there was no priest. Father O'Flanigan has disappeared."

Declan looked puzzled. The Widow pointed her stick towards Lough Gartan.

"I may have been the last person to see him. He was wailing and praying at the Stone of Sorrow night before last. I was making my way home and thought I'd stumbled upon an injured creature."

"Did ye speak to him?" asked Declan.

"Well, I asked him what was troubling him, but he didn't make much sense. Said there was too much pain in the district. First the Great Hunger, then the evictions and now these men with guns. Kept repeating the bad men with guns."

"Ah, did he mention me?"

The Widow squinted at him.

"He muttered about Ribbonmen but I mentioned ye. I said, 'sure wasn't it good news that the police won't be chargin' Declan'."

"And what did he say to that?"

The Widow closed her eyes as if in thought.

"'Twas a strange reaction, since I always thought he was very fond of ye. He covered his face with his hands and began to wail again. At that I went on my way."

Sinead looked at him and slipped her hand into his.

"Ah well, we'll just have to find another priest to marry us."

Declan digested the news and her pretty face. When he found his voice again, he smiled and squeezed her hand.

"We'll find a better priest."

For months after the ambush on the Adairs, Declan worried he'd betrayed his brother by not killing the landlord and he had a repetitive nightmare in which he fired the gun at Adair and then turned it on himself. He'd wake up in a cold sweat, shouting in his sleep. Sinead was always there to calm him and whisper gently so as not to wake everybody. He never told her what the dreams were actually about and let her think they were terrors from the war. As the nightmares continued, he moved out of their bed and slept by the hearth, out of fear his rolling and flailing would injure the unborn child. As her bump grew, they all treated Sinead with kid gloves. Cara would often come home from a day's work at the rectory and insist she would do the cooking and cleaning. Ma did her part too, going daily to the well and taking their eggs and butter to the market. Declan smiled and thought how it seemed they were all having this baby. He yearned for a place of their own but the rectory cottage was better than any hovel he could afford. Da would be relieved that his grandchild wasn't being raised in the workhouse.

In January, Michael Daniel Conaghan was born and Declan's nightmares stopped. He stroked the baby's clammy, pink skin while Sinead held him in her arms and wondered at the miracle of this tiny new life. He'd spent so many years staring at death that he felt unsure how to nurture this helpless little creature. His son. Michael's nephew. Ma's grandson. For weeks he would come home and just sit staring at the baby in the little basket Sinead had woven out of reeds from Lough Gartan.

"He *is* yours, ye know," Sinead said quietly one evening when Ma and Cara weren't in.

Declan looked up, surprised. "I never doubted ye Sinead. I just can't help staring at him, it's like I can't believe he's real."

"He's real alright when yer stuck here all day with him crying," she said, rolling her eyes.

He laughed but didn't confide in her his worries at being able to look after them.

The community braced itself for reprisals for the attempt on Adair's life but in the weeks that followed were surprised instead by an outpouring of generosity. First a donation arrived for Gartan school "to acquire books and necessary equipment". Then a substantial donation arrived for the church. A newly ordained priest was installed to replace Father O'Flanigan, whose whereabouts remained unknown. The young, bookish new priest, Father Kair, read a letter from the pulpit one Sunday.

"We have received a donation for the parish from Cornelia Adair on behalf of herself and her husband. She has suggested it be used for Poor Relief funds and church repairs. She also states…" He peered over his glasses. "…

'On a brief visit to the graveyard I noticed there is a mass grave for famine victims, marked by a flimsy wooden cross. I would like some of our donation to be used to erect a more sturdy headstone to honour the deceased'."

That spring Father Kair held a small memorial service for the unveiling of the headstone, which most of the parish attended. The Conaghans held hands in a row as the priest blessed the headstone and Mairead began sobbing quietly as Dan Conaghan's name was read out. Declan felt a sense of peace as he saw the engraving of his father's name but the peace was quickly shattered by the squawks of the new-born baby who was oblivious to the solemnity of the ceremony in honour of his grandfather.

Cornelia's presence continued to be felt in Glenveagh as she had engaged a local sculptor on a project, which fuelled wild rumours that a statue was to be erected of the landlord. The rumours were quickly dispelled by Reverend Maturin who revealed to Cara when she was serving his tea, that he and Father Kair had been consulted by the new landlady on an appropriate inscription on the sculpture.

"One that will unite the community and give them hope," wrote Cornelia in a letter to the clergymen.

"We immediately seized on the most famous figure to emerge from Gartan, if not from this island," the reverend explained to Cara.

Several months later the finished work was positioned next to the Stone of Sorrow, not far from the site of many of the evictions. A seven-foot high, granite Celtic cross towered heavenward and around its base was the inscription:

Preserve with each other sincere charity and peace – St Columba

Declan stood at the foot of the cross one hot July day and marvelled at the impressive piece of stonework. As he pondered the inscription, he understood better why Mrs Adair had defended him to her husband. He thought of what she had endured in the civil war. Despite her wealth, she too had suffered. He fiddled in his pocket with the brief letter he'd received from Mrs Adair inviting him to see her at the castle about a job. He wasn't the most sought-after labourer given his stump and the work he'd got from the Sweeneys tended to be seasonal so there was no denying he could use the money as the joy of having a son had quickly turned to worry at being able to provide for them.

"Sincere charity and peace," he muttered to himself and took the path to Glenveagh Castle.

Chapter 40

It was a beautiful, cloudless day. The kind that made him glad to be alive. Bees were buzzing in the bright yellow gorse and a choir of birds called cheekily to each other from the trees and hedgerows. He passed the stone ruins of cottages that lay like tombs across the landscape, but he'd long forgotten who had once lived there. Flocks of sheep covered the lower slopes, more than he'd ever seen and in the distance was his destination, the grey stone turret of Glenveagh Castle. The workmen that had swarmed the castle last year had all but gone and as he walked past the stag-head pillars into the yard, it was very quiet, as if no one was home.

Declan straightened the brim of his cap as he stared at the castle, confused by all the doors. He gazed up in wonder at the Adair coat of arms and the meaning of the inscription "*loyal au mort*". The foreign words together with the gleaming black door and its large lion-faced knockers sent him scurrying to find the back entrance. As he followed the new gravel path to the castle rear, he heard a rustle in the bushes, which he dismissed as birds and simply quickened his pace. But then a sudden high-pitched squeal followed by blood-curdling yelps caused him to stop dead and he stood back against the wall as footsteps came pounding towards him. A massive head-dress of feathers came rushing around the corner waving a stick in the air. Declan stared in amazement. The creature was no taller than his waist but was making a whooping sound, patting his hand frantically across his mouth. The child caught sight of him and came to a halt. As he did the bushes erupted and a slightly bigger child leapt out wearing an American cowboy-style hat. He pounced on the feathered boy and started pummelling him to the ground.

"Ahh, get off, get off!" shrieked his victim rolling on the grass.

"Take that Big Chief, see who's the best warrior now!" the cowboy yelled back in an American accent.

"Get off, Arthur. Look behind you!" the little Indian moaned.

Declan watched the scene with a mixture of amusement and nervous anticipation. The cowboy's hat slipped off his head and hung around his neck. He turned around and Declan noticed his pink ears redden when he realised he was being watched. He quickly scrambled to his feet, releasing his squirming, feather-clad brother.

"Excuse us," said the blonde cowboy. "We were just playing. What happened to your hand, sir?"

Declan stepped forward and stooped to address the red-faced child.

"Ye must be Mrs Adair's sons. I saw ye boys some years ago in Geneseo at the start of the war," he smiled and patted his shoulder. "That's what happened to my hand. I lost it in the war."

The feathered boy had risen to his feet but had removed his head-dress revealing an even more startling mop of brown curls. He walked up to him.

"Were you a soldier, sir?" he said, staring with his large blue eyes. "Our father and our grandfather were soldiers, but they died in the war. Did you know them?"

Declan hesitated. It was such an innocent question from a child and the answer seemed so unlikely.

"As a matter of fact, yes, I knew them both," said Declan, ruffling the Indian's brown curls. "They were very brave men. Yer grandfather was a famous general."

The boys continued to stare at him … or mainly at his stump.

"I am Big Chief Running Water. Was my grandfather as famous as the Indian chiefs?" asked the boy.

"Oh, far more so!" Declan laughed, enjoying their accents.

"He's called Running Water 'cos he wets the bed," sniggered the cowboy.

"Our stepfather brought me this," said the little Indian. "He got it from a real Indian on his travels to the Plains. He's been, you see, to the Wild West!"

"Well, boys, I see you've found our visitor."

Declan looked up and was startled to see the neat figure of Cornelia in a long, lemon dress and sun bonnet. He quickly removed his cap.

"He's a soldier, Mama, fought in the same war as Papa," said the Indian.

"Yes, I know, Monty, thank you for finding him – now why don't you pair run to the nursery and wash your face and hands for afternoon tea? I'm sure you're both hungry from running around."

"Starving, Mama! Bye mister soldier, sir!" said the cowboy, and the pair ran off towards the castle. Declan watched them run away and half-wished he could follow them.

"Shall we take a turn in the gardens? Well, what is to *become* the gardens," she said.

"I'd be obliged but does the lady not need an escort?" Declan mumbled.

"Oh, there are servants everywhere. Don't concern yourself, we are being watched."

Declan looked over his shoulder and noticed a face at the window.

"Ye asked to see me, ma'am, about some work?"

She walked a little ahead of him across the courtyard and up a number of steps into what appeared to be a ploughed field. He dutifully followed. She stopped dead at the top of the steps and turned to face him.

"I want this to be the kitchen garden interspersed with some foliage and a rockery to make it pretty, and down that slope over there I want a lawn and some hidden paths for my visitors to enjoy the fresh air." She gesticulated with her hands as she described her vision. Declan smiled, her enthusiasm was infectious.

"I will employ a team of labourers to do the heavy work

and I thought with your army experience you could manage a small number of gardeners. As head gardener a cottage will come with the job." She fixed her gaze on him. "Don't you think a castle with such an aspect as this ought to have beautiful gardens to go with it?"

Declan wanted to say, *you have the castle, the lough, the valley, what more could you want*, but found himself nodding in agreement.

"You don't have much to say, Mr Conaghan."

He looked nervously at his feet.

"How is yer husband, Mrs Adair?" He surprised himself as the question tumbled from his mouth.

She paused and then smiled. "He is very well, thank you for asking. He won't be at Glenveagh this summer. He's tied up with some business interests in Texas."

"Ah, the Wild West – yer boys were telling me that's where they got the Indian head-dress."

"Yes, there's a ranch there we're interested in acquiring but my husband's having some trouble with the natives."

Declan felt himself relax a little at the news that Adair was not around when suddenly the tone of the conversation changed.

"Mr Conaghan, I mean you no harm," said Cornelia, her confident manner starting to crack as she raised her voice. "I was troubled by your sudden appearance at Glenveagh last summer. I had wanted an opportunity to speak with you and talk about your time with the Wadsworth Guards but then there was that awful night … I had only just learned about the extent of the evictions and then I was stunned when I recognised your name from the letter…"

"What letter?" asked Declan, puzzled.

"My husband Monty wrote to me after he had secured my father's body from the prison hospital," she said, taking a deep breath. "It was one of his most vivid letters – and his last. It had been a difficult task crossing enemy lines, never mind the emotional devastation of retrieving my father's body."

She pulled out her handkerchief and Declan could see she was trembling. He wanted to reassure her but he knew he couldn't touch her.

"He described in his letter the bravery of you soldiers who tried to help my father in Wilderness. He felt terrible leaving you in the prison hospital with your wound and how wretched you were from losing your brother. He said the sight had made him more determined than ever to get the war finished." She paused. "His last words were 'Men must do their utmost to prevent conflict'."

"He was a good man, yer first husband," offered Declan.

"Indeed he was. It pains me to think of what he could have achieved after the war, and my father too. So much suffering and loss."

She stopped and looked closely at him.

"It saddens me that your family were caught up in the war, that you should even have been fighting in it. I understand it may be difficult for you but I pray you do not harbour grievances against my husband John, if not for my sake for your own family's sake…"

Declan looked away beyond the castle towards Gartan Valley.

"I have a young son now. We named him after my

brother."

"I'm glad. Hard as it can be, life goes on," she said quietly and dabbed the handkerchief to her neck. The sun glinted off the diamonds on her ring finger, which caught his eye.

"They didn't get all your rings—" He stopped abruptly.

"They ... No, he got one but you stopped him from taking the rest."

Declan found his face burning beneath his beard but he stayed silent.

"I know you were there that night," Cornelia said softly. "You froze when you saw him pulling off my rings, didn't you? I think Monty's spirit was protecting me."

Declan stared straight ahead with a haunted expression. He then began to gush.

"There were ghosts about that night. I could feel them all around me whispering 'kill him', 'don't kill him'. I went numb ... but the sight of ye and my memories of yer family, well I couldn't go through with it."

He stopped and looked around anxiously, expecting the police to appear. But it was just the two of them standing at the steps facing the lough.

"Why did ye protect me? Why did ye not have me hanged?"

She pursed her lips and frowned at him almost like she was scolding her children.

"And what good would that do? You showed us mercy that night, I merely returned it. I – that is my husband and I – just want to end this battle."

Declan stared at her in awe. She met his gaze and said

with a harder glint in her eye, "All I ask is that you and your … associates will not threaten my husband again. Whatever you think of him, he is the new father of my children and has treated them like his own. I can assure you that while I'm lady of Glenveagh it shall be a place of peace."

Declan felt a lump form in his throat.

"Thank ye for yer kindness to the whole estate, Mrs Ritchie— I mean, Adair," he stammered. "The headstone especially means a lot to my family. I hope this will be a new chapter for Glenveagh."

Cornelia smiled.

"That is my hope too. So, Mr Conaghan, will you help me create my gardens? I want Glenveagh Castle to be the talk of Donegal, indeed all Ireland."

Declan looked down at the cap in his hand.

"Can I think about it please? I just…"

"Of course you may. I will be here all summer. And know this, you would be working for me, not Mr Adair. My husband has given me carte blanche with the gardens."

"Carte…?"

"Complete freedom, Mr Conaghan."

Declan felt a lightness in his step as he left the castle and walked alongside the sparkling blue waters of the lough. At a bend in the lane a fox appeared and stopped to stare at him with its yellow, hungry eyes. They watched each other for a minute. The fox didn't seem menacing in the sunlight and with a swish of its red, bushy tail, it disappeared.

Author's Note

The Wilderness Way is mostly based on a true story.

John Adair was the landlord at Glenveagh from 1858 and his cousin Townsend Trench designed the castle which is now a major tourist attraction in Donegal, as part of Glenveagh National Park.

Adair clashed with his tenants mainly because he began filling the estate with sheep. His land steward, James Murray was brutally murdered in November 1860 – a crime that remained unresolved. This led to the Derryveagh evictions in April 1861 when as many as 244 tenants, including 159 children were evicted over the course of three snowy days.

There was a family called Conaghan among those evicted but I had little information about them other than they were a widow with two children, a sister and brother-in-law.

Of course, there are lots of examples of cruelty by landlords throughout Irish history. What made this fascinating to me was the timing – 1861 – and the fact Adair married an American Civil War widow.

The evictions took place in the very month the American Civil War erupted. Many Irish who emigrated to America in the 1860s were drafted into armies, on both sides, to fight a conflict they understood little about.

It was also just a decade after "the Great Famine or Hunger" which devastated the Irish population and from which it has never recovered. An estimated one million people died and another million left the country, many for the United States.

After the war Adair married Cornelia Wadsworth Ritchie, the widowed daughter of a very wealthy Civil War general, James S. Wadsworth who died at the Battle of the Wilderness in 1864.

The Adairs eventually owned homes in New York, Texas, London, Queen's County (now Co Laois) and of course Donegal. Cornelia had so many choices but spent most of her summers at Glenveagh Castle. It is a stunning place, with breath-taking scenery.

Beside the National Park you can still find the large Celtic cross erected by Cornelia in the same small field as the Stone of Sorrow and views over Lough Gartan – the scene of the evictions.

The fact it is so remote makes the dramatic history and its connections to far-flung places even more incredible. And this is just the first chapter in the history of Glenveagh Castle.

Dictionary of phrases

Barmbrack (brack) – Yeast bread with added sultanas and raisins
Boxty – Traditional potato cake
Céilí – Form of folk dancing
Galluses – Pair of suspenders for trousers
Gulder – Ulster Scots word for a shout or yell, used widely in the north of Ireland
Great Famine (Great Hunger) – From 1845-52, the main cause was a fungal blight that ruined the potato crop. The infestation was first observed in the United States. It quickly spread to Europe but because Ireland was so dependent on potato for food, almost one million died and a further million emigrated. The Irish population size has never recovered.
Hardee hat – Regulation dress hat worn by enlisted men in the Union Army
Keening – Wailing in grief

Laneway – A narrow roadway

Lough – Loch or lake

Loy – Long narrow spade used for digging turf

Oat-tatties – Boiled potatoes coated in butter and toasted oatmeal

Porter – Style of beer, well hopped and dark

Poteen – Whiskey with very high alcohol content, made from potatoes

Ribbonism – 19th century Catholic secret societies that were opposed to the Protestant ascendancy and English governance which mainly played out in grievances against landlords

Scraw – A sod of grass from a bog; the poorest form of turf for burning

Shebeen – An illicit bar where alcohol was served without a licence

St Columba and Colmcille – one and the same monk/ saint from Gartan. Columba is the Latin name, Colmcille his name in Irish meaning 'Dove of the Church'

Stirabout – A very thin porridge consisting of oatmeal or cornmeal

Sutler – Civilian merchant during American Civil War who sells provisions to soldiers

Some Irish words

Acushla asthore machree – 'O pulse of my heart' or my love in Irish

Bodhrán – Celtic drum held in the hand consisting of a circular wooden frame covered with a goatskin head on one side and played with a stick

Dia Linn – 'God bless' in Irish

Gleann Bheatha – Glenveagh, meaning Glen of the birches

"In ainm an Athar agus an Mhic agus an Spioraid Naoimh. Amen." – The sign of the cross in Irish: In the name of the Father, and of the Son and of the Holy Spirit.

Rath Dé ort – An Irish blessing 'Grace of God on you'

Sláinte – A toast in Irish meaning 'health'

Acknowledgments

I am grateful to everyone who has encouraged and supported me to write this book. It has been a long journey from inception to publication – not so much due to writer's block but, like many authors, trying to juggle writing with a full-time job. There were many times I didn't feel like opening my 'Epic' file on the computer but as my dear journalism lecturer Brendan Anderson reminded me, "So much of writing is about sitting down at your desk!"

I want to thank Marion Urch from Adventures in Fiction. After winning the Spotlight First Novel Award, her mentoring helped to shape the novel that's now in your hands.

There are so many different styles of writing. News reporting is very different from creative writing, so I would like to acknowledge those who inspired me over the years at creative writing classes and events at the Crescent Arts Centre in Belfast. I also benefited from the wonderful libraries we have in Northern Ireland, from the one I went to as a child in Glengormley (where I devoured all the Topsy & Tim books!) to the awe-inspiring Linen Hall Library in the centre of Belfast since 1788.

I would like to thank all the historians I've met who have sparked my interest in the subject: Edward McCamley at

Belfast Royal Academy; the late Éamon Phoenix; Dr Benjamin Thompson and Prof Joanna Innes from Somerville College, Oxford; and the late esteemed American historian, Duncan MacLeod from St Catherine's College, Oxford.

A special thanks to my friend and former colleague Jenny Lee at The Irish News for all her encouragement and for introducing me to prolific author, the lovely Emma Heatherington.

Thanks to the team at One More Chapter, especially publisher Charlotte Ledger, for making this dream come true.

While writing can be a lonely profession or pastime, I have never felt alone. I couldn't have written this novel without the love and support of my parents, Tom and Marie Madden and my three amazing sisters Fiona, Jill and Claire.

Finally, I want to thank the wonderful woman who has been with me throughout this epic novel-writing journey and all our trips with our dog to beautiful Donegal, my soul-mate Heather.

The author and One More Chapter would like to thank everyone who contributed to the publication of this story...

Analytics
Emma Harvey
Maria Osa

Audio
Fionnuala Barrett
Ciara Briggs

Contracts
Georgina Hoffman
Florence Shepherd

Design
Lucy Bennett
Fiona Greenway
Holly Macdonald
Liane Payne
Dean Russell

Digital Sales
Laura Daley
Michael Davies
Georgina Ugen

Editorial
Arsalan Isa
Caroline Scott-Bowden
Charlotte Ledger
Jennie Rothwell
Kimberley Young

International Sales
Bethan Moore

Marketing & Publicity
Chloe Cummings
Emma Petfield

Operations
Melissa Okusanya
Hannah Stamp

Production
Emily Chan
Denis Manson
Francesca Tuzzeo

Rights
Lana Beckwith
Rachel McCarron
Agnes Rigou
Hany Sheikh
Mohamed
Zoe Shine
Aisling Smyth

The HarperCollins Distribution Team

The HarperCollins Finance & Royalties Team

The HarperCollins Legal Team

The HarperCollins Technology Team

Trade Marketing
Ben Hurd

UK Sales
Yazmeen Akhtar
Laura Carpenter
Isabel Coburn
Jay Cochrane
Alice Gomer
Gemma Rayner
Erin White
Harriet Williams
Leah Woods

And every other essential link in the chain from delivery drivers to booksellers to librarians and beyond!

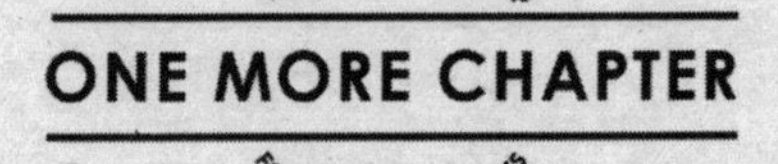
YOUR NUMBER ONE STOP
ONE MORE CHAPTER
FOR PAGETURNING BOOKS